REALITY

With a background in psychology, social work, leadership and management, Ray Glickman has heard more sob stories, sat through more meetings and written more memos than is good for anyone. His first novel, *Reality*, is an expression of his tortured past.

REALITY

RAY GLICKMAN

 FREMANTLE PRESS

CONTENTS

When you know what I have done, you will want to judge me. I know you will. I am neither evil nor benign. What I have done is no more malevolent than innocent. I am a product of my time. These days we cast aside pointless moralities and received opinions. Instead we crave opportunities to exercise our freedom. I have merely exercised mine.

I'm going to tell you this story. It's about these people – I think you may have heard of them.

Kathleen Alice Theresa Murdoch

Garry Troy Scoresby

Hannah Esther Temple Baumgarten

Julia Lee

Mario Nikita Martinelli

Dr Robert Guy Mills Hetherington

My story took a year to unfold. A year ago these were ordinary people. Not special in any way. Not suspecting I had something planned for them.

To them it seemed like an ordinary early summer Sunday when it began. But I knew better. Sunday is where my story begins.

REALITY CONCEIVED

1 PROGRESS

It was good coming over for the job. I achieved a lot. From time to time, doubts crept in about what I'd really changed in the face of such appalling bureaucracy. But I shrugged them off. Let's face it – the Department was a demolition job. I had to take it apart piece by piece. It turned out to be much worse than I'd been led to believe. Every time I touched something, the foundations were rotten underneath.

From the very beginning they knew I'd arrived. Things changed big time. Some of them didn't like it, but they grudgingly admitted it had to be done. But, the rest of them. Jesus. They were the kind who wouldn't know if their arse was on fire.

I didn't make myself popular. But then, I don't set out to be Mr Nice Guy. If people won't face facts, that's their look out.

All in all, it went pretty well. The smart ones could see what I'd achieved. More importantly, the Minister was happy. She thought what I was doing mattered.

It didn't, of course. What counted was that I was in a new city. And a new city is a perfect place for delicious diversions.

2 EDGY

Kathleen felt that telltale frisson of excitement at the prospect of her meeting. This case had come her way in circumstances she still barely understood. She found it all intriguing. Lovely and edgy.

She arrived early at Milkd – her favourite coffee hangout. She loved everything about the place. Sarah and Pablo knew her by name and would have her double shot skinny cap ready almost before she sat down. The décor was funky and cute. There were brightly coloured tables and chairs on the footpath and the prices were written neatly on the blackboard menu as 20 without the cents.

She liked her hip neighbourhood too. The Perth metro area has five or six of these suburbs at its core. Kathleen imagined cool places like these to be circling their wagons against cultural attack from the city's endless urban sprawl.

Yes, she loved that feeling when life might be teetering precariously on the edge. She sipped absent-mindedly at her arabica blend and passed the time checking in with friends online and checking out the guys passing by. Some of the dudes showed signs of a heavy Saturday night. She felt a bit musty round the edges herself.

Fortunately, Matt had been satisfied that morning with a sleepy wake-up fuck and then had made himself scarce so she could concentrate on work. Concentrate on the new client that serendipity had dropped right in her lap. She was up for this meeting and saw from her reflection in the shop window that she looked great. It wasn't her fault she was a budding hot-shot lawyer who looked damn hot.

3   THE SHITS

I remember waking up on that Sunday morning fair quivering in anticipation. It was exciting. After so much planning and preparation, the day of days had finally arrived. The initial phase of the Master Plan was now complete. I was more than satisfied with the overall approach, the strategies and the individual tactics. We were moving into the implementation stage.

Then I spoke to Mark and that stuffed everything. I was up for some positive diversion on this auspicious day, but instead I got Mark-style negative frustration. I knew when I came over here that hanging out with Mark again would give me the total shits. Just my luck that the only old friend I had on the west coast of Australia would be unreliability personified.

I had a great day planned out. I would go to the gym, draft the discussion paper for the following day's Executive Management meeting and then relax and unwind over a couple of drinks with Mark. But then the *Markness* intervened. He texted me to say he couldn't make it to the pub as certain things had cropped up.

What things? Mark didn't have a real job. He didn't even really have a life.

4 MOONLIGHTING

Garry came to around seven thirty on Sunday morning. He opened the blinds to a blast of dazzling sunlight. It was going to be a hot one. He liked his brick and tile house. His wife and kids had their lounge and family room and he had his double lock-up garage with space to park the boat and set up his workbench. Average family home or not, it cost an arm and a leg in Perth and the mortgage repayments were getting out of hand.

Garry was determined to have Sunday free of thoughts of money troubles. He wondered if this could be the beginning of summer at last. The morning easterly was full of promise and his thoughts wandered to getting the boat ready for action. Then he remembered how much he hated the routine of hitching the boat to the trailer, carting it down to the boat ramp, waiting for a lifetime to launch it and then going through the whole bullshit again in reverse just to get home.

He remembered not to forget he had a quote to do for an old lady later that day. Sunday or not, he thought, a fireman's two or three jobs are never done.

He considered re-entering the battle zone called kids eating breakfast but there was no way he was volunteering for a further tour of duty in Perthghanistan. He had served his country yesterday so Kirsty could go shopping with the girls. Today, leave in the form of reading the Sunday paper was the least he deserved.

He slipped quietly from the heavily fortified barracks of the bedroom but didn't get far before ambush from enemy fire.

No, sweetheart, I can't take the kids to your Mum's. I have to do that quote I told you about. Garry pecked her on the cheek, groped her still-cute bum and made a run for it.

I think it's helpful if you get to know me.

I'm an analytical person so I encourage understanding. Understanding breeds appreciation. Please don't confuse my desire for understanding with a quest for your approval. That really is of no consequence to me.

I've been told I have winning ways. Sometimes it's called charm or even charisma. People like me in spite of themselves. Remember the kid at school who was good at everything? Remember how hard you tried to hate him? But you couldn't, could you? That kid was me.

When I do things, I do them well. Actually I do them better than anybody else. It stems from innate ability but it's more than that. I'm more driven than other people. It's genes and guts. It's the deadly duo of nature and nurture humming like a well-oiled machine.

On reflection, I can see that having a drunken, degenerate bum for a father was the best thing that ever happened to me. Obviously, it didn't seem that way at the time. Certainly not when he beat Mum up and scared me so much that I shit my pants.

My dad would drink away the rent money and terrorise the neighbours, so we found ourselves constantly on the move from one rental to another. From time to time, he would 'go away' and Mum would drag me to see him in Melbourne's Pentridge Prison. I can still remember how cold it was there. Even in the heat of summer, those thick stone walls and inmate stares chilled me to the bone.

When I say my *dad* was like that, he was the man I called *Dad*. I never met my actual father nor was I told a thing about him. My mum kept up the pretence about my paternity throughout my childhood, but Axe (yeah, he was huge) made sure I was reminded when he and I were alone that I was literally a pathetic little bastard.

Mum remained fiercely loyal to the abomination of a man I was forced to call Dad, as do so many women who've been battered by their so-called men. I speculate that my real father was a Greek or a Turk. I have olive skin and what people describe as swarthy good looks. So I am rather handsome and, as I told you before, I have a certain charm. Axe was neither handsome nor charming. He was an ugly, ignorant brute with all the charm of a spitting cobra.

So my childhood experiences weren't great. But I am thankful for them now as I can trace my toughness and determination back to those formative years. All in all, I'm a self-made man. Maybe this will help you understand what drives me to be the very best.

Let me share something else to put you in the picture. I crave admiration. Don't confuse that with approval. I use words precisely and I do mean *admiration*. The admiration I refer to is the shock and awe reaction when people witness amazing things. I'm the kind of guy who wants to take your breath away. I want you to marvel at me. Like when the dashing hero rescues the damsel in distress. Or when the thief brazenly robs the bank in broad daylight.

As a consequence of moving from house to house, I also had to constantly change schools. Thanks to my indifferent home life, I was malnourished and always the weediest kid in my class. Interestingly enough, I was never bullied. When they first saw me, the Neanderthals in the back row would lick their lips. At the first opportunity, they would get me alone in the playground to do their worst. The funny thing was they never did. They would look at me and I would look at them. They were bristling with menace and I was supposed to be scared. The trouble was, I wasn't.

I've thought about this a lot over the years. Why didn't they go ahead and bash me? The fact is they were scared of me and not the other way around. Gradually, I would weave those boys under my spell. Before too long I would become their leader and they would do my bidding. At that time, neither they nor I could understand why.

As I made my way through university in Melbourne, the influence I had over others endured. Not that I was threatened physically by anyone. Instead we competed for the grades and the girls and the crown of king of the cool. I took what I wanted and I was the sun around which all the lesser planets orbited. If anything, the force field has progressively strengthened. These days I can fully harness the attraction. My gravitational pull is simply irresistible.

I'm confident I can get what I want. Working out what I'm going to attempt is the trickier thing. But, once I found myself here in Perth, a new man as it were, I quickly found a purpose. Something that would interest me and challenge me and justify the move to Wait-Awhile WA. Something that would combine tower rescue with bank robbery.

It all started in earnest on the very Sunday you're reading about now.

6   MAYBE A LITTLE IRREGULAR

Robert loved this time of the year now the weather was really warming up again. He sheltered his eyes from the rising sun as he waited to brief the new guy on the mass of maintenance work around the property that was now way overdue. Things were getting out of hand and that's why so much activity had overtaken his Sunday morning.

Robert and Jack introduced themselves to each other and exchanged pleasantries. Robert had just joked for the millionth time that being a gynaecologist was like being a mechanic, but with a much better view. He chuckled to himself as he always did. Luckily, Marjorie wasn't there to tell him off this time.

He oriented Jack to the features of the site. There were paddocks with sheep to do the gardening, rows of fruit trees in the scenic valley, verdelho and chenin blanc grapes planted in the perfect terroir of the gravelly, loam soil and a market garden area let to the neighbours. One hundred hectares with breathtaking views was bloody great, he told him, but having no time to do things was a problem. A busy practice, you see. The basic maintenance was getting him down, let alone the hassles with the hopeless people from the viticulture collective who were supposed to be developing his vineyard. Perhaps he was getting old, he thought, but fifty-four isn't that old these days. The new forty-four, he said to himself, as ever amused at his own joke.

Robert left Jack to it and wandered back towards the house. He noticed that the BMW Sports Z4 needed a clean. He wondered if he could fit in a clean-and-go before his appointment. It was a little irregular to see a patient on a Sunday, but she seemed desperate. She also sounded alluring. Her verdelho voice conjured up lime and honeysuckle so intensely that he could almost taste it.

At worst, it would provide a decent excuse to drop into the bar. Owning a bar by the river was fun. Something to play with, Marjorie said. Cruel but fair. Nothing wrong with a bit of fun, especially when there were young girls to ogle. It was a licence to print money too. Yes, the bar was a winner all round.

7 BRAVE NEW WORLD

When I told people I was leaving Melbourne, they were shocked. To go to Perth of all places, that made them laugh. That's what they're like in Melbourne. Superior and complacent.

The trouble is, complacency suffocates risk. The complacent classes, with silver spoons stuffed in their mouths, would rather choke on them than taste freedom. But people like me aren't afraid to take a chance. We boldly go where we've never gone before. We star-trek to another city where we know no one (except for Mark, who is too unreliable to count).

Despite the sneering looks on the faces of my colleagues, I could tell they were jealous as hell. To get head-hunted from interstate to run a whole Department, a whole service for the entire State – that was something they would only ever have dreamed of for themselves.

They thought I was heading West just for work. They didn't know it was also an escape. Not from anything bad or from any sort of scandal but more so from the confines of myself. People like me can get dragged down and diminished by the stifling conventionality of a smug, established city.

What better place to allow the spirit to run free than the most isolated capital city in the world? Where better than a new frontier to explore one's potential for great things?

Hannah couldn't understand how she got to be eighty-two. That was no great surprise. Last year, she couldn't understand how she got to be eighty-one.

When she looked ruefully in the mirror that Sunday morning, a withered old lady looked back. Inside she was still herself as she had always been, but now she was locked inside some ghastly shell.

People often commented that she still had her marbles. Hannah resented this ageism just as she had rejected racism and sexism before it. Not only was she anti the *isms*, she was one of those pioneering women who led the movements against them.

And yet it should come to this. Only a few years ago, she would have done the work herself. She renovated her own bathroom when she was seventy-five and it got her headlines in the local newspaper. Some achievement that – to be a DIY celebrity in the *Community News*! That's what currently passes for fame for a world-renowned Viennese pianist, celebrated Jungian psychiatrist, revered feminist flag-bearer and refugee from the Nazis, whose entire family had been butchered before her eyes.

She didn't waste time on regretting the past but, justifiably, she had come to resent the present. How cruel it was for a woman like her to have to ask a man for help. Now what time was the young man coming round again? It was written on that scrap of paper near the telephone table in the hall. Here it is. Damn these infernal glasses. Here we go. Two o'clock.

9 MARK

I spent a fair bit of time with Mark when I first came over. At first I wasn't entirely sure why. I thought it might have been out of nostalgia. But I soon realised that it stemmed from what you might call forensic curiosity. For me, spending time with Mark was like looking at the world through one-way glass, paradoxically coupled with the reflective benefit of looking in a mirror. When I was there with Mark, I was a dispassionate observer of life. Strangely, that helped me develop and realise self.

He seemed pleased to have me around in that special Mark way. That merely meant that my presence was, on balance, welcome. If I'd told him I was heading straight back to Melbourne, he would have shrugged his shoulders and said what time do you leave?

Mark hadn't changed much from university days but then I guess none of us do. It's not hard to understand why parents find it all so depressing. They enslave themselves to their kids for twenty years, fork out a small fortune to bring them up and then the brats turn out just like they were going to anyway.

As the Britney generation would say, Mark's parents would so-ooo feel like that. I once came over to Perth and visited him in their impressive house in their leafy suburb. Mark's parents spent the whole time apologising for him. A genius he was without a doubt, but he was as erratic and lazy as he was brilliant.

I was the only one amongst our college mates who had much time for him. I enjoyed Mark mainly because he could mount lucidly philosophical arguments even when drunk or stoned. Being a cynical bastard, he didn't believe in much. That gave him the intellectual freedom to adopt the best available argument for any issue at hand. The amazing thing was that his bullshit lines from the night before weren't actually bullshit in the morning. I would shake my head in wonder at how someone so fucked up could conceive an argument that was so fucking brilliant.

So there I was – reunited with Mr Unreliable himself. And do you know what? The experience helped open my eyes. I wouldn't tell him that because he wouldn't be interested. Anyway he probably wouldn't listen.

But, credit where it's due, Mark set me on my incredible new path. It was at the weird and wonderful University of Mark that I discovered how diverting my new life in the Australian backwater could be. Mark gave me the vision for how I might entertain myself over here and, more importantly, how my talents and capabilities could be honed to their sharpest points.

Mario inspected his thinning hairline in the bathroom mirror. He looked like shit, that was his conscious thought. Never mind about that. More importantly, was he receding faster now? Still, looking on the bright side, the hair he had left was good and black, with not a hint of grey.

He'd been told that sons inherit heads of hair from their fathers. His father was bald as a coot, dammit. But, hey, Mario was nothing like his father. Joe was a retired market gardener, a rabid communist in his day, short and thick-set, content to eat *spaghetti* with *polpetti* every day and happy to drink coffee with the same old *paesani* forever and a day.

Mario saw himself as the exact opposite. A risk-taker, an opportunist, someone who could see a good thing and grab it. Very good with the ladies, as indeed he was last night; not real good with the ex-wife. A loveable rogue, that's what they called him.

Sundays weren't his favourite day, not by a long way. For on that hallowed day, duty called for a man with no sense of duty. The plan as usual was to clap eyes on the Bitch for as short a time as possible, disengage the kids from the apron strings and then take them down to Macca's for some real kids food. Be smart this time, Mario my son, don't tell them any secrets to parrot back to the Bitch.

After returning the poor kids from day release to the Bitch's detention centre, he would trek down to Mum and Dad's, drop off and collect some washing, eat too much and try to think of something to say to them.

No, not his favourite day, especially in the current circumstances. Maybe he had overstepped the mark this time. Perhaps he was playing out of his league. Don't think like that, Mario reminded himself. Things will work out. After all, this was him he was talking to. But he *was* getting anxious and his palms were sweaty like they were when he'd been in trouble at school.

Still, he had done something about the problem now. He had jumped on his bike and started pedalling fast. No time like the present, he'd said, I'd like my appointment yesterday. He'd bunged on the urgency in the time-honoured fashion mastered by all Italians to jump queues. And it had worked. He would take back control of his life this very day.

11 RELIGION

I'm not sure what Mark would have done if he hadn't been lucky. Or was it talented or both? Anyway, for whatever reason, his mega-wealthy dad gave him a bunch of shares and the cosmos gave online share trading to the world. Mark used these gifts to good effect. Very good effect, actually. He made mega-bucks. When he got up before trading closed, that is.

I was pleased for him when I heard about it, genuinely pleased. I'm not naturally so generous of spirit. I just recognised that Mark would have gone loopy if he'd been expected to make an ordinary living like everyone else.

Given the extremely short working hours he kept, Mark was always available. After he'd forgotten to turn up at the pub once or twice, I would arrange to see him at his place. I preferred the unique chaos of what Mark called home to waiting round like a loser some girl had stood up.

It came as no surprise to discover that Mark's world, when he wasn't sleeping, stoned or 'working', revolved around TV. He was addicted to *The Simpsons* and split the rest of his viewing time between terrible old movies, obscure documentaries and reality shows involving ordinary folk cast into extraordinary situations.

I'm normally moralistic about TV. As a child, I didn't have the luxury of sitting around. As an adult, TV strikes me as an utter and pathetic waste of time. Why else would people feel the need to make excuses for watching it? You hear them claim not to watch it much. I only watch the ABC, they say. I bet these people only buy *Playboy* for the articles.

Yet TV came to fascinate me. In the bizarre company of Mark, I let myself succumb to the experience without resistance or guilt. I caught myself actually enjoying it. I realised that I wasn't enjoying watching the programs as such. It was more that I was enjoying the experience of watching TV with Mark.

I was like a novice introduced to a new religion. Seeing something of what the true devotees were seeing but with new and different eyes. In the company of Mark, I suspended judgment and I didn't criticise. I just lived life for a while through a different catechism – a spiritual posture second nature to others, yet totally alien to me.

Out on court one, Angelica was thrashing her hapless opponent with her customary casual arrogance, while on one of the outer courts, young Jasmine was fighting tooth and nail to match it with a much better player.

Julia felt guilty about the way her older daughter treated each new adversary with such disdain. This emotion battled against the pride she felt that Angie had inherited her figure, looking a picture of blonde perfection in her little tennis skirt. But guilt won in straight sets as she looked at poor Jasmine. She was stocky and dark like her dad, but carried it, regrettably, with none of his self-confidence.

It was a cracker of a day. From the tennis club, there was a gorgeous view of the sea and today it was like glass, thanks to the easterly morning breeze doing its early summer thing. This was the view she could get from their upstairs entertaining veranda. She adored it and she would never tire of it.

Although the vistas were totally different, the experience of looking out across the water reminded her of childhood and the smelly green and yellow ferries that plied Sydney Harbour. Julia's early years were framed around keeping up old-money Sydney appearances and concealing the sad truth of their barren family life. Her mother was a busy socialite, flitting between tennis at the club, charity performances and cocktail parties. Her father was hardly ever at home, working long hours and travelling interstate and overseas, building his reputation as the leading Australian avant-garde architect of the post-war era.

Julia grew up to be a beautiful young lady, a virtual clone of her own mother. She was blonde and blue-eyed, with a taste for classic twinset fashion. Outwardly Julia was serene and respectable, but inwardly she blazed with anger. Julia recognised and resented her parents' neglect from a young age. She was happy to take all the material pleasures her life offered, but deep down she felt like an orphan in her own home. In later life, she reflected on how the breathtaking architecture of the house had deflected the eye and the attention of the viewer from the true nature of the household. The toilets throughout the mansion were constructed with glass walls. They looked magnificent and modern, but to live with them was a misery of embarrassment. While the imaginative design filled the house with light, none of it penetrated her soul.

Julia was one of three sisters. Her oldest sister was more like a mother to her, working in partnership with the nannies and housekeeper to run the house. Julia was far and away the prettiest of the three and, maybe because she was the youngest, was also the most wilful and rebellious. Naturally, there were tensions and jealousies between the sisters. Most of the disquiet was directed at her.

Curiously, all three girls serially dated one particular guy. In retrospect, Julia saw this as a re-run of Cinderella, with Prince Charming working his way down the list until he came to the most dazzling of the three. As in all good fairy stories, Cinderella ended up marrying the king's son, Prince Stephen in this particular case.

Julia imagined that the white speck of the Bathurst Lighthouse on Rottnest, just visible thanks to the sparkling sunlight, was the tower of a medieval castle. She thought about her decision to marry Stephen. While he had a certain charm, he had been nowhere near the most handsome or wealthy of the boys who courted her. She'd recognised recently that his true appeal lay somewhere else. He'd been appointed to a good job away from Sydney and the fact of the matter was that he could deliver something none of his rivals could. He had the power, indeed the need, to take her away.

Julia jerked herself back to the moment. To the tennis and the girls. But between Angelica's perfect topspin executions and Jasmine's endless chasing down of balls, she could no longer avoid the truth that things had changed between her and Stephen. The thought of the approaching big four-o had probably started it, but she wasn't imagining things. Stephen had recently emerged from a decade of benign indifference and had noticed her slipping away. Why otherwise would this predictable, forty-five year old businessman have pulled the crazy Chinese stunt?

Julia felt sure now that Stephen had sniffed the air and smelled that something with her was not right. His plan was simple – re-tie her to the kitchen sink.

She ignored Angelica's current tantrum at the latest dubious line call from her opponent and wondered if today's appointment was really such a good plan. Especially, conspicuously, on a Sunday of all days.

At this moment she longed for the comforting anonymity of a proper big city. In London, New York, Paris or even Sydney, you don't have to worry that the simplest inquiry, the most basic exploration, will somehow find its way back to you over coffee with the girls or will be broadcast via the old boys' bush telegraph to the nineteenth hole chit-chat over an ice cold beer.

Still, she had badgered the poor man, name-dropped and fluttered her gorgeous eyelashes metaphorically over the phone to secure the unusual appointment. It was all too confusing. Should she go ahead with the meeting? Was it too late to back out?

I spent a fair while sitting there with Mark in the early days of my new life. Like two blokes in silent harmony bringing to life the beer ads. He would drink a Rogers or a Nail or some such 'tasty beer' and I would bring a great shiraz and sip it indulgently by myself. That was the way it was with Mark. You could spend time in his company but you could never be with him. In parallel but not in series.

We viewed. He out of habit and me out of curiosity. I saw average people aspire to non-average lives. I saw people crave to fulfil potential that their low cards in the deal of life would otherwise prevent.

In these people, I saw me, but unfortunately for them, without the driving *me-ness* of me.

I saw people trust unseen and unknown multinational conglomerates with the daily minutiae of their lives. Your life in their hands. Your free will freely given. Signed over in small print contracts that they never bothered to read. YES PLEASE ... I agree that I want to be locked in a house with perfect strangers for months on end. YES ... I want to be sent to a desert island with no food or water. I want to vie for the affections of a rugged but moronic outback farmer. I want to swap my cultured wife for a busty slag whose culinary skills extend as far as heating baked beans.

But, for reasons that I couldn't at first comprehend, I didn't mock them. I didn't scoff. I didn't shitcan it. I made no comment, even to myself. I got into it. I enjoyed it. It was different. It was what I had come for – a new life!

Hannah doubled up in laughter at the anti-terrorism security warning – be alert but not alarmed. She doubted that her adopted countryfolk, disarmingly innocent and complacent as they were, could ever raise sufficient energy to scrutinise their brown-skinned, bearded neighbours over the back fence to check on large orders of nitrates. However, the phrase summed up perfectly the way she had to lead her life these days. She was mentally tough but physically frail. So she needed to be alert.

She sat the prospective handyman down for the third degree knowing he would take her for a lonely old bat desperate for someone to talk to. That was fine. As far as Hannah was concerned, perceptions of senility were there to be milked for all they were worth.

He seemed like a nice boy. But he had something on his mind that was distracting him. She asked questions that were more direct so as to focus him. She knew that a father of young children would be attention-deprived. So she asked him about himself and what made him tick. As expected, he responded well to the luxury of talking about himself for a change and he was present and engaged. This gave her a much better opportunity to assess him.

She took the man slowly round the house showing him the work that needed doing. All the while, she was chatting to him and asking him questions. On his way out, he searched through his pockets like a man who'd lost something. Although Garry was perplexed, Hannah knew exactly why. She hadn't lost her touch. She had pickpocketed his life in thirty adept minutes of the sweetest interrogation. She now knew what she needed to know and she could read this man, his motives and his dreams like a book. There was Garry fiddling in his pocket, thinking he had lost his keys. Something of his was missing but he didn't know what.

Hannah had just committed the velvet crime.

15 ACTIVE PASSIVE MODE

After three months in town, things were going OK. I'd taken the standard time to evaluate what was happening at the Department. Actually, I'd been clear about what needed doing from day one, but it doesn't look good to start changing things straightaway. If you do that, people get anxious and even the good guys start to feel aggrieved. Then you run the risk of the good performers finding common cause with the non-performers – the fucked, foolish and forgotten – as I like to call them. So I was taking my time. I was getting to know people and getting to understand the culture of the place.

As good leaders should, I kept a professional distance from my staff. Some of them tried to befriend me but I suspected they were just sucking up. I was content to rely on Mark for company, if you could call it that. After a full day of vigorous public service, I was happy to slob around with Mark in front of the goggling machine. I was becoming addicted to mindless spectatorship and found myself looking forward to watching the lives of the manipulated unfold. I marvelled at the tolerance of people who, deprived of their liberty for endless weeks, or physically and emotionally shattered from building a cut-throat business from scratch in a month, sat passively by as the play-makers introduced new camera-friendly stooges at the eleventh hour to deprive them of their hopes, their dreams, their dignity and the pot of gold at the end of the rainbow.

Having imbibed freely of the vine, I'd sneak home the back way to avoid the baited breathtesters, not dissatisfied with my day, fully active and fully passive as it had been.

The guy hoped and prayed that the gorgeous creature sitting alone in the café might turn out to be the lawyer he was meeting. He preened himself a little, fiddled with his shirt collar and his neck chain and went for it.

I'm really hoping you're Kathleen Murdoch, he said very truthfully.

She looked up from her double-thumb texting. Yes, hi Mario, she said, shaking his hand firmly.

During the initial pleasantries about finding the café, the weather, the choice of coffee, no breakfast for me etc., he thanked his lucky stars that she was her and thanked his sunnies that he could perve on her shamelessly without getting caught.

Glossy jet black hair (straight out of a Sunsilk ad), great tits accentuated by the low v-neck of her green silk top and definitely luscious legs unfortunately hidden below the table. And to think he had conjured up an image of a frumpy redhead! An easy mistake to make given her name was Kathleen Murdoch.

Kathleen, by contrast, was amused to the point of cracking up by the caricature of Mario Martinelli that sat in front of her. Thinning black hair, black shirt, gold chain, ostentatious gold rings – basically an order of wop with the lot. She knew he liked the look of her and really, if he had some cool dress sense like Matt, she thought he could even be cute in a puppy dog sort of way.

Eventually, he stopped paying her compliments and trying to impress her and looked ready to talk about some real business. Kathleen sat forward with interest and watched him drain the last sips from his espresso. Mario leaned forward until he was conspiratorially close, shifted his stained coffee cup to one side and rested his elbows on the table. He removed his sunglasses and locked onto her eyes.

Kathleen, he said, I find myself in a bit of a fix.

17   SHARON'S WISDOM

As I started the change process at the Department in earnest, I was struck by the parallels to be found between the practice of management and the TV shows I was devouring at night.

The Department was paralysed by inertia and stultified by archaic rules and regulations. Like so many institutions, people started off as a junior in their own field and then found themselves progressively promoted on seniority to become supervisor and then manager and even executive manager. Promotions beyond competence were the Department's forte.

These petty bureaucrats had a vested interest in keeping things the same and dreaded the thought of being exposed to something new. Individually, they were masters of inactivity. Collectively, they were a champion team from the school of management indecision. As soon as a younger person came through with ideas and enthusiasm, the execs would transfer them to the organisational equivalent of Siberia to neutralise the threat. So nothing ever changed and the needs and desires of each new wave of clients (that's government-speak for people) never got a look in.

My job was to break this culture of ineptitude and crack the system open. I knew there were two ways to do this. Go long and slow and spend years bringing people on side, getting them on board, working for their trust and support, blah, blah, blah. Or there was the much quicker way to which, you will understand by now, I was much better suited. This way required more courage and a considerably thicker skin.

And bugger me, if I wasn't sitting there, glass of Knee Deep shiraz in hand, watching decidedly non-ABC TV with Mark, when I saw these two alternative strategies played out to perfection by two nineteen year olds in the lock-up house. I sat forward in my chair. Darrell was seeking the approbation of the group – weak wanker that he was – and quite appropriately got voted out. But Sharon took a different approach. She was a genius, a natural born winner.

There and then, I chose the Sharon School of Management for myself.

Julia resolved to stop glancing at her watch. She wished she hadn't parked the four-wheel drive directly over the road. After all, on a Sunday there wasn't one car in the row of parking spaces directly outside. This parking spot made her look suspicious and only intensified her deep sense of guilt.

She resisted the strengthening impulse to leave the scene but couldn't resist a further check of the watch. She glanced nervously over at the consulting rooms. The Victorian city-edge house stood out like a sore thumb amongst the chrome and concrete office blocks. At that point, an electric blue BMW sports car pulled up and a George Clooney look-alike jumped out.

Robert felt flustered and unprofessional to the point of serious discomfort, having made a death-defying dash down from the hills and having parked his convertible without bothering to slide the roof closed. First, there was this ridiculous appointment out of normal hours he had agreed to and then he had arrived late, something it was against his principles to do. Fortunately, the patient was late too and this allowed him to organise his room, switch on the computer and straighten himself up in the mirror so he looked the part.

Julia allowed herself to be ushered into the consulting suite and was surprised to find it more like a hotel than a medical room. She had practised the next bit dozens of times so that she would manage to keep it all together. Then Julia forgot the discreet story she'd prepared, burst into tears and blabbed the whole truth into hospital-strength tissues handed to her one after the other from the gallant man's outstretched hand.

19 OPERATION SHARON

This was one of my glory days. As such, it stays in my mind as a reel of images of the greatest clarity.

I'd spent the requisite time gaining the trust of the senior staff. Brian – the dull but loyal head of corporate services; Beth – the earnest and academically brilliant director of service centres; and Tim – the young trail blazer in charge of new business.

I called them in for a routine meeting of the senior team. Their expressions were priceless when I told them I had finished my structural review and that they, in all fairness, would be the first to learn of the outcomes. That wasn't entirely true as I had run my intended course of action past the Minister. She, ever eager for blood and change, had declared it 'spot on' and whispered collusive encouragement for me to stick a bomb up there where the sun don't shine.

You'll love the next bit. I placed their three copies of the report on the table in front of me, but didn't distribute them. These are the moments we all live for, aren't they? Who could resist such an opportunity to torment the weak?

Anyway, instead of circulating the documents, I referred to the contents by leafing through my own copy. I delivered each point with the measured certainty of a tennis pro mechanically rolling out serve after serve with practised efficiency.

The other delightful part was that it took me forty-five minutes to run through it all. My colleagues were desperate to play, but the weight and gravity of my delivery prevented them. Beth, being the gutsiest of the three, almost returned serve once or twice by way of interjection, but my demeanour prevented her from getting the ball back over the net.

Like an expert commentator before the Australian Open final, I balanced the positives and negatives of the performance and potential of each of them in turn. I watched the seesawing emotions etched on their faces. They relaxed when I threw them a short ball of encouragement, but soon their hopes were dashed by a centimetre-perfect lob of underlying concern.

At the end of the match, I was looking cool, calm and collected and they had played the full five sets.

Then, with Federesque timing, came match point. I played it nervelessly and majestically and the result was a foregone conclusion. Game, set and match.

I uttered the sentences most reviled in the bureaucrats' lexicon. Total departmental restructuring. All jobs to be contested.

You should have been there.

Yes-ss, yes-ss, praise be to God for this glorious moment. Yes-ss, yes-ss, praise be to Sharon.

Kathleen added more hot water so she could lie soaking for a good deal longer. The gushing stream refreshed the strawberry and nettle bath gel so that the bubbles swelled, popped and hissed back to life. That was quite a session with her surprising new client. They'd each had three cups of coffee in the process and he must've got through a dozen cigarettes.

At moments of quiet contentment like these, where the body is warm and relaxed and the thoughts are gorgeous and beguiling, she always thought of her mum. Her beautiful darling Mummy with whom she could share any secret in the world. When something good happened to her at school, when perhaps an influential girl in the social scene had included Kathy in her group, she would rush straight home to tell Mummy the news. She'd loved her daddy too, but he was a reserved unemotional type, better suited to his role as a Dublin commercial lawyer than to parenting a girl.

And then on one mild spring day around three in the afternoon, a piece of masonry the shape and size of a football took a mind to dislodge itself from the heritage façade of a building in Temple Bar, Dublin to which it had adhered for over a hundred years, and fall on Mrs Anne Murdoch as she was hurrying home.

Anne never got home that day. In fact she never came home again as the woman she had been. Physically she seemed OK, but she took to sitting around with a vacant expression on her face. From then on, she never spoke to anyone unless spoken to and, even then, would only mouth platitudes such as 'Yes, dear' and 'That would be lovely, thank you'.

Kathleen's father was bereft, but he never talked to Kathleen about how he felt. He soldiered on, employing a carer and a cleaner-cum-cook so that he could continue to meet the demands of his legal practice. When Kathy started on her classic teenage rebellion, he astounded her and the world by announcing they were to emigrate to Australia. Kathy was dragged literally kicking and screaming onto the boat.

She found her new home in Perth alien and disorientating.

Somehow she found it easier to tolerate the loss of her true mother in these new and unfamiliar surroundings. Taken away from the bad influences in Dublin, she was able to settle back into study and toe the line just enough to be tolerated at home. Eventually, she resolved to study law because she couldn't think of anything else to do. But, even though she was the daughter of a conservative lawyer and was studying law in the straightest of university settings, she kept her counsel as she had always done about everything since her real mother 'went away'. Kathleen was resolved to be a lawyer, but the lawyer *she* wanted to be.

Kathleen lowered herself until she was completely immersed in the soapy froth and dragged her mind back to the business at hand. Mario was a sweet boy really. An enthusiastic puppy who had stupidly stuck his head in the chow bowl of a much bigger dog. Scary for him maybe, but exciting for her. This case had brilliant potential. Do a good job, don't overplay the hand and, with the canine metaphors let off the leash, she could imagine some seriously big dogs taking notice of the new bitch strutting her stuff down their street.

It was clear as day to her that Mario was way out of his league. Left school at fifteen, did a number of odd jobs, gagging for something more exciting than his dad's life of all work and no play. Mario did some drugs in a gentle sort of way, got done for dope – just growing a plant or two, nothing much. Someone threw the seeds over my fence – as a lawyer, she couldn't believe he'd actually trotted that line out in court!

But, in the Italian community, Mario found himself endlessly rubbing shoulders with those who had bigger fish to fry. This made him envious, but he knew he could be just as smart and cunning as them. So he kept rocking up where he didn't belong, running an errand or two for family and older friends, making himself useful, always using his nous. Eventually, the distant cousins let him help out from time to time. And then he got to mind the car yard over lunchtime or when they had an important appointment to attend.

Then one day, when his big opportunity came along, a smart boy like him knew exactly what to do. He remembered the guy as if it were yesterday. He was a cocky young buck with a goatee beard wearing a bright red T-shirt that read (for some unaccountable reason) *No Reason* in large, barely decipherable gothic letters.

Anyway *No Reason* drove out of the showroom with a shiny used Holden ute having come in with his heart set on a Falcon sedan. Mario rang the finance company, followed their instructions, signed him up and got a more than acceptable selling price for what was no more than a suspect piece of shit.

The cousins were well pleased when they came back stinking of booze. From then on Mario had a job, a business card and a certain standing in the community as well as down the pub. Kathleen smiled at the thought of his animated rendition of his working life. As his life story rolled out, she was often on the verge of asking him to come to the point. But she restrained herself. There were worse ways to spend a Sunday morning.

Eventually, the purpose of the autobiography did become clear. The boy was good at selling cars. He had the gift of the gab and was a suitably blokey bloke to treat the guys like a mate and the girls like supermodels. But, as good as he was with the motor sales, he was better still with the loans. In due course, his talent was recognised and the finance company made him an offer he couldn't refuse.

Mario diversified from the car game to the debt game. Many of the loans were still for cars, but his enterprise also specialised in unsecured loans. She knew the ones – ridiculous interest rates for desperate customers with insufficient patience. Global meltdown specials as they came to be known.

Then out of the blue, he got another unexpected break and that, she mused, was his unlucky day. A day that she hoped would turn out to be the opposite for her.

She really quite liked Mario – he probably was, as he claimed to be, a loveable rogue. Mind you, not so endearing that he was the reason for her to slide her hand between her soapy legs.

As it happens, at that very same moment, Mario flicked his ash out of the driver's window as he waited for a change of lights and daydreamed delightfully about exploring that very same place.

I'd agonised long and hard about how to implement the required changes at the precious Department. I'd consulted the usual management gurus – Tom Peters, Peter Senge and Peter Drucker – and the change experts John Kotter and Kurt Lewin. In the end, it fell to Sharon to show me the way.

Sharon had a coherent management strategy. She set clear goals: to stay in the house and win the money. She identified the key decision-makers: the viewers, who could vote her in or out. She then developed the strategically aligned tactic of seeking to undermine her competitors in the eyes of the decision-making public.

Sharon's implementation was very professional. She did not waver from the plan. She was consistently cooperative with her housemates, caring for each of them in a unique and special way. But at the same time, she was doing them in. She was every inch the smiling assassin. Her watchwords were: be naughty, look nice. If that ain't good management, I dunno what is.

It was the perfect plan for me and it worked like a charm. The Department Heads were essentially my housemates. OK, so we spent eight or ten hours a day together rather than a whole day. But just like the housemates, we were thrown together by a million rolls of the dice, a zillion moments in our lives when fate sent each of us this way or that and eventually threw us in together.

Just as Sharon did, I developed a tailored strategy for each of the Department Heads – Brian, Beth and Tim. However, I had a common outcome in mind: to put them off their guard and bring them down.

For Brian, the stodgy accountant, I adopted the old if-you-don't-know-I'm-not-going-to-tell-you strategy. Brian dutifully reported on alarming operating deficits without proposing any solutions to bring the budget back into the black. I regularly praised him for the accuracy of his reports and for the clarity of his spreadsheets. He didn't see solutions as part of his role and I didn't disabuse him of the notion. I wondered how the hell a

Head of Finance could calmly preside over horrendous figures like those. I wondered. Just to myself, mind you.

At times I felt a pang of guilt over Brian. He was dull and unimaginative rather than bad. But Beth was a different kettle of fish. A very smelly one actually.

Beth was an appalling I-know-what's-best-for-the-customers type. She was forever spouting on about the good old days when the patrons truly appreciated what the Department had to offer. She interpreted declining attendances as a sign of dropping standards amongst the clientele. Beth was perfect for the old give-her-enough-rope-and-she'll-hang-herself manoeuvre. I was well aware that the Minster only cared about bums on seats and couldn't give a toss about the purity or quality of the services. So I gave Beth considerable autonomy and encouraged her to speak out in public on matters close to her heart. Go for it, Beth. Speak up, Beth. Just you wait, Beth.

In contrast to my feelings for the loathsome Beth, I rather liked Tom. He lived at an address somewhere near the real world. To his credit, he was trying to implement new things, trying to develop some attractions that might appeal to youth. However, we disciples of Sharon don't have the luxury of indulging in emotions like these. Liking someone in the house isn't reason not to do them down.

The problem for Tom was that, as hard as he tried and as creative as he was, he had no idea how to succeed in a world full of bureaucrats, Brians and Beths. So I encouraged Tom to give full vent to his ideas. I advised him to be bold and brook no argument from the naysayers and the fear-merchants. Unfortunately for him, when you remove all of them from the ranks of the public service, there really is nobody left. Still, he did have *my* full support.

Yes, different strokes for different folks.

How comfortable they had allowed themselves to become. Shame about the total departmental restructure.

It was a routine renovation by anyone's standards, but in these old houses everything is hard work. Garry had to bang his way through some very hard walls and lever off what seemed like centuries of plaster. By now he had hacked his way through most of the destructive work and was almost into the cleaner and more creative stage of the job.

Although the work itself was regular handyman stuff, Garry was pleased that the smoko times here were something else. For a start, he had successfully negotiated his first Wedgwood bone china cup. As his stubby, calloused fingers couldn't possibly fit through the hole, he had mastered the challenging art of gripping the delicate cup between his forefinger and thumb. He hadn't really liked tea until now, but somehow he had to agree that this ritual with the old lady was unreal. And there was more to it than just the tea-drinking. He found that, just when he was getting the hang of things and starting to relax, the old lady would unsettle him again and put him right off guard.

One day, he complimented Hannah on the ritual of the tea and asked her if she'd learned it from her mum. She burst into most unladylike laughter.

Young man, you must be deaf, she guffawed. Can't you tell my accent is from Aus-tria not Aus-tra-lia? Europeans don't drink tea, the English do.

Then she gave him that wicked wrinkly smirk he was growing to like. Damn it, I like tea and that's that!

He was glad Hannah was a hundred and ten because otherwise Kirsty would've got jealous. After working at Hannah's, he would go home and rave on to Kirsty about everything Hannah had to say. He didn't normally feel comfortable sharing his thoughts with his wife. It occurred to him that Hannah was drawing out his feminine side. He'd heard that blokes had such a thing, but hadn't looked for it before for fear he'd find out he was a poof. He grinned to himself at the prospect of telling the guys at the station that he'd found his feminine side. Within half an hour, they'd have bought him a bra and booked him in for a leg wax.

At other times, Garry wondered whether Hannah really was exposing his femininity or was he just learning to talk? Somehow, at Hannah's, he'd come to understand what was meant when people said the art of conversation was not dead. Real conversation, as in speaking to develop a point of view, had never been a feature of his life. When he was a kid, nobody spoke during dinner time. They knew their dad would go ballistic if he couldn't hear the telly. Not that it was very different in his own house. Dinners weren't stuffy affairs round the kitchen table, but the family ate off their laps in front of the box. He wondered now if that was really such a good thing.

That was it, he decided, he was enjoying talk for talk's sake. Hannah made him feel like his opinions were valuable. For the first time, he felt he had something worthwhile to say. Not just about the footy. Not the usual whinge about the pollies. He had thoughts and feelings about the world. Sometimes he spoke for ages and Hannah just beamed at him and listened. She said he was becoming a raconteur. He looked it up.

He was a raconteur. Surely Kirsty had noticed that.

23 BOXING BY MYSELF

Just as Operation Sharon had required the quiet cunning of a panther, so enacting the departmental restructure required the swift, decisive movements of a hawk. Alas, I am sorry to say, while the initiation of Sharon's devilish approach with the Department Heads had been mouth-watering and inspiring, by contrast the total capitulation of my foes in the face of pressure was as boring as batshit.

In truth, I didn't need Brian, Beth or Tom to exist because I could have played all the parts myself. Yes indeed, they all reacted just as I thought they would. Brian just crumpled. His low level of confidence was now totally shot. One grey morning, he walked nervously into my office and handed over a creased white envelope. How tedious to open – yes, he had decided to resign.

Just as predictably, Beth had decided to fight. She called in the Union, she called in the Institute of Bureaucrats from Hell, she petitioned the Minister, she leaked stories to the press about staff unrest and so on and so forth. But I was ready for it all. I made sure all processes were in keeping with the public sector rules. The alarming deficits and declining client statistics justified urgent action of this kind. The Minister declined to involve herself with staffing matters and the press was less than sympathetic to overpaid and under-occupied State employees bellyaching about their lot. After all the kerfuffle with Beth, I felt duty-bound to ensure that she became one of those public servants who were just a tad difficult to place.

As for Tom, he accepted the reality of change and threw himself upon my mercy for advice. Tom accepted the reduced role of Service Co-ordinator and gave up his executive status, car and perks without resistance, let alone a fight.

The trouble was, once I'd finished enacting the total departmental restructure, I felt completely let down. It was a total anticlimax. I felt like an Olympic boxer who'd done all the hard work, trained himself to a peak, fought his way through endless tough rounds to make the final and then had won the gold medal fight on a walkover. Sure I was Olympic Champion and I deserved it, but there was no glory to savour. There was just an empty feeling inside.

As depressing and disappointing as this feeling was, it was another revelation point as well. I had to find a bigger challenge to make my mark.

A major challenge such as a Master Plan, in fact.

Robert's first thought was that he should never compromise his professional principles again. However, his second contradictory and more powerful thought was that he could let himself get struck off for such a woman. It was not so much a verdelho she reminded him of, now that he could see her in the flesh, but her hair and skin conveyed the ripe fruit and elegance of a sauvignon blanc.

Just when she thought she might sob for eternity and the handsome doctor might give up and leave her there, Julia somehow got a grip on herself and falteringly began to speak. Her words gushed forth in a blubbery stream of consciousness.

I'm so ashamed of myself, Doctor, I'm ashamed of everything. How did I end up here like this? How can I be such a pathetic mess when I steeled myself to be strong? There must be so many unmarried young girls out there who really need a doctor's help. Pregnant girls – desperate and frightened. And here I am with everything any woman could want in the world and I'm begging you for help.

She told Robert how kind he was to see her on a Sunday, how generous he had been with his time to respond to her urgent cry for help.

Then the teary monologue continued.

It all seems so silly really, when you say it out loud. Stephen is a decent man, a successful businessman and an attentive father for the girls. We've been married now for nearly twenty years. I only avoided being a teenage bride by a matter of months. We've done so much together. We've brought up our wonderful girls and built our business up from nothing to become a roaring giant riding the crest of the wave of the resources boom.

The doctor kept handing her the tissues.

We've got a beautiful house in Cottesloe and the beach house and the winery. And we've got such dear friends.

Julia painted him the full picture of the bored housewife from numerous British feel-good movies she'd seen. The doctor seemed to take her tale of woe in his stride. That was until the abrupt shift in the plot that planted a look of horror on his face as if he'd switched channels to watch *Saw II*.

A few months ago, Stephen returned from yet another of his business trips to China. We went out to dinner. He paid me compliments and told me I looked beautiful. He told me of his exploits and how he'd sliced through all the oriental red tape. But then he told me with a twinkle in his eye I hadn't seen for ages that he'd been on an adventure.

He had been to Shanghai for several days to secure the business coup of his whole life. He was animated and seemed triumphant, but it was all so complicated that I couldn't really grasp what he was saying. All I could really understand was there was something dazzling and special, and it was a present for me.

That night Stephen made love to me like a tiger and it was very arousing. But the passion didn't last and he soon settled back into his peck on the cheek routine. As time went by, I dismissed the Shanghai coup as some drunken delusion and even wondered whether he'd been to an opium den before getting on the plane.

Then one Saturday morning, he got up too early for his regular golf routine. He woke me up with breakfast in bed, which was most unusual. But before I'd even dipped the spoon into the fruit salad, he begged me to get up. I threw on a robe and let him lead me down the stairs with my eyes shut.

I was quite excited and really didn't know what to expect. Then, with suitable hoopla, he told me I could open my eyes. Stephen made this stupid *tah-dah* sound and I found myself staring at this little slip of a Chinese girl who looked no more than sixteen.

May I present Mai Ling? Stephen said.

Don't think me crazy, Doctor, Julia said, but I knew I had just met the nursemaid for the baby I didn't know I was going to have!

For me, life has to be about challenge. It has to involve pushing yourself to go that extra step.

I certainly wasn't getting that from my job. Sure I had to pick up some slack from the sad departure of my three senior colleagues. But they'd been so slack themselves that even their slack was slack.

Eventually the glacial process of staff appointment by public sector rules moved imperceptibly to some finality. Due process was followed. We satisfied ourselves that no one with a disability and no member of a suitably disadvantaged group had been discriminated against. Just to be safe, the HR Department assured itself that no animals had been harmed in the course of the interview process. The favoured candidates survived the onslaught of form filling, medicals and psych tests, and the three shiny new executives were appointed.

It's always nice to have your own direct reports in place. They owe their allegiance to you, their goals have been set by you and best of all they know nothing of the way things used to be done in the past. On this score, I'm pretty sure Moses led the children of Israel into the wilderness for forty years on purpose. In my book, anyone who can part the Red Sea is a leader worth following. Anyway, he clearly had his shit together and led the Jewish tribes around for all that time so that, when they eventually got to the Promised Land, no one would be saying we didn't do things that way when we were in Egypt.

My new guys settled smoothly into their roles. They were loyal and fairly competent. The problem was I had even less to do. I was truly like the public servant in the joke who dares not look out of the window in the morning for fear of having nothing to do in the afternoon.

While on a biblical theme, I recall looking at what I had created within the Department and I saw that it was good. While even I wouldn't be so arrogant as to compare myself with the Almighty, I could relate to how He/She (excuse the crat-speak) must have felt after He/She'd created the world in just six days. The Creator must have wondered what the hell He/She was going to do after a well-earned break on the seventh day.

That's exactly how I felt. Where is the challenge now? I asked myself. Then a voice echoed from the heavens, or maybe a thought just entered my head, and the message was awe-inspiring.

Now is the time to play on a bigger stage.

Mario drove himself on autopilot to a bar he would rarely frequent. Well, never frequent. He didn't remember the journey or making a decision to go to that bar. But he silently praised his subconscious. It was the right place. He needed to think, away from his mindless mates at his usual haunts.

He sculled a sambuca and was now straight onto a beer. Once he'd met with the lawyer, he had expected to feel reassured. But now, the reality was that he felt shit-scared. What was it that was unnerving him like this?

Part of it was the skank Kathleen. No, the truth was that *all* of it somehow related to the Irish tart. God, she was really something. It was very confusing having her as a lawyer. Life with girls was normally simpler. There were girls to listen to and other girls to screw. Even to him, it felt filthy to want to give your lawyer one. It was like his saintly mamma fancying the parish priest.

But feeling guilty didn't stop it from being the truth. What made it worse was that she was also disarmingly smart. And that wasn't everything. Somehow, she was also scary. She obviously had balls. She didn't flinch when she heard his story and her approach had something so macho-man about it that he felt sick to the pit of his stomach. She had the *cojones* to take on these boys.

He shook his head at the prospect and broke the habit of a lifetime by allowing his mobile to ring out. He recalled that she didn't take her eyes off him for one second while he laid out the sad story of his fix. Did she even blink? He didn't think so. She didn't even blink.

He'd lit his fifth or sixth ciggie and just started his second or third espresso. He'd been flying and had let it all tumble out.

You see, I've been doing very well recently and without being big-headed I've got a really nice car and a nice apartment and some respect, which I think is something everybody needs. Although I was pleased to get out of cars and into finance, at first I was dealing with Mickey Mouse stuff and to be honest with you I wasn't making much at all. It was one of my mates down the pub, actually, who put me straight on things. He said I was wasting my time arranging finance for Mr and Mrs Average because the loans were always secured against property or guaranteed by some rock solid relative. There's no margin in those, he said. Get into unsecured loans, you mug. High risk, high rates of interest – high returns for you, my son, he said.

Well, it got me thinking and because, if I say so myself, I'm pretty smart, I added an important twist to my mate's line of thought. The banks and finance companies make all the money and all I get is the commission. A bit more from some and a bit less from others, but at best only a minimal return. So it occurred to me that I should cut out the middleman and loan people the money direct. I have some relatives and associates who can't necessarily put their money in the bank. So I thought they might be pleased to have someone use it for a while for a return.

Anyway, to cut a very long story short, my new venture went very well. I got a standard contract drawn up – essentially a copy of those used by the finance companies. Most of the punters thought it was a dinky-di contract with one of the fancy firms, but it wasn't *my* fault if they confused my company with some other larger outfit with a similar name. Anyway, I was reasonably cautious to start with and, being a good judge of character, I didn't really get myself burnt. Most of my customers were genuine people down on their luck and eventually their money really came through. They were sincerely grateful to me, as it happens. Fair enough, maybe I ripped them off with the interest rates and sign-on fees, but let's face it they knew they weren't going to get that kind of money from anyone else.

Unfortunately, typical Mario, I got a bit ahead of myself and lent money from the wrong people to the wrong people and that's how I got in the shit.

You see this guy from our village was coming out to Australia and by all accounts had made it really big over there. He had a factory selling shoes to Milan and, as you would know with your beautiful dress sense, the fashion scene up there is big bucks. He needed to set up a business over here to satisfy the immigration people and had to make a substantial investment in a venture within a fairly short time. As his money hadn't come through, people put him onto me to see what I could do.

Naturally, I was pretty keen to get involved. He was someone the family knew, was obviously successful in business and I thought he'd be a great contact for later if I looked after him well. Anyway, I arranged a loan a lot larger than the ones I normally handled. Five hundred grand to be precise. I signed him up on one of my contracts, which I'm sure are quite legal, I might add. I borrowed this money in dribs and drabs from my contacts because I thought they might refuse me if they realised how exposed I was to one punter. Needless to say, bending the truth with these boys is a little more risky than telling fibs to the ANZ bank.

A beautiful, brainy lady like you would have guessed what happened by now. The guy set up his new shoe factory and was doing very well, but so far has declined to pay his debt. He kept saying he would, but time after time he failed to come good with the cash. Eventually, I had it out with him, which I was very reluctant to do because his father and mine go way back. Anyway, he told me that my contract was flawed – *legalmente non valida* were the words he used – as it infringed consumer protection laws, was unstamped and a couple of other things I've written down for you.

Mario recalled his language getting away from him at this point and apologising for speaking like that to a young lady. After telling him in a strangely serious tone she wasn't a lady, she'd got all professional with him, asking him for a copy of the contract and such like. Her tone of voice had made a big impression on his dick, but he knew he had to concentrate.

She explained, in true lawyer style, the legal processes that applied to contracts of this kind, the legal remedies that might or might not exist and the practical difficulties of getting owed money back from people through the courts. On a more positive note, she said her firm and she herself had found ways of getting people to settle out of court and she was confident, depending on the detail of course, that she could help.

Then Kathleen crossed her legs and sent a Sharon Stone quiver up his spine. She smiled at him in a wise and knowing way and then said something as mysterious as it was troubling.

To be honest, legal issues might be the least of your concerns.

27 WHAT THE FUCK AM I DOING HERE?

I clearly remember the moment when I finally admitted to myself that I was bored. It was one of those balmy nights in Perth when all should have seemed right with the world. I was squinting at the outdoor cinema screen trying to read the subtitles of an art film from Tibet (free ticket, in case you were wondering) when I thought what the fuck am I doing here? Much to the annoyance of the hunkered-down film buffs, I struggled my way along the endless row of deckchairs, tripping over bottles of wine and picnic baskets, and exited into the deserted gloom of the park next to the Fremantle Film and Television Institute.

I realised the question *what the fuck am I doing here?* didn't just relate to the tedious film. It referred to my whole life. I strolled to the café strip and ordered a latte at a table outside so I could get lost in the hubbub of the chatter and the thumping music from the boy racers' cars.

What the fuck am I doing here?

It didn't mean Perth. It didn't mean the isolation that was evident for someone who counted Mark as his friend. It wasn't the maudlin brooding of someone desperate for love. It was none of that. There was no self-pity. I was asking myself why the fuck am I here in this job which is now such a breeze when I am cut out for much greater things.

It was time to tally up the ledger of my achievements against my potential.

Robert snapped off the surgical rubber gloves and tossed them in the fresh, empty medical waste bin. He washed his hands thoroughly in his time-honoured manner of right hand washed by left hand first and then vice versa.

Soon Julia emerged from behind the modesty screen, having adjusted her clothing and obviously retouched her make-up for good measure. He always thought it was daft that women went behind the screen to put their knickers back on after he had already looked up their fannies.

He smiled his most reassuring smile and switched on his most polished bedside manner. He told Mrs Lee, Julia, what she clearly wanted to hear. There was no reason why she couldn't have the procedure she was seeking. A tubal ligation would be routine in her case. He explained that a day procedure in his affiliated private hospital was the usual modus operandi these days but that some people still preferred an overnight stay.

The next part of his process explanation would normally roll automatically off the tongue. He would check the mental and emotional state of the patient to ensure that this procedure would not exert undue trauma on her or her family. He would also check on the family supports available to the woman and warn her against physical exertion too soon after surgery. Where he had detected emotional disturbance or marital discord, he would urge caution and recommend counselling to make sure there would be no comeback on him. But this time, he knew he didn't want to go there and he also knew exactly why.

He tried to put the inner conflict he was feeling out of his mind. He prided himself on his professionalism and conscientiousness as a surgeon and physician. Yet he had compounded the sin of an irregular appointment on a Sunday with his failure to satisfy himself that the patient was in a fit mental and spiritual state to go ahead. However, he had no intention of stirring up a hornet's nest with a delicate flower like this, who had just fallen into his lap so fortuitously.

So, instead of doing what he knew he ought to do, he satisfied himself with the superior alternative of doing what he wanted to do. In for a penny of unprofessionalism, in for a pound.

He suggested to Julia that she ring his rooms on Monday when she had decided what to do.

But then he found himself powerless to resist the forbidden urge.

Now that the consultation is over, he said, cranking up the charm, I think you and I seriously need a drink. By the way, did you know I own the Riverside Bar?

The look on her beautiful face betrayed confusion and reluctance. He quickly realised he had to normalise the proposition and render his invitation casual rather than threatening.

I've got a couple of things to check on down there and on a Sunday it's just a five-minute drive, Robert said.

He could tell she was on the verge of declining and he was a man to whom women did not say no.

Robert changed tack once again. Would a half hour appointment on a Sunday be too much for *me* to ask of *you*?

29 LOTTERY BALLS

We are all creatures of our time. Once I had decided to put a Master Plan into play and to set myself a challenge worthy of my talent, I understood that the experiences of the current moment would shape and scope my scheme.

My small-screen heroes of the day, craving remuneration from manipulation under the public gaze, were merely representatives of the common people as a whole. Fate had propelled those particular individuals into the limelight. Millions of others stood ready and willing to take their places. The Sharons and Darrells were of the common people, they weren't any different from them.

These days people subject themselves willingly, or maybe out of ignorance, to the forces of fate and manipulation. They seem happy enough to finish up where they may.

That being so, I thought I might as well get involved. The only difference in my case was that I thought I'd get involved a bit more than most.

We are after all just lottery balls in the air machine. It is the calling of some of us, rather than others, to get more involved in the draw.

30 LIFE AND DEATH

Hannah had long been philosophical on matters of life and death. She had seen so much horror in her early years that she felt somehow inured to pain. She was not insensitive or unfeeling about the hurt of others; she merely saw pain as a normal part of life. While Hannah's responses were largely typical of those who have been subjected to brutal acts in their childhood and beyond, she differed from most of those victims in one significant way. She bore no hatred for the perpetrators and never wished or sought even the most modest act of revenge.

Hannah generally believed that these characteristics had been present in her from a very young age and had shaped her desire to enter the field of psychiatry. At other times, she wasn't so sure. She was open to the possibility that she'd merely been numbed as a child and her equanimity was simply a construction of her trained adult mind transferred to her feelings at a younger age.

Whether it was as a result of experience or professional training, she was unmoved by life and death. She was curious about the prospect of her own death, rather than scared by it. She wondered what the moment of death would be like. She had something of a professional curiosity, one might say, and it amused her in this context that curiosity had reputedly killed the cat.

There were practical aspects of living and dying, however, which had to be considered. Hannah had no living relatives and these days no meaningful friends. In these circumstances, she wasn't sure whether to leave her possessions to the dogs home (classical outcome, but wasteful), the government (very stupid idea), the Viennese Concert Pianists' Foundation (relevant, but hardly necessary), Oxfam (who would actually get the benefit?), Anglicare (but she was Jewish), or to no one (irresponsible).

Of late, she'd had a better idea. She could leave it all to Garry. This appealed to her sense of the ridiculous. Handyman chances upon rich old lady to do renovations. As soon as the house is ready, she drops dead and leaves him a fortune.

Hannah entertained the idea for a while. It wasn't so silly. Why not help an ordinary chap, a simple chap, an honest Joe to get ahead in life? Was this any less worthy than any other of the more normal alternatives she had?

No, grooming Garry as her heir didn't seem such a bad way to go. But, as good an idea as it seemed, Hannah decided not to rush. How could she satisfy herself that he was worthy?

Maybe the best way was to set him a test.

I knew exactly what to do, but I didn't know how. Just make a start, I thought. Get the raw materials together and then think it through from there.

It would be a challenge, that was for sure. If I didn't know how to go on, I could at least make a start.

I ask you, how do you make a start on anything, be it grand or simple? How do you make a start to go shopping or go on holiday or maybe invade Poland?

It's easy. First, you make a list.

REALITY INITIATED

Hannah surveyed the man at the doorstep. He looked incongruous rather than dangerous. His appearance didn't fit, that was all. In different clothes, he might have looked like a gypsy or a gigolo. But, dressed as he was and addressing her in his educated way, he seemed distinctly harmless. And also rather charming, she thought.

So she overcame her reluctance and invited him in. It was, if nothing else, an unexpected and exciting event for an elderly lady on an early evening during the week.

He wanted to write an article about her!

Goodness gracious, she said, why on earth would you want to do that?

Not that she meant it. What she really meant was why would a young man like this take an interest in her, now?

He said she was a fascinating subject. She liked that. He said her life story was remarkable.

Feel free to schmooze me, she encouraged him.

He said he'd researched the articles about her in the European magazines from the eighties and found some references to her giving conference papers in the nineties. He beamed her a smile full of reassurance and spoke softly in a manner designed to secure her full attention.

You're going to be my gravy train, he said. Your life story is utterly amazing. But better than all that, you are my little secret in Australia.

Well, let me entertain this nonsense just for a while, Hannah said. Let me assume for a ridiculous moment that you are a freelance journalist as you say you are. Where do you propose to sell this wonderful story? Which of our illustrious periodicals is going to salivate at the prospect of the story of an eighty-year-old immigrant who lives in a nameless suburb of the great non-entity that goes by the name of Perth?

She had to hand it to him – he was as cool as a cucumber. Totally unflustered by her challenge and totally in control. And he was absolutely self-assured. A beguiling combination of swashbuckler and professor.

I'm glad you asked me that, he said, with the knowing look of someone whose answer would be well thought through and well rehearsed. *The Post, West Weekend, Scoop, 60 Minutes, Australian Story* and quite possibly, but I can't promise this bit, Channel 4 in the UK.

She noticed him sit back in triumph like a poker player laying down a full house.

Is that all? she asked, laughing until the tears ran down her face.

She'd always been a sucker for a good line. When she'd been young and pretty, it had cost her dearly many times. But now, what was the worst thing that could happen to her? He could hit her over the head. But he wasn't going to do that. Sure, he was after something, but his eyes betrayed no menace. This young man was cunning rather than violent.

She fished out the hanky that was tucked into her sleeve and looked him in the eye. She dabbed away the remaining tears.

Well, young man, when shall we start?

I remember that I had come across a fabulous chardonnay. I was normally a red man. But, from time to time, I would taste a chardonnay so smooth and mellifluous, so steeped in malolactic fermentation, so strongly suffused with French oak, that it deserved the much-abused label 'better than sex'. Not that sex means that much to me. Sex was violence where I was brought up. My mother screamed in agony rather than ecstasy when my father came home late at night. He would force himself on her with his loathsome breath. She succumbed to this revolting fate rather than risk the more violent alternative if she refused him. Maybe you can understand now why I don't get my major kicks out of sex.

By the way, I get plenty of offers. Don't think I don't. People like me, remember. Particularly girls. But I can take it or leave it. I can take them and leave them too when I feel in the mood.

Well, I did find this delicious drop, a Goundrey Reserve Collection. I poured myself a glass. I sliced myself some smoked salmon to place on my pumpernickel bread. What could be more agreeable? I unfolded the random number pattern that I had downloaded from the internet for my purpose that night. I smoothed it out. I savoured the moment. It was *moment-ous*, I mused – the pinnacle of achievement for a moment!

Then, from the sublime of the chardonnay and the smoked salmon, I reached for the ridiculous of the print copy of the Perth telephone directory, residential section. I took six random numbers and converted them into page numbers and then column numbers and then ran my finger down the requisite number of entries until the corresponding name revealed itself in all its sudden glory.

What a vertiginous moment it was when the names appeared. They emerged one by one but gelled immediately in my mind as a group. I laid out the mental welcome mat to each of my new honoured guests:

Murdoch, T
Scoresby, G
Baumgarten, H
Lee, J
Martinelli, M
Hetherington, Dr R

Welcome to the next part of my life.

Five fifteen was Robert's favourite time at the bar. The Riverside Bar was a pleasing jetty structure raised over the riverbed on great wooden stilts. The wake of the jet boats and ferries would slosh and slap the water against the pilings. There was a generous outdoor deck with brightly coloured umbrellas bearing the alcohol sponsors' names. Flags fluttered and clanked their rigging against their metal posts. Inside was a cooler, darker wooden bar with candles in lanterns and wooden crates and stools for tables and chairs.

What better way could there be to unwind after a continuous parade of women's troubles from eight thirty in the morning without a break? How marvellous it was to look out over the expanse of the Swan River under the Perth sky, as blue as a fashion model's eyes. A glass or two of his better wines didn't go astray and nor did the warm inner glow of proprietorship he felt at relaxing in his own licensed premises.

I own this, he would say to himself. I fucking own this, he would bellow in pride without making a sound.

Robert particularly liked the tranquillity at that time of day before the office workers were set free from their chrome towers in the adjacent CBD. The living was easy and one could comfortably strike up a conversation.

Things could be worse, eh? someone would say to him peering into the blue.

Or Robert would say, not a bad spot for a Thursday afternoon.

On that day, he found his new drinking buddy pretty interesting. In fact Robert found him more than interesting because he seemed to be well-connected. He wasn't the usual type at the bar. Mostly he found himself conversing with brash young suits from the city, whose egos seemed to have survived the latest meltdown or corporate scandal unscathed. But this guy, who wore a suit as well, was different. Like the others, he was self-confident, maybe even a bit cocky. But, he was substantial, that was the word, in a way that the common or garden corporate high-flier types never were.

He was much more of a literary, educated type than those other guys. It was uncanny really that a complete stranger would love the books of Gabriel Garcia Marquez, just as Robert did. That conversation turned his mind in a strange way to the subject of rivers, so much a feature of Marquez's books. Could there be a starker contrast between the pristine river at their feet and one of its steamy, murky, ominous South American cousins?

This guy was one of those enthusiasts who absolutely *lurved* the bar. Robert always chose his moment well with those punters. Not too early and not too late, he would confess with studied modesty that, actually, he owned the bar.

You're shitting me!

No, it's true. I've got a business partner of course, but yes, I'm happy to say, this bar is mine!

This guy, one would have to say, was particularly impressed. Robert had picked him as an *expander* and that turned out to be the case. Expanders were those patrons who had great plans for the place, if only it were theirs. Most of them had no idea about customer expectations, planning issues or the dreaded liquor licensing regulations, but waxed lyrical anyway about their grand plans hatched with other people's money in mind. But, this guy was refreshingly different.

Instead of pontificating on what he would do with the place, he was intrigued with what Robert and his partners might have in mind, given the fabulous potential of the location. These were actually timely questions as the partnership had recognised the need to make some key decisions about the bar now that it was performing well, at least during the warmer months. After chewing the fat with this guy for a while, Robert felt his mind was clearer on the subject. That wasn't an outcome he'd expected when he'd parked his bum at the bar an hour before.

You've earned yourself a drink, Robert said, thinking aloud.

He called out to Todd to bring him a bottle of the Spy Valley sauvignon blanc and a couple of glasses as a well-earned reward for them both. Towards the end of the second bottle, inebriation and sobriety kicked in with equal measure. OK, he was pissed, so he would have to shell out a small fortune for a cab to the hills or crash in the flat above. Either way, Marjorie would have a piece of him. That prospect justified one more drink.

He hadn't quite worked out what the guy did, but he was obviously well in with investors, maybe bankers, who were cashed up and ready to move. Perhaps this *was* the answer to Paddy's reluctance to put more money into the bar. Do it without him. Potentially, if he sold some equity or took on some judicious debt, he could expand the decking and ramp up the profits without stick-in-the-mud Paddy having to shell out any more himself.

It was definitely worth a thought. If Marjorie let him live long enough to think it through.

35   A MAN WITHOUT A HOUSE

It was a thrill to randomly select those names. There was some science in the random number process, but it was otherwise a blue-collar affair. The true skill and the real challenge stood on the road ahead, beckoning me and winking at me like two tarts looking for trade. They were attractive and repulsive at the same time. I had to buy and taste the pleasure, but what if I failed, what if my Master Plan couldn't get it up?

Yet I was born for this. I would make it happen and I would fulfil my potential. I reminded myself sternly of my status as a true disciple of Sharon. Maybe, to be truthful, I was more like a virtual Sharon, maybe an avatar Sharon or perhaps a potential Sharon. I had found myself some housemates, but alas, I had no house.

In this case, the only way to make a house for us all and to pull us all together was to find a way to contact my random not yet acquaintances.

After the guy left, Kathleen realised that she'd done it again and taken work she really didn't want. OK, work's work. But there are limits.

The guy had intrigued Kathleen. He was rather dishy in a Mediterranean sort of way, but didn't respond to her as cute guys were supposed to. He didn't talk to her tits like most guys and he didn't even look at her arse when she went to answer the phone. She wondered if he were gay, though he wasn't registering on her gaydar. She acknowledged to herself the appalling arrogance of labelling him gay. Sure, she *was* up herself a bit, but she was dealing with it.

This guy was being less than truthful and that, as usual, excited her. He had a pissant landlord and tenant case to pursue in Melbourne. Some guy, a real estate agent of all people, had done a runner owing him rent. Heaps of rent, actually. He'd tracked him down using collection agents, but couldn't get the dude to turn up to court.

What's more, he was selling the house and wanted the debt collection and the conveyancing handled in the one place. And locally too, so he could talk face to face with someone if the need arose.

She told him he needed a Victorian law firm to deal with it, but he knew that, he said. He was a busy man and he knew from bitter business experience that lawyer-to-lawyer communications worked much better than lawyer to inferior human being interactions. So, he wanted a local law firm to make it all happen, even if it had to be via an intermediary firm in Melbourne.

Those were his reasons for wanting a lawyer to handle it from the West.

Why *me* then? she asked him.

He avoided the question, like some politician or someone connected to politics. He chose to respond in a different way. It was in a way, she reflected now, that seemed calculated to push the right buttons. But how could he know?

The fact is, he said, and I'll be truthful with you, the fact is that I want to see how you handle this.

And why is that may I ask? she said, with her head at that alluring angle she'd perfected just to flirt.

He ignored her come-on completely. I'm connected to some people, influential people, who have a regular amount of advice and support they need in relation to their business dealings and I've heard of your firm and particularly of you.

OK, she was sucked in, she admitted it. She liked the sound of influential people and she loved the idea of helping with their 'business dealings'. Straight, boring people don't say 'business dealings'. They say what it is – property, investments, currency or whatever.

So she took the stupid little rent evasion job and the equally demeaning conveyancing work in the hope of much better things to come. She knew he might be shitting her but went into it with her eyes wide open. Obviously, nothing might come of it. But, she didn't think so. He was a guy of substance even though he was spinning a line. He wanted her for some reason.

Maybe he was just pretending not to fancy her.

My Master Plan would have been impossible before the information age. Just think of that. That's presumably why no one had attempted this insanely clever stratagem before! Information is power – that's it. In a nutshell. And how do we find information these days? With the stroke of a key or the swipe of a screen. In a couple of seconds, all of the world's information can be literally at your fingertips. You can find anything you need to know about people. Most people, anyway. Well, let's say most worthwhile people.

Imagine how fucking insignificant you would have to be these days not to show up on Google? Can you believe there are still people out there like that? That's the problem with random selection. You can get anybody. Well, that's the idea – you *do* get anybody.

It was a challenge, I won't lie to you. And it worried me in anticipation of getting into it. What if one of my housemates wouldn't Google? What then?

Well, the answer is – that's where the brains come in. That's what makes this a Master Plan. To succeed, you have to be smart, resourceful, innovative and persistent.

The thought occurs to me that we could be the first and last generation capable of a masterpiece like this. What would generation Y do if the housemates weren't there on the internet? Would they know what to do? They'd probably just give up and go back to texting somebody or tweeting to the world what they had for breakfast. Technologically savvy Gen Y may be, but what good is that if you have the attention span of a goldfish?

They'd give up, for sure.

I didn't.

The grapevine's an amazing thing, Garry thought. Particularly at a time like this. Booms and busts come and go, but there's always demand for a moonlighter. Sometimes he worried that his moonlighting was overtaking his firefighting, but the mortgage and the other bills just kept mounting up.

At first, Garry didn't think anything of the call. This bloke had somehow met the guys from the Freo fire station at the pub and they'd referred him on. Garry invited him over to his place to discuss the job. They retreated to the back yard to escape the kid noise. Garry looked him up and down. His clothes looked expensive and he spoke very well. University-educated, Garry guessed. The guy had just bought an investment property, pretty run down it was, and he wanted to turn it over for a quick sale. A beautiful old place, he told Garry, with some great features to the house.

By the way, you don't do leadlights, do you? he asked.

Leadlights, really? Garry gushed in an excited manner that would have embarrassed his daughter. Now you've got me.

Yeah, the leadlights need some work, but they're a fantastic feature of the house.

I'm a leadlights junkie, Garry confessed.

Fantastic! But better still there's five grand on top for you if you can help me turn this over for a really quick sale.

Garry could barely contain his excitement long enough to let the guy disappear out the side gate before rushing to find Kirsty.

Kirsty, you'll never guess what, he said.

What? she said sarcastically.

I said you'd never guess what.

He gave her a cuddle and a light-hearted kiss on the neck to get her in a mood to match his own. How does a five grand bonus for a job sound to you?

He could see she was impressed. The trouble was he could also tell she was already working out what to spend it on.

And that's not the good bit, he said. He wants leadlights done.

You and your leadlights, she said as she always did with a blend of affection, pity and amazement. You and your leadlights – I'm surprised you're not doing it for free!

39 JUST ASKING AROUND

As I contemplated my search I asked myself the question, what did we do before computers? I know that sounds like one of those world-weary, atavistic, wasn't-life-better-when-it-was-simpler total crap questions. That wasn't what I meant. I actually know the answer to that one. Obviously back in those days they had their own losers harking back to a previous golden age that was just as bad.

No, as the internet couldn't meet all my needs, I genuinely needed to revisit how we used to find out things and locate people back in the day. The answers were illuminating. We went to the library! Fuck – no wonder nothing got done. We went to the newspapers' offices and looked at back copies on microfiche. Jesus. We hired private detectives – that was a bit more exciting.

But the real answer to my self-posed question was that we used to ask around. I realised with regret that I would have to do this, and frankly I was not keen.

I hate asking people things because it puts you at such a disadvantage. The *askee* has all the power over the *asker* because they have some information or knowledge you want. Nowhere is this more evident than in India. Nobody there ever says they don't know. If you ask for directions, they will tell you where to go whether they know or not.

Those Indians know who holds the power in this complex social phenomenon and they will not give it up.

Armed with this knowledge, I determined to even up the ledger when I started asking around.

I would ask certain people questions, but the great thing was – they would have no idea who I was or why I was asking. To my mind, that would give the power back to me.

When Julia bumped into her best friend Lisa with her new man, she was taken aback. Lisa and Julia had laughed about the new guy being Lisa's toy boy, but faced with this dark and handsome younger man in person, Julia found that jealousy had cut her to the quick. She tried not to show it, but envy kept welling up and spilling out beyond her control.

Julia was ashamed of her reaction as she had never seen herself as one to begrudge a friend their happiness. She steeled herself to get over it, to get on with it. She shot furtive glances Lisa's way to check if her meanness had been registered, but that was a waste of time as Lisa was totally focused on her guy. Julia eventually wrestled the green devil into submission and began to chat and joke just like her old self.

Afterwards, as she walked past the boutiques and homewares shops to her car, Julia could see the attraction. He was good-looking, in a Southern European sort of way, but she was not jealous of the physicality. No, that wasn't it. He was much younger than Stephen, but that wasn't it either. The thing about Lisa's man was his naked power. He oozed influence from his every pore. Not the pull and sway that comes from high birth or having gone to the right school and university. No, he had supreme inner self-confidence that gave him the attractive air of a man in complete control.

Julia chuckled to herself and gently shook her head as she walked. She was lusting after the confidence of her husband Stephen of old. But, this guy was different from Stephen, she thought. This guy is purposeful. He's the sort of guy who knows what he wants and will do anything to get it. He perspires purpose. Stephen didn't sweat at all. He sweated so little that sometimes she wondered if he was really still alive.

What did he see in Lisa? she wondered. What a terrible thought! Lisa was pretty and bubbly. But, he didn't touch her, didn't hold her hand, didn't smooch with her or anything like that. He didn't look at her with lust in his eyes. And how did she look at him? Like a teacher? No, not quite. Like a guru? No, not with so much reverence. Like a storyteller? Now, that was close. She hung on his every word. She wanted to know where he was headed. Julia got it. Lisa was turned on by his sense of purpose, too.

I was standing on the edge of a diving board. That's where I was. It was bouncing up and down with a vigorous creaking motion and, at the moment of my choosing, I would plummet to the depths of my destiny.

I was itching to get on with it once I'd found myself some housemates. But it was going to take a moment of courage to make that decisive move and entrust myself to gravity. Even for me.

I was poised there to leap just as you now surely are – to leap to judgment. Try not to do that. Admire, don't judge.

And for God's sake, don't try to label me. Don't dive for the term control freak – that is so pejorative. If you're striving to understand, why not entertain the term *interventionist*? It has a certain descriptive accuracy. All men may be born equal, but they sure don't end up equal. Interventionism – I always wanted to invent a movement and give it a name – is the (admittedly arrogant) imposition of powerful active interveners on the lives of those whose destiny it is to be mere objects – in fact to be intervened upon.

The diving board soared and dipped. My toes gripped the very extremity of the outermost molecules of the fibreglass. Gravity was about to merge with destiny.

From the vantage point of his morning café, Mario kept an eye out for his eleven o'clock appointment. Mario liked this espresso bar. Its décor hadn't changed for years and nor had its regulars. It was frequented by rusted-on Freo types who were supposed to be looking for work. Mario knew them all and shared their basic values. He did as little as possible too.

There was a guy hanging around outside the entry to his upstairs office, but he didn't look the type he was expecting. On the other hand, no one else seemed to be showing up. Mario knocked back the molasses of the dregs of his espresso, grabbed his mobile and fags and skipped though the traffic across the road.

The guy recognised him straight away and greeted him cheerily.

Hi Mario, he said stretching out his hand, you look exactly like the photo in your ad.

I should do. No one else has got this beautiful face!

Mario led the way up the old-fashioned staircase to the classic antiquated office over the shopfronts. He puffed his way up the two fairly short flights of stairs.

I'm getting a chair lift with my frequent fagging points, Mario said breathlessly over his shoulder to his appointment who was clattering his way effortlessly up the hard wooden staircase behind him.

Mario liked his little office. It wasn't flash but it had personality. It had the usual filing cabinets, a PC and enough space for two chairs on the other side of Mario's desk. His desk had belonged to his grandfather and was made of dark mahogany. There was a faded leather blotter in the middle of it covered in scribblings, calculations and doodles on the thick absorbent paper that it framed.

The best thing about your own office, Mario often mused, was that you can light up whenever the fuck you like. So he did.

The guy may not have looked like the voice over the phone – Mario had imagined a classic Aussie – but he clearly was the same bloke, confidently launching into what he wanted and what he expected in terms of a proposition.

A friend of mine is prominent in the hospitality industry as well as being an eminent person in his own profession. My friend is keen to expand some of his operations and is looking for investors.

And you want me to fix you a loan so you can put up some capital, Mario chimed in triumphantly.

Not exactly, well not even close actually. Have I got an opportunity for you, he went on in a mock Yiddish accent.

Mario was beginning to like this fellow – he had some devil in him and he was up to something. Mario liked that in a man.

I am here to suggest that you *invest*.

I don't *invest*, Mario sniffed, taking a long, slow puff on his fag. I don't invest, I *lend*.

You're not the Mario I expected, the guy retorted, with a knowing smirk.

This sounds like a challenge, Mario said.

It is. He leant forward to engage Mario's full attention. What if I told you I'd lend you the money so you can invest?

Mario laughed and coughed at the same time, convulsing from the shock and shaking his swivel chair with his chest tremors. This guy wants to lend *me* money, he mocked once his hacking had subsided, as if to some audience that had suddenly crammed itself into his tiny office.

Why should I let you lend me money to invest in something I don't know anything about? Mario enquired with all the Joe Cool he could muster.

Because you'll make a fortune and because I won't charge you any interest.

Mario slapped both hands down on the desk with two fractionally asynchronous thwacks. This guy I love, Mario announced to the imaginary onlookers. Then he got up, gathered his mobile and smokes and said let's go to the pub and talk.

Mario slapped him on the back as they negotiated the stairs. You're up to something, buddy, and I wanna know what it is.

By the way, the guy added as their footsteps rang out on the stairs, there's one condition.

Now we're getting somewhere.

Yes, there's a catch.

A catch, I knew it, Mario whooped.

Yes, the catch is you're not allowed to tell anybody about our arrangement.

That's the catch? Mario laughed, coughing his guts out again.

Yep, that's it.

Stop it, Mario begged him, you're cracking me up.

43 SUBJECTS AND OBJECTS

The first thing I had to do was entice my randomly selected housemates towards their new reality. I made a start on Google.

Dr Robert Hetherington appeared without any fuss. Famous gynaecologist, written a few papers in *The Lancet*. Treasurer or some such thing of the Perth BMW Sports Club. Best of all, there was even a pic. He was smiling with his business partner, Patrick Michael, at the opening of the chic new Riverside Bar. My friend Robert also kindly presented himself in *Who's Who*. Married to Marjorie for twenty-five years. Two sons – both doctors – don't tell me you're really surprised.

Hannah Baumgarten – now she was a find in a random selection process. No Google entries for a good ten years or so, but there were stacks of laudatory articles and quotes about her. That's not to mention the books and articles actually written by her – autobiography, feminism, Jungian psychoanalysis and opinion pieces. This woman would have an amazing intellect, I was thinking, an appropriate challenge indeed.

Regrettably, as I've already told you, there are also nobodies in life. Garry Scoresby was googled and what did I find? Nothing, zip, zilch. The same with Julia Lee. Absolutely nothing. And what chance do you think I had with Mario Martinelli? Bugger all, that's right. Well, that's the luck of the draw and that's where the skill comes in.

Of course, it wasn't all doom and gloom. In addition to my helpful friends Dr Robert and Hannah, I also eventually found the lovely Kathleen. I was getting a tad frustrated that my nobody-to-celebrity ratio was unreasonably unbalanced, when up popped something rather juicy.

I found Kathleen in the law reports and a number of newspaper articles. I even found a photograph of her outside a courthouse with someone we euphemistically call one of Perth's more colourful personalities. For obvious reasons I won't name that person, but there she was – involved in one of his cases.

She was just a junior lawyer assisting more senior counsel, but at least I knew where to find her. I searched deeper through the

Google listings and found something very interesting indeed. I read with passionate interest what some old fuddy-duddy lawyer had to say. Dull as ditchwater QC was suggesting that some of my new lady friend's associations had seriously prejudiced a case.

Robert. Hannah. Kathleen. I had located three of my housemates. That still left three to go. The obvious thing was just to ring them up, but I had decided in the careful planning phase, that direct contact from the outset would be a last resort. I wanted to meet them in due course, but preferably at a more strategic time. Instead, I adopted a more cloak and dagger approach. I had their addresses from the great book of life and the obvious thing was to spy on them.

Garry was relatively easy. To track him down, I had to hang around in my car at some godforsaken hour in the architectural desert that passes for a suburban street in Perth. And it was not a mercifully short sojourn, either. I waited for a bloody long time until a thirty-something guy emerged in a white ute from a standard, appalling double garage.

It was thrilling following somebody after watching so many movies with car chases. Follow that car! I instructed myself. So I did and, fifteen minutes later, I found myself at the Fremantle Fire Station. That was an excellent outcome. I knew a fireman and I reckoned I could predict his way of life.

Julia's suburb was far, far and even another far, more salubrious than Garry's. So it was more uplifting waiting in *her* street one classic, blue-skied West Australian morning. I felt a bit of a fool when an Audi TT convertible sped from the driveway around seven-thirty. I got my A into G and tailed the car onto the main road until it stopped at the lights. I pulled up alongside to check out my prey and saw to my horror that it was a man!

I made my way back, hoping I hadn't missed her. Around eight-twenty, a Merc four-wheel drive appeared. Sure enough, it was a blonde-haired woman with two uniformed girls in the back. One of them was a little carbon copy of herself. I followed them, but it was hardly *French Connection II*. At the main road, we drove straight into the snooty girls private school. If the girls had walked, they would have got there quicker.

It amused me to think that the girls probably got chauffeured to save them from predatory men. And there I was, stalking their mother. What a hoot!

People are predictable, you know. I pursued Julia out of the school environs and not five minutes later, she pulled up at the local gym. A gym wife – as if I couldn't guess! But there was no time to linger. I had made some progress, but on that particular day, I had an audience with the Minister and she didn't like you to be late.

I was, in my usual fashion, beginning to think this venture was too much of a breeze. By googling and following, *foogling* perhaps, I had made an impressive start. I just had Mario to go.

The next day, I stationed myself in a street where every house was guarded by plaster lions, perched incongruously like eagles overlooking the front gate. It was one of those scorched-earth streets that, ironically, migrants from the most beautiful homelands sometimes inflict on their adopted country. Not a blade of grass was to be found in a concreted or paved front yard. Not a worm survived to pop up a quizzical head. Not one stray leaf floated to earth to lodge maliciously in a pristine gutter.

There I waited and no one appeared. So I came back and waited and no one appeared. I had no choice but to show my face at the house next door. A curtain parted, but the owner of the eyes was content to just inspect me rather than open the door.

I'm looking for Mario, I mouthed to the face.

Maybe she couldn't hear me. I'm looking for Mario, I shouted through the window.

The old lady let the curtain fall back in place and walked away from the window. I was angry and felt like banging on the door until she gave in. Just as I was weighing up my options, she opened the door and kissed me on both cheeks. She greeted me like the prodigal son returned and then alternately abused me and rained kisses on me with her fetid garlic breath.

I figured it out. The woman was demented and she had me pinned for the moment as her son Aldo.

Aldo, Aldo she cried, hugging me to her bony bosom.

I was feeling desperate. Like Queen, I knew I had to break free.

I oriented my mouth to her ear.

I'm looking for Mario who lives next door, I enunciated in my clearest diction at decibels that would rival Freddy Mercury at his loudest.

The words took a few moments to sink in. Then there was a look of recognition and, after that, there was a scowl so full of loathing and venom that I may never see its like again. Then, out of the mouths of babes and old widows, came a stream of foreign language invective that sounded fit to make waterside workers blush. I imagined it wasn't all good.

As I couldn't understand a word, I was forming the opinion that, somehow, what I'd said in English, meant can I fuck your grand-daughter in Sicilian and her powers of cognition had just kicked back in. Fortunately, a weathered old man of diminished stature appeared from the house. He motioned to me to stay put while he escorted the cursing old nonna back into the house.

He reappeared and explained to me in broken English that Mario didn't live there any more. He told me their daughter, Mario's long-suffering wife, got fed up with his cheating and his gambling and his drinking.

She threw him out, he said, and good luck to her.

Where did he go? I asked. The man just shrugged. Does your daughter still live there?

No, she moved.

Can you please tell me where they've gone? It's important.

He looked me in the eyes as he may have one day back in Palermo. He pointed to his nose and said, I minda my beesnez, maybe you minda yours.

And then he turned on his heels and went back indoors. Just like that.

The frustration at not finding Mario ate away at me for a while. I racked my brains as to how to locate him. I entertained the stupid idea of asking around for him in Freo and I pondered the criminal notion of breaking into his ex-in-laws' house to rifle through their address books to track down his ex-wife. In the face of this exceptionally trying state of affairs, I felt a yearning to confront a friendly frustration of my own. For the first time in a long time, I went round to Mark's place. Naturally, I went there unannounced, as there was more chance of being struck by lightning than not finding him home.

Mark was strangely animated for him and I wasn't sure I liked that. I was relying on Mark to be his usual, predictable self. It unnerved me to find him the exact opposite. Can't you count on anything these days?

He was excited and wanted to talk. Mark had been staying on the Gold Coast of all places. I couldn't imagine Mark going to the Gold Coast, let alone hanging out there. The land of outward appearance and front. Mark had so little front that he was only back. Anyway, he told me that he had gone there because he won a competition – that would be right – and while he was there he had bought an apartment.

How fucking ridiculous was this? Mark, who wouldn't move from his computer if a tsunami was bearing down, was suddenly becoming a gold-shoe brigade property investor. This would definitely end in tears, except for the fact that crying was something a little more active than Mark could realistically contemplate.

Fortunately, he told me the full story of his purchase and then I felt a lot better. The world wasn't turning upside down after all. He bought the apartment in the most absurd of circumstances and so, in a funny way, had been true to himself.

He was sitting in a piano bar having a quiet beer when the guy who was packing up the tables for closing time struck up a conversation with him. The guy explained to him that he was not really connected with the bar – he just lived upstairs and helped out now and again. But the best bit was that this guy was an international real estate salesman and had the business card to prove it. And the guy chatted with Mark for some time, which is no mean feat. The guy explained to Mark the ins and outs of the Gold Coast property market – what was a rip-off, what was a steal, which apartments attracted tenants and which sat empty. He recommended to Mark that he shouldn't buy an apartment and then an hour and a half and a quantity of ales later, Mark bought an apartment off the guy who clears the tables at the bar but only does so because he lives upstairs. And really, why wouldn't you buy real estate from an international property dealer who had a business card to prove it? And, moreover, why wouldn't you buy an apartment from a guy who'd told you he wouldn't recommend you buy an apartment? Why to both? – because you're Mark.

By the end of this story, Mark had done the trick and I felt far less frustrated. What's more, thanks to the saintly act of sitting patiently through Mark's real estate adventure, the gods deemed me worthy of a massive and breathtaking stroke of luck. I was flicking through the local community newspaper while Mark displayed his legendary inability to find things by giving up on the corkscrew I needed. (Yes, screwcap wine bottles were invented for Mark.) Then an ad caught my eye. There was a guy with a cheesy grin and a guilty smile offering loans to people who couldn't get them from anybody else.

Don't sit in front of the telly, come see Mario Martinelli.

Mario Martinelli of all people! Maybe there was a God after all.

Buoyed by the news, I took myself off to the bottle shop to get a good drop with a Stelvin cap. Never did a glass of red (Zonti's Steps shiraz and viognier) taste so good and never was Mark's company (even of the rather animated sort) so alluring.

I remember the elation well. This is what success tastes like. This is what it's like to win off the last ball or win the Grand Final by a point. This is achievement you can taste.

I had found all six of my subjects, if I may call my housemates that for a moment. For they *are* my subjects right now, unwitting as they are, and I am their king. Perhaps, they are actually my *objects* because I will be doing things *unto* them very soon.

Anyway, who gives a shit? As they say, you know who they are. But the beauty of it was that they didn't – not yet.

I had something of a red-wine head. Actually, it was a thumping bad one. The one where the histamines have colluded with the many headed gods of *de-hydra-tion* to make you swear off the demon drink and promise God faithfully, with your fingers crossed behind your back, that you'll never ever, ever drink again.

But, in spite of this, as they say in the James Brown classic, I felt goo-oood, so goo-ood! I was underway. I was on the scoreboard. There were varying degrees of difficulty, but nothing I couldn't overcome.

Kathleen Alice Theresa Murdoch – a lawyer, so fairly easy. Think up a case, go to see her, suck her in. No worries.

Garry Troy Scoresby – a fireman, lives in the suburbs. Have to get to him somehow, so a little bit tricky. But, hey he's a fireman, a known quantity. All firemen are the same. No problem there.

Hannah Esther Temple Baumgarten – a famous, elderly female icon. Famous people are used to strangers approaching them. Just need an angle, something that flatters them due to their celebrity. Shouldn't be that tough, but age factor could be a risk. What if she's sick and won't see anyone? Could be a problem. At any rate, she's bound to be wary of strangers at her age. Will require subtlety, this one. But then, subtlety is my middle name.

Julia Lee – tracking down process was time well spent. I know a few of her haunts. Making the actual contact could be a challenge. Turning up at the house unannounced is an absolute last resort. Will have to follow up a lead – either the school or the gym.

Mario Nikita Martinelli – I feel good about finding you, my main man. Have a pic of you, too, right out of the local paper. Seems like a piece of piss. Might have to take out some kind of loan for losers and get ripped off like the poor people do. But, hey dude, I can afford it for the sake of a Master Plan. But, wait, wait just a little minute. There could be another way. Yes, there really could. Maybe I'll loan *you* some money for a change.

Dr Robert Guy Mills Hetherington – finally, good old Robert. Dr Robert, I should say. What a way to make a living. Well, it tcould be worse. He could look up men's arseholes. He also has other irons in the fire. In hospitality, indeed, on the banks of the Swan. There must be an opening there. It might cost me a vino or two to find out. Yes, things could be worse.

Robert tried very hard to consign the following thoughts to a part of his brain that Marjorie could never penetrate. They had to be archived within a cerebral area that his medical sons couldn't probe to generate an image on a large electronic screen. He wanted to savour Julia's sweetness like a late harvest riesling. He wanted to lick Julia all over.

He tried not to let a plethora of guilty thoughts spoil this wonderful moment. He shouldn't be doing this (even in thought) to Marjorie; he shouldn't be thinking these thoughts about a patient; he shouldn't be contemplating this given Julia's emotionally vulnerable state; he certainly shouldn't have manipulated Julia into having this drink with him after the consultation.

Ooops, these thoughts were distracting him.

What was that again? he said affably.

He felt good that her husband Stephen was such a bastard. Fancy pulling that Chinese maid stunt so he could bang his wife up. Despicable. Really he'd be doing her a big favour if they got more acquainted.

He tried not to stare. No doubt about it – she was absolutely delicious. He liked the obstinate wrinkles around the eyes, the beginnings of the dreaded crows' feet. No amount of creamy, nourishing, botoxifying, anti-ageing, night-time lotioning could prevent the inexorable march of these wrinkles. Why bother anyway? They were adorable. Her little blondey femininity was adorable.

She was probably very interesting to listen to, but he realised his adoration had blocked out every word. Time to get into the game, he realised. How fortunate that she was asking how long he'd owned the bar.

To a man like him, such a question was a gift. He could tell Julia the story as he had to so many of the fairer sex before. In its telling, she would discover Robert the wealthy, Robert the entrepreneur, Robert the risk-taker, Robert the hedonist, Robert the dashing, Robert the suave, Robert the Mr Fucking Irresistible.

Sir Robert the Licker All Over.

46 OPPORTUNITY KNOCKS

My head felt better already having tallied up the scores. In my estimation, Kathleen, Mario, Robert and Hannah were ready-basted turkeys ripe for shoving in the oven. All I needed for them was an angle – for my analogy, the stuffing? – and then I could grab them easily enough and prepare them for their destiny on my festive table. But, with Garry and Julia, I still had to go to make their trussed-up acquaintance before I could bring them home. I needed some sort of friendly neighbourhood butcher to unite me with my coveted, plump birds.

On one fine Saturday morning, I decided that Julia was the place to start. Certainly, between her and Garry, Julia was a more salubrious place to take off. All rich and delicate and perfect, not rough and average and mundane like Garry was. She was after all the classic middle-class, middle-aged MILF who was sure to be up to no good. Not on the surface, mind you, because everything would be perfect. But, there would be a dark and sinister underbelly that someone of my skill and creativity would be able to discover and exploit.

To begin with, I knew three things about her. I knew where she lived; I knew where her girls went to school; and I knew where she went to the gym. OK, so I also knew she had a guy in her life, presumably her husband, but that seemed rather inconsequential.

I had already ruled out visiting the house, except if all else failed, so that left with me with two choices. I could sniff around the school, but I knew that I would stick out like the sore proverbial in the Anglo-Saxon, lilywhite, cottonwool environment of the genteel ladies college. That being the case, my least worst option was obviously to go with the gym.

Actually, this espionage stuff is much harder than it looks. I realised that I would need to spend time around Julia to probe for an opening. But, at the same time, I couldn't get too close to her or even so close as to become some sort of blip on her radar. As well as all that, I was conscious not to ignore her altogether, not to make the classic mistake of the office romance where the lovers suddenly start avoiding each other when once they would share a joke and a laugh at the water cooler.

I started casual sessions at her gym. I made sure I worked out in her vicinity, while at the same time keeping my distance. I had a sly perve on her just as any non-stalking guy would. I remained alert and kept my eye out for opportunities. And then what should happen? In walked my opportunity. Opportunity on legs. Opportunity in a leotard. Opportunity in a pump class.

In case you didn't already guess this, opportunity had a name. It was called Lisa.

47 THE IRRELEVANCE OF LAW

Kathleen caught herself working on the Martinelli brief at home on the weekend. She would sit there in her minimalist black and white lounge chairs, sipping from elegant Riedel glassware and staring into space deep in thought. Instead of facebooking and tweeting up a storm, she was neglecting her friends and the world at large to mull things over. She wasn't sure what this unusual behaviour signified exactly. What intrigued her so about the Martinelli case?

She'd read through Mario's so-called contract and looked up relevant cases in the office so as to rack up a respectable number of billable hours. As lawyers tend to, she felt the case could go either way.

If Mario hadn't been such a wise-guy, smart-arse dinghe would have had a proper contract drawn up that would have left no doubt. On the other hand, if he'd been the sort to do the standard, sensible thing, he probably wouldn't be so sweet. Anyway, the fact remained that it was a pretty lousy contract against which to lend someone half a million bucks. And there were definitely arguable loopholes. However, Your Honour, she thought, there was clearly an implied contract there to lend money on clear terms outlining how the money would be paid back. But, like so much of her work, it was impossible to tell how this would go without testing it in court.

She hated telling clients this because people want their lawyer to be like a doctor. They want you to diagnose their problem and they want you to cure it. But most of the time, you feel more like their bookmaker because you end up advising them they have to go to the judicial racetrack to find out if their horse will win. What makes it worse is that they have to pay you, win or lose, for the privilege of having been told that they have to go to the track.

She knew Mario would look at her with his big brown eyes like a seal about to be clubbed. Maybe it would do him good to look at her like an endangered animal rather than a beast on heat. She walked to her glass and metal sideboard and poured herself a Jim Beam to round off the wine. This legal bullshit really missed the point. Resolving the legal case might take months or years. Anyway, this guy from the village with the shoe factory would have a family trust that kept his wife in the lap of luxury but ensured he had no personal assets. In fact, if Mario were to sit back and allow the process of law to run its interminable course, the chances were he'd end up sliced and diced way before any verdict was handed down.

Kathleen realised that this impeccable logic was taking her to places that she didn't, but really did, want to go. How do we divert the attention of the heavies away from Mario and onto the shoe guy where it belongs? Was this a legal challenge, she wondered, or was this something a little more interesting and exhilarating?

Matt was coming round in a minute. Regrettably, Matt was far too straight to understand.

I didn't know her name then, but the woman who always smiled at me in the pump class was a good friend of my soon to be very good friend, Julia. Every morning, once they had sweated it out, she and Julia would meet at the foyer of the fitness centre and head off down the escalators, out of the swanky shopping centre and across the road to the café strip where all the gym wives liked to congregate.

I noticed that Lisa wasn't a gym wife as such, as she was wearing the telltale ex-wedding ring on her right hand. She was the perfect prospect for my purposes – a gym divorcee. Lisa was that bit older than Julia and her beauty had faded that much more. She had more wrinkles, more weight around the middle, more make-up, more gold jewellery and, as a consequence of that, more of an air of desperation. Compared with Julia, Lisa was more open to people, more out on the prowl, more ready to put herself out there, more attentive to what was around. In short, I concluded with glee, she was looking for a man. How thoughtful and convenient of her!

Call me arrogant if you like (I know you want to) but I knew I could pull this chick. The question was not if, but how? And then, while I was still weighing up my options, the solution literally landed in my lap. I had taken up position next to her for that morning's very crowded pump class in the hope it would give me the opportunity to say hello. Then, right in the middle of 'Get The Party Started', she overbalanced and tumbled in my direction, propelled in a downward, sideways motion by the impressive weight she was pumping. I don't know if I actually tried to catch her and I don't know whether she actually tried to stop herself from falling on me, but within a split second she tackled me to the floor and we landed in an ungainly, sweaty heap.

She apologised profusely and we collectively shooed away the crowd of well-toned well-wishers. On my way out, as I was towelling away the rivulets of sweat, she caught up with me and tapped me on the shoulder. I spun around and smiled my most disarming smile in mock surprise at who it was.

I'm so terribly sorry, she said. I'm so embarrassed. I'm totally mortified, as a matter of fact. Anyway, I'm Lisa, she said towelling down a clammy palm before offering it to me.

Hi Lisa, I said, I'm *very* pleased to meet you.

Hannah was exulting in her favourite Mozart concerto, letting its warmth and virtuosity envelope her. She was contemplating how to test Garry's worth now that the renovations were well progressed and fairly soon would be at an end. She was fairly sure they should have been finished some time ago, however, her once shy and inarticulate protégé was now waxing forth on the most outlandish subjects and extending tea breaks for hours on end. Perhaps that was the test. Perhaps she just had to wait to see if Garry still charged her the quoted price, given that the job had taken much longer than he'd originally estimated.

She shook her head and laughed at the absurdity of testing a tradesman's honesty by the accuracy of the bill.

Obviously, she needed something more challenging. Something that would tempt the most honest of people to do the wrong thing. She loved a moral dilemma. She needed to come up with something akin to the perfect crime. Some situation where doing the wrong thing would be easier than doing the opposite. Some circumstance where, if you chose the side of darkness rather than light, no one would ever know what you had done.

A favourite passage from *Eine Kleine Nachtmusik* broke her chain of thought. Once she refocused, she found herself searching for the inner truth. Why did she feel the need to *test* Garry before leaving him everything? Why was it better to leave her money and assets to a saint rather than a sinner? What did it say about her that she needed to make these moral judgments, to play God like this? Since when had she become so bourgeoise? She knew from a lifetime of work and study that questions like this, from the moral domain, had no answer. To solve her problem, she thought up a new question, one much more susceptible to an answer. Why do I need a reason to put someone to the test? The answer to this was as easy as it was rhetorical.

At my age, you don't need a reason to have a bit of fun!

I never expected my so-called cousin Neville to prove useful to me, but there you go. I say so-called because he is a blood relative of my so-called father, Axe.

I had the misfortune to spend time with him at a wake for a distant so-called relative. We shared dog-eared ham sandwiches and a couple of beers as we shuffled uncomfortably from one foot to the other wondering when we could legitimately make a break for it.

The conversation was less than riveting, hence my designation of the encounter as unfortunate. However, as things turned out, the experience later more than proved its worth.

Anyway, Neville was a fireman at a suburban station in Melbourne and was good enough to tell me about his job. By the sound of it, his inarticulate babbling was about as interesting as actually being a fireman. According to Neville, they hung around, played pool, polished equipment and hoped against hope that they wouldn't be called out. Neville told me all the ins and outs of daily life as a fireperson. This was trivia for which I had no use – at the time.

The human brain is a wonderful thing. Once I'd tracked Garry down to the Fremantle Fire Station, Neville's half hour of drivel came flooding back to me. I knew exactly what I had to do next. I took myself around to the only hotel left in Fremantle's once multi-pubbed West End. This would be the spot, I thought. If I don't find Garry himself, I'll find his mates.

It took a bit of patience, but eventually my plan worked out. I spied a group of blokes who looked the part, talked the part and a couple of them even carried the latest FESA issue manuals to confirm their suspected identity.

Hi, I said, interrupting the endless piss-taking that passes for conversation amongst blokes.

I'm Neville from the Footscray Station in Melbourne. I thought I'd try my luck over here in the West.

51   WHAT MUST I BE THINKING?

No sooner had Julia sat down at the beautiful, trendy bar down by the river than she was offered a crisp white wine. No sooner had he set off for the bar to get it than her brain went into its customary spin. In no more than a couple of minutes, her mental iPod shuffled through the entire playlist of worries, fears, guilts and regrets. Chasing cars around her head, as the song goes.

Of course, she shouldn't have seen the doctor and of course, she shouldn't have agreed to go for a drink with him. What would she say if someone saw them? What excuse would she make? What if Stephen was bonking the Asian maid? How would the girls cope without their father, if things come to a head?

And so it went on until Robert reappeared silhouetted against the late afternoon sun. It took her a while to come round and realise where she was and who she was with. Next, she found herself doing what she always did when she was nervous. She prattled on about the first thing that came into her head and instantly regretted asking if he had his own boat.

What a stupid question, she scolded herself. It's obvious he's trying to get off with me and now I've encouraged him and made him think I was sizing him up for his wealth and his worldly goods. God, I'm a mess, she thought, what did he say in reply? Has he got a blessed boat or not?

She had to admit, though, that she liked the distinguished sweep of his waxed grey hair and the air of rakish abandon that defined him. How delightful it was to have a handsome man focus all of his attention on her as if no one and nothing else existed in the whole wide world. She realised he probably charmed women like this all the time at his impressive bar, but quite frankly, madam, at that moment, she didn't give a damn.

Then she did it again. She asked him the wrong question. How long have you owned the bar?

So he told her, at length. She was suitably impressed, silently confessing that a bit more glamour in her life wouldn't go astray.

What are you thinking? he asked her.

Oh God, he must have seen through my eyes that my mind was

all over the place. But it was a good question, she thought. What must I be thinking? she asked herself.

And then out of a fog of confusion, and with no connection to any train of recent thought she was aware of, she said: I was thinking that I'd like you to do the procedure tomorrow, if you would be so kind.

I quite enjoyed life as Nev for a while. A counterpoint persona, I'd call it. I played Nev as the exact opposite of myself and I found it a blissful release from my managerial responsibilities. Of course, it was a guided release, not a frivolous, moronic one. The incarnation of Nev was a masterstroke, an immaculate conception, if you like. Nev had an important role to play in advancing the cause. In fact, an immaculate deception.

Early on, I was nervous that Garry would appear and cruel my plan not to meet my prey before due time. But I quickly cottoned on from the side conversations that they saw Garry as the hen-pecked type. That means a bloke who rats on his mates by going home to be with his family rather than doing his duty and propping up the bar like a man.

I was impressed, I have to say, with the way the blokes from the station accepted Nev. You wouldn't have thought they would be the most tolerant guys in the world, would you? Of course, someone more cynical than I might attribute their ready acceptance of him to the frequency with which Nev's hand went into his pocket. But, for whatever reason, it suited me well that I could infiltrate the group so easily and thus segue into the life of my intended target.

Although I'm not naturally that way inclined, referring to boys' talk in the pub of course, I'm pretty bloody good at it, if I say so myself. While it didn't exactly excite me to leer at that sheila with big knockers at the bar or to wax lyrical as to why Aussies can't bat, bowl, putt, serve or cycle like they used to, I didn't find it that difficult in a good cause.

Nev was expected to be a footy expert, coming from Melbourne and now propping up the bar in Freo. But it was OK because I was full bottle on all of Carlton's premierships. I also praised the achievements of the Clontarf Football Academy to add a dash of local colour, so to speak.

Gradually, bit by bit, session by session, I found myself being welcomed as a fixture at the bar and I began to get to know the boys. More to the point, I got to know who does what around the station and who aspires to climb the greasy extension ladder of success as opposed to sliding down the fireman's pole of failure. It was just as well I was making headway as I was putting on weight swilling beers with my fireman mates like it was free from the hose.

Well, what do you know and are you surprised? Fireys in Perth are just like Nev and his mates, the fireys in Melbourne. They're restless spirits on account of sitting around all day, waiting for fires or hoping against fires, whatever the case may be. They can't sit still all their lives so they have two jobs and three women and sometimes the other way around.

And, guess what. I found out Garry does handy jobs and maintenance in his spare time. Not only that, but he has an esoteric passion. He loves leadlights. It was very helpful to know that. Information is power.

Perfect, Nev, absabloodylutely perfect.

53 THERE MIGHT BE BETTER WAYS

She was getting to him. After all, it wasn't every day Mario came across such a posh and tasty tart. Unfortunately, he hadn't yet come across her in the way he really wanted to. That was usually just a matter of time. But, with this bird, he had a nasty feeling things could be different.

He'd just got back from his second meeting with Kathleen. Mario was regretting the distraction of his permanent stiffy because he could have done with listening to her more closely than he had. He wished lawyers, or was it chic chicks, or possibly both, didn't talk in riddles all the time. He felt like asking her several times to spit it out, to come to the point, to put it out there in simple terms. But, it would've been uncool to do that as she might have thought he was dumb.

Anyway, the gist of the message seemed to be that he had a case and he didn't have one, that he was definitely morally in the right, but that didn't count for anything, that he could take the cunt to court if he wanted to, but knowing cunts like that, they didn't own anything in their own names, and that even if he did win, which he might not because it would depend a lot on the judge at the time and there was no way of knowing which judge it was going to be, he would be up for something like a hundred grand in legal costs, which could very well be a lot more than he could actually get from that cunt, unless he was awarded costs of course which would depend on a lot of things and then there was that issue again of what if that cunt had no money anyway?

He desperately wished at this point that he hadn't asked Kathleen for her advice on what to do because he knew before he asked it what she would answer. Of course she said she could only provide the facts and assess the risks for him, but she really couldn't enter into the question of whether he should go ahead with a case or not.

He lit up another calming smoke and looked out over his local suburb from the veranda of his ridiculously overpriced apartment. If all that lawyer shit hadn't been confusing enough, she then proceeded to fuck with his mind by heading off to riddle-land.

He scratched his head, wondering what she meant by *there might be better ways to resolve this*. That was if the guys he borrowed the money from to make the loan didn't turn nasty on him any day now. Which was on the cards, he had to concede and it made him sick in the stomach just thinking about it.

He twisted the top off a Hahn to settle the unpleasant churning in his belly. She's not suggesting heavying the heavies who loaned me the money, is she? No, she couldn't be, surely. Or is she suggesting setting *those* really bad cunts on that cunt of a shoeman? Yes, that could be it. But, how could she and why would they? The foot fetishist cunt doesn't owe *them* a cent, after all.

Mario was getting really spooked with all this, but he could also feel time slipping away. The nasty boys could knock on his door any day now and pay him what's called in the trade, a friendly visit. And they wouldn't bring cream cakes, that was for sure.

And that wasn't the only thing that was bugging him. He really didn't understand this snooty lawyer chick thing one bit. Should he ask her out or send her flowers or some such shit? Wouldn't she in real life just pull the lawyer–client privilege thing even if they conveniently forget that stuff on the box? In pretty much every TV show, lawyers and doctors and judges protest that they can't get involved with their clients in the very scene before they actually do. So, maybe she would go out with him after protesting that she couldn't? Or maybe that was just TV land and this was real life. This really was doing his head in.

Maybe there was a better way with her? She might be a snooty lawyer chick and all that, but she was a skank as well. He of all people could pick that up. Perhaps he shouldn't join in with the round-the-houses, talking in riddles stuff and should just get to the point? Something more direct could work with her. Maybe he should just reach out and stick his hand up her skirt? Or even better, perhaps he should just SMS her and tell her to clear her desk.

Make it fast, his text would say, I'm on my way over for a fuck.

54 PUTTY IN MY HANDS

After Lisa so conveniently fell into my lap, she was pretty much putty in my hands. I know it sounds awful, and it is, but I thought she was pathetic. Where's the self-respect that's supposed to go with age when a mid-forties, wealthy woman literally and metaphorically throws herself at a guy like me? As desirable as I may be.

When she saw me on the day after the lap-dancing incident, the apology dam burst all over again. I was magnanimous and forgiving, of course, and then I trotted out a cliché pick-up line that would make even the Marks of this world cringe.

You can make it up to me, I said, by letting me buy you coffee.

It took all my resolve not to puke on the spot. But, surprise, surprise, Lisa's face lit up.

Sure, she said, I guess it's the least I can do.

As I had an early meeting after the workout that day, we agreed to meet for Saturday brunch right there on the coffee strip.

It was tactically important to make an impression on our first *date*. So I selected my coolest shirt – the Desigual, with its swirling, brightly coloured, circular patterns. The pants and jacket I matched with it were denim blue and sharp as a positively dangerous tack. I felt confident I would take a first positive step with Lisa that day that would lead me, just a short walk later, straight to juicy Julia's door.

When Lisa arrived, I saw an approving smile creep across her face and I returned the compliment to her. She looked like she'd spent the entire intervening period at the day spa. Talk about coiffed and buffed. She'd whiled away so much time with her face caked in mud and her eyelids weighed down with cucumber rounds that she seemed like an airbrushed mannequin rather than a real creature made of flesh and blood.

Anyway, suffice to say that we (*we* in a technical sense that is) got on like a house on fire. We chatted at length about Julia – very useful indeed.

You surely would have noticed her – don't lie, she enthused.

Only after I stopped looking at you, I replied (bring me the bucket please).

Lisa chatted freely about her work as a real estate office manager and I got chapter and verse on the local gentry and their house buying proclivities. (These people clearly do have more money than sense.)

I played it mysterious and intellectual and I could sense from the beginning that it hit the spot. Who'd have thought she'd be more into Andrew Denton than Matt Damon? More George Negus than George Clooney? Anyway, there's no accounting for taste and, thanks to my skill and verve in reading people's minds, I had picked the right persona first out of the box.

So that was good. I talked about world affairs, global hunger, global warming, climate change, regime change, the resources boom, and all that sort of stuff. Name any earnest subject about warming or cooling or changing or all of those put together, and I was into it. I was authoritative, maybe masterful, but deeply and sincerely compassionate. I could tell she was impressed.

Let me sum up how well the first meeting went. I almost said *date* again, but caught myself this time. I could have had a root by two o'clock. That's how well it went. But I chivalrously put off the evil moment in a manner Sir Galahad himself would have endorsed. I shook her hand and then kissed her lightly but lingeringly on the forehead.

I like you, Lisa, very much actually, I said.

Then I turned on my heels and in my case walked, rather than rode, off into the distance.

Garry found he wasn't exactly whistling while he worked at the old girl's house any more. He knew why, too. He'd been growing as a person under Hannah's watchful eye and he was far from ready for it to stop. It wasn't just that he enjoyed the opportunity to exercise his brain and talk about how he really felt. It was more a recognition of fear, which was something he wouldn't have been able to identify in himself in the past. The fact was that he didn't want the job to finish because he was terrified he would slip back and lose all the gains he'd made. Hannah was a fix to which he was now well and truly addicted.

He thought about offering to come round for tea now and again. He imagined himself letting the idea drop one day, presenting it as some sort of gift from the young to the old. He would offer the prize that the lonely yearn for most – some company. But he knew the old bat would be on to him in a flash. He knew before long she'd slowly but surely extract a confession from him that would be truly embarrassing. Yes, it's true. Can I come and visit you because I want to? Or even worse, he sometimes imagined himself saying because I *need* to.

He couldn't bear the humiliation of being found out like that. The alternative was to be straightforward and honest. Just tell her what good she was doing him and ask if she would mind seeing him once a week for a while. It wouldn't be easy to say that and he was by no means sure that he had the guts. But the real bugger was that she wouldn't buy that either. She hated dependency with a passion. Even at her age. So, if he gave her a message of pathetic desperation like that, she would break things off quick smart, probably before he'd even finished the works.

There was nowhere to go with this and so the black dog of his mood couldn't be chased away. Not only that, but his neck was aching doing the delicate brushwork overhead on the architraves. He stepped gingerly back down the ladder and massaged his neck with both hands. Then he remembered Hannah had asked him to shift some old files and papers from a storeroom into the wood-panelled office. Some variety was what he needed right now with a sore neck like this.

He made various trips with arms full of box files, manila folders, monographs and magazines. He was covered in dust in no time. These piles hadn't been disturbed for years, if not decades. After manhandling a particularly large mound out of the way, he discovered an ornate, red lacquer box. It looked Chinese but it had old-style German writing on it that he couldn't understand.

He reassured himself that no one could resist having a peek inside a treasure trove such as this and graciously gave himself permission. He found old, decaying letters, sepia photos of a beautiful young girl that he knew instantly must be Hannah and then the most amazing diamond ring encrusted with massive red stones in the shape of a rose. It was like nothing he had ever seen before. At the very bottom was a bulky envelope that had become unsealed.

It contained twenty thousand Australian dollars in cash.

All in all, it had been a pretty good few weeks' work. Lady Luck had smiled on me with Mario's ugly mug appearing in the paper like that. But, don't they say you make your own luck and you get the luck you deserve?

And it's not as if I didn't put in the hard yakka at this delicate time. I had to work bloody hard impersonating Nev. It's not easy wheedling your way into the trust of true-blue Aussie blokes. Well, it is, actually. How come these tough, macho types are so naïve and impressionable? It's a fucking paradox, that's what it is. What kind of screwed-up world is it where only the indoor, sensitive types like me are tough enough to manipulate and deceive people?

In any event, I had to put plenty of time and work into being Nev. And it was the same with lovely Lisa – my train ticket to station Julia. I challenge you to tell me that wasn't a labour of love.

Connecting to the others was what you might call, middling. Internet track-downs aren't too arduous. Hannah was the easiest of them all. Track her down. Make an appointment. Flatter her and butter her up. Move onto the next one.

By contrast, Kathleen had presented certain challenges. It's not so much that she was hard to find. It was rather that the pitch to Kathleen wasn't entirely convincing. Even though she seemed to have swallowed it for the moment, I continued to have nagging doubts about it. I had this uneasy feeling that something was going to go wrong with Kathleen, but I couldn't put my finger on why.

What if she smells a rat, smart and sassy cookie that she is? What if, what if, what if? The two most valuable, yet futile, words you can juxtapose in the English language. On the good side, the question *what if* is the engine of innovation. After all, nothing much would change if nobody bothered to ask *what if*. But, I'm not so keen on the insidious function of those words as a vehicle for self-doubt. What if he doesn't love me? What if the stock market crashes? What if the sky falls in? What if we don't waste any more time speculating about things that may never happen?

Fortunately, Robert was a lay-down misère for a class player like me. He was easy to track down, easy to locate at the bar, easy to engage in conversation and, best of all, easy to suck into a line.

My main man, Mario, well what can you say about him? He's a scallywag, an Iti-larrikin, a wolf in sheep's clothing. I reckon everybody likes this guy. At school, they probably liked him even when they were flushing his head down the toilet. But, really, what's the point of being liked? It doesn't get you anywhere. You can be liked and pitied, liked and abused, liked and basically fucked. In real life, the Marios of this world are always fucked. Fucked by everyone, actually. Fucked by the nasty, just as much as they are fucked by the nice.

I do have the odd soft and tender moment, as you would by now have observed. I had quite a lot of them actually while, armed with notebook and smartphone set to record, I proceeded to interview the old girl.

I caught myself looking at Hannah sometimes and then pulling myself into line. Damn it, she was an elegant woman for her age. Her hair, clothes, jewellery and the understated make-up she wore were always just so. It struck me after a while that she always dressed in shades of grey (but not so many as fifty). Her clothes somehow blended perfectly into the silver-grey colour of her hair. She was a work of art, I would catch myself thinking, and then I would snap out of it and get myself back to business.

She spoke to me non-stop in that funny accent of hers from the kitchen area where she was making the tea.

You don't want coffee, do you? she insisted in a way that made me think I was being offered nothing at all.

But then she waddled off to the kitchenette and I surmised, from the rattling of cups and saucers, that she was backhandedly offering me tea.

I could get the drift of her conversation from those sentences I could hear that wafted my way.

I wish I knew what you were up to, young man. Now, don't deny it, I know you couldn't possibly really want to interview me for articles and the TV. I think you said the movies too, didn't you? Did you say the movies?

A documentary, I corrected her.

Yes, well, that's all a cock and bull story if ever I heard one, but never mind, I will get to the bottom of this, young man, mark my words if I don't.

She smiled at me as she handed me the wobbling cup on the saucer. It was the smile of a chess player who secretly sees checkmate a few moves away. I responded with my most confident and reassuring expression. Game on, I thought.

Let's not let the suspense build up any more, shall we? she said, with a lip-curl full of irony. Why don't you switch the recorder on? It will make you more credible, you know.

Good idea, I agreed.

I then set about interviewing her in the measured way a real journalist would. I drew out her history. I explored in depth the periods of significance. I quizzed her on any hint of inconsistency I found.

We enjoyed ourselves. It was exhilarating. I liked her, but I was cool and didn't let it interfere with my purpose. She liked me, I knew she did. But she wouldn't drop her guard. She stuck to her guns, probing every element of my cover.

Without warning, I stopped the recording, stood up and looked out of the window. I rubbed my neck. I was genuinely tired.

Time for small talk, I suggested, your life's way too heavy.

Can't take the pace?

Not at all, I replied smugly. Even serious intellectuals and over-achievers must have some trivia in their lives.

The trivia's usually the most titillating part, is it not? she responded, leaving the thought hanging in the air.

How long have you lived here?

In Australia or here, here?

In this house, I mean.

Well, it's more years than I care to remember, she replied with another dead bat to my bowling.

Can I have a look around? I asked.

Why not? she conceded with a wave of her hand. By the way, you don't need to open the back door to let in your accomplices. Be civilised and get them to ring the doorbell.

Now you've offended me, I chided her, grasping an opportunity for the upper hand.

I didn't realise you were so sensitive, she snorted with dismissive contempt.

Quite a bathroom, I shouted down the corridor, in genuine admiration.

That brought the sound of chair legs scraping against the floorboards as she got slowly up. She shuffled her way in my direction. I saw an emotion in her I hadn't seen before. Wow, it was pride.

I did this myself, she announced boastfully. At the grand young age of seventy-five, actually. Back when I was a young girl with a crazy dream.

It's magnificent, I said in genuine appreciation.

So it is. In utilitarian surroundings such as these, what could be more appropriate than lifting the spirits from the level of the lavatory?

Is that a special rose? I asked about the motif running through the hand-made tiles.

A long family story, she said.

Very enigmatic, I said, as I pushed on down the corridor. Not so flash along here, though. Did you run out of steam after the bathhouse?

Very amusing, young man. I did, as you suggest, regrettably run out of energy. But, not out of intent, she said pointedly, arriving in the doorway. I'm going to get this area done up very soon.

Home handywork. Now, there's a thought, I said to myself.

Good idea, I responded to Hannah, holding out my elbow in an extravagant gesture, offering to walk her back along the hallway.

Tut-tut, she said reprovingly, I never hold hands on the first date.

Julia looked round the dinner table and hated everyone she saw.

She knew it was her hormones, her guilt or something, but it was true that right then, at that moment, she pretty much hated them all. How could Jasmine still eat with her mouth open at her age? If only Angelica could hear herself speak. A loathsome, spoiled brat whingeing about the gay colour choices for her mobile phone. And as for Mai Ling! She was nothing but a waste of air. What with her abysmal English, her nauseating politeness and her zero-value contribution around the house.

And then there was Stephen. She suspected her current feelings for the girls might be temporary. But, with Stephen, she was pretty sure she hated him long-term. How could he do this to me? What a pathetic joke. The very thought of Mai Ling caring for a baby! Ridiculous. She wouldn't have a clue. I'd be doing all the work again, barefoot and child rearing, just as he planned it.

Still, as early as tomorrow, it would be fixed. Once and for all. She felt like telling him. It would be easy really, particularly in this mood. Let the kids disappear to go on Facebook while pretending to do their homework; ask Mai Ling to organise the dishes later. And then just come straight out with it. Tell Stephen she knows his little game. Tell him what a despicable shit he really is. What a selfish prick he's always been. Tell him not only is she not having another baby, not soon, not ever actually, but better than that, he can kick the tenants out and piss off and live in their apartment in the city from now on.

I'm not in the mood right now, she responded to a question from Stephen.

What was he on about? A walk on the beach or was it going to the movies? What a nerve to go on as normal, Mr Perfect Husband. I'm going to chain you up like some dangerous dog, but every so often I'll throw you a bone and then I expect you to be really, really grateful. Yes, thank you so much, Master, I would love to walk on the beach or hold hands in the back row at the Luna. What a thoughtful man you are!

God, what would have happened if she hadn't woken up to it?

What if she hadn't been put onto Dr Robert? Ah, Dr Robert – best not to think of him right now. But, really, what would she have done? Thank God for Lisa, everyone needs someone like Lisa. A person who is there for them unconditionally. Julia had been dreadfully tipsy that night at Lisa's, but what if she hadn't been? What if she hadn't blurted it all out that night? How embarrassing that Lisa's guy was there. But, what if she hadn't? After all, it was actually his idea about how to solve her problem. Thank God he happened to be there.

Mario should be on *This Is Your Life*. He tells you his life story in fifteen minutes. It would make the program shorter too and that would be a blessing. From an info point of view, you get double value with a guy like Mario. You get the verbal outpouring of what he knows and what he's got to say, but being a people-person as I am, I also get the equal half he doesn't say, much less does he know, even about himself.

So, we went across the road to the pub. It was the sort of place that didn't know its own identity. It was part old and part new, but with no logic as to why that would be. You went from rooms that had remained undecorated from the time the pub was built to extensions that were ultra-modern with the latest electronic gadgets to help you pay your bill. You'd walk from one incongruous space to another wondering if you belonged in the grungy or the chic. Eventually you'd find you'd crossed more design zones than a jetlagged architect.

There were lots of back-slaps and high-fives being exchanged between Mario and the boys. It was a modern mix of good, old Aussie camaraderie and the insidious new American version. (Of course, all camaraderie could be French, but the only other word we've got is comradeship and that's been commandeered by the Russians.)

Anyway, Mario seemed to know everyone in the pub. From the inner city townhouse set to the down-on-their-luck wannabe clients of his own financial services.

A beer, mate? he asked.

Nah, a shiraz – out of a bottle, I insisted.

He grinned from ear to ear. I won't be shouting you again.

He returned soon enough and plonked the drinks down on the table.

Red wine fresh from the cow, he announced.

He laid out his keys, smokes and mobile as if he was a starting a Find the Lady card trick. He reached for a cigarette and lit it. Then he remembered the new nanny-state laws that forbade him from giving himself cancer in a public place.

Let's go outside, he said.

We made our way out into a concrete wasteland that passes for a beer garden in some establishments in the port city. We could have gone to the flash, chrome-bedecked landscaped area on the other side of the pub, but we didn't.

Mein host lets us smoke in this courtyard, he winked. Anyway, laws are meant to be broken.

He took a long slow drag like someone who'd just quit quitting and blew smoke rings just for the hell of it.

OK, he said, so you want me to invest money, not lend you some.

Sort of, I said, but my plan is more fundamentally about making you and me some serious money.

That sounds tops, I must say. But why *me*?

I gave him points for that – the critical question, and sooner than I thought. But I had no intention of going there yet, not before we had built up what we call, in the bullshit trade, rapport.

I went straight to suave and cool. I wordlessly conveyed the age-old truth to him that rushing headlong into business like that simply isn't done. By way of foreplay, I said, raising one eyebrow in a way I had practised heavily at uni, tell me first about the finance business.

Well, I don't want to give away trade secrets, he smirked, but I make things possible for people that others reject. Like that John West ad pretty much.

He warmed to the subject, just as I'd hoped.

So, it's a form of public service really. No, really I mean it. These are basically good people who've had some bad luck or have strayed from the straight and narrow a little bit and I help them get things together, get back on the right path. And do you know, you won't believe this, but I could count the bad debts on one hand, I really could. If I could count that far, he added, with a return of his great wide grin.

I guess you've been in the game for a while? I continued, to let more line out to reel him in later. Being a talkative type, he took the bait. He chatted away and we had another drink and he told me about his early days at the car yard and about his wife (the Bitch) and his kids and his parents. Then we had another drink and he asked me about me. And I told him what I'd carefully prepared for that moment.

I'm in real estate in Melbourne, trying my luck in the West where the money's to be made.

We had one of those discussions that suburbanites love – capping the other's story about house prices going up and down. I told him of some properties I was going to buy to do up, including one with these magnificent leadlights.

Why don't you buy them on your own? he asked, trying to get me back to the critical point.

But, of course, I'm really good at this bit. These are after all the moments Master Planners train for.

A few reasons, I said, rolling them out like a professional presentation at work.

By the way, a rudimentary understanding of human nature would tell you that guys with gold chains will do anything not to pay GST. And, as for those truly dirty words, income tax and capital gains tax – merely to contemplate them would be akin to spitting on your grandmother's grave. So I got to work.

First, I said, playing my trumps straight out, I'm not a big fan of the Federal Treasurer so I look out for projects that don't involve paying any tax. Secondly, I need to be flexible so I can get in, make money and get the hell out.

You're talking my language so far.

And thirdly, I said with the solemnity of a magician revealing the prestige, I know from bitter experience in business how essential it is to have local knowledge, local contacts and local clout.

OK then, he said, adopting a professorial tone, I'm with you philosophically on this, we're singing from the same hymnbook, so to speak. But, something's still troubling me. Except for the fact that I know more than a local yokel or three, I still don't get why me.

I'm on the lookout for someone who is really well connected – with the important, rich people of the moment – tradesmen, brickies, chippies, that sort of thing. But, I'm also keen to bring on board someone connected with finance. Not the banks and the form-filler type of big four banking, you understand, but back-up cash without paper trails just in case some project or other should fall in a hole. So, Mario, if I'm not mistaken, you would appear to me to be such a man.

Well, not that I'm blowing my own trumpet mind, but I would say that I qualify, yes.

Before I could continue, he gestured airily to indicate he still had the talking-stick firmly in his hand. Correct me if I'm wrong, but I'm not the only guy who fits the bill. So, my good friend, kindly enlighten me as to why you chose *me*.

I savoured the moment as a strategic opportunity to disengage.

I'll get one in, I said and set off for the bar.

I used the time to steady myself because there I was, in my meticulously planned little scheme, at a point where I had to take a chance. Naturally, I pride myself in the tennis match of life on playing the big points really well. I had rehearsed this moment a number of times, but had been careful not to over-practise and run the risk of stifling spontaneity.

This is a point so many so-called managers fail to understand. They are happy to label themselves as creative or strategic as if one or other quality will suffice. You need a forehand and a backhand obviously to be great and having both has really helped me set myself apart. Sodding strategic and fucking flexible – that's me.

I set the drinks down – our third or fourth round it was by now. I went for the play.

You come highly recommended, as it happens. By your family, broadly speaking, if you know what I mean.

I calculated on two things working with this line. It would lend itself, if I needed it to, to encouraging him to guess. What's more, with ethnic guys like this, family can mean almost anything.

In no way was I prepared for his reaction. He stiffened and backed off three paces even though he was actually sitting down. He stroked his chin in an agitated way and shot me a tense smile. He swigged some beer and lit up another personal incendiary device. He looked up, clearly a less confident, in fact almost a broken, man.

There was time for think music, lots of it.

Fair enough, he responded at long last, so quietly I barely heard what he'd said. Let's work something out. Yeah, we can work something out. Course, we can. Actually, it's very ingenious of you, my friend, he said with some animation returning to his soul, a very smart way of solving our little problem now I think of it.

This result was good, but I knew from instinct, that it was also very bad. OK, so I had him hooked into doing a deal with me, but I didn't know why and I knew deep in my guts this route would lead to lack of control – a state of play this Master Plan cannot abide. I moved fast and totally from instinct. I had to resort to my ultimate fallback position and run the risk that it would blow the total scene. I just couldn't afford for him to take me into some sort of scary twilight zone of his I didn't comprehend.

Jesus, Mario, I said, you can't hate the old fucker that much!

He looked up from his beer totally perplexed and confused.

You can't hate your ex-father-in-law that much.

Who? he said, almost outraged.

Your father-in-law.

That old mongrel, he whooped in visible delight. Do you really mean that old cunt?

I nodded sagely.

Why would that dickhead recommend me, he hates me, the cunt.

It wasn't for your benefit obviously, I told him calmly.

Ah, for the Bitch!

The light globe I needed switched on.

He wants the Bitch to get *more* blood out of the stone.

Then the penny dropped. Well, a penny dropped, anyway.

Melbourne, of course, he said. Uncle Sal, everybody deals with Uncle Sal! Fuck me, he said, with the broadest of broad smiles on his face, you really put the fucking wind up me then. Shit, let me but you a drink, my very good, very friendly friend.

He returned with yet more drinks.

I owe you an explanation. I'm in a bit of bother right now, more than a little bit actually. And I thought, well never mind, I thought you might be someone else.

But, you're not. You're OK, he said. You're fucking OK.

Garry felt sick in the stomach the whole way home. Not only that, he'd felt just as sick packing everything away. Perhaps the game was up already because surely steel-trap mind lady would have noticed his odd behaviour at once. It was normal for him to have a laugh and a chat with Hannah before he hit the road. Sometimes, he'd have a quick sherry with her. That drink sure was an acquired taste. But, this time, he'd upped and he'd gone with a quick cheerio and a feeble excuse about needing to dash to pick up the girls.

He didn't mind being stuck in traffic at this point for what seemed like ages. It gave him time to think. Maybe he was worrying too much. Perhaps his fear stemmed from guilt rather than from any real cause for concern. Really, there was no reason for her to suspect anything. Why wouldn't Hannah believe he had to pick up his kids?

And as for the valuables, surely, they were long hidden and forgotten. If not, why would she have asked him to tidy up that mess?

As he pulled into his neatly concreted driveway, he felt more relaxed, even a little elated. After all, what a find it was! The ring was the most amazing piece of jewellery Garry had ever seen and then there was the stash of what must be thousands of bucks in cash. He shuddered at the memory of his impulse to count the green and yellow notes right there in the house. What a stupid idea that was. Well, only stupid if he was planning to pocket this windfall without letting on.

Of course, an innocent, honest and upright man, which Garry was, or perhaps once had been, would very likely have rifled through the notes and quickly understood the significance of his find. And then, he would have beamed from ear to ear and rushed down the corridor calling Hannah's name. And then, what would an honourable man have done? An honourable man would probably have hidden the secret hoard behind his back and teased Hannah about it for a while. Finally he would have made her guess what he'd found before producing the bounty in triumph.

Her face would have been a picture. Would have been.

Garry grabbed the garden hose, uncharacteristically for him when he got home from work. He set these thoughts aside and diligently watered the lawn, the flowerbeds and the herbs in their gaudy pots. He calmed his racing mind temporarily, buying himself some precious time. A fireman, even if it's for a few short seconds, analyses the problem and the available options before rushing in and perhaps, literally, fuelling the fire.

At this point, the way he saw it, he had three options. Keep it all and say nothing. Risk assessment: unknown. Or put it back, devise a way to re-find it again and declare the haul to Hannah. Risk assessment in the intervening period: very low. The third choice was to fess up and admit he was tempted and took the loot, but hand it over in a flood of apologies. Risk assessment: admission of guilt, but Hannah, being a complex person, might secretly admire a man who eventually found a way to do the right thing.

As tempted as he was over dinner, he couldn't risk, just yet, letting Kirsty in on the deal. He slept on it, fitfully. But he sat bolt upright in bed at 3.27 a.m. precisely and realised that there weren't only three options, there were four. Re-find and declare the ring, but hold on to the cash.

This was a good compromise, he concluded. What Hannah would probably call a moral equilibrium. Yet his conscience was alert to the furtive footsteps of dishonesty on the march.

That would be a despicable act, it told him.

61   SPOT THE FRAUD

I'd put a fair bit of work into the business plan that Robert was studying so thoughtfully across the table from me. I told him there was no rush as I was quite happy taking in the scenery and chilling out to the gentle sound of the river lapping against the pilings. At that moment I felt at peace with my adopted city. It was affording me such creative possibilities on top of these delightful views.

Of course, business plans are my bread and butter and this one was effortless for me in many ways. But I still needed the raw data about the business to frame the parameters of an enticing proposition. I had Robert email me some basic information to the address I'd linked to the website I'd set up for my scheme (www. realityrealty.com.au – try it now!)

To build confidence, I suggested he preserve commercial secrecy by not including real turnover and margin information in his email. I told him, once he'd understood the model, he'd be able to plug the real figures into the spreadsheet to assess the proposal.

Anyway, I waited for Robert to absorb the detail. I used the same Melbourne realty cover I'd trotted out for Mario. It was a natural shell for this particular crab as it had several directors who had since scattered to the four corners of the globe (which is of course spherical, but never mind).

He asked me some pertinent questions re access to funds and contractual arrangements. I put my cards on the table. I spun him a line I knew would appeal to a man of his age, background and mentality.

I always do business on the shake of a hand, I told Robert with a suitable tone of gravitas.

Amazing in this day and age, he responded predictably.

Sadly so, I agreed, but I pride myself on my ability to read people well and I have no hesitation in trusting you.

I'm flattered, I really am, Robert responded looking mighty pleased with himself.

So, in your case, I will be happy to provide you with the funds in cash with no contract. That way the risk is all mine. We can also shake hands on a return for my investment as I know you won't let me down.

You're quite right. I won't let you down. But I should level with you as well since you are being so genuine and honest with me.

Fantastic. If only every deal could be like this.

Actually, this sort of arrangement suits me down to the ground, Robert explained earnestly. Paddy is a great bloke, but an awfully tedious guy to have as a partner. This way, I'll be able to talk him into the development as there will be no risk for him.

That makes sense, I encouraged him.

Robert's enthusiasm showed in his voice. Look, I think the way to proceed with this would be for me to match your investment fifty-fifty, he said. In fact I'm quite confident doing that because I estimate that expanding the deck over there will probably double what we get from the bar. And, what's more, we'll be able to expand our food lines with that space and that will have a big impact on turnover.

Robert was excited. I was excited. But that's where the equality started and ended.

No, come to think of it, there *was* some equality between Robert and me. Despite what people might think from outward appearances, Robert is a fraud. You know he's a fraud. I know he's a fraud. You know I'm a fraud. I know I'm a fraud.

At that point, Robert didn't know I was a fraud.

62   HYPOTHETICAL PERSON TALK

Kathleen had slipped her black Honda Accord Euro into the one free parking space at the back of Wheels & Dollbaby and had then helped herself to an armful of potential purchases to take into the curtained-off change cubicle. A girl who felt as good as this deserved to go shopping.

Kathleen's little tête-à-tête with her managing partner, Max, had gone very well. Very, very well, actually. She really admired Max, possibly even hero-worshipped him, she mused as she skilfully pulled a shimmery little Melanie Greensmith number over her head without disturbing a single hair. Yes, he was a hero. He was terrific at the law, but more so at the edge of the law. Max and she were kindred spirits. They both understood that a lawyer's duty to the client is to win. To win at all costs. To be prepared to do what it takes to win at all costs.

Everyone knows the law is an ass and has nothing to do with justice. The law is about process and justice is about outcomes. So if you're interested in a good process, use the law, but if you're after a positive outcome, put your faith in something more likely to get a result.

The great thing about Max was that you could talk freely with him about trying to get a result. About getting a result for Mario, for example.

Dear old Max. He wasn't old, but he was no longer young. The poor guy was as ugly as sin with his pear-shaped dome and his aquiline nose. He looked every inch the human eagle. But looks weren't *everything*. Max was damn smart. And, better still, he had the cunning of a rat.

So that was Max. He was a brilliant yet unorthodox lawyer. He was a stickler at work about his appearance and demeanour, but a total sleaze if he met you in the pub. She'd let him get his hand in her knickers once or twice, but only when she was drunk and he'd earned it.

But there were no such goings-on today, she recalled, abandoning her first try-on but full of hope for the merchandise that was left. All business in his office, it was. As usual, he'd listened intently. Asked the odd question for clarification; made the occasional observation; quizzed her on her understanding of relevant cases; assessed her conclusions and agreed with them, give or take a subtlety or two.

Then he'd set forth on his diatribe, pacing up and down his office to give suitable emphasis to his oratory and delivery. This was Max at his best. Imperious and theatrical; hamming it up to make Kathleen smile.

If a hypothetical person ... of ethnic persuasion, Max intoned with the studied pomposity of a judge, winking at Kathleen to get her in the mood. As I say, if a hypothetical person of ethnic persuasion, called Luigi or Mario for example, found himself in a contractual situation where he was at a financial disadvantage in respect of another second hypothetical person of a similar ethnic orientation who had failed to pay him, and was morally in the right but, unfortunately, legally in a very uncertain place ...

Max was warming to his task and strutting his stuff with his thumbs tucked into his lapels ... *and* if this Luigi or Mario was also under pressure of time and at risk of what one might call unfriendly acts from other persons of similar ethnic composition but of a less pacifist disposition who had advanced him funds, *then* that person, Luigi or was it Mario, could do worse than try to persuade those robust types who had funded him that the quickest path to regaining their readies plus interest might be via making direct and vigorous representations to the second ethnic person who was actually the cause of everyone's difficulties.

Max paused for dramatic effect. Kathleen's attentive face was all the encouragement he needed to continue.

Now, as you might very well point out, *if* those robust moneylenders were to respond to our friend Luigi or was it Mario to the effect that they have no interest in what he did with their money but merely have interest in the principal plus interest, as it were, as a principle ... (followed by a classic Max smirk) ... *and if* our Luigi or Mario were unwilling to confront the second hypothetical ethnic person who owes him the money in a suitably robust fashion, in a dark alley or some such poorly lit venue, *then* the course of action for his hypothetical legal practitioners would be quite clear.

Kathleen eventually controlled her giggling and asked the question Max was clearly waiting for. And that course of action would be what exactly?

Max deemed it time to step down from the stage to ensure his protégé fully understood what he was saying.

On your client's behalf, my darling, we will need to persuade the suppliers of funds to get their money back from the shoeman direct or we will have to persuade the shoeman himself that his best interests lie in paying up. Either way, my learned friend, that is where you and I come in. Naturally, either choice takes us down a path that is unconventional in legal terms, so we will need to proceed with discretion. I'm sure you would agree that persuading the moneylenders to apply pressure to the debtor would be the simplest and best course of action. So, my sweetness, I'd suggest you get off your pert bum and persuade your client of the wisdom of our counsel, set up a 'legal conference' with the mafia types and warn Luigi or Mario or whatever his name is that these types of semi-legal services do not come cheap, but come at a fraction of the real cost of what might happen to him if he does not get this matter resolved in a timely fashion.

You do follow me darling, don't you? Max asked, giving her a conspiratorial hug as she left his office.

Yes, I think I do, Kathleen said in a tone that left the matter in doubt.

Kathleen knew full well that she was trying on those skin-tight pants with that barely-there lace top because of the thrilling nature of her interlude with Max. Should she ring Matt to take her standing up, right there in the confines of cubicle one?

No, Mario more like it. He'd be there like a shot.

I'll level with you. I didn't realise how useful my Melbourne real estate connection was going to be. It's not to say that I couldn't have found another way, or to imply that I lacked planning. My admission just reinforces my recent point. Well-organised people shouldn't be so rigid that they can't go with the flow.

For my follow-up appointment with Kathleen (which, as I have already admitted, I was concerned I wouldn't get), I wore my most conservative and official suit. The game plan here was clear. I needed to convince her that my total affairs were of great substance. Indeed, of such significant proportions, that it would be worth her while taking on a loss-leader of a piddling interstate conveyancing job for me.

The good news, my friends, was that I really was selling a property I owned in St Kilda. The even better news was that it was actually owned by the property company I'd referred to when we first met. After a minimum of small talk, I got down to business. I was very grown-up. I took the relevant papers out of my impressive leather briefcase. I had brought along a glowing glossy prospectus on my company that I had knocked up for the purpose of our meeting.

I explained what I needed done in Melbourne and then took the opportunity to discuss the further business in the pipeline that I would bring to the firm. I described the exciting hospitality project I had well underway on a highly sought-after riverside site and I explained that the first of my investment properties was soon coming on-stream.

Kathleen was cool and distant. I feared, at any moment, she might teeter over the edge and knock back the work. It might have been on the tip of her tongue to do so, but the Lord saved me by making the phone ring. She apologised for taking the call and then indicated with her eyes that it was important so she would have to keep going. From the *mm*s and *ah-ha*s and serious tone, I gathered it was something that had reached a delicate stage. On a couple of occasions, she was on the verge of hanging up. However, the client clearly wouldn't let her go. I had the strong impression that, if I hadn't been in the room, this conversation could've become very heated indeed. With me there, she was keeping her cool, but only just.

I decided to go for broke, as this sort of opportunity might never return. I stood up. Out of courtesy, she asked the person to excuse her for a moment and then she tried to apologise to me. She promised she wouldn't be long. But, I was gallant and full of understanding in the circumstances and indicated by my expression and demeanour that there was nothing to apologise for.

You've got the paperwork now but don't hesitate to call me if you need more, I said, easing myself out of the door

No really, she protested.

No, I corrected her in firm tones, I won't hear of it. Deal with your call – it's clearly important. My work can wait.

I made my way out. She shrugged her shoulders. She seemed appreciative, yet frustrated.

Courtesy costs nothing, eh?

At this stage, I will accept your plaudits. I have progressed really well. In a relatively short time, I have established a relationship with each of my randomly selected housemates.

Hannah doesn't trust me, but she likes me and is cooperating nicely enough. She's even letting helpful little snippets of information slip my way.

What about Robert? His eyes are positively lighting up at the prospect of someone stupid enough to invest in his pretentious bar, with no collateral required.

And Kathy? She's found herself handling my little property sale in Melbourne. Not because she wants to, but because a tasty carrot has been dangled her way in the shape of juicy, lucrative legal work that she thinks could be hers. There may be something about Mary, but there's also definitely something about Kathleen.

Then there's the lovely Julia. Why is the lovely Julia like an M&M? Because there may be some hardness on the outside right now but she's nothing but soft centre inside. And what a treasure my darling Lisa has turned out to be! Fancy her organising for me a little interlude in Julia's company that fateful night. That night when Julia was oh so tipsy and oh so garrulous and oh so vulnerable with a capital V. And did I make myself useful being the resourceful sort of dude that you know I am? I surely did. I made that little suggestion. Most helpful to her and most expedient for me.

And were we talking of expedience? Well, obviously mirthful Mario needs a friend or two, as we speak. The more I hear of his predicament, the more I know I'd be calling for the brown trousers if I were him. That's a nice little mess he's got himself into. Gee, does he need a good mate right now! And, lucky boy, he found me! How timely of me to put a lucrative little deal his way in this hour of need. But, money isn't everything is it? No, a man in his situation needs support. So I've given him friendship too. Someone he can turn to for advice. Someone he can trust.

Now let's talk about Garry. Is *he* someone we can trust? Well, I sure hope so. Did I tell you he's agreed to take on my job and he's positively wetting himself with ideas about restoring the leadlights. And, of course, putting in a few more. A proposition, in the circumstances, I could hardly refuse. I hope he's not the type to rip someone off. Someone innocent and unsuspecting, like me.

So far so good then. I've made the acquaintance of the housemates and we're all getting along famously. What's more, my new executive team is absolutely perfect and my achievements steadily mount. The iron law of masterly inactivity is proving itself over and over again. The less I actually touch and interfere with as a public servant–leader, the more magnificent are the outcomes I'm seen to achieve.

Yet I am conscious that I have so far negotiated the shallowest incline and that scaling the tallest mountains lies ahead. The achievement is planting the flag atop Everest, not making it to base camp one.

Indeed this strolling around in the foothills to date has been relatively unsatisfying. Selecting and engaging my fellow-dwellers has had its challenges, but it has been rather one-dimensional. Everything has reverted to me.

I have been using any downtime well. I'm now fully trained for the next stage of the ascent. The next climb will be far more interesting and demanding. You see, by some coincidence, pairs of these randomly selected people will start meeting each other on the same day or thereabouts.

What a coincidence indeed!

If she'd made some sort of normal appointment to have her procedure in a week's time, Julia would have had Lisa there literally holding her hand. That would have been very comforting. The swanky private hospital she was now heading into was a far cry from Robert's quaint consulting rooms. His rooms gave off a sense of old-fashioned reassurance. Just then, Julia felt very alone as she stepped into the marbled frigidity of the flagrantly for-profit hospital.

Julia hesitated at the electric sliding doors before conjuring up a memory of the hateful dinner she had sat through the night before. That bastard, she said to herself, and felt steeled to get on with what she now had to do. The hospital receptionists were cool, snooty and efficient. Within minutes, she had filled in the forms, appropriately hesitated to write Stephen down as her next of kin, conveyed her Medicare and private health insurance numbers, consented to the tubal ligation and had signed small-print forms exempting the hospital and its servants (curiously) from any liability for any unexpected outcome known to patient.

Once these formalities had been attended to, she was whisked away into something akin to a Qantas Club lounge and then half an hour later found herself in a surgical gown in a tasteful pastel cubicle waiting for her surgeon. A butch nurse with spiky red hair had written on her thigh in indelible ink her name and the procedure she was having.

At the moment of truth, Julia found herself feeling quite calm. She'd always been that way. She was prone to be a ditz and a drama queen when the sea was as calm as a millpond, but lots of people didn't appreciate that she was ice cool when the waves were smashing themselves against the shore. All those years ago, she had turned on the histrionics when her parents were about to leave her with the nanny once again, but little did her mother and father realise that she'd soon learned to put her fears and anxieties behind her once their Bentley had disappeared around the sharp bend in their driveway.

Indeed, she had always been the one to stay cool when the chips of family life were down. Weren't those the times when big, strong Stephen looked queasy and sat with his head between his legs? She'd never forget the twenty-four hour labour she'd been through with Angie. Of course, Stephen had been the model of a sensitive new-age husband and had attended the antenatal classes, helped her practise the breathing exercises and had held her hand through most of the excruciating labour. But then the business end came and the epidural was ordered. Where was Stephen then for the insertion into her spine? In the corner, looking away, feeling dizzy and sorry for himself.

And then there was the horrible time when Jasmine piloted her bike over the parapet on Rottnest Island and plummeted in slow motion freefall onto the rocks and stones below. It was one of those moments where life unfolds frame by frame. The promenading masses looked on aghast and everything fell silent. No one moved, Jasmine made no sound from below and the spinning wheels of the bike somehow drowned out the distant crash of the waves. Only Julia sprang into action. She leapt the parapet without thinking of the drop. She whisked Jazzy away, held her broken arm straight, consoled her and ordered her to be brave, sent some passers-by off to the nurses' post and others back to fetch Stephen. She was in complete control when the going got tough.

Robert paused outside the cubicle. He saw Julia, undressed and vulnerable. As much as he longed to play doctors and nurses, he instinctively assumed the role of all-powerful surgeon, sweeping the curtains aside to make an impressive entry. His bedside manner was impeccable. Informative and assured – his manner always instilled confidence in the patient, without him needing to show an ounce of emotion or betray the slightest inkling that he cared.

Edicts delivered, instructions to nurses clearly imparted, he swept out of the cubicle in the same decisive, heroic manner in which he had entered.

With the last whirr and clatter of the curtain rings against the metal of the steel rail, Julia's courage drained from her body. Robert's cruel distance had cut her to the quick.

At the same moment, Robert felt sick to the pit of his stomach. He cursed the stifling expectations of his role and standing in the world. Why should he have to bury his deepest feelings under this veneer of haughty surgical disdain?

I loved *A Beautiful Mind*. Russell Crowe really showed what he could do in that film. I empathised deeply with his character. I could put myself in Russell's place because of the intricate diagrams and connectivity plans he used in his imagination to decorate the walls of his shed.

That was how the small office in my apartment looked. Russell knew that having good data was the key to solving complex problems. He had all the key facts and information right there at his fingertips. And so I had clippings and photos from the internet and in some cases from magazines up on my wall. I had Lisa's loving home-printed photographs of her, Julia and me. I had the certificates of title of the properties I was dealing on. I had council plans of the Riverside Bar. I had Mario's garish brochures and Garry's homemade handyman business cards. I had the transcript of the interviews with Hannah with the salient points of her life highlighted in lurid pink.

As you can imagine, the most difficult part – and I'm sure Russell would support me on this – was connecting the light blue tape from one person to another. It might be a simple task with your relatives or your schoolmates to work out who would work out best with whom. But, how do you go about matching people up when they've been selected from a random sample of humanity? Why should X be linked up with Y? And how could they be introduced? And how might they be successfully linked up like so many puppets on a string without even the faintest whiff of the aftershave of the puppeteer reaching their nostrils?

I developed numerous scenarios and tested them with the mad scribbling of a mathematics professor, scrawling the rationale for their connection and the substance and complexity of the artifice required to connect them. The plan would stare back at me from my office room wall for days on end and then, one manic night, I would storm into the operations room at three in the morning and, as if mesmerised by the murmurings of some Communist spy, I'd rip the diagram to shreds and commence a new scrawl of connections, supported by suitable intrigue, to take their place.

I lived liked that for several weeks. At one level, as mad as Russell had ever been, but at another, as analytically brilliant as his character dared to become.

Hannah had no right to feel so girlishly excited at the prospect, but this was a moment to be savoured. She made her way steadily along the corridor to where Garry had relocated her pile of junk. Damn these knees, she thought, as she squatted down on the floor to commence rummaging through what she thought of as the residue of her life.

Did she want to find the ring and money untouched or did she not? She didn't know. She wasn't sure. How stupid to have set up a situation that might leave her unsatisfied either way!

If the booty was there untouched, how would things be? Well, she would know Garry to be an honest man and that would be good. Undoubtedly, it would be good, but it wouldn't be fun. She couldn't even know for sure he'd found it. His mind might have been miles away, thinking about work or his children or the sports results or any damn thing. Hidden away like that, he could even have missed them. So, where would she be if she found the valuables? Precisely nowhere. And even worse, she would still be bored.

But if he'd taken the money and the ring, that would be another situation entirely. How marvellous! But, how disappointing! To be let down by your enthusiastic puppy dog is no good thing. Garry would have messed in the corner just when he was considered house-trained.

It would be sad, too, wouldn't it? What a sad reflection on modern life. What a sad reflection on this ordinary, nice young man who had blossomed so, once given permission to talk. And yet, it would be fun. Rapturous fun.

If Garry really had taken her valuables, she would engage him in one of her philosophical dilemma games designed to test right from wrong. She would be very subtle, of course, as only she could. But she would make him suffer the torture of a thousand ethical cuts, morally mutilating his flesh one tiny incision at a time.

While Hannah was painstakingly sifting through the abandoned artefacts of her long life, Garry was blowing another opportunity to bring his guilty secret into the light. For once, he and Kirsty were alone, and both awake. Garry desperately wanted to share the problem with Kirsty. Every night since the discovery, he had slept badly, with his mind endlessly exploring what he should do. Now he had the opportunity to share the burden with Kirsty. A burden shared, after all, is a burden halved. But, he couldn't bring himself to do it. Why not? At last he knew the answer to that. He was too ashamed to tell her what he'd done.

It was obvious he should say nothing and just put the stuff back. The trouble was, he didn't want to do that. After all, putting the money back was plain stupid when they were desperate for cold, hard cash. He was very confused. He was ashamed of himself for what amounted to stealing, but not honest enough any more to do the right thing. He was in mental conflict yet he knew deep down there was more to his moral turmoil than that. There was another problem preventing him from telling Kirsty. He was ashamed of this thought too, although he knew it was indeed the awful truth. The fact was, if he told Kirsty about the loot, he was certain she would have no qualms about keeping it. That was the second problem. He was scared that Kirsty was not as honest as she ought to be. Not as honest as *he* once thought himself to be. While he didn't want to put the money back, he couldn't let Kirsty make him keep it just like that. Without agonising over it and without questioning right and wrong.

What did it say about his marriage if he couldn't own up to his wife and tell her honestly what he had done? For better or worse. For richer or poorer.

So that opportunity to unburden went begging too. As he drove to work the next morning, these conflictual thoughts still haunted him. No, there were only two options from here, he thought. He could slip the money back and hope Hannah hadn't missed it or he could tell Kirsty and let that action drag him where it may.

He responded belatedly to the insistent beeping of the cars stuck behind him now the lights were green.

Waiting for a colour you like? an irate motorist shouted at him with the rude finger held aloft.

Fuck you too! Garry responded in kind.

What a fucking mess. He wished to God he'd never found the

bloody stuff and that his life could somehow go back to the way it had been. He wanted an uncomplicated cuddle with his wife. He wanted a leisurely chat over tea with his mentor. He wanted back to when he had only minor cares in his world.

As he pulled into the fire station, it was clear what he had to do. He would tell Kirsty tonight. He would give it to her straight and he would not be bullied or blackmailed into doing what was wrong. And he would put the money and the ring back. His tension eased. It would be wrong to deceive Kirsty just as it would be wrong to keep what he'd found. If he did the right thing on both counts, his conscience would be clear and he would have a chance to turn back the clock.

Better search through it all again, Hannah muttered to herself breathlessly. He wouldn't have taken it, surely? Not a nice boy like him.

At that time, I was like a matchmaker. I connected and re-connected the blue tape between my grooms and brides, searching for a set of marriages truly made in heaven. I can be a little obsessive, and for a while matchmaking dominated my thoughts. So much so that I decided to undertake a little action research.

I thought it might be educational for me to sign up with a dating agency. I wanted to learn their trade secrets. I also thought it might be a source of fun. I wondered what these experts in the relationships of the lonely, poor and lost might make of a successful, handsome and wealthy guy.

I completed the forms online, gave my American Express details and waited for The Loveline to contact me within twenty-four hours. I was duly contacted by my appointed Heart Consultant, but it was disappointing that it took them all of thirty-two hours to get back to me. On the next day I met with a well-groomed young lady by the name of Joanne and then I filled out more forms and then we met again and she told me about the kind of guy I was and then summarised the kind of woman I liked.

I was unfalteringly polite while I pondered the supreme irony of a twenty-two year old checkout chick doing a psych profile on a man like me. When I sat down with the multiple-choice questionnaire in front of me, notwithstanding the fifteen hundred bucks I'd just coughed up, I couldn't resist creating a fantasy personality for myself just for the hell of it. I let her tell me the results, knowing they were total bullshit. For the record, I couldn't stand the creep she told me I was. A loving, nurturing, sensitive man committed to achieving a meaningful relationship with a like-minded girl. Wow! I looked round the room to check that she was talking to me.

But while I sat there, I was taking it all in. How do you match people together effectively? Does the computer just spit out the attributes so there's no human skill involved? Does it follow that Jack will love Jill because they are compatible on

The Loveline's standard weighted psychological pairing test developed in accordance with Hatfield's matching hypothesis? Does psychology outweigh chemistry after all? Truly, what's love got to do with it? And there was I thinking all along that Jill loved Jack cos he's got a flash car and Jack loved Jill cos she's got big tits.

As I walked away from the city office contemplating whether to meet some woman called Diane from a suburb I'd never heard of, it occurred to me that this research had been worth every cent. Having observed Joanne very closely, I had some evidence-based learning to work from. Despite company policy, she didn't treat the Hatfield and the computer as God.

Joanne was a rebel – a humanly flawed rebel. She didn't link the people together that the computer said. Instead she matched up the people she liked with the other people she liked, and with the people she didn't like she did the same. On this basis, I wondered what Diane from Dog Swamp could possibly be like to end up being paired up with me. It was almost worth meeting her to find out.

Thanks to Joanne, I recognised that I'd been striving too hard for scientific pairings, without letting the human factor in. I thought it unprofessional to mix and match without a logical basis. Now I felt free to go along with gut feel to seek a solution for my longstanding problem.

I allowed myself to go with the flow of what felt right. Which pairings appealed to me? I liked Kathleen with Robert – that would have got his juices flowing. I liked Julia with Garry for the sheer irony of it. It was very Mills & Boon. Julia's flawless skin at the mercy of his rough, sinewy worker's hands! And, of course, who could resist Hannah with Mario? What a show!

But, then what about Mario with Julia or the temptation for Garry with Kathleen? The possibilities were great but one permutation of pairings would be the best. I had to strive to find that one.

To be the best – that is after all the whole point.

Oh yes, Mario, you are da main man, you are the gigolo all the hos want.

Mario was mixing his ethnicities and metaphors freely. He combed and re-combed his hair to cover up the thinning areas. You look real good, if I may so, very hot indeed.

He splashed on the duty-free cologne his brother-in-law had brought back from his trip to Palermo and worried for a fleeting moment that it might explode on contact with his smoke. He was taking deep nervous drags between coiffing the delicate strands of his still immaculately black hair.

He skipped to the lift and down to his underground car park. He fired up the beast and roared out in celebratory style, missing the rising security grille by centimetres. Fancy her ringing me, eh? Now, that's nice. So, I haven't lost my touch after all. She sounded a bit serious with all that I've got to talk something over with you stuff. But then she sounded all sultry and sexy too, what with that I'm at a loose end right now so why don't you join me in Subi for a little chat?

He felt up for it all right tonight. Full of himself in every sense of the word. He gave himself a little rub at the red light as his filthy thoughts were causing pressure on his zipper. G-strings for sure, he thought, no question about it. All lacy and silky too, cos a lawyer type doesn't shop at Target for her smalls.

She was deep into her second daiquiri when Mario walked into the dimly lit bar and peered through the gloom like a miner starting his shift below. He did look sweet squinting like that, she thought. Eventually, he tracked her down and stood beaming beside her.

You're not really a lawyer, darlin' are you? Mario said. You can't fool me, you know, no one as gorgeous as you would waste their time poring over dusty old books.

He made a huge fuss about going to the bar and insisted on getting her a cocktail. He came back with an over-priced imported beer for him and a cloudy, frothy number for her with an umbrella and a spiked glace cherry. He pretended to have a sip through Kathleen's straw.

Just so our lips will finally touch, he said with a schoolboy grin.

Before you get carried away, Mr Martinelli, she said with mock severity belied by a flirtatious grin, we are here for serious business.

Business before pleasure it is then.

Well, I've had a conference with one of our partners about your situation and we think there's a clear, preferred course for you to follow.

He perched on the perspex cube next to her and somehow resisted the temptation to slide his hand under the table onto what would be a taut as titanium thigh. He was admiring his self-control in the face of the palpable pressure in his underpants when he felt his ardour subside in a hurry as she began to speak.

Now, about your friends. We have considered a range of options from a legal point of view and also as much from a risk management perspective.

Mario didn't like the sound of that.

We feel that far and away the most practical way forward would be to approach the originators of the loan directly and suggest that their interests would be best served by recovery from the ultimate defaulter on the debt.

Look, beautiful, don't take this the wrong way, Mario interrupted, but if I understand your meaning correctly and I think I do, I actually place a strong value on my nuts, particularly in your sweet company, and I'd like to keep them quite a bit longer, thank you very much. Basically, if I go to these boys and try to direct them onto someone else for the money I owe them, I will be as welcome as a mullah at a barmitzvah.

With due respect, Mr Martinelli. There she was being stern and professional again and it stirred him even in these circumstances. His mind wandered momentarily to how much he liked women in uniforms and starched business suits. We are not suggesting that *you* approach them at all. We are proposing that our partner and I seek a conference with the gentlemen concerned on your behalf and seek to persuade them that you are the innocent party in this matter, but more importantly, that you don't have the money they need to cover the debt so it would be more productive to approach the shoe manufacturer directly.

Yes, but they'll still know that you're doing this on my behalf and so there's no telling what they might do to *me* regardless, Mario spluttered. But she took him by surprise and changed her approach 360 degrees.

Look here darling, she said mocking him expertly, these Sicilian bastards are going to knock on your door one early morning soon anyway so you have sweet fucking nothing to lose, if you know what I mean, darling. And what's more, we have some expertise in negotiations of this delicate nature and we charge a proverbial arm and a leg for it because we are fucking brilliant at what we do, *capiche*?

So, when do we start? he said with his characteristic smirk, sliding a hand under the table onto a leather-clad, thigh that felt as taut as titanium.

Start *what*? she said, placing her hand on his.

You know what, he said, trying to shift her hand and his to the place of no return.

I know *where* to start at least, she said, standing up and grabbing her bag off the vacant stool. Coming?

Mario sped to get in front of her. He opened the door for her with an elaborate flourish of his right hand that finished up on her bum as she led the way through the door.

Men are so predictable, Kathleen thought. That must be why I like them.

It was time to make a decision. I favour the Japanese management decision-making approach over the western version any day. Western management is so adversarial. Decision making in the west is a contest about who can win. There are protagonists and opponents and they fight it out until a decision is made. At that point the winners and losers are declared.

However, in the east, decision making is an evolutionary process. A decision is reached in its own good time. Decisions aren't forced to satisfy the impatience of those who seek to win. They say that when a decision is needed, it will come.

So the time had come for me to decide. I was in the shower – the place where I make my best decisions. I let the thoughts flow over and around me with the hot water. Thoughts and ideas came and went. The good ones clung to me with the soap suds and the crap ones were washed down the plughole with the Garnier and the pee.

I was ready for the decision now and it was there.

Robert with Julia; Mario with Kathleen; and Hannah with Garry.

As you know, there were equally attractive pairings to me and I was tempted, very tempted, to go with others. I didn't. In the end, when I needed to make up my mind, I simply chose the pairings I liked best.

And why not for fuck's sake? It was my Master Plan. It was my choice to make.

So I did.

I was allegedly making good progress on the old girl's article. Hannah was opening up to me. I didn't fool myself that she was fooled by me. But she found me intelligent enough to bother to answer my questions and sensitive enough apparently to tell me about the most personal and harrowing details of her incredible life.

I actually did feel like writing about some of it. The parallels with modern wars and totalitarian domination of people's ideas and beliefs were inescapable. In a funny sort of way, modern man of the twenty-first century can relate very easily to the experiences of less-than-modern woman of the mid-twentieth century. But, notwithstanding my ability to relate and even to care when I choose to, my true nature came to the fore and I trivialised the tragedy of Hannah's experiences in a breathtakingly callous fashion.

She was telling me about that cold winter's day when the Gestapo came to call. They banged on the front door and a dread chill ran through the bones of Hannah and her sisters(!), her three brothers, her father, her mother, her grandfather on her father's side and so the list went on. They all closed around her father for whom the nice gentlemen from the Third Reich were coming to call. Hannah was despatched to open the door as the least likely to meet a violent response. As fate would have it, the grandfather began to pray in Hebrew at the very moment the leather-coated captain swept into the room followed by a horde of jackbooted flunkies.

Josef Baumgarten, you are to come with us, the *hauptmann* announced.

The group closed around the head of the family and, without a hint of insolence or defiance, remained standing there silently refusing to give up the quarry. The soldiers corralled the group with their rifle butts and shepherded them towards the French doors that gave onto a tiny courtyard. The tight knit group shuffled inch by inch backwards towards the high stone walls overgrown with creeper.

The captain stated calmly that Josef Baumgarten should now make himself known and leave with the soldiers. He added, or there will be consequences. Not a member of the family moved; not even Josef himself, who must have known that he was putting all of his loved ones at risk. Despite the fact that he knew perfectly well which one of these wretched people was Josef and, if he hadn't known, could have worked out who it was from the way the crowd was protecting him, the captain removed his pistol from its leather holster and executed the family members one by one until his bullets were exhausted. He then motioned to his Gestapo colleague, who finished off the remaining two people, including the grandfather who was the only one to utter a sound, the sound of Jewish prayer said without conviction or defiance.

Having concluded their carnage, the soldiers turned on their heels and exited through the front door and past Hannah who was still standing there holding the wooden door handle, not having moved and not having spoken.

When Hannah finished her story, I switched off the tape recorder with what seemed a deafening and definitive click. I know that you wouldn't have turned it off at that point. I know exactly what you think of that. I know exactly what you would have asked her at that point. But, you're no better than me and no more moral than me, although right now you might think so. Your curiosity would have been born from prurience and not from compassion. Hannah may have an opinion about why they let her live or she may not. She might want to tell you and she might not. She might have told you why they came for Josef. Maybe not.

But, I didn't ask her that.

Instead I said: By the way, you know that renovation work you want done? I've got a moonlighting fireman I can recommend for it.

There's nothing else for it, Robert concluded.

He'd exhausted every other approach. He'd tried everything he could reasonably do without raising Marj's antennae and getting her nose twitching in that way that scared him.

Robert swished the dregs of his red around the now stained wine glass. He'd phoned her God knows how many times, he'd emailed her under the pretence of impeccable, post-operative customer service and he'd even had his secretary schedule an unnecessary follow-up appointment that Julia hadn't kept.

Maybe she was just using him. It would serve him right, he conceded. Maybe she just wanted the procedure pronto, incognito, finito and that was that. Once she'd had her way with him surgically-speaking, well that was that. He couldn't reasonably believe it. He was a doctor for fuck's sake, a people-person and he could read people. So he knew that Julia was crazy about him, weak-kneed about him, knickers-wet for him, so there had to be another explanation he just wasn't getting.

And since that had to be the case, he determined to undertake that desperate act and put his professional reputation, his obviously Hypocritical Oath on the line for the sake of a dalliance with a bit of blonde, and not even a young bit of blonde at that. But, she was worth all that. This bit of blonde. She was class, she was delectable, she was tailor-made for him and like all the others she would have to be his.

So Robert walked up Julia's driveway, observing that her car was there in front of the cedar-wood garage. The gravel crunched under his feet, but he did not hear it. The security cameras recorded his arrival, but he did not notice them. His mobile phone vibrated in his pocket, but he paid no attention to it. Instead, he rang the security entry phone at the wrought iron gate that protected the shady courtyard that served as the entry to the front door.

He expected to hear Julia's voice over the intercom, but instead he heard the door open. She must have been standing right there. Robert looked away as if to close his eyes in anticipation of a breathtaking present.

Hi, can I help you? a quizzical male voice inquired of him.

I made it my business to spend time with Mario as I had tagged him as a loose cannon, an unpredictable type who could bring my plan undone if a close eye wasn't kept on him. Keep your friends close and your enemies closer, as they say. Not that he was an enemy as such, but I was very aware that he could unwittingly bring me down.

I'm not getting sentimental or anything again, but I rather liked him. I found our little sessions at his local nothing if not entertaining. I liked sitting there while he held court. There was a veritable conga line of passers-by who would sashay up to our table when he was seated on his grubby red-padded throne. I accused him of paying them to rock up to make him look popular.

Believe me, my friend, if I wanted to impress you I'd get a few tarts with big knockers to hang off me like that Playboy bloke, what's his name.

Hugh Hefner, I volunteered.

Anyway, paid or not, they would descend on Mario and I'd lose him for a while to his subjects. They asked after his nonna, they gave him racing tips, they offered him 'cheap' mobile phones and laptops and they stroked his ego in the hope that he'd shout them a beer.

My favourite amongst those granted an audience was an ex-alcoholic ex-actor who had just got back from climbing Kilimanjaro. He regaled us with his intrepid adventures, the peak of which, so to speak, was the death of one of his party of eight on the mountain.

There was me, he said, who's never done any serious exercise in his life and three flabby partners from some big law firm, a batty granny in a green tracksuit, two Pommy beer-swilling plasterers and an ironman from Queensland. And who do you think fucking died from altitude sickness on the way up?

Mario and I looked at each other uncertain if he expected an answer.

Yeah, the fucking so-called ironman, he roared. There is a God, boys. There really is divine justice in the world.

And this jovial tone would persist for a while until the evening wore on. Then gradually, the drinkers would disperse to their homes and their lives, leaving the playing field to the hard-core drinkers with no wives and no lives. Inevitably the tone would deteriorate and melancholia would become cocktail of the week. Thus it always was with Mario. Once the bonhomie faded and the acolytes departed, Mario would become morose and his fears and anxieties would tiptoe out of hiding in the shadows and form a line at our table every bit as long as the supplicants only hours before.

What do you think was top of the shit parade for Mario? It was his little venture with the *Mafiosi* and the shoeman, wasn't it? Eventually his head would sink into his hands and he would declare that he didn't know what was for the best. He felt like smashing the little fuck's face in, but he knew that wouldn't solve his problem. Presently his dial would appear again with a grin and he'd say maybe I should go to Siberia or Brazil or somewhere like that and start a nice life with Ronnie Biggs and the gang. But the comic relief would never last very long and he would sink into despair again.

Then one day he broke from the usual pattern and looked at me earnestly.

Come on you're a smart bloke, he said. You know a thing or two about this and that. What do *you* think I should do?

I sat in inscrutable silence for a while.

Well, Einstein, what advice have you got?

As it happens, I do have something for you.

Wow, fantastic. Come on, spit it out.

Well, I've happened across a lawyer who I really think could help. Before you interrupt me, I insisted, waving his impending objection away, this lawyer is different. This lawyer is street-smart, this lawyer moves in the right circles to talk turkey with your frightening friends. This lawyer will hit the mark for you, I know.

OK then, let me lick your arse for a while with a proposal like this, he said perking up visibly. Does this guy have a name?

Yes, this guy does have a name, I said. This guy's name is Kathleen and what's more, this guy is a dead-set spunk of a lawyer in a tight-fitting suit.

The moment had arrived for Garry. Self-respect demanded that he grasp it, come what may. He steeled himself to get the job done in spite of the domestic distractions and red herrings that were worthy of a crime thriller. There was bath time, supper time, talking to grandma time, putting away the toys time, watching a DVD time and finally story time.

Eventually, Garry found himself seated opposite his impossibly elusive wife. He bought a little time to regroup. He forked his peas one by one and then he started cutting his beefburger into small cubes until even he found the whole thing laughable. He threw down his knife and fork with much more intensity than he had intended. Kirsty was taken aback.

We have to talk, he said. He realised that he'd completely stuffed up the intro and she now expected him to confess to a torrid affair with Nina, the elderly next door neighbour.

Sorry, sweetie, it's nothing terrible or anything, but I really do need to tell you something.

And so he told her. He left out all the stuff about his relationship with Hannah because he knew he would make a mess of that. So he stuck to the facts of the events of the fateful day where he became richer than he had ever been and at least twice as unhappy.

He noticed Kirsty's face tensing up, showing the recently acquired wrinkles around her eyes. He watched her hand inch centimetre by centimetre (if that's possible) onto her forehead to accentuate her look of disbelief.

You're joking, you're not joking, are you? she said.

Garry was unsure whether to agree or disagree and with which part. Fucking unreal, eh? Then he remembered the game plan was to leave no uncertainty. I'm just gonna put it back tomorrow and hope the old girl never noticed it was gone.

Show me the ring, Kirsty requested.

No, it's not a good idea, Kirst – we've got to give it back.

Don't you trust me or something? I've gotta see this ring.

Reluctantly, Garry went to the bag he'd stashed in the garage and returned with the money and the ring. He spread the notes and the ring out on the battered kitchen table and he instantly knew that was a stupid thing to have done.

Garry watched Kirsty shake her head as she took in the beauty and intricacy of the antique jewellery.

Jesus, she sighed softly. This ring is incredible. Look at the work that's gone into it. Look at the diamonds in the rose. This must be a family heirloom.

Probably German or Austrian, I suppose.

Kirsty changed tack without warning. How much cash is here, Gaz?

Twenty grand, he whispered reluctantly.

Game over, he thought as he watched Kirsty gather up the notes.

We need to give it back, Kirst. She's a lovely old lady and she's been through an awful lot in her life. Unimaginable things. I know we could use the money, I know it would be a godsend really, but we're not that like that and we need to give it back.

The ring's gotta go back for sure, she said, that must have sentimental value. But not the money, Gaz.

Kirst! he protested firmly, responding instinctively to a fire getting out of control.

But Kirsty was having none of it. She must be loaded to leave this lying around and she wouldn't even know she's got it, believe me.

I couldn't look her in the face if I kept the money, Garry said.

Suit yourself, Kirsty said raising her voice, you always do. Sometimes, you're really stupid, do you know that? We can't even afford proper furniture for this place and you're going to give the lottery winnings back!

It's not right, Kirsty, that's all. It's not right.

You're always right, that's the problem, she said, slamming her plate into the sink. I dunno why you bothered telling me about it in the first place if you'd made up your mind, as usual. We need some money, Garry, we can't go on like this. I'm too embarrassed to ask our friends round here, do you know that, to sit on this clapped out shit we call a sofa. We need to do something, Garry, she shrieked, do you hear me, Mr Fucking Saint?

The door slammed rattling the door frame. The house shook and the kids woke up crying.

Fuck, fuck, fuck, fuck, Garry said in despair.

He cleared the remains of his beefburger into the pedal bin. It was a disappointment, but not a shock. He knew Kirsty very well, of course. He knew from the start what she would say. Now, he had to work out what to do. But, from hereon in, he was on his own.

And the stakes were impossibly high.

I pictured myself as a double agent. But, in my case, it was *Tinker, Tailor, Soldier, Cry*. At that moment, under deep cover or, as we say these days, embedded, I seriously could have wept. My seemingly dismembered hand was intertwined with Lisa's perfectly manicured counterpart in an outward display of affection. To her, I think it was more an outward display of *couple-dom*, which as we all know is the station one stop down the line from *bore-dom*. Anyway, suffice to say, I had to put up with her mauling to get close to Julia as often as possible.

While men have an uncanny ability to avoid talking about anything, their penis-deprived earthling companions have an extraordinary ability to talk about nothing. All that was expected of me was to maintain tactile engagement with Lisa. This was required at all times. For good measure, I added an affable facial demeanour and a judicious occasional nod and a yes and a wow to avoid detection.

However, behind the eyes of this spy, I was imagining myself in sepia tones in a run-down hotel room where the overhead fan was spinning and creaking. Just like in the old spy movies, I fantasised that my book of Shakespeare had been transformed into a transmitter with my toothbrush screwed in as an aerial. My hairbrush had been separated into a morse sender and into two ear muffs for decoding. Vast quantities of my data crawled their way across the ether to a man with a croupier's eye shade, elasticated clips to keep his shirtsleeves up and a thick coating of brilliantine on his hair as if it was going out of fashion (and it was).

As hard as I slaved away at my espionage activities, there were slim pickings indeed for the boffins back at base to work with. If you ever wondered what people with no problems talk about, I can tell you that they talk about their problems. As it's logically impossible, you can't help but admire the ability of the women of Perth's western suburbs to do this. These conversations defy logic as well as beggar belief. I soon realised that there was no need to be distracted by the lines themselves and that I was free to concentrate on listening between them.

Over a couple of sessions, I was confident that HQ must have been piecing together intelligence on the supporting cast at least. Stephen, Angelica, Jasmine and Benjie (the Dalmatian, no less). This group began to form itself in my febrile brain like an alternative troupe of the seven dwarfs. Stephen was Dopey; Angelica was Happy; Jasmine was Bashful; Benjie was Sneezy; Julia was Ditzy; and I was definitely Sleepy. I needed a seventh person of diminished stature. I ruefully cast Lisa as Horny.

So I sat through these events stupefied under a cloud of vapour. On this particular day, Lisa was to take me to the movies.

We're going to Luna 3, she gushed. It's so civilised, you can take a glass of wine into the cinema.

But then she rang me in a cloudburst of apologies explaining that Julia had called her and sounded funny on the phone.

What do you mean by funny? I asked.

Well, she didn't sound like herself, nothing like it actually. I'm worried something must really be wrong.

So, Lisa expected me to be a sweetie and give up the flicks. I know you'll believe me that nothing would have been more welcome than this reprieve. But, being a double agent as it happens, I kicked back.

Well, no, I'm not happy about it at all, I protested. I've changed various plans and stood people up to go to this movie that you said we absolutely had to see. And what's more, I was really looking forward to seeing you tonight.

You're so sweet, she tried to pacify me, and I don't blame you for bring ticked off. I know, how about this? I'll get Julia to meet me early in some bar near the cinema and then you can join me at nine and we'll still make it in time for nine fifteen.

I grudgingly told her that sounded like a plan. But I sent the following message back to camp: Development stop; possible crisis stop; opportunity stop; wouldn't miss this for anything stop; need to arrive accidentally early stop.

And so I did. There was Julia all puffy and red-eyed.

You're early darling, Lisa said.

No I'm not.

You are – I said nine.

Bugger it, did you? I thought it was half eight. Julia – are you OK? – you look dreadful.

I feel worse, she said gulping down her wine.

Whatever's the matter? No I shouldn't ask.

Give us a bit more time, be a sweetie, Lisa pleaded.

No, it's OK, really, Julia said firmly. I don't hate *all* men.

Then the Julia floodgates opened. Outwardly, I let myself be washed away. My eyes said expertly, Oh my God, you poor thing, what a bastard, are you sure, yes, of course you are, a Chinese nursemaid, Jesus Christ, no the film doesn't matter, I think you need some friends right now, and I'm your friend too, it's not just Lisa, it's me too, and I'm a man, a good man, a caring man, and a man who will stand by you through thick and through thin.

And behind my expert, compassionate eyes I said, You little fucking bewdy. I waited for a lull in the maelstrom of anguish. Lisa went to the loo and Julia sculled another glass of red and snivelled into an overused tissue. I gave her a relatively fresh one from my pocket and I also gave her a napkin from the table. But this was not for her nose. It was for her salvation.

With a suitable preamble of not knowing her well and not wanting to pry and not wanting to interfere nor wanting to presume, I slipped her the napkin with a name on it.

I looked her in the eye and said to her with an air of authority. In my view, he's disempowering you. He's counting on you feeling too impotent to respond. But you must not acquiesce. You must be proactive. If you don't want more children, make sure you really can't have them. I overheard my PA give glowing reports on this guy.

Is that Hetherington? she snivelled.

Yes, Dr Robert Hetherington, sorry about my handwriting. Put it in your handbag or Lisa will tell me off.

I sent my final report home: Abandon plan for Riverside Bar introduction stop; can now infiltrate deep inside enemy lines stop; as deep as you can go stop.

Kathleen felt like she was babysitting very naughty twins.

Mario's pacing up and down was getting on her nerves. She didn't dare look at the ever-intolerant Max.

I hope to God this thing never ends up in court, Kathleen found herself saying out loud.

I know what you mean, Max responded in his habitual sardonic tone.

What *do* you mean? Mario inquired mournfully.

Well, look at you, she said, doing your caged lion act. You need to pull yourself together right now or leave it to us as I advised you.

Regrettably, her intervention only made things worse, with Mario slinking off to light up right in front of the *No Smoking* sign.

Despite paying out on Mario, she was acutely aware that she and Max were nowhere near as cool, calm and collected as they appeared. Max was in one of his foul moods and she would have to be prepared to intervene at some point should the haemorrhaging from his diplomacy bypass need cauterising. Normally Max's debt recovery strategy did not end up with lawyer-to-lawyer contact of this kind and this departure from the normal course was making Max super-cranky.

Max had been cocky as usual after his initial call to the hoods. He'd used his best UWA law school training to propose a meeting to see if things couldn't be resolved. As required by the Law Society, he'd asked the men in black for the name of their legal representatives so everything could be done *according to Hoyle*. This sham of rectitude had worked wonders in the past in getting to meet the clients without their lawyers present. Most people were reluctant to run up their legal bills just for the sake of a chat. But these guys didn't do that. They just shot back the name of their lawyers. And who would it be, as if this was any surprise, but the guy everyone knows represents Perth's *Mafiosi*? Even more than we do, Kathleen had observed to Max, with sincere regret.

So, there was Kathleen doing adult childcare on the thirty-eighth level on the Terrace with a sweaty-palmed client fagging in front of the pricey artworks and a petulant partner ready to punch their client on the nose.

Kathleen breathed more easily once they were led into a leather-book-lined boardroom designed with deliberate indifference to both intimidate and relax. She allowed herself the luxury of wishing her firm had impressive surroundings like that.

Mario sat quietly, tuning out like a kid covering his ears so as not to hear how much trouble he was in. He tried to distract himself with scarcely more palatable thoughts about how much this legal talkfest would be costing him.

If Mario's brain had been working, he would have registered the following: the arsehole's advocates think my lawyers' legal arguments are shit; they think the argument that a case against me could take a long time to get to court is totally irrelevant shit; they know the whole idea of this matter going to court is total shit; they know they don't have to bother with the law to recover their money and shit; they can't see any reason to dirty their hands on that shit who didn't repay me; they're going to make me pay them or eat shit.

As it was, he just sat there feeling scared shitless.

When the interview was over, Mario slumped into the café armchair in the foyer of the office tower. Instinctively, Max ordered him an espresso. Mario ignored another *No Smoking* sign.

I think that went according to plan, Kathleen said.

Mario was speechless.

I agree, Max said.

Mario was speechless.

D'you reckon they'll do it, Max? Kathleen asked.

I think they will.

Mario was speechless.

It's the obvious thing, Max added.

Yeah, I think we got that across, Kathleen agreed.

Mario was speechless.

If we look at the their options, it makes sense, Kathleen

continued. Legal track – definitely not. Putting the heavies on our client? – risky now that we're involved and have fronted their lawyers. Go the soft option of the shoeman, it's obvious.

Absolutely, Max said with an air of finality.

Mario was no longer speechless. He told them quietly and calmly and without swearing the story of Nick Conti from the island of his birth. As the country songs go, he had done them wrong. They taught him a lesson.

His wheelchair worked pretty well, apparently.

Woody Allen's metaphor in *Match Point* was pretty apt, don't you think? Fate places us at the mercy of events where the tennis ball of life teeters precariously on the top of the net and it could fall this way or it could fall that. And of course, the ball could have a hard landing or it might be soft. And how will we know which result was for the best? Sometimes we rejoice at unexpected success. But for how long? Often the wisdom of hindsight proves those celebrations not only premature but also absurd in its cold retrospective light. And conversely, don't we just as often curse our bad luck at a lost job or a missed liaison and thank our lucky stars down the track that some God or other was looking our way back then?

And so it was for my little tribe. Dear old Hannah needed some work done. I helped her. I gave her Garry's card. To Garry I gave Hannah. She helped him too. Did I set the little test for Garry? No, I did not. Was it me who exposed his weakness? No, it was not. Did I ask him to marry Kirsty? Not that I can remember. Which way will his tennis ball fall?

Do I get the feeling juicy Julia's marriage is in trouble? I think I do. Is that my fault? Certainly not. Did I send solid Stephen off to China to bring back Lucy Liu? No way. Did I want Jules up the duff? Not me. Did I make rich and rakish Robert really randy? I did not. What if I did give Julia a bit of a nudge in his direction? You know me – I only did it to help. What else was the poor darling going to do? Who says Robert won't make her happy? Who says Julia's arrival won't make long-suffering Marjorie happy? Who is to say that they'll even get it together? Which way will the tennis ball fall?

How long ago was it that I met mournful Mario and caressable Kathy? A matter of months? So it couldn't have been me that made Mario the merry moron that he is. Did I go up to him and beg him to borrow big bucks from big blokes and lend it to a shaman shoeman? I hadn't even met him then, had I? And was I hard at it with Kathy's red-haired mummy while Daddy was hard at it at the office so that the bouncing babe was born into the respectable

Irish household that she was? Maybe it was the parish priest but it sure as hell wasn't me. Did I create this smart but rebellious bint? No, sir. Is it my fault that dangerous deeds get her juices flowing? Cannot be. Sure, I put Mario onto a good lawyer. An appropriate lawyer for his needs, as it happens. I was there to help. Is that a crime? Did I give him legal advice? Not qualified to do so. Which way will his tennis ball fall? And, which way will hers?

And what about you for that matter? Which way will your ball fall? Look at you now sitting back and judging me, sitting back and judging them. I told you not to judge me, didn't I? I don't care if you do. I'm just advising you against it.

I don't want you to look foolish. You might condemn when you should congratulate. You might admonish when you should admire. You might reject when you should revere.

And the beauty of it all is that this is a true story that you actually know. It's gorgeous, isn't it? It might be at the edge of your memory somewhere, but you definitely know it. Maybe you get flashes of recollection and bits and pieces come back to you. You can't hold onto them can you? That's the trouble. You know you know this story from somewhere and yet you haven't got a fucking clue what is going to happen.

To be fair, you might not recognise the tale told as it is. It's like looking at one of those concave mirrors or like looking at a 3D film without the silly glasses on. Everything is familiar but you can't quite see it. I'm letting you see it through my prism. I'm letting you see it from the inside out as it were and not from where you're used to – outside in.

You wouldn't have known that an unseen, controlling hand created their destiny. You wouldn't have known that there was another reality. Let me roll some more out for you. Maybe the light will switch on soon? Or maybe later?

REALITY ENGAGED

Garry was particularly annoyed with himself. He was painting, but the brush was moving in automatic strokes. He was remembering an event when he was fourteen and distracting himself from his distraction from the painting, to wonder why he could recall a particular event from so many years ago. It was pre-season footy. There was a life and death struggle for the school team in a really good year. It was the final practice match and the places were up for grabs. It was late in the game. He had two set shots for goal. He fluffed them both. He'd practised the same shots probably hundreds of times. He was supposed to be ready. He obviously wasn't. And to add insult to injury, a kid called Ducky took his place. Fancy missing out to someone called Donald.

So, he absentmindedly flexed his wrist this way and that and the white matt paint progressively covered the now perfectly prepared ceiling. How could he be there and not be ready? How could he have rocked up and still not known whether to return the stuff or not?

It may have stemmed from paranoia or just plain guilt. But Garry had the sense that Hannah was undressing him with her eyes. No, not like that. He felt that his every movement and gesture was transparent to her on that day. He felt like a butterfly whose number was up. There he was lying in an undignified position, pinned through the backside, having every pore examined under the penetrating gaze of a microscope.

As the day dragged on, Garry became more and more convinced that Hannah was torturing him for his crimes. He tried to shake the image of her searching desperately for her valuables. But it was so vivid. There Hannah was, scrabbling around like a bag lady on the dirty floor, panicking at the loss of her mother's wedding ring and the nest egg she was relying upon to eke out her few remaining years.

It was clear as day to him that Hannah had no intention of loosening the screws on the rack. Every few minutes she was interrupting him, just by chance, to show him some curious knick-knack she'd discovered in the pile of things he'd kindly moved for her the other day.

Then Hannah pottered down the hall again to call out to him.

Garry, I've got a nice surprise for you. I've made some apple strudel.

He knew for sure this act of kindness was designed to cut a man with a guilty conscience to the quick.

It's my speciality so I want you to give it a try. Anyway, you must have a stiff neck by now craning up at the ceiling like that. Come on, pop down and join me in the kitchen.

Garry took his time. He dragged himself down from the ladder and mooched along the hall like a condemned man taking the long, last walk to the gallows. He waddled like the disconsolate duck that trudges across the TV screen when the batsman's out for nought. So his time was up. After weeks in the cell, thinking about this moment, contemplating oblivion, telling himself to smell the roses because today wasn't the day, today had finally arrived and now he was going to face his execution and he still didn't know what to do.

He sat down on the bentwood kitchen chair while Hannah prattled on somewhere in the suburbs of his brain. So, this is it. This is the moment. What is your decision? My decision is, he said to himself leaving ample time for a drum roll to build the tension, my decision is ... I'm going to put it all back and pretend it was there all along.

He felt heaps better instantly. Oh yes, that feels good. There'll be hell to pay when I get home, but I will bask in the glory of having done the right thing. Shit, how close did I come? How fucking close was that? He'd been just centimetres from hitting that other car that sped through the intersection. That's how close he'd been. This was one to tell his mates. Well, maybe not. But, it was over now.

Apple strudel?

This is grouse, Hannah!

Yes, I know, you Aussies can't tell the difference between cake and small Scottish birds.

Hannah was unusually quiet and that unnerved Garry again. But he felt so good to have made some decision that he willed himself to stay in the moment just as Hannah had taught him to. He ate more strudel. Lots more strudel. He chatted. He engaged. He conversed with Hannah about her heirlooms and then he went back to work.

It had been such a good day up to that time. Actually, a fucking brilliant day, Mario thought. It might have been his best to that point. That was when it turned ugly, of course.

It did have a shitty start thanks to another blue with the Bitch over the phone. About something petty again, like leaving Olivia's shoes behind at the park. The park that's a hundred metres from the Bitch's house, mind you, so she could've gone back there and got them and done something useful rather than give him an ear job that wasn't going to get the shoes found anyway.

But, hey, it's water off a duck's back. Nothing's gonna change with the Bitch; if it's not one thing it's the next. Lucky she didn't notice the socks were missing as well.

Boy, had that Friday morning improved. It was a case of going from the darkness into light. That beautiful messenger, his umbellical mobile phone, had pinged in reply just as he picked up his car keys to head off to work. Wow, he could hardly believe it. Fuck, he didn't believe it actually – that's why he re-read the text at least five times.

I guess I could squeeze you in for an appointment at two o'clock, it said. At the Llama Bar of course and all expenses to be paid by the client – my usual terms.

So, you see, my son, he said chirpily to himself – a bird's a bird, posh and hoity-toity or not. Yes, my man, they are all the same. None of them are immune to your charms. Texting birds is a work of art, mind you. Yes, it is. Not anyone can do it, even if it might look easy. You need charm and subtlety and a big dose of inyourfaceness to get over the line.

He'd chanced his arm with this one.

Any chance of some lawyer–client privilege anytime soon?

A masterpiece of a text it was. One to be hung in his hall of fame, next to his bar by the pool table. One to take pride of place. Especially as it had worked and got such a beautiful response.

So there he was, in the swanky restaurant-bar, a little bit early, hoping that didn't make him seem too needy. And there she was, not there. But she did rock up. They sat at the bar for a while. On the trendy bar stools made from old road signs. They were both sitting on the number 40. Kathleen looked great, too. Smart, crisp work suit, but sexy too. Silky little top underneath as usual. What an eyeful he got every time she bent over to sip her drink.

Do you know what the number forty stands for, darling? he said.

Go on, she responded cautiously.

In my case, it's my IQ and in your case it's your tits, Mario spluttered through an explosion of laughter that degenerated quickly into another uncontrollable coughing fit.

And lunch was good. Lunch was fun. Even if he wasn't her regular type, he could tell she really liked him. Probably because he was different. She probably gets bored shitless by lawyer talk all the time, he thought, with stuffy blokes in striped shirts and silk ties. And he felt himself letting go a bit. Relaxing. Dropping the charm offensive. Not that there was such a gap between his image and himself. But, he was winding down and being cheeky and being flirty, but just not being OTT. Not needing to be larger than life. Just being himself. It was fun for a change to be himself.

The time was absolutely ripping by. A couple of bottles had gone down smooth as silk and they were still chatting away when the office workers started pouring in, undoing their ties, kicking off their heels, digging in for a session after a long working week. He could feel telltale danger signs in the pit of his stomach. Bugger, she's going to notice the time. She's gonna pick up her bag. She's gonna peck me on the cheek and fly out the door. God, is that the time? I'm late, really late, so I've gotta dash, sorry to do that to you. I'll have to bill you for my time, you understand, and with a wave and an embarrassed expression on her face, she'd be gone.

But Kathleen didn't go. She did get up as if to go, but she said, c'mon let's go to the Vic and kick on there.

And so they did and that was fun, too. And they were getting smashed and giggly and of course she knew lots of yuppy, lawyer types who wanted to drag her away from him and take advantage of her themselves. She didn't introduce him and that hurt. But, he understood it. It wasn't that she didn't like him, it was just a lawyer thing, being a bit careful, not flaunting a relationship with a client, that's what it was.

Mario proposed another drink. This time she tried to say no, but Mario was having nothing of it. As he waited at the bar, well somewhere near the bar given the Friday night crowd begging the models-disguised-as-barstaff to serve them next, his vast experience of such things told him he would have to make a move. Like a skilled and committed coach, he'd already reviewed his performance at the wine bar a couple of weeks before. Somehow, he'd misplayed that one. Was it the hand on her bum on the way out? Was it the *Your place or mine darlin'?* line that he thought he'd said in the right way to take the piss out of the cliché? Or, was she just a more expensive prick tease than he was used to?

He was getting a bit shirty to tell the truth, stuck there in the queue and watching the corporate types hit on his bird. He almost gave up a couple of times to return to home base to defend his property, but that course of action would have brought the moment of truth to a head that much sooner. So, he cooled it, starting chatting to the other blokes in the queue as they joked about what sort of funeral they wanted as they would be dead before they got served. He joined in the frivolity, but his heart wasn't in it. Should he make a direct move or should he insist they take a taxi and let fate take its course? The stakes were fucking high and it was making him nervous. After his wipe-out at the wine bar, this session had to deliver a fuck.

When he eventually returned to the table, Kathleen was texting someone – not a good sign. When he plonked the drinks down and he was just about to launch into his experiences in the beer queue, she hopped up, gathered her things and said c'mon let's go. Mario was in no doubt that if she'd been a bloke, he'd have clocked her one. But, she'd disarmed him, or more accurately enarmed him by slipping her arm through his to lead him out of the door.

I think I've had enough drinks, she said, steering him back in the direction from which they'd walked earlier.

He realised that the moment of truth was now.

I'll call us a cab, he suggested.

No, don't do that.

He pushed on now he was committed to this line of attack.

We need to get a taxi, beautiful upholder of the law, as we are both, as they say in the classics, totally shit-faced.

Well I probably am, she conceded, but I thought you, Mr Martinelli, were an out-there sort of a guy.

The realisation dawned on Mario that she expected him to drive, that she wanted him to drive. What with her being a lawyer and everything and him being totally pissed. Even he didn't want to drive, not that he didn't push the boundaries of 0.05 nearly every day, but this was asking for trouble in the state he was in.

You're joking, he said, trying to sound hip and nonchalant about it.

I'm not, she corrected him, with that flirty smirk that sent electric current to his balls. What's more, she added, there could be a reward in it for you if you're man enough to drive me home.

Well, what could he do but hope and pray that the Virgin Mother would cause her countenance to shine upon him and let him stay away from the blow-in-the-bag killjoys? He wasn't about to pass up what was going to be, without question, the fuck of his life. He tried to keep his mind off her pussy and on closing the deal while he drove with the exaggerated caution of the driver who's drunk.

And what a perfect moment it turned out to be! How glad was he that he puffed out his chest to impress the girl and showed he had the guts for a little bit of the old drink and drive? As it turned out, it wasn't a fuck, but it is the absolute truth to say it was the next best thing. No sooner had he slipped the park brake on outside her apartment and breathed a massive sigh of relief than her pale and delicate hand reached across into his seated lap. And then it proceeded with practised skill to pull down his zipper and then receive instructions from high command that the space was too confined so appropriate assistance from the other hand was required to unbuckle his belt. And so flabbergasted was he at this turn of events that he didn't do what he wanted to do which was to stroke her hair as she worked with her head bowed to prepare the site. She pulled back to make space so he could shuffle his pants and jocks down towards his knees.

He'd got a glimpse of the painted nails closing around the shaft of his dick and so far it hadn't produced the premature reaction that he always feared. She stroked him and he did what any man would do and reached down to feel up her tits. She responded to the tug on the hem of her lacy top by pulling it over her head so he could make direct contact for the first time with those much dreamed of breasts. And then she'd blown him in a mind-bendingly, bone-janglingly, better-than-sex-if-it-wasn't-actually-sex sort of way until he'd spurted gratefully and desperately into her enveloping mouth.

And if that wasn't a fucking good end to a fucking brilliant day, he didn't know what was. He drove himself home because now he knew for sure that today he could do no wrong. And then of course, it happened and life stinks that something should happen to dampen his spirits on such a day. And just when he thought he was home free to add prized new footage to his mental blow-job highlight reel, it did happen and it's not what you think.

They didn't pick him up for drink driving or anything boring or inconsequential like that. When he pressed the button for the lift from his basement garage, he was greeted by two gentlemen with ponytails dressed entirely in black. He squinted at them in the vain hope that they were figments of his inebriation. But, he could see that they were not. And he could see more than that. He saw something clearly in their eyes. They meant to hurt him.

And they did.

OK, so she'd gone ballistic at him for calling round to her house of all things. And getting Julia uncontrollably angry certainly wasn't part of Robert's preferred script. But there was a definite upside. She'd made contact with him, when before she'd been incommunicado.

At first, he was mortified at her storming into his consulting rooms and making a scene in front of his already anxious patients in the waiting lounge. What on earth will everyone think? But he found himself relaxing. After all, what could be more normal than a stressed and obviously emotional woman venting her spleen on a specialist doctor who had after all only done his best to put right some complex gynaecological problem that nature had unfortunately chosen to put awry?

He handled it like he would have for a real patient. Well, she was a real patient, but a real patient with some rather special circumstances. So, he asked Erica the receptionist – the one with the true people skills in the practice – to show Mrs Lee into the spare consulting room, the one that was doubling as a storage room, the one that was piled high with boxes of medical supplies so you could hardly walk into it. The one that had been empty since Dr Mackenzie had gone back to Edinburgh and the one that in retrospect was hardly likely to pacify an irate patient with special circumstances.

He excused himself from Mrs Harley in his typically charming and ultra-caring fashion – would you mind terribly if I left you for a couple of moments to attend to one of my patients who is clearly distressed? – and steeled himself momentarily before turning the doorhandle. He found Julia brimming with anger but scarcely visible over a pile of sterilised, sanitised (and as he often said in more jovial times bloody-pasturised) plastic gloves.

He feared a stream of invective followed by fisticuffs that could have been deadly in a cramped space like this. His years of training kicked in instinctively and Robert said, in a masterful we-are-facing-an-emergency-right-now-so-do-what-I-say-without-questioning tone, Follow me.

He unsnibbed the other door from the office that led into the private car park and directed her to his car and then the passenger's door that he opened in a fluid, commanding gesture.

Having contained the potential for collateral damage, he braced for the full impact of the blast. The sports car was not a perfect venue as the space was confined and he was virtually cheek by jowl with a mad-eyed harpy. The invective lashed his face and the venom he ingested surged through his veins. The eye of the storm came and went and the anger boiled over like a seething torrent. The force eventually spent itself and the twister passed.

He felt much the same as he imagined someone caught in a cyclone would. It was over in a blur and he couldn't remember any of it very clearly. He could recall the words *selfish, pathetic, arrogant* and *disgraceful* soaring and dipping in the wind. Once it was over, it surprisingly seemed really to be over. She wiped her eyes and blew her nose and paused waiting for him to say something.

There hadn't been much to say, except one thing. He was scared to say that thing because, out of any combination of words in the language that could possibly venture forth from his mouth at a time like this, this particular combination was tailor-made by the finest house of linguistic couture to make things worse and start up the tempest again. So, he said nothing. But because he'd said nothing and she had now stopped in the full expectation that he would at least say something, and in fact the least he could do was to actually say something, she wasn't prepared to leave it at that because she was entitled to have him say something given the pain she'd been through to spew forth what she'd had to say.

Aren't you going to say something? Julia said.

So now he said what he knew he shouldn't say. I can't help myself around you because you are so delectable.

She turned to look at him in what must have been a calculated way, but had generated a face so inscrutable that Confucius himself would have had no idea what it meant. She got out of the car and closed the door in a way that was neither relaxed nor angry. She walked up the slope of the car park towards the street with a gait that was neither fast nor slow. She looked back in a way that was neither longing nor dismissive. She disappeared over the horizon.

He sat in the car for a moment to compose himself. The way forward was obvious to a man like him.

Go for broke, old son, go for broke.

Hannah couldn't work it out and that was unusual for her. *Can I have misread him so badly? I thought that silly boy was an open book to me.*

Her mind wandered back to strudel-time. She'd deliberately eaten in silence to create space for the grand confession. Several times, she'd thought him on the verge of owning up, but those moments had come and gone. And then he'd got back to work and been singing, mind you, singing – the absolute chutzpah!

Somehow he'd cleared his conscience, but how did that happen? Then it occurred to her and it seemed so obvious really. He'd put everything back. Of course he had. He'd taken the coward's way out. He hadn't progressed as much as she thought. He lacked the strength to own up to his moral failing.

So she got down on her painful hands and knees again to scrabble around amongst the papers and the artefacts she'd previously turned over a good three times. But there was still nothing there. No money and no ring.

She propped herself up against the wall to catch her breath and think things through. *Perhaps he put them somewhere else? Maybe he thought he could get away with putting the stuff back in her dresser or maybe he'd snuck into her bedroom and slipped it all into a drawer? My God, these things could be anywhere.* The thought made her feel terribly, terribly tired. She didn't have the energy to search any more. A glass of brandy and bed was the only answer.

But the next day brought no better luck. Refreshed by a sound sleep and encouraged by a sensible plan that would see her undertake a search little by little of every possible place, she went about her business with renewed hope. But, as the day rolled by, and the obvious hiding spots gave way to searching the ridiculous and preposterous nooks and crannies of her house, she noticed the progressive deterioration of her mood. Hope and compassion had finally given way to bitterness and anger.

Finally she slumped wearily into her favourite armchair. She cursed in several languages at having sat down before pouring herself that brandy she'd been longing for. She muttered and spluttered and hauled herself up out of her chair and then grabbed the bottle so as not to make the same mistake again. Her mood was foul. The full array of emotions competed for ascendancy. Anger and bitterness, of course. But betrayal, self-pity, contempt and disbelief were right up there too.

She drank too much and that meant a sleepless night lay ahead. She tossed and turned, a helpless victim to her turbulent thoughts. As much as negative and wasteful emotions were anathema to her, she felt morally weak and emotionally powerless to prevent blame from being apportioned. She possessed the rare ability to forgive on the grand scale. She didn't hate the Nazis, after all. But, she was never that strong on the small stage. Paradoxically, the minutiae of life got to her every time. Come morning, she knew she would be looking for a showdown. It would either be time to shoot the vain old woman for playing games with a helpless young man or time to shoot the man for being nothing more than a common thief masquerading as a mensch.

Hannah felt like death when she eventually woke up after a dreadful night's sleep. It might have been a blessing if she'd died in her sleep. She beat herself up. What a stupid, stupid game. What an appalling thing to do, to tempt a poor innocent family man in this manipulative way. Yet he'd violated her trust and stolen the most precious object in any woman's life – her mother's wedding ring. What loathsome, spineless creature could do such a thing?

But, a new day had come, as unwelcome as it was.

Action needed to be taken. Hannah treated herself to some strudel for breakfast and the strongest of heart-starting coffees to ease the pain. Then she picked up the telephone and dialled the number without hesitation. The matter had to be resolved. The phone was answered.

I need to report a theft, Hannah said.

Kathleen was terrified. She hadn't felt that way for the longest time. Life wasn't supposed to be like that any more. And for the first time in her life, Kathleen felt responsible for something truly, truly awful. That feeling sucked.

Her mind switched onto autopilot. Without thinking, she grabbed her bag, rummaged inside to find her car keys and ran out the door. She didn't check what she was wearing, didn't look in the mirror, didn't check her lippy or go through any of her normal routine. Instinctively, she navigated the car to West Perth. She was in luck. At that time of night there was a car park right outside Max's apartment block.

She buzzed the intercom and Max clicked the door open for her. In the enclosed surroundings of the lift, a moment of sanity prevailed. What if Max has got one of his conquests with him? Was this a bad idea? The lift arrived at his floor and opened before she'd finished thinking that through. There was Max standing in the doorway to his apartment. He was still in his business suit.

She started to blurt it all out. Max handed her a bourbon to calm her nerves.

He looked her straight in the eye. Who the fuck are we talking about here, girl?

A couple of swigs of the spirit burned Kathleen's throat on the way down, but did the trick. Gradually she got through the tale of woe with Mario.

How do you know all this? he asked.

Mario phoned me from the hospital.

Did he now? Max clearly disapproved.

He still has his weird sense of humour, Kathleen said, choking back tears. He said at least they were giving him drugs.

Max stared out of the window, sipping at his Scotch, while she let it all hang out.

He waited until he was sure she had finished.

I think you might be leaping to conclusions without the full facts, he said. A bad habit for a lawyer, even one in distress. It could have been anybody with a guy like him. I mean, a smart-arse like him would probably have a queue of petty crooks, thieves and bikies wanting to put the boot into him.

Kathleen was filthy with him. Get off your fucking high horse for once in your life and face up to yourself, she said. Max, you're no fucking saint yourself and you're not fucking infallible either.

Steady on.

No, Max, sometimes you actually fall for your own spin. We fucked up. I fucked up. You fucked up. Yes, I mean you Max!

Kathleen sat silently for a while. She broke down once the anger had vented completely from her system. She sobbed uncontrollably and Max sat down beside her on his fashionably uncomfortable sofa and hugged her to him. Her tears ran down her cheeks and onto his shoulder. Then she snivelled into one of Max's lurid handkerchiefs that he persisted in wearing as an affectation in the breast pocket of his suit coat.

Shit, I've just cottoned on, he said. You like this guy don't you?

She nodded and snuffled. I do, I think I must.

Eventually, the waterworks subsided allowing Max to pour a second round of stiff drinks. They talked the issues through, gradually returning to a more normal mode of lawyer interaction.

Max tried to sum up. We don't know for sure who did this and we don't know why.

Kathleen was about to protest.

Bu-ut, he continued cutting her off, it's a reasonable assumption to make that it's our friends in black. If we assume it is them, we will clearly need to engage a third party to progress things with the debtor, and fast. We cannot risk what we do next being traced back to us.

Kathleen went to the wall mirror to check herself out. I look ghastly, she said.

Never mind that. Maybe we have read this one wrong, after all. I just don't get it. We've handled these sorts of things dozens of times and these low-lifes don't normally get an itchy trigger finger so quickly, especially for a lousy half a mill. Plus a fair bit of interest, I suppose, but it's still not sheep stations, is it?

What other choices did your boyfriend Luigi have, anyway? Max speculated as he paced up and down.

Mario, she corrected him.

Max ignored her. They wanted their money, they wanted it badly obviously, and he didn't have it. I guess he could've borrowed it from a legit lending source. But banks and the like are swear words to black economy types like Luigi, aren't they? I mean, to these guys, getting a bank loan is like farting in church.

Kathleen applied make-up while Max pontificated.

It's a fucking no-win situation this one, Max concluded, as he freshened up their drinks again.

It's now a fucking lose-lose-lose situation, Kathleen responded. Our good friends still haven't got their cash. Mario's in a hospital bed. And, to add insult to his literal injuries, the cops will soon be crawling all over him wanting chapter and verse.

True to form, Max eventually switched to action mode. He resumed his prowling back and forth like an American TV lawyer.

Normally, I'd just let things run their course, he said. I'd take the view that we're not responsible for the problem and the worst we can say about our intervention is that it didn't work. But in this case, my sweetness, you are obviously not indifferent to the pain and suffering that might come your Italian stallion's way. So, we'd better intervene with Mr Shoeman directly, don't you think? I think our special debt collector can be as persuasive as the Men In Black's hired help and recovery of the money would be the very best solution to Mario's probs right now, and more importantly, to ours as well.

Kathleen was surprised and elated. She hadn't seen a sympathetic response like this coming.

You're an angel Max, you really are, she said pecking him on the cheek. I know how risky this is and I know you're putting a lot on the line for me.

You see, I am a saint after all!

Yes, you are an angel and a saint, she said, snuffling back a tear and beaming back at him.

Max held her gaze and then held out his hand to pull her up. You may reward me now in the customary fashion, he said.

Kathleen allowed herself to be led.

Hand over those knickers, Ms Murdoch, or I'll subpoena them!

Kathleen let Max get her into bed.

A good fuck might help me sleep, she thought.

There was that particular day, Julia remembered, when she walked up Cottesloe beach. The remarkable thing that happened was the catalyst for change in her life. She took it as an omen.

There she was in the middle of the city, at Cottesloe beach, slap in the middle of Perth's affluent western suburbs. This beach was safe home turf for her. It was clean and pristine and solid. It was the centre of her universe and everything that happened there and everyone who went there could rely on the familiar rhythms of the day to unfold. The tide came in and the tide went out. Young joggers arrived early in the morning followed by middle-aged beach walkers followed by young sunbakers followed by after-work strollers and so it would go on, as it should, predictable and pleasant.

And yet, on that day, at about one in the afternoon, a tiger snake slithered its way out of the bushes that separate the beach from the boardwalk and made a beeline, if reptiles can do that, straight for the surf. It drew a crowd of onlookers as it traced its body shape into the massed sand and then etched it more clearly and deeply into the wet sand at the water's edge.

It was amazing how the beachgoers stopped in their tracks. Each person stood dead still. Many just shook their heads. Incredulous, they watched the snake go for a surf and then disappear beneath the crashing waves formed by the cooling Fremantle Doctor, blowing hard and fast in the early afternoon.

Nobody said a word. Eventually the bystanders dispersed, with each person looking forward to telling someone their tale about the beach and the snake and the surf.

That was not the message Julia determined to deliver when she got home. While all the other beachgoers may have been confused by what they'd just seen, Julia knew exactly what she'd witnessed and it made perfect sense to her. She'd just seen a frightened, cornered, frustrated creature make a desperate break for freedom despite all the risks. Not only that, but she'd seen it escape from its hiding place there in Cottesloe, where things should be safe, things should be predictable, where people were reliable, where lives unfolded in perfect middle-class respectability, where silly women didn't make fools of themselves by running away from it all. Well, not that often, anyway.

There and then, Julia made up her mind to do what she had to do. The serpent may have led Eve astray and tempted her there in the Garden of Eden, but this snake had done the opposite. It showed her the true path and it gave her the courage to do what was right, not what was wrong. It also taught her how to undertake the unthinkable act.

She had mentally rehearsed every possible way of telling Stephen that she wanted him to go. In her mind, she had practised the act of writing to him, emailing him, even texting him, sitting him down and breaking the news, broaching the subject while they were out together somewhere. Every possible scenario she had tried and tested, over and over, and each of them had come up wanting.

None of these scenarios involved the girls, as was only right and proper. But she knew for sure that as soon as she told Stephen, he would trample her in the rush to be the first to tell the girls in that appalling, childish, accusatory tone of his she had grown to view with such disgust. And yet she still couldn't tell the girls first. Even *she* couldn't do that to *him*. Despite the fact that he would use it against her, immediately and without hesitation.

Now she saw the way forward to involve the whole family at once. This approach would work and it would at least be quick, if clearly not painless. She would tell the gathered throng at next week's pizza party. She would ask for silence. She would hold it all together, as she did when the going got tough.

She was clear what she would say. Hey, everyone, I've got something important to tell you.

Stephen would look condescending, as he always did, and would imply by his body language and the expression on his face, that his wife was half-cut again. The girls would squirm where they stood, waiting for their mum to embarrass them again.

Once the chatter from her friends and family had subsided completely, she would have her say. Stephen and I are getting a divorce.

Then she would walk into the house, across the polished

jarrah floorboards, through the front door into the street and she'd keep going, going, going down to the beach and into the frothy, bubbling, cleansing surf.

Garry had only dealt with the police on a professional basis before then. As equals, both on the same side of the law. There'd been fires and road accidents, one or two of the grizzly kind. He recalled them labouring together, hand in glove, consoling and reassuring some seventeen year old girl whose legs were pinned and crushed in the mangled wreckage of her boyfriend's car. They dodged the plaintive questions about the boy's welfare, directing her to stay focused for a few minutes more as they positioned the jaws of life to cut through the twisted metal and blood-smeared upholstery to free her legs. They chatted to the girl together as a team. The endless chatter was as much for their benefit as hers. Nobody wanted to see what they would see when the oxyacetylene had done its job.

But they had not all been mates and cobbers and equals that day when two of them, in plain clothes, paid Garry a visit. How could fellow professionals be so insensitive as to front him at the fire station? Not in the privacy of his own home? They could have made a polite phone call to ask him to drop down to the police station when it was convenient. But they didn't have the decency to do that. These two blokes just rocked up at the fire station, declining to explain who they were, just saying it was a personal matter and they would wait for Mr Scoresby if need be.

Maybe his workmates hadn't twigged to who his visitors were. He thought that was possible. But, *he* wasn't fooled. He felt it right in the guts when Macca poked his head round the office door and said there were a couple of blokes to see him and they wouldn't say what it was about. The dread probably showed on his face.

Told you to pay those gas bills, Macca quipped on his way out.

Garry went down to meet them. They introduced themselves as Detective Sergeant someone and Detective Constable somebody else. He must have invited them to come through to the office, judging by the fact that they were following him noisily up the creaking staircase. He must have offered them a drink because they both declined. He must have had enough presence of mind to excuse himself to go to the gents. He breathed a huge sigh of relief once the bathroom door had swung closed behind him. He splashed cold water on his face to regain some composure and kick start that dull, numb brain of his back to life.

He struggled desperately to get his head straight during the few minutes' thinking time afforded him by the pit stop. Should I say nothing without my lawyer present or does that just make me seem guilty? Should I pass it off in some light-hearted way? The old girl asked me to have the ring cleaned – don't tell me she's reported it to the cops! Better not deny it as they may have searched our house already. Just took it home for safekeeping, actually. She's getting really senile, you know, lovely old lady that she is. She was going to throw this whole pile of papers and rubbish out when I discovered these valuables were part of it. I told her to be careful and that she needed to sort it out. But, she would have none of it and insisted that she would throw the whole lot out. So, I chucked the papers away, but obviously kept the ring and the money and I've been trying to find some relatives to contact about Hannah going downhill like this and about the valuables and the money and God knows what else might be lying around in drawers and cupboards and old boxes around the house.

When he came back, Someone and Somebody listened attentively to Garry's story. They both made notes and took it in turns to ask questions.

Did you not think to report this situation to a social worker, her GP or even to us? Someone asked.

It definitely occurred to me, Garry replied, but I didn't know what to do because she is really on the ball most of the time. I didn't want to upset her and create an unpleasant scene or anything. So, in the end, I thought it best to try to find a relative first before going through more official channels.

Can you give us details of the people you've contacted so far about this? Somebody asked.

Well, I haven't contacted anyone yet because I've been having to sneak looks in her old telephone directory and in her desk drawers to find someone to talk to. The trouble is that Hannah seems to lead a very isolated life these days, like lots of old people do, and I was beginning to think that all her relatives had been murdered in the war. She's an Austrian Jew, you see.

How did you say you became involved with Ms Baumgarten again?

I was doing some decorating for her, you know how it is with us fireys, and I think she must have got onto me from word of mouth. I can't remember how exactly now, but it might come to me and if it does, I'll let you know.

Someone or Somebody gave him his card and directed him to report to the Fremantle Police Station within three hours with all of Ms Baumgarten's goods. Then the other guy took over and told Garry he'd be required to attend the station again within the next forty-eight hours to make a statement.

As the detectives headed for their car, Garry called out to them as a parting shot that he'd just been trying to help an old lady out. He regretted it immediately as it made him sound guilty.

As guilty as the snivelling arsonists he hated so much.

Julia waited in exactly the same parking space as the first time she'd met him. On that Sunday the street was dead as a dodo. But this was a weekday early morning and the street was buzzing with office girls and suits, cars and cabs and buses, everyone rushing somewhere with a take-away coffee cup in hand.

She was nervous this time too and part of her wanted to cut and run. That part of her secretly hoped Robert wouldn't be at the surgery today. But Robert did arrive. Her heart rate went into overdrive as she saw him ease the BMW down the sloping driveway to the sub-ground car park etched so vividly in her memory from their recent encounter.

Once he disappeared from view, Julia's courage deserted her. She turned on her ignition ready to speed away. She pulled out suddenly and lurched across the carriageway drawing the angry hoots of oncoming traffic. But it proved a fruitless, almost pathetic gesture. She slowed down almost immediately, drove round the block and slipped the car back into the same space she'd fled from a couple of minutes earlier.

And so, now, this was it. This was the moment her faithful friend Lisa had begged her to avoid. Julia checked her make-up in the rear-view mirror, straightened her beautifully cut clothes, slid from her leather driver's seat, skipped across the chaotic city street and faltered once again, this time at the door of Robert's consulting rooms. She took a few deep breaths and regained her composure as she always did at the moment of truth. She pushed open the heavily curtained glass door and was crestfallen to find a waiting room full of people, even at this ridiculously early hour.

However, she felt in control now. She hovered near the reception desk until the receptionist finished her phone call and looked up at her.

I don't suppose Dr Hetherington could squeeze me in for just five minutes, could he? Julia asked in a tone that sounded suitably desperate.

Is it an emergency?

Not exactly, no.

Would you care to sit and wait and see if someone fails to turn up?

Julia was unsure. She decided to play it safe. Yes, I think I might for a while, thank you, she said.

She sat there, flicking through meaningless women's gossip trash, not taking in a single word (and thereby not missing anything, of course) for twenty minutes or so. Then a horrific scenario crossed her mind. How bad would it be if he appeared to call his next patient and saw Julia there without understanding the significance of her presence? What if he shrugged his shoulders and cast her a withering look as if to say what do you expect me to do, right here, right now, in front of all these people?

She couldn't be passive. She needed to act now. Julia asked the imposing figure behind the counter for a piece of paper and an envelope. She looked in her handbag for her Montblanc and was surprised and relieved that it came easily to hand. She wrote three words only before folding the *With compliments* slip that seemed too commonplace on which to write such a momentous note. She licked the envelope that carried Dr Hetherington's qualifications illegibly embossed in gothic script, and sealed it down.

At 5.46 p.m. exactly, Robert read the note. That was many hours after Julia had resigned herself to being rejected, embarrassed and scorned.

It read *Take me away.*

Kathleen tried to convince herself that life was essentially the same after the incident, but deep down she knew was kidding herself. *Trying* to kid herself would have been more to the point.

On the surface, life continued as normal. Breakfasting at her usual café, texting as if it was going out of fashion, catching up with the girls, putting up with Matt, working long hours, texting some more, buying new shoes, having her hair done, buying more shoes, watching arty movies, facebooking, getting hopelessly drunk, guiltily eating chocolate – everything the same.

Who am I kidding? At last she faced facts, sitting in the same café, at the same table, at the very seat in fact where she first met up with Mario. She smiled at the thought of him before the incident. What you see with him is what you get. He's not like all those smarmy, devious lawyers who are always hitting on me. He has the hots for me and he just sits there with his tongue hanging out.

She felt like a different person now. That was the truth of it. The bashing had sobered her up and had made her serious, even boring. It had changed her outlook on life again. Life could be brutal and nasty, as she'd known as a child.

While she was finally ready to acknowledge the change, she refused to accept it. Serious did not suit her. Boring wasn't an option. Pain was definitely out. She'd watched her mum do pain after the accident. And how! Kathleen would go to any lengths to avoid that fate for herself.

Clearly life had to be returned to normal. It needed to be restored to that comfortable, desirable state where life really was just a game and yukky things happened to others. Unpleasantness was supposed to happen to clients.

Mario was a client. But he had become more than that. Mario was a friend and things that happen to friends cut deep and inflict pain. Therefore, logically, the source of that pain needed to be removed. Things had to be put to rights and the way to put this thing to rights was exactly as Max said. Dealing with the shoeman was the thing.

So she and Max had rocked up to the shoe factory to put the matter to rest. Naturally, with this game plan, they had not rocked up alone. Sebastian Maitland-Webster was there with them. Seb was a London boy. In his case, he had suffered from the peculiar handicap of being born on the *right* side of the tracks, but to a family that couldn't keep on the right side of the law. His parents specialised in white-collar crime. They taught Seb wrong from right. To them the important right was their divine right to other people's wealth.

He'd grown up, messed up. He shot up. He wouldn't shut up. He fucked up. He dropped out. He broke out. He came out. He fell in with some bad company. He fell from grace. He fell for some serious scams. He became a male prostitute. He was destitute. He would do anything for money. He did everything for money. He could always get you money. He was right on the money. He was there to get the shoeman's money.

Naturally, Max did all the talking. Kathleen paid attention. Seb was the epitome of inattention.

Max introduced their group as the Martinelli legal team. He asked the shoeman for five minutes of his time. He then asked him if he wanted his own lawyer present. To both questions, the skinny, balding, middle-aged man reacted with the merest shrug of his shoulders. As he had neither agreed to a meeting nor refused one, they sat down in his dingy office. He reluctantly followed suit.

Max didn't speak for long. He made a few simple points to the man of shoes.

You owe our client a considerable amount of money. His legal case is very strong. However, before we commence legal proceedings, I wanted to show you a photograph of our client.

Max handed the man his mobile phone.

So, you see, our client now finds himself incapacitated and I'm sure you would now feel as sympathetic towards poor Mr Martinelli as we all do.

The shoeman did not react other than to return Max's phone to him.

Given these unfortunate circumstances, we have come here today as a sign of our goodwill to see if we can't resolve this matter amicably without recourse to the legal system. We feel sure that there must have been some misunderstanding between the two of you. We have therefore approached you today to propose mediation and to introduce you to our mediator. We commend him to you because he is very good at what he does. He gets things resolved very efficiently and effectively.

Max waited for the man to respond. His eyes wandered across all three of them, lingering longer on Sebastian as was intended. Still he said nothing.

Very well then, Max concluded standing up to leave, our mediation specialist here will be in touch very shortly to get the process underway.

Kathleen's thoughts were a jumble as they drove back to the CBD in silence. Only Max had spoken. She hadn't said a word. Seb hadn't said a word. The shoeman hadn't said a word either. Did the shoeman have a clue what mediation in this case actually meant?

She switched into her own car at the office and set off for home. Kathleen felt disorientated and confused. Her life was still spinning way off course. On an impulse, she screeched across Loftus Street to get into the right-turn lane. She changed course to head for the hospital. She would tell Mario that Max had taken steps to put things right. She'd tell him that things would get sorted. She'd reassure him. She'd reassure herself. Life would be fun again, she'd tell Mario.

Life would be fun again, she told herself.

Recently Hannah had been finding life tiring. It had been a trying time. Of course, this was nothing compared to the life and death events (in fact death and death events) she'd survived. But she wasn't as young as she used to be and emotional events these days really took their toll.

She'd been examining her own behaviour of late. It was like watching some decrepit old hag on TV. True enough, the hag looked like her when she dared to look in the mirror, but the shared identity with that thing was hard to accept. Hannah dismissed those unwelcome thoughts and settled down in her favourite brown leather armchair for yet another nap. I'm sleeping such a lot these days. Maybe I'm practising for the future.

She was roused from her slumbers by a series of sharp rings on the doorbell. There was no way she was getting up. Not for anybody. The ringing persisted. She was not moving. But it continued in that insistent way that is hard to ignore. Every soundwave started to scream EMERGENCY! Intellectually, she knew there was nobody left she cared for, so what manner of emergency could really be visiting her? But the ringing wouldn't give up and she was left with no choice but to seek to know for whom the bell tolled.

Slowly and painfully Hannah raised herself from the plush cushions and made her way wearily along the corridor. She could make out the silhouette of a woman through the stained glass panes of the door. The woman was leaning on the bell with her body turned to one side. It was impossible to recognise her or even place her age.

The silhouette then turned to face the door as the sound of slow, awkward movements became audible. Hannah slowly unhooked the security chain and eased back the pin of the door lock. She peered through the door she'd opened ajar to stare at a young woman, a pretty little thing actually.

Can I help you? Hannah asked, conscious for some reason of the incongruous sound of her European accent.

I'm sure you can, the pretty little thing replied in a censorious tone that lacked something in authority coming from such a slip of a girl.

How so?

By way of an answer the girl introduced herself. My name is Kirsty Scoresby.

Erica made light work of all the appointment rearranging that had to be done for Robert. His partner Nick was grateful for the extra caseload and, being the ambitious young buck that he was, planned to snaffle each of Robert's patients for his own in return for doing the old boy a favour.

Indeed his highly discreet and professional receptionist hadn't blinked an eyelid, Robert recalled, at the notion of him filling in at the last minute for the suddenly indisposed keynote speaker at The International Society of Gynaecologists Annual Conference at Nusa Dua, Bali. He couldn't say the same for Marjorie. Not that she cared particularly if he took himself off somewhere all of a sudden. The timing was a tad problematic, though, on account of Nathan's engagement party.

Accordingly, Robert enlisted Nath to his cause in advance of breaking the news to Marjie. He knew Nathan wouldn't give a shit whether his dad was there or not, but the problem with Nath was that he always took the line of least resistance with his mother. That's how this double-headed monster of a party got organised in the first place.

Only Marjie could come up with a plan that involved a cocktail party for the old folks followed by a band and dancing for the youngsters (and of course the coke, the ice and the fucking) that the old folks would (regrettably in Robert's view) not attend.

No worries, Dad, whatever you need to do, Nathan responded. As long as you don't forget the generous pressie, he added with that twisted smile of his that meant I'm pretending not to mean this for the benefit of onlookers but I know you know full well that I do actually really mean it.

Would I let you down? Robert replied, regretting the remark almost immediately as he didn't want Nathan pondering the answer to that question.

Still, he was safe with Nathan. Nath wasn't the type to ask questions. God help his poor patients, Robert muttered on the way back to his car.

Eventually, Marjorie got over it. In her own way. It was just the latest in a long string of Robert's disappointments that she swept under the carpet. As usual, she put on a brave face to the outside world.

Bobby's so desperately disappointed about it, she would say, but you know what he's like when he's asked to help, he's just an old softy.

By contrast, for internal consumption, she gave Robert the cold shoulder.

How could you do this to me? she wailed at him in private. How could you do this to Nathan?

From time to time, Robert would plead his case. You know Nathan actually doesn't have a problem with this, don't you?

But she would swat Robert away like a pesky fly. You have no idea what Nathan thinks about this or thinks about anything else for that matter as you haven't bothered to get to know him – yet.

Robert stretched his legs in pleasure like a big cat released from a restricted cage. He revelled in the ecstasy of having made it to the luxurious safe haven of business class. All of that nonsense was behind him now.

Gin and tonic please, he said.

Soon he was swishing his glass around just for the hell of it, just to hear that satisfying clink of ice on glass that said that he was home free. He allowed himself the luxury of getting pissed on the grog that's laughably referred to as free given the ridiculous price of the fare. He was expectant. He was nervous. He was excited about what lay in prospect. He was looking forward to letting his hair down at long last. Yet he was anxious about how it would all turn out.

The private limo whisked him away from Denpasar airport in air-conditioned comfort, sheltering him from the noisy trucks, the litter-strewn streets and the half-finished concrete shells of more hotels or shopping centres. Wayan carried his bags and ensured that his obvious intoxication didn't register on the consciousness of the resort staff. The busboy escorted Robert to his poolside suite.

Robert didn't dare ask the obvious question at reception. He wasn't prepared to risk the answer he didn't want to hear. The short walk through the leafy compound in the tropical heat seemed to take a lifetime.

He couldn't put off the question in his own mind any longer. Had Julia come?

As Mario couldn't think of anything good in his life lying there in his hospital bed, he was comparing the shitty bits to see which was the worst. The candidates that came to mind were the pain in his legs, the pain in his balls, the pain in his face, the pain of seeing his mum every day, the pain of having a fugly nurse and the pain of the Bitch actually rocking up to the hospital with the kids.

OK, so it was no contest – the pain of seeing the Bitch was easily the worst. As for the others, well the pain in his legs hurt more than the other two physical pains. The pain in his face didn't hurt that much, but the anxiety associated with damage to his rugged, Italian good looks was cause for concern. Needless to say in relation to the pain in his nuts, the ouch-factor was bloody high and the anxiety level associated with it was extreme. It had recorded 8.5 on his Erector scale against which the dangers to his crown jewels had to be measured.

He tried to distract himself with games like this. It succeeded up to a point. It got his hazy brain working and occupied it with something suitably frivolous. Best of all, it stopped his mind from replaying in super slow motion the events of that horrible night when he'd seen the unusual shadows near the lift well in the basement car park to his apartment block.

He was startled at first to find other people down in the basement at that hour. Startled, but not in any way concerned. Why would he be? He was totally full of himself thanks to Kathy's delightful oral attentions and come to think of it Kathy had been full of himself too once she'd finished with him. At one level, his brain did compute something strange when none of the shadows moved to get into the lift that had just arrived. Not that his befuddled brain was functioning all that well what with the booze, the tiredness and the euphoria. So he barely noticed when the hand came from nowhere. It was like one of those horror movies where the pale, bloodless hand, dismembered from its host body, has been condemned to let its fingers do the walking for eternity.

But this hand merely stopped the lift door from closing with Mario inside. After that, despite his repeated efforts, his recollections came back to him no more clearly than the jerky frames of an old cartoon. The ponytails swished and the iron bar swooped and cut him down from the knee. The steel-capped boots thudded into tissue and fingers so laden with rings that they appeared made of steel dragged his bleeding body upright against the thinly corrugated lift interior. The fists whirred, thudding into his belly and grinding metal into his face. Gnarled hands supported him when he crumpled and a bony knee crunched into his groin as he slumped now unsupported to the floor. The only other thing he could remember clearly was the resigned comfort he'd felt as the warm liquid flowed over his battered body. The acrid odour of urine had never smelled so sweet.

So things were fuzzy. But this endless reflection and distraction, reflection and distraction was itself a desperate game of hide and seek from the truth. The trouble was not only were the events a blur, but everything he looked at was literally a blur.

He panicked at first when he couldn't see. He could bring himself to be the usual good old Mario and crack jokes about his other injuries. He could even joke about the wife's best friend coming good in due course! But, after a couple of weeks, his vision was really blurry. That fat nurse Sarah could be a stunner for all he knew.

Mario had no choice but to do what any self-respecting male would do in these circumstances. He did his best to pretend it wasn't happening. Anyway, nothing was happening, yet. Not until the specialist saw him again to tell him the news. So, at this stage, he couldn't see, but there was nothing wrong with him.

Not officially and not yet.

REALITY REVIEWED

**QUESTION: What, if any, insights can you provide in relation
to your personal experiences arising from the 'Reality' event
and/or your attitude towards the perpetrator?**

Transcript 1 – Dr Robert Guy Mills Hetherington

*Incredulous, I guess. Yes, that would be the word. I couldn't believe
it when it came out. I didn't want to believe it, either, to be honest. I
didn't want to believe that I'd been taken in like this. I think it must
be like being in a freak accident or being the victim of a terrorist
attack or some such thing. Obviously, I'm not trying to compare my
fate with people who've had something horrific happen to them.
But, it feels unreal just like it must for those poor devils.*

*At one level it was a relief, too. When I look back, I realise I made
lots of bad decisions during that time. Not that I regret them, life's
too short for that. I miss Marjorie, though, I really do. I didn't
appreciate her at the time. That was her fault as much as mine,
mind you. She's the sort of person who begs you not to appreciate
them. So reasonable, so helpful, so polite. So bland, basically. But
a good sort for all that. That's why I miss her. I always had that
dependability behind me. It gave me an enormous sense of freedom.
Not that I attributed that to Marj then. But I do now.*

*Yes, so it was a relief in a way when he revealed the whole kit and
caboodle. A relief because not all the bad choices had really been
my fault. Well, not entirely my fault, let's say. There was joint
responsibility for what was happening. I was not entirely my own
master, even though I didn't realise it at the time.*

*I admire the guy despite what he made me do. You have to admire
that sort of thing, don't you? I know I'm going to appear to everyone
to be a selfish oaf and that hurts. But then, I wonder what any other*

man would have done running into Julia – so beautiful and so fragile at the same time. How many men could have resisted her? Resisted helping her and then wanting her for himself? What I'm trying to say, in my usual roundabout way, is that I admire him for the most basic of reasons. I admire him because he is so much like me.

Unfortunately, I think I'm doing my usual thing with what I'm saying here. I'm trying to come across as magnanimous so that everyone will like me. But, obviously, I hate the bastard, too. Why wouldn't I? After all, look what's he's done to me. He's deprived me of the two things that have defined me for the last thirty years. My family and my work.

I guess I'm confused. Because he's also given me something incredibly precious, something I would never otherwise have had. And he's redefined me. That's the flipside of losing my identity and my past, I suppose. I've just had a funny thought, actually. Thanks to him, I'm like someone in the witness protection program. I've been given a new identity and a new life. And, that's exciting. But on the other hand, I've had to give up the old life, completely. I can't go back to it. I can't even reminisce about it because it's soured and it's gone. It's pretty tough actually. I get teary sometimes. But then, of course, there's the joy.

QUESTION: What, if any, insights can you provide in relation to your personal experiences arising from the 'Reality' event and/or your attitude towards the perpetrator?

Transcript 2 – Hannah Esther Temple Baumgarten

Actually, this sort of experience makes you glad to be alive. Well, it certainly does for someone of my age. It's convinced me that I am still young, you know, and that's a remarkable thing.

I think everyone involved will go through a range of emotions with something like this. It will test the ego strength of us all, I'm sure. I've sat in the groups with the others and looked at how they were coping and, mark my words, some of them have a lot of work to do on this before it comes out all right for them. That might apply to me too, of course. But, out of all of us, I suppose I am the one with the least to lose. I mean to say – what difference does some embarrassment and some financial loss make to a woman of my age?

In a funny way, the experience has brought back a lot of memories for me. I think it's the realisation that your life can been taken over by another influence or source of power. I think we all felt this when our worst fears were realised by the Nazis. There we were, fearing the worst but hoping for the best. Our desperate optimism overpowered, no, more than that, blocked out our fears and so we allowed ourselves the delusion that it would never happen. And it's incredible, but the world, your world, can tip on its axis in a split second. One moment life is normal and the next tanks are rolling into the city while you are still sitting there in the corner park having a family picnic.

It was the same with this, really. We all had our own lives and we all had our challenges. Then, suddenly, the world flips over and Garry and I have been thrown together by circumstances that were not merely chance. It was another unreal experience in my life, that's what I'm trying to say.

Look, I don't want to create a false impression about the Garry thing. I'm not proud of what I did to him, but I'm not ashamed of it either. I did what I chose to do. That's all there is to it. I could have done otherwise. I could have done things that other people would have judged to be more moral in the circumstances. I could have done those things, but I didn't choose to.

At the end of the day, this is all we can say about a human being. A human being does what a human being chooses to do. In my practice and in my study and teaching, all I have learned to do is to probe for the reasons why people choose what they choose to do. This is a matter of diagnosis and comprehension. It is not something in the realm of judgment. We do not, after all, help someone by judging them. We help them by holding up a mirror for them so they can look within themselves. Through understanding, and by coming to terms with past choices, people can free themselves to make choices that fulfil them in the future.

Let's not forget that Garry is a player with self-determination, too. He had choices to make and he made them. Many of them were interesting to me and indeed surprising. They said a lot about his life and his relationships. But, they were genuine. They were authentic choices. They were his. And, of course, the consequences flowed for him as they do for us all.

Clearly, looking back, and bringing the background and theory to my life that I do, I am in a position to offer some few words of supposed wisdom. First amongst these is that regrets are a pointless state of mind. If, for example, regret is a statement of intentionality towards something that has not come to pass, then the only worthwhile thing to do is to strive with every bone in your body to make that thing happen. And, if that thing cannot happen, then what on earth is the point of having that regret?

The second thing I'd say is do not waste energy on the sentiment of hate. I'm pretty sure some of the others will hate that young man for intervening in our lives as he did. But why? All he did was change the environment, change the circumstances for us. He didn't make our choices for us, nor could he. And, anyway, none of us can know what the environment would have been like for us if he hadn't taken it upon himself to get involved.

You know, I listened to the indignation of some of them with amusement. What right did he have to do this? None at all. But, what right does someone have to fall asleep at the wheel and stray onto the wrong side of the road and smash into a hapless family of six driving safely and doing nothing wrong? None at all. What right does someone have to meet someone else by chance on a train and fall in love with them? None at all. Things happen. Two words basically say it all. Things happen, whether by chance or manipulation and we respond. We make choices for ourselves. We face the consequences and we face them healthily if we have no regrets and particularly if we have no hate. We can't be healthy and hate someone for the choices we make.

And, before anyone asks me, I will answer the question before it is asked. I do not hate the Nazis because I do not have regrets about something I cannot change and I do not hate other people for the choices they have made in the circumstances they had to make them in. Those people, butchers as some of them were, may well have hated themselves. That is quite likely. They may well have been unhealthy and unhealed. But, that is not the question that you would have asked.

And so I do not hate him. Rather, I thank him. What he did was no ordinary thing. He did not lead an ordinary life by any means. He has tried to be extraordinary. He delivered me interesting choices to make and intriguing situations that have been good for me at my age and at my stage. I thank him, but I suspect I will be the only one who does.

QUESTION: What, if any, insights can you provide in relation to your personal experiences arising from the 'Reality' event and/or your attitude towards the perpetrator?

Transcript 3 – Mario Nikita Martinelli

He's a cunt. Since you ask, and of course you're not the only one who has. In fact, sometimes, I think it would be easier to count up those who haven't asked, but since you ask, as I say, he's a cunt.

Now, fair enough, I'm no angel, I admit that. I have done a few shady things in my time, quite a few in fact, and maybe some of those may have been on the other side of the law. And some say that I didn't treat the bitch well enough, although as it turned out, I reckon I was a saint for sticking around as long as I did, but anyway, I admit that I'm not exactly perfect. But, there are rules of the game – even in villainy. In fact, I'll go further than that – there are rules of the game even in secondhand car dealing. So basically, I put my hand on my heart and say Mario has never done anything to rival this in cuntery.

Pardon me for getting all superior about it, as out of character as it may be for me, but even I can't tolerate deception. Cowardly deception, you might say. Believe me, it's quite different when a party comes in for an old banger or they need a loan when no one else will give them one. They know pretty much what they're in for. They know the operation's going to be a bit iffy, that the price will be a bit over the top, if not a rip-off, but they are up for that because this is the pool they swim around in. If they could buy a new Merc or front up straight at the Commonwealth Bank and demand a loan, or just get the funds from their internet facility in bloody Switzerland, they would. But they can't, cos this is the murky pond they swim around in. At least they can take comfort that there are rules. There are limits. They know where they stand, more or less. Their goodwill won't be abused.

Abuse – that's it, that's what this cunt does. And not the good variety in self-abuse, either. He abuses people. He abuses their trust. He abuses their good nature. I mean, what about that sweet old lady, very brainy as she clearly is, but how can you take advantage of an old lady? Well, cunts like him can, obviously.

And, by the way, it doesn't make me feel any better about him, not the slightest bit, that thanks to him I got to meet Kath. That's a case of what my nonna always says – out of bad, sometimes comes good. And anyway, I made that into good, if you know what I mean. Because, well let's face it, their legal advice was total shit and didn't exactly do me a lot of good, in the short-term at least, so the good that came from Kathleen, and it was very, very good, was all due to me. All due to my unique masculine charms and not thanks to that abusive fucker.

I know some of the other guys have a different view of this. They're entitled to their opinions, but I think that makes them a bunch of wimps. You see, I do have some principles behind me and I will name two of them for you right now. Don't abuse people in that bad way and don't be a wuss who forgives bastards who really don't deserve it. That's the world according to Mario.

QUESTION: What, if any, insights can you provide in relation to your personal experiences arising from the 'Reality' event and/or your attitude towards the perpetrator?

Transcript 4 – Julia Lee

Look, I can't make sense of anything these days so I've no idea if anything I say here will make sense either. Obviously, he's a swine for using my best friend the way he did. What's that word? – he's a cad. And, you see, I'm confused already with this because sometimes it's apparent that women like a cad, even need a cad I suppose. I guess I might be speaking for myself in saying this. I shouldn't talk about what women think, should I? Actually before all this, I think I could have spoken for all the girls. I was a typical one, I think. OK, a wealthy one. But, I thought what women think. Now I don't know what I think.

Anyway, he was obviously a bastard for treating Lisa that way. God knows, she was fragile enough before all this, so it was the last thing she needed. It set her back quite a bit, actually. And my situation didn't help either. I wasn't exactly in a stable emotional state to help her with her problems. Also, what made it worse was that I've worked through my issues and found some level of happiness again. Fleeting as it might turn out to be. That's not to forget about all the pain and hurt, but I think that was coming anyway. I think our friend's little game just sped things up. But, thinking about Lisa, well there's always some sort of competitive thing between best friends, isn't there? Especially between women. I'm not sure that men have the same competitiveness between mates – but I'd better not set myself up as an expert on men now either.

But, you know, returning to Lisa – and I know you want my opinions on him – but I'm working round to that in a funny sort of way. With Lisa, and I feel sorry about saying this, but she does ask to be hurt by men. I'm glad that we have the guarantee that these comments will be kept confidential because otherwise I couldn't say what I need to say. But, Lisa's like a puppy dog when a new man's on the scene and she holds nothing back. She smothers them, I think. And, not surprisingly, after they've got her in the sack a few times, they head off for someone who might be a tougher challenge. I feel horrible in saying this. But, I never thought that guy was right for her and I never trusted him. So, what I'm saying is, I guess, that while he was a total bastard to her, it wasn't entirely his fault.

But, getting back to the subject, well what can I say? I don't know. He was like the hand of fate, somehow. I know that sounds pretty silly, but that's what I think. The older I get, the more I believe in fate. I think certain things are destined to happen. But the timing somehow depends on when the planets align, I guess. I'm not talking about that astronomy nonsense, or is it astrology?, that you read in women's magazines. What I'm trying to say is that fate needs conductors to make the contacts to influence people's lives. I guess our friend was one of these fate conductors. And so, he was as much fulfilling his own destiny as influencing ours.

Actually, I believe he thought he was an orchestra conductor, calling the tunes and directing all the players when to come in and when to go out, and how loud or soft to play. I'm pretty sure that's how he pictured himself. But he wasn't an orchestra conductor, he was actually a fate conductor and he didn't know it. He was creating some reality that in reality was being created for him. That's quite philosophical really – for me!

QUESTION: What, if any, insights can you provide in relation to your personal experiences arising from the 'Reality' event and/or your attitude towards the perpetrator?

Transcript 5 – Garry Troy Scoresby

I'll put it this way. It felt like someone tore up the script for my life and flushed it down the loo. I never imagined there was an actual someone involved. It was a figure of speech.

Anyway, that's what it's been like. Everything in my life had been orderly and in its place. Too orderly and too much in its place, I was thinking at the time. But that was just an early midlife crisis, I reckon. I'd give anything for my life to go back to where it was before all this.

It was a typical life in the suburbs, I would say. Met my childhood sweetheart, just about the prettiest girl in our year, by the way. Got married. Got a steady job with the Fire Service. Had the two kids. Got a mortgage that was far too big for us to manage, but we had to have the four bedrooms, the double garage and the home theatre like all our mates. Worked extra jobs to pay for everything. Lusted after some of the young mums I did jobs for, but never did anything about it because I loved Kirsty and because I didn't have the nerve, to tell you the truth. Got pissed with the boys now and again and went to see the Dockers and basically did all the ordinary things you do in an ordinary life. People like me just get on with it really. Nothing special to say. Dependable good citizens we are. I suppose now I should say we were. I have trouble getting used to that.

And then, overnight, without warning, somebody tore the script up and, as I say, flushed me with it down the toilet. And I meet this amazing old lady and I got to love the old bird, you know. I really did. It opened my eyes about so many things, especially my attitude to older people. And I came on and I grew as a person and I was feeling good about myself and I was actually allowing myself to think that I could change my ordinary life a little bit to make it more challenging and more fun for Kirsty and me.

And then what happens? Shit happens. But not random shit, which I think would be easier to take. I mean shit does happen to people, but they have nobody to blame. Sure, when it happens, like at a bad fire, they lash out at everyone. They curse their luck and they search for scapegoats. But, over time, the pain heals and they get used to the idea that shit happens. The worst part for everyone, and I've seen this so many times at work, is the moment of realisation that shit doesn't only happen to other people, it actually happens to you. And that's the depressing truth. I now know because it happened to me.

So, what happened to me is like what happens to victims, but it's different. Bucket loads of shit have rained down on me from a massive height. Not thanks to bad luck or my number being up, but thanks to him and thanks to her. I probably shouldn't put them in the same category. It might be wrong to lump them both together. But, in their own way, they both played games with my life. So, from that point of view, they are both the same.

In a way, you know, I hate her more than him. I mean, he's just some kind of sicko. Some guy with a small dick. Like the fucking arsonists who light fires to make themselves important for five minutes in their lives. At one level, though, you can almost excuse them because they are mostly losers with nothing going for them. What's his excuse with a good job and lots of money? But anyway, he's just a sicko, as I say. But, when I found out that she'd left the valuables lying around as some sort of game, well I did my nut I can tell you.

What kind of game is that? I felt terrible guilt through the whole thing and I hated Kirsty for what she made me do. I know she didn't handcuff me to stop me putting the stuff back as I'd planned, but I didn't do it in the end because I didn't want to face up to all the aggro with her it was going to cause. I didn't want all the grief. I realised that I was spineless and weak and I hated myself and Kirsty for our stupidity and our greed. I should have put it all back – full stop, no discussion.

I've had plenty of time to think about the ring. Actually, I've kind of come round to Kirsty's view that the loss of the ring was the thing that made the old lady do what she did. But, that's no justification for playing around with my life in the first place. When I was first told that it was some kind of test, I refused to believe it. I couldn't accept that someone I looked up to, someone I admired like a guru, could behave in such a hopeless and pathetic way. It just goes to show that we should choose our heroes more carefully, that's what I think now.

So, he doesn't bother me that much. Really, his bastard act pales into insignificance compared to hers.

QUESTION: What, if any, insights can you provide in relation to your personal experiences arising from the 'Reality' event and/or your attitude towards the perpetrator?

Transcript 6 – Kathleen Alice Theresa Murdoch

Cool. Really cool, actually. I've had a ball with the whole thing, so I've got no complaints. I don't think some of the other guys were quite so happy, but I guess that's their problem.

You know, I never trusted the guy from the start, so I at least give myself credit for that. I never wanted to take that stupid real estate job interstate and I was doing my best to knock the work back. From memory, he managed to catch me off guard with it. Yes, that's right, it's just come back to me. I was on the phone to a client, and that was one of those hairy, shady cases we had at the time and he just plonked the paperwork down on my desk with a cheque and split. So, I basically got stuck with it. A clever ploy on his part, it has to be said. In retrospect, I suppose that's what you would expect from a gross manipulator like him.

I give him credit for a lot of things about his little game. You know, he had me worked out to a tee and he played me superbly. You have to hand it to him. He was landed with all of these diverse people at random and then had to get into their skins and more or less work out how to pull their strings in his little creation.

But then, you meet people like this quite a bit in the law. Actually, most of them are lawyers! No, I didn't mean that, really. Obviously, you end up meeting lots of people as your clients who have had something go wrong for them and I think the common denominator between them is that they're all trying to be too clever by half. I'm not trying to lump them all together. Obviously, you have your out-and-out conmen who would sell their grandmothers into slavery for an extra ten dollars, but there are also lots of fairly ordinary people who have tried to push a deal that bit too far, basically tried to extract that extra bit of goodness out of a dollar. Well, let's face it, we had a global meltdown thanks to that.

I guess that's Mario down pat. There's not a nasty bone in that guy's body. He's a classic wouldn't-hurt-a-fly-guy and yet he gets himself into so many scrapes. Just from being a bit too smart, being a bit too gullible, being a bit too much of everything really. Mario must have been a godsend to our learned friend because you can basically get Mario to do anything you want. OK, I know what you're thinking. I admit that I could too but the point is that guys can do that with him too. He's a sweet boy, he really is and I don't think this whole affair did him that much harm, to be honest.

So all in all, it was a lot of fun and the whole circus that has surrounded it has done wonders for me. I'm a bit of a celebrity now myself— you should see how many Facebook friends and Twitter followers I've got. And my name now rings a bell with people in the legal community too, which is great.

As for the guy himself? He's a clever dude, that one. Attractive in his own way, but he's definitely not hot in case you were going to ask. In fact, he's cool and that's what I said to start with.

QUESTION: Has the 'Reality' event had any lasting impact on your life?

Transcript 7 – Mario Nikita Martinelli

To be honest with you, as you can probably realise, I'm getting pretty shat off with the question. Basically, I'm not going to answer it anyway because I wouldn't give him the satisfaction of watching this or reading this and knowing that I'm giving him that much credit, either way.

As I said, the man's a cunt and that's all that matters. There's no way I'm going to play along with this whole game and let him think he won. Finito. End of story. Next question?

QUESTION: Has the 'Reality' event had any lasting impact on your life?

Transcript 8 – Hannah Esther Temple Baumgarten

No, of course not. I'm pretty sure I have answered that point already. As I said, across all my years of practice, I met so many people who came to me in profound sadness and asked me, in fact begged me, to do something to change their lives. And, naturally, that's impossible. Only the individual can change his or her own life and then that can only really be done when the individual has developed sufficient understanding of his own life and its meaning to date. This is basic logic. You can't change something, if you don't understand what it is. Just as you can't go somewhere if you don't know where it is.

So, no, I can't say that this young man changed my life. But, I would go this far. The context of my life was clearly changed by what he rightly calls his intervention. This is a very different thing. Put this way, there is no implication that 'I' – the me entity – has lost causality, has lost control over my own decisions and my own destiny.

Don't think me rude or impertinent, will you, but I think you might be asking people the wrong question.

QUESTION: Has the 'Reality' event had any lasting impact on your life?

Transcript 9 – Robert Guy Mills Hetherington

Unequivocally, yes. In fact, nothing much in my life is actually the same. I guess I still have contact with the boys. And, of course, I still have the Riverside Bar. But even those relationships aren't the same. The boys see me as a betrayer and the bar's become home from home really now that I don't travel up and down to the hills every day.

I'm not one for this esoteric philosophical stuff to tell you the truth. I don't mind saying that he changed my life. I've listened to what some of the others have said of course about nobody being able to change someone else's life but, as far as I'm concerned, that's a load of bollocks. Anyway, who gives a flying fuck? My life is not the same thanks to him. So, yes, he changed my life.

QUESTION: Has the 'Reality' event had any lasting impact on your life?

Transcript 10 – Kathleen Alice Theresa Murdoch

No, definitely not. I've thought about this question from time to time, actually. It must be the legal training kicking in that leads you to consider the impacts on others of people's actions. Lawyers are used to dissecting events in minute detail and pulling them apart like the wings off a fly. So, I've developed a metaphor around this. The metaphor of the movie of my life. You see, in my movie, and of course I'm still barely past the opening credits, these events might take up a few scenes at the very most. What's more, I don't think these events will even feature significantly in the overall plot of my life. That's not to say that they won't be dramatic and that people might not think it's awesome to have been part of it all. But, it's going to be a few megabytes in the total DVD of my life. Something interesting, maybe even thrilling at times. But inconsequential in the scheme of things for Kathleen Alice Theresa Murdoch.

QUESTION: Has the 'Reality' event had any lasting impact on your life?

Transcript 11 – Garry Troy Scoresby

Well, ask me yesterday and I'd have said yes. But, today, I don't know. I'm pretty upbeat today and, to tell you the truth, I don't really know why. I suppose I have to say he changed my life, but as I said before, I still think the old lady changed it more than him.

I don't know if I told you this the other day, but I'm having a bit of counselling at the moment through what's called the employee assistance program run by the Fire Service. And it's helping me a bit, talking to the young sheila about what's happened to me and what's happening to me day to day. I suppose that might be the reason I'm feeling a bit more in control of things.

Anyway, although she keeps asking me questions, which is a bit annoying after a while, I think she's angling at the fact that I was always too laid back and passive in my relationship with Kirsty. And it's kind of making sense because it's making me wonder what would've happened if I'd put my foot down and done the right thing in the first place and said absolutely no way am I having anything to do with keeping any of the old girl's loot.

So, the reason I'm crapping on about that, is that questions like this about someone changing my life now make me ask the obvious question. Did I do enough to change my own? And, more importantly from now on, am I going to do anything to change it in the future?

QUESTION: Has the 'Reality' event had any lasting impact on your life?

Transcript 12 – Julia Lee

No, I wouldn't say so. That's not the way I see it. A lot has happened, of course, but these things were going to happen inevitably, I think. I would have found the courage to leave Stephen in the end, I feel sure of that now. The more I think about it, the more I consider myself typical of the modern middle-class, middle-aged woman. We were born in a different era when we received everyone else's view of a good life and did our best to conform to that. I know that I just put up with an unhappy situation because I felt it was my duty and my lot. Of course, the girls were a major factor, a major constraint on my freedom. I don't mean to suggest that I resented them for that, but it's a fact of life that they were an impediment to freedom. But I'm confident that I was already feeling my way, groping my way along a dark corridor, towards changing my own life. Our friend turned out to be a catalyst for me, not a prime mover or a saviour. Just a catalyst.

REALITY CONFRONTED

I didn't hand over the story to my fishies because I wanted to. I did it to achieve balance. I thought you might be sceptical about my version of events. So I let them speak for themselves. I granted them free speech. They got to tell you their side of the story. They got to share their interesting perspectives. Did you find them interesting?

I'll be honest with you. I found their opinions and so-called insights rather self-serving. I had them snared and wrapped up like fish and chips from the local takeaway. They didn't have a clue that they were being played. Played by a master. Hook, line and sinker. And yet, when you listen to them, well, what do you hear? I did this and I did that. I think this and I think that. Yes, he manipulated my life. No, he didn't change my life. He's an arsehole. I admire him. It's all *me* and *I* with them, isn't it?

And what did they all do towards our heroic outcomes? Nothing much. They just lived their lives and drifted with the prevailing currents. They swam around, darting from rock to rock, from reef to reef, and that's nothing compared to the pressures the angler faces to select the best lure, opt for the correct line and reel and above all find the best place to anchor the boat to snare his catch.

And that brings me to my other reason for letting the little sticklebacks speak for themselves. The beauty is that now you know firsthand what they're like. If I hadn't granted them the opportunity, you would have been sitting there in your living room, on the train, at the beach, in bed half asleep or wherever you might be, making judgments about me. And you would have said, how could someone do that to these poor unsuspecting people? How could anyone do that for his own gratification? And you'd have let them off for what they did.

I've given you access to them now. You've had a direct line to their inner thoughts and feelings. So now you know what they're like.

They exercise their own freedoms, but seek to blame others for the outcomes of their decisions. You know that they are weak and they are simple, just like everybody else. They are deceitful and they are personally dishonest, perhaps just like you. They are small people, all of them. Barely deserving of their own reality, in fact.

I'm glad you know this now. But, the question I've been asking myself of late is this. Once you've walked a mile in their shoes. Once you've looked them all in the eye. Once you've been exposed to their foibles and their frailties. Will you care enough about them to want to know what happened to them? Will you give a rat's arse about what happened to them? About how their realities unfolded?

I've been asking myself this. I've been scratching the designer stubble on my chin as I write. I've been walking round the block to think this through. I've been sampling the Will's Domain chardonnay to nut this one out. I have been on the verge of reading the tea leaves in my cup for inspiration.

And I've concluded that I *should* tell you. The emphasis is on the 'I' here, by the way. *I* will tell you what happened to them. And the *should*. It is something that I ought to do, so that ultimately you can understand and marvel. So I will tell you it straight. Without embellishment from them, without allowing them the embarrassing self-justification that you now realise they are quick to wallow in.

In any event, I have concluded that you will want to know. Not for any good reason, of course. It's merely because you, or at least nearly all of you, will turn out to be exactly like them. You will be interested in the little lives of little people.

But, fear not. Your edification will not be neglected. There are gems yet to be revealed and there will be ample opportunity for you to rise above judgment and marvel at achievement. For now, though, let me tell you how they swam purposefully in that direction, submitted to the pull of the current in this direction, turned left instead of right from that deep, dark cave to be drawn inexorably together to become one. Now *I* will tell you that.

Are you sitting comfortably? Then I'll begin.

The old lady was nothing like Kirsty had imagined. As she entered the stuffy, wood-panelled hallway, she realised she had no idea what Garry meant when he described Hannah as the typical Jewish mother-in-law. For some reason, she had this mental image of the old lady as one of the characters from the *Golden Girls*. But, of course, that was ridiculous. It was empty-headed, silly nonsense for her to think that people were going to be remotely like the characters on TV. Hannah wasn't blonde. Hannah wasn't middle-aged. Hannah was old, very old. But she was startling too. Kirsty couldn't take her eyes off this stunningly elegant woman.

Kirsty was exactly as Hannah imagined her. Slight, blonde, pretty, timid but feisty, fashionable in a discount store sort of way, uptight and resentful.

Hannah motioned to Kirsty to sit down in the kitchen. Naturally Hannah offered her tea. Equally naturally, Kirsty declined.

Young lady, I have a feeling that this meeting will be difficult enough for both of us without making it worse through the absence of tea.

I don't drink tea, thank you.

Nonsense, you will have some Earl Grey tea, which is flavoursome and very non-threatening.

Hannah's voice trailed away as she shuffled across the kitchen. To Kirsty, the clinking and clattering dragged on for an eternity. What could possibly take someone this long? With every mounting second, she became more and more convinced that this delaying tactic was another of those games Garry told her about. She would not put up with this nonsense like Garry did. By the time Hannah returned, rattling the tea things precariously on the old wooden tray, Kirsty was blazing with rage.

There was no opportunity for Hannah to go through the niceties of taking the cups and saucers off the tray for an appropriate afternoon tea. Kirsty pulled the trigger straightaway. She gave Hannah both barrels.

Look, lady, you're not fooling anyone with this helpless routine, you know. Garry might have been taken in by it, but you don't fool me for one second.

Hannah put the cup and saucer she had in her hand back on the tray. She wiped her hands on her grey pinafore, eased herself into the chair, spread her fingers out in front of her on the table.

She looked up at Kirsty with an expression on her face that said go on, I'm listening.

You should be ashamed of yourself. Especially at your age. Garry might be a gentle man, but that doesn't entitle you to take advantage of his better nature. He doesn't deserve this, you know. He wouldn't hurt a fly. He wouldn't rip off an old lady either, even though he obviously could. Do you think you would've noticed being charged for an extra bag of cement, some extra pots of paint, some extra hours he hadn't done? Of course you wouldn't. But Garry wouldn't do that because he has a conscience, he has a sense of right and wrong, if you know what that is being a psychiatrist or whatever the hell you are. So, I'm really interested to know how you could do this to him. I've got plenty of time and I'm all ears.

Kirsty folded her arms to indicate that she'd finished. Hannah smiled in genuine affection at the young lady who was starting to remind her of herself at that age. Hannah said nothing, but with her body language, indicated that Kirsty's outburst had changed nothing. She set to work to lay out two bone china teacups with matching saucers. There was a matching milk jug and a sugar bowl in the same pattern and they were patiently laid out. Two plates, with an identical pattern but one different from the tea set, were unloaded from the tray. Each had a thick, moist slice of apple strudel on it, a generous dollop of cream and a pastry fork.

When Hannah had finished arranging the setting for tea, she picked up her teacup, nodded to Kirsty and said, Do you want to continue or do you want me respond to you?

Kirsty refused to look at her for fear of flying off the handle again. I want you to explain to me how you could treat Garry this way.

Hannah collected her thoughts and took her time before responding.

There is a simple answer to your question. It was a test.

What the hell do you mean, a test?

It was a test for Garry. I was testing him.

What exactly makes you so high and mighty that you can give him tests? What makes you think you're so fucking superior that you can be some damn schoolteacher and give people tests if you feel like it?

I didn't do this to make myself superior, as you put it. I did it because it was important for me to find out what sort of person Garry really was, and for that matter, what sort of person his wife was.

What the fuck has it got to do with *you* what sort of people we are? What the hell does all this have to do with you leaving valuable stuff lying around as if it's a pile of garbage? Basically, I think you're just ducking the question with all this test nonsense. I think you're just too ashamed to admit what sort of person *you* really are.

Hannah sighed. She encouraged Kirsty with a wave of her hand to drink her tea and eat the delicious strudel. She wanted her to calm down. Hannah felt torn about what she should say. She felt a strong pull to tell Kirsty the whole truth. To let her in on the secret that she'd been thinking of making Garry the main beneficiary of her will. She wanted to explain herself, to show she had good reason, even if the method may not have been the wisest thing in retrospect.

But she felt an equally strong impulse to hold back. By now, hadn't this whole stupid idea gone so far off the rails that it couldn't be retrieved? Didn't her inclination to be honest with Kirsty emanate purely from a need for self-justification? Really, what was the point of coming clean now? Would Garry really believe she was going to put him in her will? What hope was there that the vexatious Kirsty would embrace this?

At the same time, Hannah was aware that a darker motive was also lurking and dragging the chain on her making a clean breast of the whole ridiculous saga. What would the police make of it all? What would they conclude about a silly old bag laying a trap for some innocent young man just because she was thinking of including him in her will?

How could she explain this to one-dimensional folk like the police? How could she then expect them to understand why she had reported her prospective heir to them for theft? How could they possibly comprehend that she'd done that because he'd let her down? She knew they would dismiss her as another silly old fool who'd lost her marbles. That was a tag she could never bear to encourage, much less one she could tolerate applied to herself.

So, Hannah decided not to tell Kirsty the truth.

I know you want to label me as a bad person and to dismiss me as a distasteful individual, Hannah said. But, I am not. Truly, I am not. I needed to set a test for Garry out of the best of motives. I had the greatest respect for Garry. I liked him a lot and I had high hopes for him. Sincerely, it was a test and not a trap. I really wish I could tell you why it was necessary to give him this opportunity via the test. I want to tell you, but I cannot.

Lady, I think you're losing the plot. You're talking in riddles and do you know what – it's all crap!

I can understand why you say that, but I'm sorry that you think that way. I am old enough to know by now that people will believe what they want to believe. I understand that it suits you to consider yourself better than me right now. I accept that. I accept your right to that sentiment. However, all I can say is that I'm as sorry as anyone could possibly be that Garry did not live up to the expectations I had of him.

Kirsty rummaged in her handbag and looked up at Hannah with a face filled with contempt.

I came here thinking you were evil, and nothing you've said to me has changed my mind. In fact, you've just confirmed for me that you're a total witch. Well, never mind all that because thank God not everyone is like you. Some of us have got some decency, even if we don't know all your fancy words. So, take this and make sure I never see your revolting, wrinkly face again.

Hannah's ring skated and skittered across the table, bunted up against her saucer and deflected at right angles off the edge of the table. Kirsty closed the clasp on her handbag and got up to leave. On her way, she lowered herself until her face was within inches of Hannah's. Out of her mouth came a froth of undiluted invective.

Take the ring, but you can fucking well whistle Dixie for the money. There was no fucking money, you understand. Just the ring that Garry got cleaned to provide a lovely surprise for a dear, innocent old lady. Some ridiculous accusation about missing money would be nothing but the ravings of a demented old woman, who doesn't know what day it is, let alone where she might have put her bags of money.

The door slammed behind Kirsty. Hannah slowly got down on her knees to retrieve her precious jewellery. To think there would have been so much money for both of them. So much money in such bad hands. Thank God I set him that test!

As you know by now or at least should have guessed, I was happy up to a point. It was nine months or so since I'd arrived in the wild west of Australia. My initiatives over the last six months had set some interesting things in motion. Some momentous things at that. I had created the linkages I sought. But they were simple ones and they didn't satisfy. Well, they did. But they didn't satisfy nearly enough.

To gratify myself further – and I am conceding this to you because this is the terminology I know you seek – I needed to add layers upon the layer I had successfully established.

It wasn't enough that the innocent renovations at Hannah's had led to such interesting possibilities, that Robert and Julia had undoubtedly met at just the right time to make their lifelines pulse, and that Kathleen and Mario had got to play in the big league to which they both so passionately aspired.

I felt rather empty because I knew there was much more scope. I would indulge in the fruit of the vine long into the night, peering at my chart of fate and the thin blue lines linking one housemate to another. Then, one night, the phone rang and jarred me awake, spilling the nearly empty contents of my glass of Shephard's Hill cabernet sauvignon down my Diesel T-shirt and onto my favourite Ralph Lauren jeans. It was the Department's out-of-hours emergency service. There had been a break-in and suspected arson at one of our major centres. Valuable, irreplaceable pieces that were being kept in storage there were feared damaged beyond repair.

OK, I'll come straight over, I said, trying to shake myself awake.

When I got to the scene of the crime, several of the other senior staff were already there. Things were not good, judging from faces that were as ashen as the smouldering remains. They all spoke at once in desperate, animated tones. But there was reverence in their voices too. It was like a funeral on speed. They catalogued the losses. They speculated on the likely consequences. The losses were one thing – tragic, even unimaginable. But, being good public servants, their concerns were centred squarely on themselves. There's bound to be an Inquiry. Why were pieces of such value stored in such an inappropriate place? Without proper security. Without adequate fire abatement systems.

A brave soul chimed in to name the elephant in the room. Will the insurance policy respond to these treasures stored in such an inappropriate way?

Negligent way, perhaps? I added, to stir the pot.

I was enjoying watching them squirm. Of course, a scandal like this would be bad for me and would be embarrassing in the extreme for the Minister. But I was confident I could distance myself sufficiently from the decision-making to wring my hands, express regret and promise to take corrective measures to make sure that never again could poor decisions like these be made without my knowledge. I'd been there, done that, before. I would get by. I could sit back, relax and enjoy the show.

When Tom arrived, he was devastated.

These pieces were to be moved next week and put securely on display in their permanent home, he wailed.

His colleagues were too engrossed in their personal pass-the-buck planning to respond.

Undeterred, Tom warmed to his task.

What a cruel twist of fate! These particular works were sent to this particular storage point after the last re-shuffle and now they're gone. As the various pieces have been needed from time to time for temporary displays, we've been moving them around the storage locations as logistics demanded. So these particular pieces haven't been here as a group the whole time – they've been in several different locations in various different combinations. Now they're gone and the others, that are more or less worthy of preservation as the case may be, were moved from here and have now survived to be re-housed next week. These are works of art and so, valuable or not, they are the artists' creative genius expressed in physical form – for posterity. It's the luck of the draw. The pieces have been stored together in different combinations and different places. Now some are gone and some are not.

I nodded sagely. Tom took it as a silent mark of respect. That's Tom's problem – he takes everything at face value. I was nodding because his moronic diatribe had significance for *me*. I couldn't give a shit why some representation of colonial Fremantle was immolated instead of some unfortunate woman with a triangular head and three breasts.

When I got home from the frenetic damping down of embers and expectations at the fire scene, I found that I had calmly, rationally cottoned on. Cottoned on literally in fact. At last I knew how to link those blue pieces of tape from one of my chargelings to the other.

My problem had been interventionism. I'd felt pressure to find the best way that *I* could establish the next layer of linkages. Although fate had commenced the whole process, I had then intervened to create the pairs that appealed to me most. Interventionism. Of course! I didn't need to put so much pressure on myself. This enterprise must be allowed to unfold at the end, just as at the beginning, on the basis of fate. The fate that poor Tom was rambling on about. The fate that combines and re-combines works of art and keeps them moving from one place to another like atoms in a cell.

The beauty of orderly chaos.

Doubtless you won't be surprised to learn that life for the professional princess had been going off script. Her existence was to be gilt-edged and guilt-free. Recent events had been thrilling enough, that's for sure. But, they had come with a price tag that was beyond what an A1 shopper like her had grown accustomed to paying. That huge debit on the credit card of life spoke one name. Mario.

Kathleen could see that Mario was trying his best to be heroic and stoic. She could tell that he was striving to maintain his boyish charm and cheeky sense of humour in the face of dressings and tubes and the unbearable bandaging of his eyes. But his customarily thick layer of bonhomie was a paper-thin veneer these days. She had to steel herself to visit him.

Visit by visit, Mario's affability was ebbing away as clearly as the fluids circulating through the transparent pipes attached to him. Fear and anxiety were giving way, slowly but surely, to desperation and morbidity. Sure, the poor boy was suffering. He was the one who might not see clearly again. He was the one who still owed the money and still faced the prospect of beatings or worse. But, *she* was suffering too and nobody recognised it. Nobody appreciated what she was going through. Against her will and her better judgment, she was wracked by guilt. This discomfort could only be dispelled by getting Mario out of his strife or by getting Mario out of her life.

Matt was the first tangible fall-out from the Mario incident. As ever, he'd been kind and sympathetic to Kathleen seeing how visibly shaken and deeply upset she was. But he couldn't understand why Kathleen, who always held herself so professionally aloof from her clients, was so devastated by these events. When she kept taking herself off to the hospital, that's when he smelled a rat. The bad smell became more rank for him when she wouldn't bonk him one Saturday night.

This Mario guy's more than just a client to you, isn't he? he said.

If you'd like to think that, she responded icily, go right ahead.

I'm getting the message here, right, loud and clear.

What message is that?

That if I walk out that door, you won't try to stop me.

Kathleen didn't react.

I'm outta here then, he declared.

Suit yourself, she replied indifferently.

And then he was gone.

Kathleen needed resolution to put her life back on track. Max and Seb were keys to this, but Max was not letting on about progress with the shoeman and he showed no inclination to do so. Kathleen knew full well that these were the rules. Sebastian Maitland-Webster business was not to be acknowledged, much less was it to be talked about. In their practice, they felt no guilt and they felt no shame about using whatever means were necessary to get a result. This was risky, risky business. These sorts of para-legal settlements spelled disbarment, ruination of reputation and certain jail. They could never be discussed. She had assumed, naively of course, that Mario's case would be an exception. Surely Max would realise that she needed to be kept up to date with proceedings. Particularly with poor Mario lying in his hospital bed. But Max's lips were sealed.

Her vigils with Mario were becoming unbearable. She needed good news and she needed it fast to get the monkey of Mario off her back. Eventually, she was resigned to having to do what she understood she must never do. She had to raise it with Max. Instinctively, she'd set up the circumstances perfectly. A drink after work. She made sure she looked good and she let Max perve at her legs long and hard. They had lots of serious legal chat and exchanged office gossip that she normally loved, but on this occasion found interminable.

There was a lull in the conversation and she needed to leap through this brief window of opportunity. Her heart was pounding, but she went for it without hesitation. She asked Max the question, straight to the point. His face flared red in anger and he slammed his glass down on the bar.

You need to grow up, you stupid tart, he blazed at her for all to hear before storming out with barely the presence of mind to grab his keys and his phone as he marched out the door.

So, Kathleen was there once again at Mario's bedside. As usual, she'd snuck in after visiting time once all the uncles and aunts and nephews and nieces and grandparents and friends of the family had swarmed out into the corridors of the hospital and been sucked through the automatic doors. Hospitals are very free and easy these days and none of the staff cared about visitors coming at any time as long as they behaved themselves.

His bedside, as she'd once joked to him, should be called *Mario Fresh*. There was every line of produce you could find in a fruiterer's as well as a respectable selection from the menu of a deli-pizzeria.

How's it going white-stick boy? she announced herself.

One is thankful for small mercies, like not be able to see the Bitch when she brings the kids.

Shame the nurses are so cute today, though, wouldn't you say?

The real shame is that they don't do bed baths like they do in the porno movies.

This was how every visit started – light-hearted, flirtatious and audacious. But, you can only keep up banter like this for so long when the situation is repeated day in and day out and when no amorous action is possible as a result. Kathleen would use all her wiles to keep the conversation at this level, but as the keeper of Mario's secrets, she knew it was only a matter of time before the jovial and flippant would give way to the anxious and morose.

Mr Plod was in today, he would change tack out of the blue.

Bummer, eh? What did he want this time?

Different day, same shit – obviously they don't buy the mugging line seeing as how I was beaten up in a security-controlled area and the punks didn't take my wallet or phone.

No mention of CCTV footage still?

Nah, I told you they never put film in that system, being the tight-arsed mongrels that they are.

Did you tell them to charge you or leave you alone, like I told you?

No, because like I told *you*, I don't get to go home in half an hour's time to my neat apartment, in my cute car, with my fat salary. In case you weren't aware, I don't need to make myself any more enemies right now, thank you very much!

She bit her tongue, wondering if she could get out of there with just her customary departure gift. But she could sense his anger was building to blow and there'd be a huge scene if she made a move right now. She was right on the money, too, because he went straight to the usual question, but in a venomous tone that was so unlike the real Mario she thought she knew.

So, tell me, Ms Hot Shot Lawyer – am I a rich man today? Am I a man who can pay his debts to his very good friends?

I don't know yet.

Oh, you don't know yet. So, you still don't know whether this brilliant solution, following on from the previous stroke of genius that landed me in this godforsaken place, this brilliant solution that this time couldn't fail, has actually delivered on one red cent of what I need to avoid my next little experience that will clearly be the morgue at an early age.

I'm sorry, but there's no point in getting nasty. It's not going to help. I did actually ask Max last night, which was something I didn't want to do. But I did because you basically begged me to.

And what exactly did you manage to extract from the great man?

Sweet fuck all, I'm afraid, just like I warned you.

They retreated to their respective verbal corners for a while to lick their wounded feelings. But Mario these days couldn't leave things alone. He had to pick at every scab.

Well, as I say, that means there's no fucking progress, in my book. If he had any bloody good news, I'm sure he'd tell you.

To be perfectly honest, whether you're a fucking invalid or not, you don't know what you're talking about. You're not the only one here with plenty on the line, you know, so keep things in perspective.

Well, it seems to me I'm the only one here who's so far had his balls on the line and I'm the only one who might be short of perspective. But in my case it might be for the rest of my life!

Kathleen sighed and bit her tongue and said nothing so deliberately that it made an eloquent statement. The old Mario would have backed down at this point to put an end to the awkwardness his personality found hard to bear. But, this time she wasn't expecting him to. And he didn't.

In fact, the conversation took a confronting turn for which she was ill-prepared. She didn't do self-pity. After living with the pathetic dependency of her mother for so long, she felt a sense of foreboding at the very thought of having someone who would be helpless but for her. She loathed people who felt sorry for themselves, but out it came. There was even a catch and a sob in his voice.

I'm shit-scared lying here, Kathy, I don't mind telling you.

Kathleen knew a normal person would take his hand at this moment and squeeze it to give him courage. But she couldn't do that. She just didn't do that stuff.

I know it's hard for you, but getting depressed will only make things worse.

Well, I'm not sure if you realise this, because sometimes I'm not sure if you really feel much at all, but getting depressed isn't actually a choice thing. You don't choose to feel depressed, you just feel it.

Another long silence enveloped the pair and sat there like a slow-moving low-pressure system just off the coast. Mario was regretting saying things to Kathy that might drive her away. After all, in his current world where he was buried down a mineshaft of dung, she was the only shining light. He realised deep down at that moment that if Kathy actually did respond to him in a way that showed sympathy and concern, it might be the last time she would ever appear at his hospital bed.

Kathy looked at her nails that clearly needed a re-manicure soon. The trouble was, Mario was right. Half the time, she wasn't sure if she felt anything for him or for anybody else for that matter. But she was searching for the right thing to say because, unlike other people, she happily accepted herself as she was. So she didn't care. She didn't do self-pity. So what.

Just when Mario thought that his ear drums might burst on account of the oppressive silence, Kathleen spoke.

Cheer up, Stevie Wonder, you can always join the Blind Boys of Alabama.

Mario breathed a sigh of relief. If I take up singing, darling, as a result of my misfortune, I will use the stage name of the Eyeless Iti. What do you think?

They laughed together, relieved at the easing of the tension. Kathy leaned over and kissed him on the forehead, whispering that she had to go. She lingered there so he could extract his departure gift. His hand found its way unerringly up her short skirt as if his sight had been transferred to his fingertips. He revelled in the heightened pleasure as if his fingers had now become the epicentre for all five senses. He explored the smoothness of her thighs, the roundness of her arse and the silky sensuality of her knickers.

As if propelled by an unseen, unheard buzzer, she declared his time was up. She pulled away and replaced his hand onto the bed covers. Naturally, he protested. She kissed him quickly again on the forehead, this time skilfully avoiding his seeing-dog hand and whispered to him that maybe next time his swelling and bruising may have gone down enough for her to use her hand on him for a change.

I let the frenzy of excitement about the artwork fire wash over me. I was good, I was professional, I was frank, I was determined that all the facts would be made public. That seemed to make everyone happy or, to be precise, happy that they could now be justifiably angry. The newspapers and the talkback worked themselves into a lather of indignation about neglect and incompetence. Ten-pound migrant steelworkers from Yorkshire waxed lyrical about the loss of art they wouldn't hang even in the toilet. But life's like that and I didn't care. I was looking forward to my selection ceremony.

I chose an Art Series riesling for the occasion as the name seemed more than topical for that time. Then I rummaged through the wire basket in my wardrobe – the one containing the flares and the waistcoat that you move with you from house to house just in case. It was a line-ball decision, but I selected the battered panama hat over the second eleven cricket cap. I cut an official memorandum on the artwork insurance situation into six pieces and then wrote an initial on each and tossed each folded slip into the hat. I made sure that I wasn't peeking so that justice would be seen to be done, should anyone miraculously be looking. Then I pulled the next exciting layer of my destiny out from the panama's canal.

G came out first and then K. The G and the K danced before my eyes. I kept myself emotion-free and dispassionate. *Que sera sera*, what will be, will be. Fate demanded that I link up Garry and Kathleen somehow.

Speaking of Garry, I'd been seeing a fair bit of him at that time as he worked on the house. Between you and me, I was glad I hadn't hired him on a commercial basis to get the place ready for tenanting. Not only was he less than reliable in when he showed up – as any self-respecting tradesman naturally should be – but he was doubly unreliable as any tradesman-cum-fireperson was bound to be.

It was cute when he apologised for being so unreliable. It was better than cute, actually. It was truthfully sweet poetry to my ears to have him explain that he was doing this reno job for this amazing old lady whom he couldn't let down and, at the same time, was being sent on this frontline management course by the Fire Service that had him gallivanting all over Perth to attend the lectures and practical exercises.

Well, what could I do but ask him to tell me more about the old lady? She sounds intriguing, I encouraged him. I would stand there in my suit on my way home from work, chatting to him while he grafted away. He would always finish his stint with some leadlighting. For him, doing the artistic, intricate work was a reward for surviving the whacking and banging. It was like having a fag after sex in the old days, when having a fag and having sex were both allowed. These days, the equivalent would be digging your organic vegetable patch after a wank.

His face would positively light up and his prose would become almost purple as he combined his two great loves. Hannah and the leadlights. What a name for a band! Anyway, he'd tell me how interesting she was. What an incredible life she'd led. How famous she had been. How insightful she was, but not in those words. How he came to feel ten feet tall by the time he went home after working there.

Now, I know that there is one basic truth in life and it is this. Nobody likes a clever dick. But you would excuse me, I'm sure, if I couldn't resist the temptation of asking him one evening how he got the job with the old bat in the first place.

I dunno where she got my name from, he said. She just rang up and asked me to come round and quote. Most of my jobs are word of mouth, just like you getting onto me, I guess.

For a while, I would catch up with Garry a couple of times a week. I'd bring him a take-away coffee and we'd chew the fat while he worked. He was getting more comfortable with me and was opening up more as I casually asked him about his family. He'd ask me questions in return and I'd spin him some yarn about this and that. I'd drop in some true facts for what I call verisimilitude or what you'd probably call it, making the bullshit believable. I'd reciprocate and tell him about my troubles. I'd tell him about my girlfriend, Lisa!

While Garry and I gossiped, I would be half listening to him and half turning over in my mind how I would effect the linking of him to Kathleen that fate had decreed. I'd been entertaining some unimpressive options such as inviting him out for a meal as a thank you for his efforts and taking him to one of Kathleen's after work haunts. But this was pathetically lame for an ace of administration like me. I'd thought about calling into Kathleen's office with Garry in tow ostensibly to drop off some papers, but that was even lamer than lame.

In truth, it was difficult to work out how to weave Kathleen into my plot any deeper because she was the one who'd let me into her life the least. I had a pretty good relationship with Robert at the bar and with the loan, with Garry via the work, with sceptical Hannah about the article, and of course with Julia via the accommodating Lisa. I got on with Mario like a house on fire. But, I'd only just managed to scam it with Kathleen. The fact was, there was no relationship there.

Then, one Monday evening, I called in on the house to catch up with Garry with the two flat whites as was my custom and the bugger didn't even front. I probably waited an hour for him, polishing off both coffees by the time I decided to split. I checked my messages as I drove away, but there was nothing. I didn't think too much of it at that point. However, I called round to the house that Sunday night and it was obvious that no further work had been done. I phoned him and got his voicemail. I left him the few choice words tradies are accustomed to hearing from their exasperated customers.

Nothing eventuated from that so I thought I'd have a look at the house the following night, it being a Monday, the night when Garry had mostly been there. I was relieved to see his ute parked in the driveway.

Hi stranger, I said in a tone both critical and matey, in other words narky but not snaky.

When he turned his head to peer down at me from his ladder, I got a shock. He looked like shit and he sounded worse, like a whole pile of manure.

Now, it's not as if I didn't quite like Garry. After all, he is the salt of the earth. Is that phrase really a compliment? If being fucking ordinary is to be praised, well fair enough. Anyway, as I say, I wasn't unsympathetic to him. But I have to say that, once I dragged his tale of woe out of him, as censored and sanitised as I later found his expurgated version to be, I could hardly contain my joy. One man's meat is another man's poison, and it turns out Garry gave me a juicy fillet steak.

You see, what Garry told me solved my problem in a most convenient way. What's more, not only was Garry's sad tale a useful means to an end, but it was also bloody good fun. Not that he told me the truth and nothing but the truth, as I intimated to you before. But, in doing so, he proved that his morality was no better than mine.

He told me a barefaced lie, the naughty boy. He told me there had been a terrible misunderstanding with Hannah. About money.

She paid me cash upfront for the work, he explained, as she didn't want it lying around the house. And she gave me quite a bit more than the original quote because I'd told her I couldn't give her an exact price until I'd got the old plaster off and found out how bad the walls were.

He sat slumped on the floor, sipping on the coffee that I had ducked out specially to get this time, not knowing originally if he was going to be there. He seemed depressed and I was concerned he might selfishly deprive me of all the gory details.

So I encouraged him in a sympathetic tone. Was it a lot of money we're talking about? Eventually, he looked up at me and replied enigmatically, Enough.

To be honest, he was frustrating me. I found myself projecting my own personality onto him. I assumed he was just playing me, just stringing me along. I could see he was in pain, but that was no excuse for this obvious cover-up. He was clearly keeping things from me, in a most unpleasant way. I was annoyed about it, but kept myself in check sufficiently to play the patience game.

I restricted myself to a simple, telling question. Why don't you return the money, or the balance of it anyway, and let her pay you on invoices produced?

He shook his head. I'm afraid it's gone beyond that stage now.

That was all he was going to say. He tossed his take-away cup onto the rubbish pile of plaster and wood and set off again up the ladder.

I was far from impressed. He deemed that non-answer a satisfactory response to someone lending him a sympathetic ear. Maybe he read irritation on my face. He suddenly thought better of it and turned to look down at me, chisel in hand.

The police are involved now, he said ruefully, and it really is becoming a mess. She thinks I took the money. I really don't know why.

Shit! I exclaimed in what was a spontaneous and genuine outpouring of empathy.

Fortunately, I pulled myself together quick smart. I shook my head and fell silent as a mark of respect. I was pondering the unmistakeable fact that as one door closes, another one opens. While it was a problem for Garry, and no doubt for his sweet and mousey, ever-trusting wife, it seemed to me to be an excellent opportunity to help a mate get a good lawyer. A bloody good lawyer, actually.

It was time to go. I invited him to contact me if there was anything I could do to help. That is what mates do, isn't it? But I was troubled as well as elated as I drove home. How in hell was I going to get Kathleen to agree to see Garry?

Robert dismissed the boy at the entrance to his suite, stuffing a handful of meaningless bank notes into his hand. He rebuffed the boy's grateful attempts to bring the bags inside and finally stood alone at the threshold with his temples pounding in a head full of blood. He stood there motionless until he had full control of his breathing and heart rate. Then he swiped the electronic lock of the door with his plastic card and stuffed it into the module that controlled the lights.

He took his courage in both hands and strode into the living quarters to find – just what he feared – absolutely no one. Maybe Julia was frolicking naked in their private pool? No such luck. Finally, he mouthed a silent prayer and entered the bedroom. Similarly, it was deserted.

Robert went to the bar and poured himself a stiff one. He ventured out by the pool to clear his head. Conflicting thoughts troubled his brain. He was distraught, yet still hopeful that Julia would arrive. He was relieved that life with Marjorie would go on in its old familiar way, but he was angry at being jilted. He was annoyed. He was confused. He was expectant. He was frustrated. He was everything rolled into one.

Eventually he dragged himself out to the resort's sumptuous dining room. He ordered up big. He spent a small fortune by Balinese standards to pick at his food and drink copious amounts of alcohol. He flirted with the beautiful waitresses. He teamed up with a handsome middle-aged couple from Sydney, dressed all in white. He charmed the wife – he was at his rakish best – while the unsuspecting husband relieved himself in the luxurious loos.

If only we were here alone, he cooed at his table partner, surreptitiously taking hold of her hand under the tablecloth. What a magical couple we would make.

He fully expected her free hand to belt him with a right cross to the chin, but none was forthcoming. In fact, she seemed to be lapping it up. For a fleeting moment, he considered whisking Cheryl away to the confines of his suite. He thought she might just do it. As he plucked up the courage to pull her up from her chair, he glimpsed out of the corner of his eye the reappearance of the dreaded killjoy Damian through the swinging wooden doors from the gents.

Through the randy fogging effect of his binge on the grog, he wondered if Damian would like to come back and join in. He was calculating the odds of this being successful, when Damian grabbed Cheryl's now relinquished hand and pulled her up announcing it was time to go. He shook Damian by the hand and bent low to kiss Cheryl's in the approved manner of a gentleman. His practised eye couldn't fail to notice Cheryl's longing glance as she was whisked away into the tropical night.

Reluctantly, Robert returned to his lonely suite. His heart missed a beat when his brain entertained the hope that Julia could have arrived in the meantime. He leapt into the apartment in a state of excitement, but his hopes were dashed. He suffered an immediate depression surpassing the opposing high. He slumped into the wicker lounger and kicked the cushion violently off the footrest.

Fuck her, he shouted, fuck the lot of them.

He contemplated visiting Cheryl and Damian and dragging her away to his lair. Cheryl had been easy on the eye. Not Julia standard mind you, but not that far short. He felt full of virile power, but frustrated to the max with his lack of female company.

Fuck them all, he repeated, that's the shot.

He poured himself another spirit and rang through to the concierge. As you would expect in an establishment like this, the duty manager was only too happy to oblige.

Robert paced his apartment until eventually there was a knock at the door. He opened it to a vision of loveliness. She was perfect. She was eighteen going on sixteen. She was pretty as a painting. As slim and curvy as an elfin child. He was transfixed. He found himself powerless but to caress her as one would a porcelain doll.

You're perfect, absolutely perfect, he repeated, tracing every delightful contour of her tiny frame.

He was roused from his sensual trance by a further gentle knocking at the door. This would be the Dom Perignon he'd ordered. He excused himself and set off to open the door personally to the room-service boy so he could remain discrete.

Excuse me, my darling, he whispered to his whore and then found himself confronted in the doorway by a vision of loveliness. She was perfect too. As totally perfect as only Julia could be.

Now I don't think I've told you yet, but the panama hat of fate that delivered the pairing of Garry with Kathy also connected the slips of paper bearing the letters R and M.

It struck me that this grouping was as simple and straightforward as the pairing of Garry and Kathy was problematic. Seriously, how hard was this going to be? I reckoned a child who spoke only Swahili could persuade Mario, reluctant consumer of alcohol that he was, to accompany him to the delightful Riverside Bar for a jar at a time when Robert was likely to be there. A challenge – not.

Getting them together was not going to be a problem. But protecting my cover until the time was right was something much more worthy of careful consideration. One option I entertained was to engineer a meeting between the parties without my being there. Given their gregarious personalities, I felt sure they would connect up and the mission would be accomplished. I contemplated hanging out somewhere at an appropriate distance, perhaps using my telephoto lens to confirm that contact had been made.

That would have been a meal of very meagre fare. And, as a gourmand of life, I wasn't going to settle for a McDonald's when I could be dining at Rockpool. No, these guys would need to meet with me present for there to be any level of satisfaction. But this was going to be unquestionably risky. Or rather, challenging and exhilarating, when I looked at the glass half full. If this went wrong, I knew the whole Master Plan could be at risk.

I was also concerned because my original overture to each of them had been about matters financial. I'd agreed to finance Robert's development plan from some real estate sales so he could avoid involving his partner. I'd also implied to him that I was able to access funds from certain ethnic investors that I enigmatically refused to name.

In Mario's case, I'd provided him with a stake in my leadlighting house as a start to a spurious financial relationship. I'd also alluded to my contacts in hospitality and had floated, in an admittedly obscure and tantalising fashion, the prospect of him being able to take a stake in a fabulous bar owned by a mate of mine.

In these circumstances, I resolved to steer the conversation well away from the financial realm. However, because it seemed improbable that this subject could be avoided entirely, I knew I would need to be on my mettle to get through unscathed.

In reality, these conversational challenges were only the start of it. You see, since I had come into their lives some five or six months before, and as ever I will bow to accept your applause right now, the behaviour of each of them had become highly erratic. Robert seemed distant and distracted. He'd been overseas and come back again and had become harder to pin down than ever. In fact, I'd begun to doubt the bar extension was really going to happen. The line of funds I'd organised for him still hadn't been accessed and he'd been brushing off all my questions about the works with infuriating all-in-good-time type statements. Naturally, it was going to be better for me if he never touched my money at all. But, I guessed the delays in the business side of his affairs were brought about by my arrangements for him with Julia that I knew were muddying the waters in the river mouth of his life.

But that was nothing. If Robert was proving unpredictable, Mario's already disordered life seemed now to have descended into some sort of schizophrenic farce. His conversations see-sawed between the anguish of his marginally requited love for Kathleen – yes, thank you – again I take a bow – and the aftermath of his traumatic experiences at the hands of the junior *Mafiosi*.

He told me he'd been in hospital after a car crash (why do these people always lie to me?) and his conversation of late had become rambling and incoherent. Mario was shifty and edgy like a man high on ice. At times, I seriously wondered whether Mario could hold down a conversation with good old Robert at all.

On the spur of the moment, one afternoon at work, I decided it was time to get the job done. It was a Wednesday, I think. At any rate, it was one of the weekdays when Robert could be found after work at the bar. I rang Mario's mobile. We chatted for a while. He was like the proverbial cat on a hot tin roof.

Hey, man, you seriously need to chill out, I said in the pseudo-hip tone I would adopt for Mario's benefit. You need a break from the drudgery of high finance and people's money troubles. I'm going to swing by in half an hour, and take you away from all this.

Once inside Mario's office, I found him in a highly gesticulative conversation with a countryman about some crap loan or other. The room was so fogged up with tobacco fumes that I considered crawling along the floor to avoid smoke inhalation. I motioned to him from the doorway that we needed to go. He gestured to me to sit down. For the next ten minutes, it was like the Marcel Marceau show. I kept signalling him to get off the phone and he kept motioning to me that it was important and he couldn't just bail on the call.

We eventually got out of there. I delivered him to the RB.

Phew, he said, not bad, not bad at all.

I bought him a drink and we chatted idly watching the boats go by. It was the same old, same old with Mario. It was Kathy this and Kathy that. It was Max this and Max that. As complimentary as his assessments of Kathy were, just as condemnatory were his opinions of the 'loathsome snake' Max.

You should meet Kathy, he told me. (I enjoyed that!) Great arse. Not sure if she's a great lawyer, but. But, this bum boy from her office, Max, if he's a Premier League lawyer I'm the Pope's fucking love child.

Then, out of the corner of my eye, I saw Robert. I excused myself from Mario and trotted off to chat with Robert for a while up at the bar. I indicated I wanted to introduce him to a business associate of mine and nodded in Mario's direction. Robert told me he'd bring over a bottle of wine in a moment once he'd been up to the office.

Presently, he arrived and sat down. I introduced them. My chest swelled with pride. I felt like the proud father of two fine, strapping boys. For a while, I beamed from one to the other, enjoying the moment. After a while, I jerked myself back into the present. I was terrified that I'd lost control, as I had absolutely no idea what they were talking about. I tuned in. Thankfully, it was where you might expect it to be. Mario was admiring the bar and Robert, with a characteristic burst of false modesty, was agreeing it was great but also claiming it was no big deal.

As it turned out, I think it suited both of them to escape from their trials and tribulations for a while and shoot the breeze about matters inconsequential. For once, Mario seemed like his old self, with the bravado coming back and the self-pity retreating to the shadows. The chit-chat may have been light, but their collective drinking was otherwise. Robert and I knocked back the vino (him voraciously; me cautiously) and Robert organised Crownies from the bar for Mario.

I began to relax. I was doing little more than a referee does with two nimble, clean-hitting boxers. I let the bout flow and just intervened now and again to ease them onto a different path. They were both steering clear of matters personal and problematic and that suited me down to the ground. I was, after all, the unacknowledged source of all that was interesting right now in their lives. For once, remaining unacknowledged across the table suited me just fine.

Having dropped my guard at the beginning of the conversation, I stayed alert from then on. All was going well, but I was concerned at what might happen once the effects of the drinking set in. After an hour or so, I'd had my fun and I was keen to vamoose. As I'd given Mario a lift there, I had some control over when he might leave. It was on the tip of my tongue to suggest that we make a move, but I had this residual anxiety that he might decide to stick around and take a cab. I backed off from breaking things up because I couldn't risk these two guys sitting around, becoming drunken BFFs and naturally enough comparing notes.

I decided to create the impression that I needed to go, without actually suggesting it. I glanced at my watch and checked my emails on the Blackberry without losing track of what they were talking about. At last, Mario showed signs of making a move. I breathed easier. However, I got a sinking feeling in the pit of my stomach when he gathered up the empties. Mario made his way to the bar. A top player like me needed to pounce without delay. I needed to get Robert to leave. What the fuck could I tell Robert? Whatever it was, I needed it fast.

Fear not, good friends. Genius is born not made. Robert opened his mouth to speak. I had no idea what he was going to say, but, in any event, I couldn't let him say it.

Robert, I interjected, I'm sorry. Look, I've just got to tell you this while Mario's gone. He's got a custody mediation with his ex-wife at nine in the morning and, if he goes on a bender this evening, he'll stuff up his chances for good of ever seeing his kids.

Robert looked concerned – this line was going to work.

Again, I interrupted him on the verge of speaking. Robert, please forgive me for being so rude, but would you nick off for a little while and then I'll be able to prise him away from here.

Robert stood up. No trouble, old son, he said, I should be on my way, anyway.

Robert shook my hand and set off. I caught up with him and clapped him on the back.

Thanks mate, I said, Mario was impressed with you and the bar, you know. Normally he never has more than one these days, but I could tell he was enjoying your company far too much to behave himself.

I sat back down and allowed myself to relax. Mario plonked himself down with all the drinks. Where's Roberto? he asked.

He's on call and his pager went off, I replied casually. Don't think he'll be back.

That's a shame, Mario said. Still, while he's looking up some emergency fanny, we'll just have to drink *his* share.

Mario was obviously not grieving for the loss of his new acquaintance all that much.

Exactly right, I thought to myself. As there's no risk now, we might as well stay and have a few.

97 OH, TO BE A FLY ON THE WALL

If my little tale wasn't so painfully true, I could embellish it at this point like one of those Hollywood movies. I could invent a van with Ferguson Plumbing (or some such tripe) on the side, that parks outside the abodes of my little loved ones, relaying back to me vision and sound. But, this ain't the movies, folks, this is reality.

In the absence of any such digital record, you'll just have to do the old-fashioned thing and sit back and imagine the scene when Garry got home to Kirsty that particular night.

Although Kirsty was still white-hot with anger about Garry, she was looking forward to him getting home. She was feeling pretty pleased with herself after bearding the lioness Hannah in her den. The visit had gone nicely to plan. True, Hannah's real-life appearance had unsettled her and the old bag's tea and sympathy routine had been disconcerting at first. But, overall, Kirsty felt she'd got the whole affair back on track. Back to where it should have been if Garry had an ounce of common sense. The ring of sentimental value had been returned. And the money? What money?

Kirsty sang along to 94.5 as she microwaved the kids' fish fingers. She was now hopeful things might turn out OK. In fact, maybe Garry's muddling might turn out for the best. After all, if he'd just come home and told her what happened, wouldn't she have felt too guilty to pocket the old bird's dough? But now, why should she worry? Grandma had shown her true colours and surely even Garry wouldn't jack up now about denying any money was found.

At the back of her mind, Kirsty was a bit worried about the police. Still, she knew Garry better than he knew himself. With his uncanny ability to put things off, there was no way he'd make the statement until they hounded him to death and she knew that, once he heard about her run-in with Hannah, he'd have no option but to fall in behind the money-what-money line.

Garry eventually came to the conclusion that, as the nightmare wasn't going away, he would have to take steps to sort it out. In the shower that morning, he willed himself to treat the Hannah events as an emergency. An emergency like any other he was trained for. Every fireman knows the steps in their sleep – combat, control, recovery. OK, so the combat response was poor. Clearly he should have reported the find to Hannah. However, be that as it may, he had to progress to the control phase. He was putting that off because it meant dealing with the police. Like some criminal. But, it had to be done.

He steeled himself to make it happen and the sooner, the better. He dressed in his uniform, waved rather than kissed Kirsty goodbye and got into his car to drive to work. He followed exactly the steps he'd planned out in the shower. He did not start the car. He did switch on the mobile. He did not check his messages. He did ring the cops. He did make an appointment for that afternoon.

Garry did his best not to think about it during the day. Luck was with him because he was called out to an incident that took a long time to resolve without proving dangerous or taxing. He could almost see the funny side of waiting there for the local police to arrive. At long last, his shift came to an end and he set off in an anxious but determined frame of mind.

He was glad he'd worn his uniform. It gave the impression he was there on professional business. In due course a uniformed copper called him in and the barest of pleasantries were exchanged. He was cautioned and sat glumly through the tedious process of his statement being typed and re-typed. He resigned himself to the fact that they were never going to spell his first name with a double *r*. The irony that he was signing his statement with the standard emergency services issue biro did not escape him. He accepted the outstretched hand of the otherwise impassive constable and scarpered as fast as he could from the heritage environment of the police precinct into the glorious anonymity of the concrete-art car park opposite.

He felt depressed and exhausted by the time he got home. It had been an emotionally draining day. He wanted to play with the kids and continue to escape from reality. But, to do so, he would have to confront the Kirsty cold-shoulder treatment. It occurred to him to go to the pub with his single mates. He was tempted but he cranked his brain back into trained behaviour mode. He willed himself to take the next step to exert some control over his life. No running away allowed, not any more.

Once his key was heard in the lock, events started to unfold as he imagined. The kids came hurtling down the hall, screaming Daddy, Daddy. They clambered all over him and he put them over his shoulder and threatened to drop them just as he had done in happier times. He gradually made his way along the hallway for the confrontation that could no longer wait.

Then events took an unexpected turn. Kirsty actually greeted him. She even pecked him on the cheek. Naturally, Garry's mood improved. It stayed that way too through a much less frosty dinner time where he was served a stubbie of VB with his lamb chops. The domestic atmosphere remained chirpy through bath time and all the way to story and bed time.

But there I go, I'm going to prick your balloon again. Maybe you should just think happy thoughts for a while. Think about reading bedtime stories to your own kids. All that bubble bath and giggling and no I don't want to get out. Or, if you haven't got kids, think about how much you'd like to have them in your life one day. Or, as a third alternative, pat yourself on the back for remaining childless and saving all that money to spend on yourself. Maybe you could remember your own childhood if it was happy. If it wasn't, think about when you first got laid. If you had an unhappy childhood and you're a virgin, do me a favour and read some other book.

Anyway, back at our typical suburban house in our typical suburban street, Kirsty and Garry slumped in their usual armchairs in a classic domestic scene. Garry was exhausted, but feeling better. Kirsty was obviously in the best mood she'd been in for a long time. The best for a long, long time, actually. She was bursting to tell Garry about her day. She contained herself and asked him about his first. He told her about the fire and how long they'd had to wait for the police to attend. She commiserated with him that it sucked. He omitted the little detail of the statement he'd given to the cops as he was desperate, just like you guys, to think happy thoughts.

Kirsty drew breath and got underway. She told him what had happened with Hannah, blow by blow. At first, he was mildly apprehensive. When Kirsty got to the part where the ring skidded across the kitchen table and bounced along the floor, he was sure he was going to throw up. A loud cry was heard in the background. A falling out of bed kind of cry. Kirsty rushed to the source of the outburst.

Garry got another beer from the fridge to try to settle his nerves. What to think? Suddenly all was peace and quiet at the far end of the house. Kirsty bounded back into her armchair and waited for Garry to settle down. She paused for dramatic effect.

I haven't told you the best bit yet, she said. I told her there never was any fucking money so she'd better stop telling such awful lies.

Garry swigged slowly from his bottle to cover the expression of fear playing on his face.

Kirsty ploughed on, oblivious. As long as we don't put it in the bank, she said, how is anyone ever going to prove it?

She celebrated the triumphant end to her story by perching on the edge of Garry's armchair to kiss him on the lips. It had been a long time between drinks. He surrendered to the moment as an antidote to the rampaging fever in his mind.

Man and wife made hungry love that night. But the love was a lie. Soon enough those typed words on the page in a battered filing cabinet somewhere in a drab office in the bowels of a police station in Freo would make them face the truth.

OK, you're all geniuses. You've worked out by a process of elimination that the hat of fate required me finally to connect Julia with Hannah.

That didn't particularly faze me. After all, I had the inside running on Julia thanks to my deep and meaningful relationship with her very best friend. Proximity brought many benefits. At any given time, I knew precisely where the lovely Julia stood. But, by the same token, being close brought me closer to risk. If I was going to get sprung by anyone, it would be by her. Even a maestro like me could forget himself. Loose lips sink ships.

Given this risk situation, I needed to plan my trysts with Lisa with military precision, even more so for when Julia would be around. From the very beginning I cultivated myself as an avant-garde, enigmatic man. A man of few words (and certainly not rash ones). I cast erudite pearls before the swine to impress them. But I never said much. Quality not quantity was my motto.

Early on, I let it slip to Lisa (and therefore obviously to Julia) that I was something of a writer. I told her of my various freelance projects, including my current secret commission to cover the life of a celebrated female icon. Lisa readily took my cover story on board.

That's why you like to listen rather than speak, Lisa concluded.

I felt reassured that my disclosed other life as an author would provide reasonable cover for me, should Julia and Hannah start chatting about me when they met. That gave me confidence to proceed to set up the play. As ever, I considered my options for effecting the introduction. Ordinarily it could have been challenging. But Julia's many trials and tribulations provided an excellent excuse for a friend to invite her out to take her mind off things.

I called her on her mobile one lunchtime on spec. This wasn't that unusual, as I had been lending her a sympathetic ear. Only to have it ear-bashed, of course. She would ramble on interminably – What should I do? My life's a mess. I've met this guy but I feel so guilty.

You know how it goes. I would lap it up, I don't mind telling you. It was beautiful music to my abused ears.

Anyway, on this day, I cut through all the crap.

Julia, enough of all that, I said firmly to stem the verbal tide. The reason I rang is that I want you to meet a friend of mine.

A friend, what friend? I can't.

What do you meant you can't?

I'm not dressed. Well, I am dressed obviously at lunchtime, things aren't that bad, but I'm not dressed to go out.

Nonsense. Come on, it will do you good, I insisted. By the way, this friend is not what you think. In fact, you couldn't possibly imagine how fantastic and how different this person is.

I gave her fifteen minutes to put her face on. I rocked up and virtually bundled her into my car. Naturally I'd taken the precaution of teeing up a further visit with Hannah for that time.

What would Lisa think of me letting you take me out unchaperoned? Julia mused, buckling up her seatbelt.

The last thing you need, Julia, is another handsome man in your life!

I regretted this repartee as it set her off on another of her woe-is-me monologues. These were growing tiresome (even if gratifying as evidence of my success). I tried to steer her onto another subject.

Guess who we're going to see.

I don't like guessing games, Julia replied.

Of course you do, everyone likes guessing games.

Oh, OK – it's your long-lost sister who was adopted and you only found out about her last night.

I laughed. It was actually funny.

How did you guess?

Fortunately, by this time we'd arrived. I wasn't sure how Hannah was going to react to me bringing along an interloper. I was pleasantly surprised. She beamed at Julia and invited us both in. Mind you, I could tell immediately that Hannah wasn't her usual self. She seemed less sure of herself, less provocative, less like an analyst and observer of proceedings and more like an actual participant. I was humbled and proud that these events of my making could have had such a profound effect on someone so self-aware and controlled.

As we walked in, I looked at Julia and she looked at me. Julia found the old lady entrancing. I smiled a knowing smile. It radiated, yes I am a man of many mysteries, a Joseph of a technicolour coat, someone not to be labelled and pigeonholed. Julia got that, I could tell.

We settled around the kitchen table as is the pattern at Hannah's house. I performed the introductions.

Hannah, this is my friend Julia. We were having a spot of lunch and I thought I would bring her along.

I'm glad you did, Hannah said with a serene smile.

Julia, this is my friend Hannah – we're working on something together. I winked at Hannah to signify that it might be best for both of us if we didn't get into specifics about what we were working on.

Hannah offered us tea, as is her custom, and as she shuffled off to make it, she turned her head from the benchtop to look straight at Julia.

You seem troubled, young lady, she said.

OK, so I pretty much knew what was going to happen. And, yes, it was painful to the max. But, that's not the point. The point was to weave my darlings that bit closer together. So I just had to grin and bear in. What an opportunity it was for *Troubled from Cottesloe* to come face to face with a super-counsellor from way back. Oh my God, did it come spewing out all over again! All over the table. All over the floor. All over Hannah. All over me.

I was comfortable that we were playing agony aunts. It represented a very low risk to my enterprise. Hannah was doing her thing, but I could tell she was off-colour. It's like a footballer slightly off his game. The average punter in the stands might not notice anything, but the footy connoisseur does. And that's how it was with Hannah. I found myself absorbed in assessing the subtle changes that Hannah had undergone.

After a period of observation, I had evaluated the data and reached a diagnosis. Hannah was engaging in the problems Julia was casting around like confetti. She made a comment here and a comment there that was very telling. Telling in more ways than one. She was offering advice. She was actually telling Julia what to do.

There was only one explanation for this and it gave me a warm, inner glow. I worked hard to keep my body language neutral. Hannah was no longer the ice queen – thanks to me. She was no longer an impeccable model of professional detachment – thanks to me. She had lost control – the thing she prized most – and all thanks to me. The pressure of the Garry and Kirsty affair had got to her, even if just a little bit. That is a win. Boy, is that a win!

I woke myself from my reverie. I was having too much fun. I snapped myself back into the here and now.

Jules, I interrupted the flow of conversation, I'm sorry but I need to go.

They conceded that they needed to stop talking and, like the *Queen Mary 2*, eventually the floating juggernaut of women's conversation turned from its course.

We were saying our farewells along the passageway. I was pretty chuffed – all had gone very well indeed. I steered Julia by the elbow to make sure she was really going to leave. Once out of the door, she turned round and gave Hannah a peck on the cheek. Hannah responded by patting Julia fondly on the back.

We were in the car, slowly pulling back and I was almost in the clear. I felt like the hostages in *Argo* once they were safe on the plane taking off from Tehran airport. Then Hannah held up her hand and ambled towards the car. I wound my electric windows down.

Come and see me any time, Hannah called to Julia in the passenger seat.

I winced.

I will, responded Julia, I will.

As I finished my reversing manoeuvre, I wondered if she meant it. I hoped she didn't.

It was true that I'd determined to let fate take its course. But I'm only human. Even me.

They say timing is everything, don't they? By the way, who are 'they' who say things like this and do all sorts of things to us like change bus timetables, build apartment blocks near the foreshore, replace bank tellers with ATMs and all the other stuff we don't like?

But in this case timing *was* everything.

It was fun getting up to his little tricks again. Not as much fun as really hurting people and watching the fear in their faces, but on a scale of 1–10, this was a 6 or 7, so not bad in Sebastian Maitland-Webster's estimation. Breaking and entering his way into the shoe factory was a cinch. Some of the larger factory units down in South Lake had nasty-looking guard dogs on site. All black and slobbery looking – canine skinhead types. Most of them had security warnings – patrolled by some impressive sounding security company with secure, or alert, or guard somewhere in their name. But this place was a joke.

Sebastian shook his head at the standard of security these days. A so-called security guard would be a sixty year old, short-sighted, fat grandpa who would patrol all of Perth on his own to protect and serve the company's customers. To be fair, these security guards were old and fat but they weren't stupid. They would park their white Toyotas near the factory gates, pop their cards in the lock and piss off as fast as possible to avert any chance encounter with some ne'er-do-well up to no good.

Sebastian was therefore free to poke around the shoe factory at his leisure. He had a stroll around the manufacturing plant and noticed, with his practised eye, opportunities to cause some problems. He visited the small showroom-cum–waiting room area but rejected this as being of limited value. Finally, he reached the office area where he'd sat in silence previously and put his boot against the door. The Taiwanese padlock exploded on impact.

The office was much more to his liking. It had made some sort of nodding acquaintance with the modern world of technology in the shape of two desktop computers festooned with yellow post-it notes, but its heart clearly lay in a bygone era where the filing cabinet, the box cards and especially the teledex reigned supreme. He looked around and smiled. Sure enough there was a fax machine that still seemed to be in use.

For a while, he rummaged in that way that men with black gloves and a big torch always do. Not that you've ever really seen anyone do that, but you know how they do it because every film or TV show you watch features some guy doing this. So, let me assure you, Sebastian did this in the approved manner. But your untrained eye would not have told you that Sebastian was a professional rummager. While he appeared to be casually opening this drawer and that, spreading out this file rather than that one, he was actually engaged in something much more purposeful.

By the way, for the more academic amongst you, Sebastian and his ilk are true professionals. They have a distinct body of knowledge. Sebastian, for example, can find the bits of paperwork and the PDFs you don't want him to find. He understands how the human brain works and how people categorise things in their minds. Knowing this, he knows where you hide things. Don't let Sebastian near your wife, guys – he'll help her sniff out your internet porn in no time.

Once Sebastian had found and copied what he was searching for – a thorough job that took an hour or more – he left the cabinets and individual files to be found in the manner that would have most impact. Priding himself on his attention to detail, he left certain documents in and around the copier to show what the intruder had been up to. He was then free to turn his attention to the other major agenda item of the night.

He wandered round again, this time assessing possibilities. This visit was designed to be no more than a warning shot across the bows. Its goal was to encourage the offending party to do the right thing, rather than inflict any serious damage. Often, this is all someone in his profession really has to do. Just show the punter that you mean business and they mostly see things differently after that. Good in a way, and a shame in a way, for him. It was good financially as you got paid fast without having to expend very much. But at another level, it was a great shame. After all, inflicting serious damage is so much more fun.

He surveyed the factory and started to narrow down his

options. What criminal damage could he perpetrate that would be the equivalent of his office activities where he'd tagged and copied their files relating to GST, super and tax? What would show them how vulnerable they were without triggering some backs-to-the-wall irrational defiance and resistance? Something old, something new, something borrowed, something blue? No, something significant, but not devastating. And something noticeable without being important.

Sebastian availed himself of the glue from the assembly area and a variety of sharp tools from the cutting floor. He chose a large and expensive piece of machinery that he fancied moulded the rubber to make the soles. He liberally poured the glue into various parts of the works and dropped the cutting tools inside to supplement the glue. He poked the lumps of metal deep into the belly of the equipment. It was important they not be seen, but rather discovered once the vicious grinding noise from the machinery had grated unbearably even on the hardened ear canals of the machine operators.

At 4 a.m., Sebastian slipped away into the dark industrial night.

At the same time, because everything is in the timing of things, Mario decided in a parallel medicated night that he really couldn't sleep and, as he still couldn't extract the soporific value to be had from a hospitalised wank, he would have to give up on the *zzzs* for another fucking night. His head was doing bog laps like his nephews round the Cappuccino Strip. Just before dawn is your darkest hour according to Ry Cooder, and Mario was entertaining undiluted dark thoughts. Even for him, of late, whose thoughts had typically been as black as a coalminer's crotch.

Mario was preoccupied with his vision or rather lack of it. Naturally he was also worried sick about his testicles and about a further visit from his ponytailed friends. But, above all, it was his blurred vision that had him spooked. Sometimes, when he was in more of an upbeat mood, he felt the fog was clearing somewhat and that he could see a fraction better. But, whenever he fell asleep, as he fitfully had that night, some particular circuits and synapses would connect and he would sit bolt upright in terror that he would open his eyes and there would be no light to be seen at all. That night, as usual, there was good news and bad news.

He had opened his eyes and he wasn't blind, but he couldn't see properly either.

The doctors were non-committal about his sight. Cautiously optimistic was the phrase his stuck-up, spruced-up, dressed-up specialist liked to use, but Mario didn't know if he should believe him. It was a waiting game essentially. This was not good for Mario, as being a patient patient was not his thing. Quite the opposite in fact. He had not been a kid to wait to open his presents. He had not put away any Easter eggs for later. He hated waiting. He shouldn't have to wait. And yet he had to. For once, there were no options to pay more, talk someone into something, bribe someone to advance him in the queue. None of these options were available this time round.

In fact, the waiting game was really getting to him by now. Mario was distinctly uptight and antsy. That night, in the sterile ward kitchenette, Mario was desperate for a drink. How frustrating for him that the café bar wasn't a real bar. He would've given anything to press one of those buttons and, instead of getting a tasteless concoction that was a very distant cousin of an espresso, be served with a Bacardi and Coke or a brandy and dry.

Frustrations with Kathleen were really getting to him too. It was his growing sense of anger with her that had him prowling painfully and sleeplessly around that night. It was all right for her. It was good fun for her and her poofy lawyer friend to play games with other people's lives. Talk about all care and no responsibility!

He could feel a new force driving him that night, to which at first he couldn't give a name. But, over the course of sipping at his bitter black beverage, an identity for this new longing came to the fore. It was called payback.

As you know, or maybe you don't, payback is the offspring of revenge. Mario didn't want these people getting off scot-free. Yes, he got his own good self into trouble in the first place, but these lawyers had only made things worse. And, to add insult to injury, his parents brought him his mail that very afternoon, and what did he find there but a bill from his lawyers that looked more like a telephone number than an amount owed. He was now in hock to them for a huge sum of money on top of his unpaid debt that they were supposed to be sorting for him.

Mario was seething with righteous indignation. In the hospital, in his lurid purple and black striped satin pyjamas. And, the strange thing was, that this feeling was so intense towards Kathy. Maybe he was now a changed man who didn't always think first with his dick. He wanted payback, that was all. I don't know if he expressed it to himself in this way. But he wanted the lawyers to honour their professional indemnity. That's how I choose to put it. He felt that they were paid for their professional expertise, but their poor advice and ill-advised decision-making had caused him nothing but trouble and damage so far. Their tactic of talking to the heavies had been a disaster. And their great idea of getting their own heavy to heavy the shoeman had obviously come to nothing, as they wouldn't even talk about it now.

And so, given the timing of things, in the early hours of the morning, Mario hit upon a marvellous new plan that would make the lawyers literally and metaphorically pay. As it happens, this was just as the loyal Sebastian Maitland-Webster was enacting the lawyer's plan to make sure that Mario would get paid – by the person who actually owed him the money. This sort of coincidence makes everything worthwhile, don't you think? It makes you glad to be alive and especially to be a player on the trading floor of that great stockmarket called life.

Once I'd drawn the names from the hat, there was enough in the volatility of the arrangements to keep me amused. In truth, I was in serious need of amusement at that point because my work circumstances had taken a turn for the worse. Not due to the destruction of the valuables or anything I had done or not done, but because the dead hand of dreary politics had chosen to intervene.

The popularity of the government had nosedived thanks to the untimely intervention of its own Crime and Corruption Authority. Everyone knows that governments are inherently corrupt. So it's obvious even to the most educationally challenged amongst us, that a government that sets up a corruption watchdog is asking for trouble. Anyway, surprise surprise, the shit hit the fan, some ministers resigned and others got sacked and then of course the party shafted my minister, the only one of the lot of them with balls, although she was a woman.

Anyway, my new boss was a bumbling fool of a party hack with four chins, John Lennon glasses and a line of rhetoric from the Young Socialists 1974. Just my luck to have to housetrain a minister, as we say in the public service, at a time when I had more interesting and challenging things to focus on.

The introductions of my charges, one to the other, had progressed fairly well. There was nothing untoward going on. Nevertheless there was an ever-present risk that relationships between them could burgeon independently and slip from my control. I was concerned that Mario might take himself off to the Riverside Bar unsupervised and that he and Robert might chitchat about topics I didn't want them to.

I still had the problem of getting Garry to see Kathleen for legal advice. I was comforted by what I was hearing from Garry about domestic discord as that seemed to play into my hands. Yet my track record with Kathleen to date didn't fill me with confidence that persuading her to represent Garry was going to be a walk in the park.

The Julia–Hannah combination concerned me most. Julia sang Hannah's praises all the way home. On reflection, Hannah's last-minute invitation to Julia was a dagger in my heart. This anxiety frustrated me greatly and deprived me of the satisfaction I was entitled to for having set up the Bermuda triangle between Robert, Julia and husband Stephen so beautifully. Just when I should have been relaxing in the control tower observing the comforting blip of Julia's plane on the radar, unanticipated interference courtesy of Hannah loomed as a distinct possibility.

Still, them's the breaks. The stewardship of this Master Plan is why I'm here.

Somehow, Garry managed to maintain some inner calm. But you can imagine the monumental frustration he felt when Kirsty dropped her bombshell about the visit to Hannah's. What rotten luck for Garry that the fates propelled him to make his statement to the cops on the very day Kirsty decided to do what she did.

Should he have predicted that? How could he possibly have guessed that she would face off with Hannah like that? How Garry's hopes were dashed! He had found an unexpectedly affectionate, in fact amorous, Kirsty on his return from work that night. But the fire of spousal warmth and love would clearly soon be snuffed out.

Garry somehow controlled his emotions, but he knew he couldn't contain them for long. He invented an excuse for a post-coital dog-walk and literally dragged the poor canine off his comfy bean bag where he'd settled for the night. When he got to the dark solitude of the local park, Garry let out a solitary scream. He emptied his lungs, piercing the silence of the night. For fear the neighbours would appear to investigate, he slumped to the ground in the shadows and propped his back against a tree trunk for support.

He sat there in silence for an eternity. The dog circled him nonplussed as to why he'd been from his bed untimely ripped for a pseudo-non-walk. Garry eventually took pity on the pooch and forced himself upright. He traversed the ill-lit lawn, striving to kick his addled brain into gear. He summoned up his training to assess and reassess the circumstances. Where the hell was he after all this turmoil and shit? Recount the facts. Kirsty has given Hannah back the ring. Kirsty has denied the existence of any money. Hannah would be happy to get back the ring. Hannah would be angry about the money. While she might live with the loss of the cash, she would never accept the denial and the lie.

He ran through the facts from his side. What exactly did he tell the police? He found a ring and a lot of money. He found it in a pile of trash. He told the old lady about it (well, hadn't he intended to?) Hannah was totally confused and he was worried she would lose it all again if he'd just left it there (well, wasn't that possible?) He was holding the ring and money in safekeeping while he tried to track down Hannah's relatives (well, he had looked her up on the internet sometime earlier, so the info he gave the police did ring true).

In his disturbed state of mind that night, he found it hard to unravel the extent of the shit he was in. I've given a false statement to the police. That might have been OK, but Kirsty has now contradicted it to Hannah. If Hannah tells the police what Kirsty said to her, then the boys in blue will conclude that one of us is lying. They'll probably decide that neither of us can be trusted. Then, of course, they'll be more inclined to believe Hannah completely and they will be highly suspicious that my statement to them was false.

He pounded the suburban pavement, exhausting his hapless hound and his own befuddled brain. Of course, none of this will be such a problem if Hannah keeps her mouth shut. If Hannah keeps Kirsty's visit to herself then the inconsistencies won't surface for the police. But how likely is that really? Even if she's in no hurry to tell the police about Kirsty's denial about the money, won't she need to tell them about the return of her precious, antique ring?

To his disconsolate dog's great relief, Garry at last turned for home. That was when the unthinkable came into his mind. Don't pretend that your thoughts haven't gone there too. Don't sit there in smug judgment of Garry and me. He entertained the thought that you're having too. What if, for some reason, Hannah didn't get to report this development to the police?

But, as his steps rang out on that noiseless night, Garry recoiled in horror from such dishonourable thoughts. There has to be another way. Some way he could maintain his self-respect. He knew full well that there was one, in fact there was a one and only way that he could go. Kirsty has to agree to give the money back. We can claim the old lady was confused again when Kirsty visited her. Surely, once everything has been returned, the police will lose interest in the whole affair. After all, don't they have real crooks to catch? Don't they claim to be desperate to get cops back on the beat being real policemen not pen-pushers?

Unfortunately, as Garry trudged wearily home, other calculations infringed on his attempts to restore virtue. There was another unthinkable issue at hand. He had to confess to Kirsty he'd made a statement to the police without telling her. This would be admitting to a sin beyond the bare truth of these facts. He would in effect be telling her that he didn't trust her enough to share his plans with her. This was unthinkable at the best of times. These were not the best of times.

Garry resisted the husky-strength pulling on the leash once he reached the corner of his street. While his head was relatively clear, he needed to cobble together some sort of speech to be delivered to Kirsty in the morning. He practised it silently.

Kirsty, we have another problem, I'm afraid. I went to the police station yesterday and made a statement. I'm sorry I didn't discuss it with you first. I know I should have, but you haven't been that easy to talk to recently on account of you being so mad at me. Anyway, my statement contradicts what you said to Hannah. I'm sorry but it never occurred to me that you would go round to Hannah's and obviously I had no idea that you would be returning the ring and not the money.

Garry could picture all too clearly the look on Kirsty's face.

By rights, you should've told me what you were planning to do. Still, what's done is done, but we are going to be in deep shit if Hannah contacts the police to tell them the ring has been returned.

He paused again. The facial expression he imagined didn't look any happier. He mentally soldiered on.

If she does go to the cops, and I can't see why she wouldn't, she's bound to tell them that you denied that there ever was any money to be taken.

He kept going for fear of conjuring up another terrible picture. There's nothing for it, Kirsty, I've thought about it every which way and the only thing we can do is for you to visit her again and to apologise about the money and return it to her. I would do it myself if I could, but the police warned me not to go anywhere near the house. You have to see, Kirsty, that we have no other choice. Our best hope from here is that the police lose interest in the whole thing once all the property is returned.

He laughed inwardly at how reasonable and logical it all came out in words. He knew it would be vastly different in practice. He gave into the dog's urgent pressure. Confronting Kirsty on this was unthinkable and it was out of the question. So what other options did he have? There was only one.

One way or another, Hannah must not get to tell the police about Kirsty's visit.

I had to wrestle manfully with the prospect of linking Garry to Kathleen. Albeit unknowingly, Kathleen seemed intent on bringing my Master Plan undone. Maybe I was a little paranoid, but I sensed this great reluctance on her part to allow me into her world.

The land transfer papers for the sale in Melbourne had been sent to me from Kathleen's office. This represented the one clear shot on target I had to take. I carefully read the documents over lunch one day when I was waiting for Lisa to arrive. She was always twenty minutes late so I knew I had plenty of time. I pondered the opportunities that the land transfer document provided me.

How could I use these documents in such a way as to lead me personally to Kathy? The standard actions such as signing and returning them would lead me to a legal clerk or a secretary or the fucking tea lady if I was really unlucky. To create a pathway to Kathleen, the land transfer had to hit a snag and a major one at that. It had to be something that would put my lawyer's dear client's interests in jeopardy and give her cause to meet with me to save me from the consequences of my actions.

There was only one thing I could think of. Accordingly, I sent the papers back with a sorrowful note. I have had some serious misfortune in the family and I can no longer sell the property. The secretary phoned me, followed by the clerk. I thanked them politely for their kind attention, and for their diligent explanations of the legality of things, but I explained that no matter what, I could not now part with the site.

I pictured Kathleen huffing and puffing when her staff reported back to her.

I didn't want this stupid case in the first place. I told that jerk to do the conveyancing in the local jurisdiction, but no, some people think they know the law better than we do! What's the matter with people that they can't see simple reason? Sally, you'd better get him to come in.

It was a night for gatecrashing, that one.

Lovely Julia didn't know what to think when the door was opened by a drunk in the foreground with a barely dressed Balinese hooker in the background. This was hardly the polite Cottesloe social scene to which she was accustomed.

By contrast, thousands of kilometres away, her husband Stephen initially felt much more at home amongst the Armani suits and the Ruth Tarvydas gowns at the gathering he'd infiltrated.

Actually, I applaud them both for their courage in rocking up where they did. To be honest, I didn't think either of them had it in them. Who'd have thought that so-nice Julia would have abandoned her perfect children to flit off to Bali for a root at a resort? And certainly, I wouldn't have given stupid Stephen credit enough to think he could put two and two together as he did and actually come up with four.

And to think Julia had been quaffing the passable Qantas business-class bubbly all the way there and nibbling on a lettuce leaf or two so she could still fit into her new Seafolly bikini, all the while imagining, in its Barbara Cartland perfection, her triumphant arrival at the darling Balinese apartment. Robert, dashing and handsome Robert, would sweep her into his arms like Clark Gable in *Gone With The Wind* and carry her over the threshold straight to the very chic bamboo and rattan bedroom. It must have been so perfect in her imagination. And then, poor darling, how would she have felt to find herself degraded with an underage common tart being paraded before her eyes?

I can well imagine Robert stumbling and stammering as he found the latest light of his life silhouetted against the moonlight there in the doorway. How Robert must have called upon every ounce of his experience gained from his distinguished career in marital deception. Yes, of course, his delicious teenage tart would have been ushered unceremoniously out of the apartment.

He would have drowned out her protests by clumsily attempting to smother the disdainful Julia in unwelcome kisses.

We can't doubt that the phrases – It's not how it seems, and of course, I can explain everything – would have leapt from his treacherous lips.

How he would have blabbered on!

I'm a bit sloshed, darling, it's true. I thought you weren't coming. I was so distressed. I was distraught, actually. Anyway, thank God, Sheena was at the resort to keep me company. I've known Sheena since she was this high. She's the owner's daughter and Jati and I go way back. That's why I always stay here. Anyway, I had some dinner with Sheena and quite a few wines and cocktails, I have to admit, and then Sheena and I were just chatting about how much things have changed here in Nusa Dua. And there you were. To be honest, I'd got depressed and made up my mind you weren't coming. I thought you were room service and I thought wow, that's amazing, here they are so soon. Just let me answer the door, would you?

And, while Robert had been thinking on his feet and trying to talk himself out of yet another clandestine catastrophe, Stephen would have gathered round with everyone else ostensibly to listen to the speeches. He'd have secretly felt very smug at this point, I would think. For one thing, he'd worked it all out, like some private dick. He hadn't lived with Julia for all this time not to know what she was like. He knew there'd be some hero on the scene, some knight in shining armour to play the lead role in one of Julia's escapist fantasies. And then, on the plane one late afternoon, the obvious clue came into focus that had been eluding his examination of Julia's mobile calls and his rifling through her handbag. The guy who'd mysteriously shown up at the door, the distinguished, handsome guy, the classic doctor-type, tied in with the gynaecologist's appointment he'd found in her diary. The man at his front door was the fanny scanner. Of course, he was.

Back to the credit card records. No problem there, just get the right month, ah here we are, Dr Robert Hetherington. Get home, fire up the internet on his tablet, get the address of his rooms, print out the bio notes, wife and two sons both doctors. Nathan

Hetherington. That rings a bell. He's a GP locally, isn't he? Look him up. There he is. Actually, he's the young guy at the Golf Club, isn't he? A friend of Harry's. That's him. I'm sure it is. Zip over to the Club. He's not there. But there's another reason his name's familiar. Have a drink. Have a think. It's something to do with the Club. Hey Geoff, what's happening with young Nath Hetherington these days? Don't mention him to me, he keeps beating me. No seriously, there's something up with him. Well, there's something big up with him, actually – if getting engaged counts, he laughed. Then over to the noticeboard. There it is – whip around for Nath's engagement to Kelly.

Not a solitary electrical impulse in Julia's brain made a connection that Robert was telling the truth. Well, perhaps with the exception that Robert knew the owner of the resort. That story about that tart being called Sheena and being the owner's daughter was total twaddle. As they say in the best cross-examinations in *Rumpole*, that story was a tissue of lies. But, unlike an earnest group of jurors straining to learn the truth, there wasn't one impulse in Julia's body that actually cared. She'd just done the bravest thing she'd ever done in her life to escape the truth – the awful truth of her loveless, tedious, pointless existence – so what value did she put on truth at that precise moment in time, anyway?

Her instincts dictated what to do next. She didn't care that he was lying, but it was important that he not know that. There was a victory to be gained here in a crucial battle that might determine the fate of the war. He would have to grovel. He would have to beg for forgiveness. He would have to kneel at her feet and lick them before he would get himself into her bed. She dismissed him.

I need a shower, she announced.

She extracted her washbag from her case that she pointedly left outside the door and then she disappeared into the bathroom. The metallic sliding of the bolt rang out over the sound of crickets in the still night.

Stephen nodded casually to several in the crowd he recognised from the Club. He bided his time. He waited patiently through the inarticulate bumbling from Kelly's father as he welcomed young

Nathan to the family and failed to resist the obviously irresistible cliché that he was gaining a son not losing a daughter. Stephen downed another scotch and importuned a passing waiter for another. His head was pounding and his temples were thumping as Marjorie Hetherington stepped forward to speak. This is it, old fellah, he steadied himself.

Good evening everybody and thank you, Edward, for that wonderful introduction to tonight's proceedings. Well, as you know, I am not exactly the speechmaker out of Robert and I ... polite laughs ... but unfortunately, as you can see, Bobby couldn't be here tonight. As you can imagine, Bobby is so upset ...

WHERE IS BOBBY? Stephen's voice rang out, WHERE'S GOOD OLD BOBBY?

Stephen's voice echoed round the room to more polite laughs.

Well, as I was going to say, Bobby unfortunately had to go to Bali at short notice.

This was the moment Stephen came here for, the moment he could not miss.

When the bolt slid back on the bathroom door and the ravishing Julia emerged with the snowy white towel around her head, Robert pounced and he was not repelled.

Bobby unfortunately had to go to Bali at short notice ...

TO FUCK MY WIFE.

The sentence that was finished for Marjorie had an authentic ring of truth, but it wasn't in fact what she was going to say.

I was more than a bit nervous – even me! – when I sat waiting for my appointment with Kathleen. There was a lot of history between us. I felt it and she felt it. I resented her for nearly scuppering my plan. She surely resented me for trampling over her attempts to resist my work.

This was another of those make or break moments for my Master Plan. I knew I would have to succeed with Kathleen at several levels. I would have to justify taking up her time with this nonsense about the land transfer. At the same time, I would have to let her talk me around so that she'd have a sense of achievement and success. And then, I would have to get her interested in Garry's plight. I knew this would be tough as she was clearly no countess of compassion. Don't get me wrong – compassion remains grossly overrated. It just happened to be a quality I needed for a while.

When I got in to see her, Kathleen was tight. Not just tight of body and tight of clothes like I remembered her, but her beautiful face seemed drawn. Even lined, maybe. She was tense and tetchy.

She launched into the issues with the transfer of land and explained why I couldn't just pull out of the sale at this late stage in proceedings. This was all pretty basic stuff, let me tell you, but I let her explain, I let her build her case as lawyers do. Eventually, she drew breath. I'd thought of repeating the bullshit line I'd fed her PA about sickness in the family, but had wisely thought better of it. I suspected her tolerance level for sob stories would be low, particularly in my case, and I had one to tell her later.

I went to the opposite extreme. I confessed that I'd told her staff a couple of fibs, but assured her that she would understand why when I told her the truth. Then I explained to her that a major developer had been buying up surrounding properties in the last few weeks and that I could potentially get double the current sale price if I could weasel my way out of the original deal. She looked interested. For the first time, she regarded me with sympathy. She recognised me as a fellow traveller with a deviant moral code.

She was silent for a while, obviously considering my options. Then she engaged.

Look, it's purely a financial calculation from here. If you dishonour the contract, you'll be up for the deposit and probably direct and indirect losses the other party incurs, not to mention substantial costs. But, it could be worth taking the hit if the windfall profit from the resale is sufficient to make it worth your while. I'd suggest you approach the developer ASAP and have a chat about how interested he is.

She advised me to move very quickly as she couldn't delay the other party much longer without telling them there was a problem with the transfer.

My interview was drawing to a close and I had to act. I had at last established some sort of rapport with Kathleen and was present on her radar right now. I had got there through being a shit and I somehow had to appeal to her on the basis of higher principles this time. I remained convinced that the bleedin' heart approach was not going to work. I ran through plans B, C and D very fast in my mind.

Hey, Kathleen, thanks very much for your help with that and for understanding where I'm coming from. I appreciate your advice and your counsel very much. If I could change the subject very briefly, I have an interesting case that I want to put your way.

I raised my eyes to check her reaction. Predictably she was on the verge of protest. I held up the palms of my hands to stop her from interrupting me.

Now I know what you're thinking. It's not a shitty property matter again, I promise you that.

She relaxed back in her seat.

Don't worry, I expect you to say no and this time I will accept your answer straight out with no complaint. But, can I describe the case in one sentence only and then I'll go?

She looked at me with an air of indifference and frustration.

Go ahead, she said.

I spat it out. I've a case that will make you famous overnight.

You'd probably say justice was being done and you'd probably crack a smile as I do when I write this.

Mario's balls were healing at last, but Kathleen hadn't visited him for days. The Bitch had brought the kids in again, but there was no way he'd be *road-testicling* his tender tackle on her.

To say Mario wasn't in a good mood is like saying Osama Bin Laden didn't like Americans. His vision was a fraction clearer, but he still couldn't see the TV clearly. Nor could he be sure of the face on the agency nurse he was chatting up on pure instinct. The police were still badgering him to tell them who'd beaten him up. No news was just no news on progress via the double-barrelled dill the lawyers had hired. He still wasn't allowed any alcohol. What's more, the hospital staff showed greater prowess at detecting grog than detecting disease.

All in all, things were not good. In fact, they were fucking bad, to use his own words. Mario was getting bitter, rather than better, and he was enjoying it. Bitterness was a new suit that fitted him perfectly and he liked it so much he did not take it off. He soon found himself accessorising, trying on resentment and malice, and they proved a comfortable fit. He now lacked just one thing to make his outfit perfect. He needed a scapegoat.

Mario revealed the identity of the scapegoat to himself and the whole world at the same time. Ladies and gentlemen, I present to you the cause of all my troubles and of all the evil in the universe. Ladies and gentlemen, give it up for – Maaaxxx!

Max was making all the bad decisions in the gross mishandling of his case. Max stuffed up the negotiations with the money-lenders. And Max had failed to exert even the tiniest amount of pressure on the shoeman to get the problem solved. How can someone who has sworn to uphold even the dubious ethics of the legal profession break that code at will and act like a common criminal, like me, only worse? Anyway, what did I expect from a preening legal wuss like Max? These angry, destructive thoughts occupied his mind as his endless hours of ward-waiting dragged on and on.

Mario determined it was well and truly time to make someone pay. But, even in his new embittered mood, Mario was troubled at the effect his quest for revenge might have on his relationship with Kathleen. She was no longer his favourite person, but he still harboured the hope that she had some excellent reason to be staying away. Even in this maudlin state of mind, he hadn't totally ruled out the possibility that she would appear at any moment – in a nurse's uniform as a preference – to salve his scrotum.

But his worries about Kathleen would not deter him from settling the score. Max would need to pay, come what may. And the beauty of it all was that it would be easy peasy to make Max pay. You see, Max, as smart as he was as a partner in a law firm in the city, seemed pretty stupid to someone as streetwise as Mario.

Mario felt sure Max would have plenty of skeletons in his cupboard and Mario had plenty of time, prostrate on his hospital mattress, to devise a spell that would bring dem dusty Max bones back to life.

I had penetrated Kathleen's defences now in two places. She seemed to accept me as a legitimate client now that my conveyancing job had developed into something more challenging. And I'd dangled some tempting fame-bait in front of her nose and I could tell she was in no mood to resist.

Having played the fame game card, she was waiting for me to make good by elaborating on the case I had in mind. But I had other plans. I needed to think the story through more carefully now that I knew that it had legs and I didn't want to blunder into something that would put her off. I got up immediately and apologised that I had to go.

There you go, I said, I am true to my word and I promised only to take up a minute of your time.

She looked irritated. I stayed on my course.

Once I've caught up with the developer, I'll come and see you briefly to plan the next step, if that's OK, and then I'll fill you in on this extraordinary case I have for you.

I'd never seen Kathleen so passive. She stood up to shake my hand and show me out.

I'll see you next week then, she called to me.

I allowed myself a little inward smile on the way down in the lift. I had at last pressed Kathleen's button and it read *fame*.

It's a lovely scenario to contemplate isn't it? While Julia and Robert were making up in the most basic, time-honoured way and were fulfilling their respective needs for intimacy and shagging, good old dependable Stephen was thrusting himself equally vigorously into the very womb of Robert's existence. But, little did they know and little did they want to know and little would they have wanted to know if someone had said do you want to know what's going wrong in your life right now or shall I leave the details til later?

After all, it is not exactly out of the pages of Debrett's etiquette manual to shout out to the mother of the groom-to-be at the engagement party that her husband is overseas poking another bloke's wife. Not surprisingly, the heckling had a somewhat negative impact on the hardly flowing elegance of Marjorie's speech. Instead of stuttering and apologising her way through her few words as she had started, she found herself entirely lost for words. It wasn't the message she'd heard that had stopped her in her tracks. After all, there was nothing surprising there in what was said. It was just that she didn't really know what she should do next. Not knowing whether to continue as planned or respond to the heckler in some way, she did the only thing a respectable middle-class woman could do in those circumstances. She stood there silently and smiled weakly at the family and friends.

At first, there was a hushed silence in the crowd like the barely audible rumblings that presage a tsunami. But soon the shock wore off and the gathered guests understood that Marjorie was not going to go on. The entire group turned to Stephen to see who could be responsible for such an incredible outburst. Stephen's first inclination was to bolt for the door, but that opportunity went begging. Now he was confronted by a sea of expectant faces, the stage lights had been turned up so he was in full view and there was an air of expectancy that he would perform – maybe Hamlet's soliloquy or say, I come to bury Caesar not to praise him.

So, what could a poor actor do when his hour had come to strut and fret upon the stage? Stephen's show had to go on. And it did magnificently. This Broadway hit would run and run.

GOOD OLD BOBBY'S FUCKING MY WIFE AS WE SPEAK, he bayed to the crowd, SO-CALLED PUSSY DOCTOR FUCKING ROBERT HETHERINGTON, PUSSY BONER MORE LIKE ...

By some silent accord, the crowd and particularly the happy couple had been hoping they could ride out the first interjection. So as not to spoil the joyous occasion, you understand. But the second contribution from Stephen was silently deemed by the group to have spoiled the occasion anyway and so, in good old Aussie fashion, it was on for young and old from that point on. I absolutely love the idea of the professional, well-to-do golfing classes turning into an uncivilised mob more reminiscent of Coolbellup than Cottesloe. And so, the doctors, lawyers, accountants and stockbrokers, hell-bent on revenge, jumped on Stephen like the proverbial human trampoline.

Meanwhile, Julia bounced up and down on Robert in perfect, unsuspecting bliss.

She wasn't sure she should let him in. As Hannah hesitated with her front door still on the chain, she felt chilled by the look in his eye.

I'm not sure this is a good idea, she said.

But, Garry was insistent, calmly insistent. We really need to talk. This matter will only get worse if it's not discussed.

Had she educated him so well that he could find the right words to persuade her to act to his own advantage?

All of us have done the wrong thing here in one way or another, Garry continued, and I think we need to clear the matter up.

She could feel Garry's message turning her. What he was saying was true, indeed it was true to himself. She felt proud of his mature expression. How could she not honour her lifetime's work of encouraging people to communicate? She could not refuse his request to talk things over. But, at the same time, she sensed there was something in Garry's demeanour that she had not seen before and it made her shudder.

They sat at the kitchen table. She asked him politely if he would like some tea and he knew he must accept even though he was champing at the bit to get on with what he had to do. She made the tea with her usual meticulous care. The silence weighed heavily on them both. What a contrast to those joyful, inspiring afternoon teas they'd shared not so long ago!

Once the table was set and the tea was all but poured, Hannah spoke before Garry could get things started the way he'd planned.

I had such high hopes for you, you know. I was so close, so terribly close, to setting you up for life.

Setting me up for life? he ridiculed her in a sarcastic tone, ruining my life more like.

I had to make sure you were worthy.

Worthy of what – being set up?

Unfortunately, your frame of mind is dismissive. Regrettably, it is preventing you from listening to me. That is a shame, a great shame, Hannah emphasised, because what I have to say will help you understand what has happened to you.

Garry made a gesture of resignation that young people know means, whatever.

Yes, it is true that what I did has harmed you. Yes, it is true that, in retrospect, I regret what I did. But, what I did was a test. And it was not a pointless or meaningless test. I had a reason, a very worthwhile reason, to test you ...

Garry bit back. What possible reason could justify ruining my life when I had done nothing to you? Nothing, when I could have done so much! I could have ripped you off, done a botch job –

Stolen from me?

Hannah instantly regretted saying that – it was cheap and it was beneath her. But she set that aside to take the opportunity to get the story out while Garry was looking at her open-mouthed in disbelief. She blurted it out while she had the chance.

I was thinking of making you my heir.

Garry was staring at her like a roo frozen in the headlights. It was as if this one last blow to the orderly normality of his life had driven him to freeze in front of the oncoming car so he could meet his maker.

I'm not exactly young any more, as I'm sure you may have noticed. However, I'm not exactly a nobody on the scale of modern day measures of a person's worth. You see, I am a very wealthy woman. Not in cash, you understand, but I have considerable assets and investments here and overseas. Of course, I have no living relatives thanks to the Nazis, as you know, and so there is no one to leave my considerable fortune to.

Garry sat with his head in his hands.

And so, I thought of you.

Hannah paused to allow Garry to respond. She wasn't sure what to expect. Comprehension, regret, gratitude? But, there was nothing. He remained slumped in his chair with his head still in his hands. In the absence of reaction, Hannah felt compelled to press on.

But I couldn't leave a fortune to a virtual stranger, could I?

She paused again, but he didn't look up. I was so impressed

with you. So impressed with how you'd grown so much in such a short time. I was amazed at your hunger for what I had to give you. For what I could teach you.

Hannah was now disturbed by Garry's inaction. Experience told her that, with men of this age, when the reaction eventuated it would be sudden and it would be forceful. Instinctively, she moved to assuage the inevitable anger.

I seek your forgiveness for my arrogance in all of this. I recognise that I have been guilty of appalling pride. I meant no harm by it, but I know that I was driven in part by my need to develop a protégé. A protégé – a testament to my skill and glory. Please forgive me for that. It was weak and it was wrong.

Still Garry sat. This time, Hannah kept speaking because she knew now that Garry would respond when he was good and ready and at a time she would not be able to predict.

I needed somehow to confirm that what I thought I saw in you was really there. I thought it was only fair for me to assure myself that my inheritance would end up in hands that wouldn't fritter it away and squander what my family had amassed through so much toil and tragedy. So, I hit upon a plan that would allow me very simply to test your character. It seemed apt and reasonable to me at the time. If you could be trusted to return the valuables to me that you had found, you would be certain to honour them when they rightfully became your own.

Garry now was staring at her wild-eyed and she could see the veins in his head bulging with blood. He might kill me now and I wouldn't blame him if he did, Hannah was thinking.

Hannah by now was in full flow in the confessional box and was going to make a clean breast of things, even if it cost her life.

Mark my words, I had no doubt that you would return the valuables to me. Not a doubt in the world. To tell you the absolute truth, a tiny part of me was hoping that you wouldn't. But that was just to add a little spark of excitement into an old woman's dreary life. And, Garry, please believe me when I say that I know that I was right about *you*. I really do understand now that if it had been up to you alone, you would have returned those things and passed my pathetic little test.

Garry lurched to his feet. His chair rocked on its legs and teetered then toppled to the floor. He stood over her with both fists clenched and Hannah locked onto her executioner's eyes, finding the inner strength to face up to the inevitable. He was squeezing the trigger, but he couldn't fire. Decency welled up inside him to fight his anger and blood lust for revenge, but he knew deep down that he wasn't holding back from hitting her because he was a good guy. The fact was he couldn't hit her because he knew what she was saying was the truth. He would have returned everything if it had been up to him.

He remained standing over her, but his hands slumped back to his sides. Hannah continued to purge herself of guilt.

Hit me if you want, I do deserve it, but I have to say what has to be said now that I have you here. When your wife came to visit me out of the blue, it confirmed absolutely that I had been right about you. I knew for sure after I had met her that you would have returned the ring and the money – all of it – but your wife's morality does not match yours.

Garry turned on his heels in the direction of the front door. Hannah couldn't stop now so close to the full story being told.

So, I couldn't leave you everything, you understand. I couldn't leave it to you and *her*, she called down the corridor to him.

He turned on his heels immediately and within seconds was towering over her again. He jabbed an angry finger into her face. I can't stand by and let you ruin my life!

Then he ran from the house.

He scrambled his way into the ute as quickly as he possibly could and then pushed down the knob to centrally lock all the doors. Garry banged his head violently against the steering wheel. He'd locked the doors to make it harder to go back and kill her. He struggled to formulate some thoughts through the blanketing fog of his anger. His heart rate slowed but he realised that calmness hadn't robbed him of his murder lust.

He muttered to himself out loud as if reciting some obscure mantra. I can't let that woman ruin my life. I can't let that woman ruin my life.

Meanwhile, Hannah sat motionless at the kitchen table, surprisingly calm. She was calm because the undercurrent of violence she had seen in Garry had further validated her behaviour. After all, she'd been right to set him a test. And now she also knew it had been the right thing to do to tell the police about the return of the ring and the denial of the stolen cash.

Seated in her swanky legal office once again, I couldn't help noticing that Kathleen was still looking the worse for wear. There were signs of black under her once sparkling eyes and her once luminous skin was tight. She snapped at her PA over the intercom and then apologised for having to go and sort something out herself. I took deep pride in her faded appearance as I felt sure it was I who was responsible.

I sipped at my Nespresso latte that far out-tasted the nasty instant coffee we serve visitors in my government office. I looked out of the window at the marvellous view over the Swan River. Naturally the best vistas were reserved for the partners, but it was impressive nonetheless. She swept back into the office, snapping me out of my riverscape reverie.

Our river's so ridiculously underdeveloped, I suggested, even with that new quay coming to life.

It's amazing but I don't actually notice the view any more, Kathleen responded.

Then she changed the subject with disconcerting speed. A case that will make me famous, I think you were saying.

Yes, I did say that.

I was intent on dragging out the suspense as long as possible. The base facts of Garry's case were so mundane that I knew they'd hold Kathleen's interest for as long as that bell tower below that had been designed to conform rather then confound. While I knew the celebrity angle could be my winning suit, I was worried she might never have heard of Hannah. I still had to go with it. Surely some rising star young female professional would include Hannah as one of her heroines? I had brought collateral backup with me in the form of magazines and books featuring Hannah. Anyway, it was time to weigh in, so I did.

This is a bizarre situation that stars Hannah Baumgarten.

The Hannah Baumgarten? she said.

I'm not sure what made me feel happier. That my gamble on recognition had paid off or the inanity of the interrogative – *the* Hannah Baumgarten? – as if it was likely there'd be two of them.

The Hannah Baumgarten, I said in huge italics.

Wow, I didn't even know she lived here. Or does she live in Melbourne?

No, she lives here.

Cool. Well what has she done and, more importantly, how does it involve you?

Well, it involves her and a builder friend of mine – a really nice guy, who's in a heap of trouble now, thanks to her.

I recounted the sorry story just as Garry had explained it to me. I now know he hadn't let me in on every sordid detail of this saga, but there was enough in it to hold the legal eagle's interest.

And why exactly are you coming to *me* with this?

Don't worry, I was well prepared for this question. It was as if the autocue was running and I merely had to look at the screen and read out the script,

I'm coming to you for a whole host of reasons. The first is because you've got balls, if you'll pardon the expression. Perhaps I should have said nerve. In other words, I know you have the spunk to take something hairy on. Secondly, Garry is not wealthy and he has a wife and two small kids to support. So, he can't afford normal legal rates with a major firm like this. And, thirdly, and this really is the clincher, what better way is there to climb a few rungs of the legal ladder than to take on a celebrity case and get yourself plastered all over the papers? Locally, nationally and internationally, I explained.

She said nothing, but merely stared into my eyes for what was an uncomfortably long time.

I'll be honest with you, she said still holding my gaze. I don't trust you. I'm not trying to be offensive in saying that. What I mean by it is that I suspect you have ulterior motives behind everything you do.

She paused to see if I wanted to react. I didn't.

OK, well, I couldn't understand why you brought that conveyancing case to me, at least at the start and I'm not buying your reasons for bringing Hannah Baumgarten to me either. What's more, I'm pretty good at sussing out men's nefarious agendas. Most of them want to fuck me and will go to any lengths to do it. But not you. I don't get that impression with you.

I responded in kind, looking silently back at her. This time I outstared her.

I'm sorry if I've offended you, she said.

Not at all, I said. Everyone has agendas that they are playing out. I have them. You certainly have them. Sometimes in business we get so used to reeling them out that we don't know how to stop. Maybe I've come across that way with Garry. I apologise if I have. It's simple really. He's a nice guy, he's in trouble, he can't afford the help he needs and I'm not a bastard all the time. Basically, I want to get some help for Garry and let's face it, a high profile case won't do you any harm.

She threw her hair back and laughed out loud. OK then, she said, bring him in but don't imagine that I trust you.

Maybe I don't trust you either, I bantered, to transform her misgivings into a game.

Fair enough then, let's not trust each other, she said enjoying the sport, things are safer that way!

I need a fucking beer with a fucking fag. No one deserved these simple pleasures more than Mario. After all that he'd been through, and now, not least after a lifetime's wait for his mama and papa and nonna to piss off out of his apartment.

Mario could not see that well, but well enough to know his place had been cleaned up and tidied such that all his things were in the sort of stupid place that some ancient person would put them. He winced at the thought of his nonna tidying up his porno DVDs and his mags, but consoled himself that she'd always loved sausages and big, well-stuffed ones at that.

A horrifying thought entered his head. Don't tell me they've confiscated my booze and smokes. He hobbled to the fridge. He was shocked. There was food in it. Mercifully his eyes settled upon a couple of Stellas lying down at the back, trying really hard to blend in with their alien companions – lasagna, gnocchi, prosciutto and, of all things, vegetables.

Thank you God, I will go to church every Sunday, Mario said, confident that a God who knew everything would know that he was joking.

He instantly regretted his hasty outburst of religious fervour, even if he hadn't meant it. After all the true test of faith lay ahead. Had the Almighty preserved his stash of smokes? No packs on the dresser and none behind the bar near the pool table. His belief in God now hung on the stolen cartons he bought down the pub. He made his way to the wardrobe and painstakingly got up on a chair like he was climbing Everest. He moved aside the suitcases. He shifted the grotesque tapestry of Venice his zia Pina had given him after her trip. And there they were, his little angels, safe and sound. His faith in God and his belief in the infallibility of the pope were now fully restored.

How great is this? he said out loud, rubbing his hands in glee. He was now back home with a cold one and a cancer stick. Fucking beautiful, it was, fucking beautiful. He alternated long, refreshing drags on his ciggie with deep, savouring swigs from the stubbie. He swished the nectar of the gods around his mouth like a wine taster from way back. Needless to say, he did not spit it out.

He blissed out for a while, but his anxieties were still at the back of his mind. Soon they muscled their way to the front. How long will it take the bad boys to find out I'm home? When will they come calling again? He was no nearer getting anything out of the shoeman, thanks to the farcical carryings on led by mummy's boy, Max. Kathy had at last found the time to visit him, but she was like a broken Pollyanna record – Sebastian will get the money out of him, he always does.

Mario was unconvinced. Thanks to battling through the pain barrier and finding the will to survive, he had regained a measure of self-belief. He was feeling confident that he was much more streetwise than these hoity-toity lawyers would ever be and maybe a bit smarter than them despite their college education and their fancy degrees.

Mario had a plan of his own. A plan that would not only solve his money problems and therefore save his life, but a payback plan that would be deeply satisfying as it was dripping with revenge. Half a million dollars would be nothing to Max. Well, even if it was an amount of concern, it would be insignificant compared to the losses he would suffer from being disbarred. Think of the lifetime of rip-off fees foregone. Think of the public humiliation at the Weld Club.

Mario had spent a lot of time thinking through his game plan. In classic style, he'd written out the various options on the back of an envelope. It was from an ill-timed begging letter urging him to give generously to those less fortunate than himself.

The plan itself was simple enough. Blackmail Max.

How hard could that be with a dodgy dude in Max's position? But then the menacing image of the double-barrelled dill came to mind. Even though he'd been as useful as tits on a bull in his own case, he wondered whether he might be more dangerous protecting his boss's back. The thought chilled him for a while, but then he thought, what the fuck? Well, what the fuck indeed? The *Mafiosi* are going to kill me anyway if I don't get the money, so what are Max and Sebastian going to do to me? Kill me again?

Mario found it very comforting that there was nothing Max could do to him that wasn't going to happen to him anyway. In fact, the life sentence hanging over him from the boys in black was actually a deterrent to Max dealing with Mario himself. After all, how would the nice boys with pigtails feel about Max if he got in the way of them collecting five hundred G that was owing to them? Mario smiled to himself at the very thought. It's worth being snuffed by Max just to think about him being slit open along the fine lines of his fucking pin-striped suit.

As an afterthought, it crossed his mind that Max could go the filth on account of being blackmailed. Would he do that? Would he take the risk? No way he'd do that. He might try to rub me out, but there's no way he'd risk the police crawling over his grubby goings-on.

So Mario settled on the simplest of plans. He left Max a message on his voicemail. From a friend. But it was a friend with Mario's voice with no effort made to disguise it.

I have drafted a letter to *The West Australian*'s law reporter, the friend who sounded like Mario said, with a copy to The Law Society of WA. I've given this letter to an acquaintance of mine and I've asked him to post them this time next week. Please give my regards to Sebastian Maitland-Whatever and let him know he'll be famous shortly, in fact almost as famous as you. I could still contact my friend with the letters and beg him not to post them. But, that really depends on you. It depends on you doing what you promised from the start but have so far failed to deliver. You said you'd fix my problem for me and for your sake I hope you do. Cheers for now.

The project was going oh, so well. So much turmoil, so much mayhem, so much heartache, so much chaos. It was magnificent. Yet I was doing it tough, I really was. I was wondering if it was all worth it. Could I really be expected to put up with Lisa for one moment longer?

Lisa drove me crazy at the best of times. But, once Julia got back from Bali, and her goings-on with Robert and Stephen started to resemble a bad episode of *Days of Our Lives*, things had become unbearable with Lisa. She was obsessed with Julia's woes and there was no other subject of conversation she would entertain.

I fought back the urge to scream at her. I know Julia's in desperate trouble. I dropped her in it, thank you very much!

Although I felt like entering a monastery or inventing a distant but very sick relative I had to visit for a lengthy period, I knew I had to hang in there and endure the unendurable. I had to keep a handle on the progress of things and I couldn't bail while the job was yet unfinished.

Eventually I had to succumb to Lisa's relentless pressure. The constant nightly shelling had got to the morale of my civilian population and, weakened by the endless sleepless nights from the blitzkrieg, I emerged from the beleaguered tube station of my sanity and surrendered to Lisa's demands for peace. Yes, I will see Julia myself alone and at least give you an opinion on how she's coping.

I didn't want to risk going anywhere near her house at this point because, by all accounts, Stephen was out of his tree. I coaxed Julia out to the new wine store that had opened to serve the idle rich of Cottesloe. I waited amongst the wine racks that doubled up as a place to drink the over-priced wines.

Eventually she burst into the joint in a flurry of lateness. I was surprised. She looked immaculate. I bought a bottle of the exquisite Cloudy Bay sauvignon blanc at a price devised by a malevolent mathematician and we perched at the uncomfortable coffee table at the front of the bar, sorry, wine store. I told her, quite genuinely, that she looked great. I did this out of annoyance that Lisa had been beating up the story as usual, rather than from a desire to flatter or flirt.

Oh, oh – this innocent little remark had in some unaccountable way extracted the digit that had been precariously but strategically placed in this dyke (sic!). The waters burst in a flood of mixed metaphors.

Well, I've just been to the day spa for a makeover, haven't I? I couldn't possibly have come here looking like death, could I?

Obviously, despair brings out the rhetorical question in people.

Anyway, what can I do? Stephen is way out of control, way beyond the pale. To tell you the truth, I dread him coming home. I tremble when I hear his car pull up. Why is he still there? I really don't know. And you can imagine what it's doing to the girls, can't you? It's a nightmare for them. You'd think they'd understand what I've been going through all these years with that man. But they can't see that, can they? All they can see is what's just happened. And, of course, that makes me the bad one, doesn't it? Look what you've done to Daddy, Jazzie actually said to me yesterday. God, it's a nightmare, I can tell you. I'm living out some dreadful American soapie!

Just as I was tallying up the score of rhetorical versus non-rhetorical questions to see if I should respond, Julia changed direction with the unseemly haste of a prime minister reading the report from a focus group.

Anyway, how are *you*? she asked.

I laughed out loud. Well I had to, didn't I? Oh God, she's got me doing it now. I couldn't help myself (there, I resisted the interrogative). It was such a ludicrous, momentary reflex of decency to ask. I didn't reply. She didn't hesitate to fill the sound vacuum.

You know, it's all become clear to me about Stephen. He's an addict.

That got my attention. I raised a quizzical eyebrow.

He's an addictive personality.

This sounded much less interesting – and alas it was. It's amazing how distressed and traumatised people, who can't at that point think clearly enough to boil a kettle, claim the most brilliant insights into their lives that they were mysteriously incapable of finding when their mental functioning was normal.

You know, at last I've nailed his problem. Stephen goes through life moving from addiction to addiction. It was sex once, then alcohol and now it's work. And of course, he's had all these obsessions – motorbikes, German cars, antiques, everything really.

Stupidly, I dropped my guard to daydream for a second.

What do you think? she asked suddenly, catching me out.

I don't know, I said, buying some time to recover from my attention deficit. Lisa's very worried about you, you know.

That's sweet. She's so sweet. She's such a good friend.

She thinks you might do something silly.

Well, that would be unusual for me, of late, wouldn't it? She laughed and then fell serious again.

I've got to do something. I have to sort something out. We can't all go on like this. I worry for the girls. I told Stephen he should move out. But he's so irrational and so unreasonable. You know, I speak to him in the most calm and reasonable way. I tell him that I've messed things up and I apologise for the hurt I've caused him. But he won't listen, will he? He must know that he has to move out. The girls obviously need to be with their mother and I can't go traipsing around trying to find an apartment somewhere in Freo, can I? Anyway, he flies into a terrible rage when I try to talk to him so I don't see how he's ever going to see sense.

Lisa sent you to check up on me then, she said with another dazzling sidestep.

Basically, yes, I replied, relieved to have my cover blown. Is there actually anything I can do for you?

Talk sense to Stephen, man to man.

Thankfully she must have picked up on the expression of total horror on my face.

I'm only joking, she added quickly.

Nothing I can do then? I pounced on the opportunity to get myself off the hook.

No, nothing.

I inwardly sighed in relief and, mission accomplished, wondered how I might high tail it out of there.

Actually, there is something.

Can you give me Hannah's number?

Actually, it's OK, she continued. I can find her number myself – I can see you don't want to get involved.

No no, I insisted, I'll text it to you.

One sirloin steak, medium rare, with the peppercorn poison, was enough to stop him in his tracks. All bark and no bite, Sebastian thought. The body twitched for a few seconds of futile resistance. The silence was deathly, now that the snapping, snarling and frothing had died away. All he could hear was the distant drone of the traffic on the Kwinana Freeway.

The guard dog was a predictable response to his earlier visit to the shoe factory. Having dragged the demised Doberman out of sight, he checked carefully for other improved security measures. He shook his head at how mean some people are. And what bad businessmen they are! He'd hoped for some security cameras to show they'd treated his first visit with due respect. He looked around the entire site. No CCTV. Nothing but the dog. The dead dog.

Once stage one was completed, Sebastian cut a hole in the chain mesh fence and slipped inside with his heavy container. He'd been to his local Bunnings hardware store earlier in the day and found the sort of canister he was looking for. He had found one with a warning that said, in effect, this stuff will go up like a fucking inferno if some stupid bastard drops a butt around here. He carried it round to the side of the unit where he'd previously discovered they piled their recyclable cardboard boxes against the showroom wall.

He didn't stint in his sloshing of the this-will-burn-your-balls-off liquid all over the mountain of cardboard. But, oh dear, what a shame, despite the serious warning to be found on the metal container, some stupid bastard was about to drop his cigarette just where he wasn't supposed to.

He continued with his preparations until he was confident the stage was set. He then slipped back through the hole in the fence to the car and made the phone call as planned.

While he waited, he smoked some weed to relax him and played some Marilyn Manson to excite him. A perfect combination of downers and uppers. In around twenty minutes, in line with his original estimate, he saw car headlights approach the factory gate. He cut the sound. This was a critical point. He saw only one guy get out of the car. The new arrival unhooked the padlock to the gate and drove in. There could still be accomplices in the car, so he still needed to approach with caution.

If the factory owner had noticed the absence of his newly acquired guard dog, he showed no signs of it. He walked straight to the front of the warehouse, opened the padlock and pushed up the security roller shutter. Sebastian waited for the owner to conclude that the call had been a hoax and then he slipped though the fence. He skirted around near the car to check whether there was any further company. Another insult – the guy had come alone. Fair enough though, he didn't know it was Sebastian.

As the shoeman stepped out again into the cool air and turned his back to roll down the shutter, Sebastian tapped him on the shoulder. The factory owner cried out. Not surprisingly, there was a look of absolute terror on his face when he found himself up close and personal with a balaclavaed man.

Sebastian motioned to him to move around the side of the building. When he turned the corner, he saw a huge pile of cardboard in full view from the security light that had turned itself on with the detected movement.

I need an indication from you now of your willingness to cooperate, Sebastian cooed in his ear. I'm sure you agree that debts must be repaid. Especially by those with cash in hand from not paying their taxes.

Sebastian paused a moment to let his message sink in.

You should also realise by now that we have the capability and the will to destroy this factory whenever we choose. What's more, you've met me now and I'm sure I don't need to spell out for you how much pleasure it would give me to cut off your dick and feed it to you before I kill you.

One end of a pair of handcuffs was dangling from a downpipe next to the cardboard colossus where Sebastian had left them. He invited his victim to attach himself to the spare bracelet and he cordially complied. He removed the man's mobile phone and tossed it some metres away. Gently so as not to damage it. He demanded the man's car keys and they were handed over. Sebastian drove the car over with the front passenger door positioned inches from the sweating man's face. He then liberally poured the remainder of the flammable liquid over the base of the fire site and struck himself a camping-style, long-stemmed match.

Terrified eyes followed him as Sebastian made his way back to the imprisoned man. Sebastian brandished the match with theatrical exaggeration.

Can I take it the debt will be settled in, say, forty-eight hours?

The man nodded. He had still not said one word.

Excellent, Sebastian concluded.

I've put the key to the cuffs in your glovebox, Sebastian called out to him, clumsily dropping the match.

He slipped back through the chain mail fence, contented with such satisfying work, started up his car and was gone.

As I reflect on my triumphs with the Master Plan, I recognise that the meeting with Julia in the wine store was a turning point. Of itself, it was a nothing sort of event. Tiresome and predictable, if the truth be told. But, the half-expected revelation at the end did have a profound effect on me.

Julia wants Hannah's number. Julia and Hannah together. Unsupervised. This was the stuff to bring me undone. Without a doubt, this contact could be averted. I could use my legendary evasive skills to see off this attack. I could refuse to pass on the number. I could kick back against the idea. I could tell Julia that Hannah would do her no good. I could make up stories about the damage Hannah has done to clients in Julia's circumstances. I could enlist Lisa's assistance with my deception. That would be easy.

More of a challenge would be to get Hannah to refuse to see Julia. I was still working on Hannah's article and we were still getting on famously. Verbal jousting, mental fancy footwork and the like. Hannah could be persuaded not to see Julia if I told her she was already seeing someone else. These medicos like to stick together to defend their pay packets so Hannah could be talked out of it with a good enough story.

So there were many options in front of me, viable ones, with which to resist Julia's objective. And yet, I felt strangely unwilling to use any of them. I put her off by saying I'd had trouble with my mobile and had lost a lot of my stored numbers. I could've stalled her for a bit longer along these lines. But, I just didn't feel like it.

Was I getting tired at the business end of a long campaign? Not really. Had I lost the stomach for the fight? Definitely not. What was it then? I let my mind wander at tedious meetings. Not only during the vast expanses of meaningless drivel, but at some more critical times. I had to snap myself back into focus. The Minister caught me out on one occasion.

So, why do you insist when you can't muster an adequate argument for it?

Because I wanted to, I stammered in response.

That wasn't like me. But, it was true. I *wanted* Julia to meet with Hannah.

I thought it through. I got back on top. I got to grips with the issue and I could see that it was all positive. It was nothing to do with any lack of will or any inadequacy. It was about moving forward. I was ready to move towards the denouement. That was exciting. That was going to get me up again. It was time to move towards the thrill of the consequences of my actions.

I could hardly wait to drive forward to the true satisfaction that I was due. I texted Julia the number just as I promised. A thrill of anticipation, and of fear to be honest, quivered through my body. I was like a kid on Christmas morning. I couldn't wait to open another present. Which one next? The one that rattles seductively or the big box? Perhaps two pressies at once. That would be the thing.

I rang Mario too. A few pleasantries. Fancy catching up with my mate Robert at the Riverside? He sounded more upbeat than of late, a bit more in control of his life. He even managed a couple of weak jokes.

Come to the Riverside? Nah.

It will do you good, I cajoled him.

You're turning into my nonna.

I'll pick her up and bring her round to your office right now if you don't come.

I surrender – see my white flag?

I picked him up and drove him down to the bar. Naturally, I chose the after work time when there would be a good chance of catching Robert. Robert was the real reason for choosing this particular grouping of presents to unwrap. I needed to see how he was going. I was so intimately acquainted with how his girlfriend was faring that I was bursting to discover how much damage he was suffering himself. I'd finally advanced him the loan a week or so earlier and so I had legitimacy in visiting the bar. After all, in a funny sort of way, it was now my bar, too.

Coincidentally, we all arrived at the same time. Robert looked as handsome as ever, but a little greyer and a little older, I told myself. I insisted on buying a bottle and I delighted in leaving

Mario and Robert together – alone.

This was thrilling. It was truly scary. I was alive and my whole body was tingling with anticipation again. I couldn't wait for the whole delicious truth to come tumbling out. How would it happen exactly? I had no idea where the first breach in the wall would occur and where the first stresses and strains in the foundations would be felt. I deserved excitement like this.

I joined the two of them with the booze and some glasses.

Don't let me interrupt you, I said.

The Horsemen of the Apocalypse were out riding now.

He didn't need to be a rocket scientist to know the police would call him very soon. So, outwardly, Garry went about his business resigned to his fate. *Outwardly* meant to his workmates and his friends. At home, a sort of unholy truce had been declared. Kirsty wasn't in his face all the time, she was just indifferent. That hurt him almost as much as her open hostility. He didn't bother to tell her about his statement to the police. He omitted to inform her of his visit to Hannah's. So Kirsty didn't know that the various stories about the ring and the money just didn't gel.

When the call came through asking if he could pop down to answer a few more questions, he was relaxed and unfazed.

Sure, he said.

The fact was that he was resigned. Resigned to his fate that his life was basically fucked.

The interview was lengthy and embarrassing. Humiliating, was the word. Garry repressed an almost uncontrollable desire to punch the detective, who reeled out the facts in a sickening is-it-the-case-that-you-said-this-but-in-that-case-how-do-you-explain-that-she-said-the-other smarmy, holier than thou, I-know-more-than-you, obnoxious sort of way.

Eventually Garry tottered out of the police station with his head spinning and his guts churning. He felt like killing someone, but he didn't know if it should be Hannah or his wife. A suspect who hadn't yet given up would at least have tried to reconcile the conflicting, incriminating stories. But he hadn't even tried to explain all that away.

He could've said the old lady had forgotten where she'd put the money after all. He could've dismissed the detectives' assertions that Ms Baumgarten had been on the ball with them throughout. He could've resolutely protested his innocence. He could even have told them the truth. But, instead he stared into the distance and said nothing. The detectives had been vaguely sympathetic to him the first time or at least had been keeping an open mind.

During his latest visit, they had been snarling, superior and threatening.

The interview was terminated when he demanded to have a lawyer present.

Fair enough, you can go, the sergeant responded with a yawn. You'd better get yourself a good one, he called out to Garry who was halfway out the door.

Garry fingered the piece of paper in his pocket that I'd given him with Kathleen's number on it, but said nothing as the door banged behind him. All he could think of was making someone pay. Someone should pay for what had been done to him. These two women between them had conspired to unmask him as the wanker and the wimp he truly was. Did he even have the courage to achieve one small thing? To make someone, anyone, pay?

Of course, Julia and Robert in the apartment above the bar had one or two problems of their own. OK, they had a fuck or two, but they also had sorrows aplenty to drown together – in vast quantities of wholesale liquor.

The apartment had been Robert's full-time bachelor pad for a week or two now. That fucking tosspot Stephen had turned everything to shit for Robert with his outrageous antics at the engagement party. Marjie didn't care that much that he wasn't really at a gynaecologists' convention on Bali. Well, not of the kind he said he was at, anyway. Nor did she really care that he went there to bonk some blonde. There was nothing new in that. But, she did seem to care an awful lot about her total humiliation at the engagement party in front of her family, her friends and all the hangers-on she knew.

Robert thought she'd come round fairly quickly, being a tough old stick. But the old girl was taking this latest turn of events very badly. She was barely civil with him, even when he was apologising to her with sincerity in his voice. He knew things domestically had hit a new low when the campaign of flowers and chocolates, and even the pièce de résistance – the new puppy – weren't improving his popularity in the polls.

In the circumstances, Robert decided to make himself scarce for a while in the expectation that absence would make the heart grow fonder. Besides, *abstinence* did not traditionally make *his* heart grow fonder and there were obvious benefits in being in town within easy reach for Julia, should she need him at any time of the night.

In truth, Julia was faring no better. Her kids were a total mess. She thought her girls, being at a private school, would take family breakdown in their stride given that the parents of their friends were all separated or divorced. But no such luck. Julia was finding them incredibly selfish, as they wallowed in self-pity without a thought for what she was going through. To make matters worse, on the rare occasions they would show compassion for a parent, they would always firmly take their father's side.

So, Robert and Julia would huddle and snuggle there in the apartment and console each other as best they could. Then something amazing happened. It surprised them both. It even amazed Robert who spoke the words.

We should get a house together.

What?

We should get a house together.

Are you serious?

Of course, I am – we'll find somewhere with a pool for the girls and close enough to school for them so it's not a total upheaval.

But you haven't even met them yet.

Well I want to, Robert responded affectionately nuzzling her neck. Bring them to the bar some time soon, tomorrow maybe, and let them meet me. They'll love me, I know they will.

Julia was lost for words, so Robert continued.

All women love me, you know that, he said tickling her until she let out a shriek and then collapsed into an uncontrollable fit of the giggles.

Fortunately, things were nowhere near as gloomy everywhere around town. Kathleen rocked up to Mario's apartment unannounced, with a very expensive bottle and a very alluring dress.

At that point, as Leonard Cohen would say, Mario's body still ached in the places he used to play. But his vision was gradually improving and the presence of Kathleen in all her glory was literally a sight for his sore eyes. Tonight, she was bright and breezy, free and easy. She was in that flirty, fun mood he loved. Mario was desperate to get into the spirit of things and have some serious fun, but he was feeling distinctly guarded. Guarded wasn't really something he did. He was probably the most unguarded creature in the universe. But, the thing was – what did she know? What did she know of the letter to Max? What did she know of this blackmail? Did she know and not just care? Wasn't she worried where this would end up for her? How could she be up for fun with the blackmailer? Maybe Max didn't tell her what was happening.

His thoughts were interrupted by the return of the goodtime girl from the kitchen. She had the bottle of Henschke open and two glasses were waving in the air.

I've something nice to give you later, she said sloshing him a glass of red, but only after you give me something first.

After Mario's purgatory spent in clinical constraint, a roll in the hay with the luscious lawyer was a source of much joy. All the more so because it was unexpected and because he was undeserving of it too. Once the deed was done and the offer was honoured, Kathleen excused herself to go to the ensuite. Then she set about topping up the glasses and disappeared into the living room to fetch her handbag.

I've got a wonderful surprise for you, Mr Martinelli, she announced seductively.

Well, while I am a sex machine, darling, as you know, I don't think I can back up for another round just yet.

Mario was getting his mojo back and it felt good. Kathleen got back into bed, took a swig of her wine and then insisted he close his eyes and hold out his hand. He told her he didn't need to close his eyes not to be able to see. She teased him by lowering him a breast for a feel and then exchanging it for a beer mug from the bedside table.

OK, Kathleen said, enough. No more messing about.

She lowered a single narrow piece of paper into his outstretched palm.

Still no peeking, she advised. OK – now!

He opened his eyes and looked down at a cheque for a considerable sum of money.

What do you think? she asked, clapping her hands in excitement. Didn't I tell you Sebastian double-barrelled would come up trumps?

Kathleen was pleased with herself. She ducked down under the covers, just keeping her head high enough to sip the wine.

You don't seem very happy, she chided him.

I'm stunned, was all Mario could say.

Mario's head was spinning and he didn't know what to think. It felt like every emotion in his fairly limited repertoire was fighting for supremacy. He felt elated, immensely relieved, flabbergasted, disbelieving, horrified and frightened. But, above all, he felt confused.

Drink up and celebrate, she said.

He didn't know what to do. Kathy was acting if she didn't know about the blackmail. Well, that was the point. Was she acting or did she really not know? Why did she bonk him and not just deliver the cheque, or even put it in the mail? Why was she hanging around in bed when she'd always resisted his desperate pleadings for an action replay in the past? What should he do? Should he play dumb and enjoy himself while the going was good? Should he explain himself to her? Should he tell her the truth that that bastard Max deserved everything coming to him? Or should he justify himself and explain that it was a stupid mistake made as a result of the cocktail of paranoia-inducing drugs he'd been taking? Or should he be a tough, real man and tell her that the cheque didn't change a damn thing and that Max was going down because Mario was just that kind of guy?

Mario said to himself unhelpfully, I've got no fucking idea what to do next.

But then, God kept his promise to the world of bringing solace to those who are suffering. God made Kathy solve Mario's dilemma, in her most seductive voice, no less.

All that silly nonsense you concocted for Max will be history now, I presume.

Oh, you presume do you? he said mockingly, trying to work his knees inside hers.

No really, before any more of this, I need to know. We delivered for you in the end, didn't we? Didn't Max come up with the goods in the end?

Mario watched his desire shrivel like a prawn – a phenomenon that usually alarmed him. But, on this occasion, it didn't seem to matter. He had a nasty feeling he'd been used.

I'll give you credit though, Mario, Kathleen said cheerily, I've never seen anyone get to Max like that. Boy, was he spitting chips! The veins were standing up in his neck just like one of those footy coaches you see on the box. I swear he would've wrung your neck if you'd been anywhere nearby. And the names he called you. Well, they were enough to make a modest girl like me blush from head to toe. And what do you think he was going to do when he'd got himself calm enough to think? Yes, he was going to contact Sebastian. He was going to make it a double act for him. Get two wops for the price of one, she giggled to herself, pouring another glass of wine.

Mario gave up on his petrified penis.

And yet, things turned out so well for you, didn't they? she continued. And I wonder why that is? I wonder who has a little guardian angel to look after his interests and keep him from harm? For that matter, I wonder who managed to talk sense into the raging bull and persuade him to let Sebastian perform his magic?

Mario didn't guess.

I told Max things would sort themselves out once Sebastian had done his stuff, and surprise surprise, I was right, wasn't I?

But Mario just couldn't play ball. He desperately wanted to make everything right and tell Kathleen what she'd come to his bed to hear. His instincts told him not to. He knew he wasn't brainy smart, but he did know something about self-preservation. His street wisdom was speaking to him loud and clear. That bastard Max and his pitbull Sebastian will be coming after you as soon as they think you're weak.

Now listen here, my lovely, he said scrambling out of bed and hoisting on his pants. Don't think I don't appreciate everything you've done for me. What with the money. What with your performance in the sack, which was top notch.

He interrupted himself, pulling a T-shirt over his head.

I certainly do appreciate all of that. But, I have to be honest. I don't appreciate the company you keep at your company. Quite amusing really, don't you think? I don't like that nancy boy Max one little bit and, what's more, I don't trust him neither. So, I'm going to bank this cheque before something goes wrong and then, once the money is cleared, and the boys in black get paid off, guess what. That's right, I'll call off publication of the letter.

This clearly took Kathleen by surprise but Mario ploughed on.

But I'm gonna keep my little scheme in place for insurance, you might say. So that, in the event that something bad does happen to me again, well, the people who should know, will know, about a certain lawyer and what a certain lawyer does that is just a few suburbs outside the neighbourhood of the law.

He beamed down at her uncomprehending face and pecked her on the cheek.

Stay as long as you like, darlin', in fact stay for a while and I'll give you one for the road, if you're a very lucky girl, when I get back.

His heart was pounding at an unhealthy speed as he slipped out of the apartment.

Hannah was feeling the same way. At my age, this stress is not good. I will need to meditate again today. The world seems to have gone mad of late. I was leading a boring but possibly healthy life not so long ago, but of late I find myself with more excitement in my life than I can handle. All this business with Garry and the money and the police. And then Julia comes to see me. She once had a perfect life and now it's in such a mess. Perfection is deception, as I've always said.

She pondered Julia's situation. What had been perfect about it? Was affluence a smokescreen for unhappiness? These days money does pass for happiness or so young people think. It's not their fault and it's not Julia's fault. Life is bereft these days of enduring culture. It is riddled instead with mass communications that dull people's sensitivity to what they've lost. What sort of marital relationship is it where the man spends most of his life travelling overseas, doing pointless deals while his wife spends most of *her* life at the manicurist or the tennis club or on some other vacuous pastime?

Hannah sighed, tired from trying to fathom the unfathomable secrets of modern life. Why has this accursed modern world found its way into my life so suddenly and with so much force? Still, I suppose my longest-held wish might yet come true.

The way things are going, I might yet die of excitement.

REALITY IMAGINED

OK, I was loving it, and much better than a Macca's.

I took the time to sit back and admire my work. I breathed in the pleasure. As idyllic as this experience was, I knew it would soon end. It was entropy. It was the natural life cycle of things. It's all too hard for humans to endure. Just when things are so good and you want more, it's taken away from you. It's the human condition.

At another level, though, I was excited about the end and not depressed about it. OK, so the journey is the thing and arriving isn't usually what it's cracked up to be. But, in this case, the true satisfaction still lay ahead of me. I was lapping up the self-adulation about my achievements, but what's the good of success if no one knows about it? A tree falls silently in the forest – so what? Where's the reverence for the conquering hero? I was winning Olympic gold in my own living room. But they don't hold the Olympics like that, do they? No, they hold the events in massive stadiums (stadia sounds like some sort of disease, doesn't it?) and every twitch of every toned muscle and every bead of sweat is broadcast into the living rooms of the multitudes. And the masses celebrate. They bow down and they worship their heroes as they should. They load them up with precious metals (engraved as well!) and they welcome them home with ticker-tape parades and then they give them what they've truly earned – massive commercial endorsements so they'll never want for anything for the rest of their lives. That's what being a hero is, and I sure as hell wasn't getting what I deserved.

The lighting of my own Olympic torch and the holding of my very own games was going to be that much more delicious than those so-called heroes get to experience. Those javelin slingers and tumble-turn merchants are just actors in someone else's play. There's nothing wrong with that. But, by contrast, what deliciousness awaits someone who is the producer, director, lighting and sound expert, and principal actor all rolled into one of his own work of art?

Yes, indeed, to bring this drama, this ultimate contest of daily living, to fruition will bring hero-worship in its purest and strongest form. It will literally take the breath away. It will generate raw emotion of a kind the players have never experienced before. It will be catharsis. It will be Kristallnacht. It will be VE Day. It will be the apotheosis. It will be the end of the world. It will be reality. Fucking beautiful reality.

Bring it on!

You can say what you like about me, but I don't lack a sense of occasion.

Once my life had got on a roll over here, what with my Master Plan and the trivia of daily work, I didn't really see much of my old mucker, Mark. What with Lisa in tow, as well – that woman could organise enough commitments to keep the entire population of China rushed off its feet. And, let's face it, there hadn't been a lot to gain from catching up with Mark either. After his unwitting inspiration in introducing me to Sharon in the first place, he was hardly likely to have added any great value to my strategy as it all came to pass.

Still, I do have a sense of occasion and I felt it only fitting that the denouement should be launched where it had all begun just a year earlier – round at Mark's. I observed the required formalities and turned up unannounced. However, I did not fail entirely in the etiquette stakes, coming armed with a delicious Pepperjack shiraz.

Mark opened the front door, nodded at me to come in and scurried back down the corridor to his computer screens. He was multi-tasking between playing Grand Theft Auto and dumping junior mining stocks, and was presumably using the correct control button for each. I thought adding a third level of complexity, such as asking for some wine glasses, was probably over the top. So I took myself off to the kitchen to have a fossick around. It looked like the entire cast of a Mel Brooks movie had run amok in there. I found a couple of chipped and stained glasses on the draining board, probably exactly where I'd left them on my last visit, and gave them a hand rinse under the tap. I thought of drying them, but the tea towel resembled a lab for cultivating new strains of microbe, so I shook the drips off them instead.

I handed Mark a glass of wine and he now dexterously manoeuvered the three consoles without missing a beat. The same couldn't be said for his mental agility. I tried asking a question or two, you know, inquiring politely about his health and general wellbeing. But I was greeted with George W. Bush impersonations, such as, What was that? and, What did you say? I melted into the background for a while and savoured the peppery wine. The strobe effect from the flashing lights was ruining the taste so I slipped away to the living room and brushed some clothes off an armchair to sit down.

Every human being is unique, especially Mark (although I know you can't strictly be *especially unique*) and eventually he proved it when he joined me in the living room. It's hard to imagine what chain of thoughts came to life in his head that propelled him away from the screen to undertake this selfless act of hospitality. I tried again to inquire as to his life over the last few months. For some reason, his brain and mouth suddenly connected.

Something amazing happened to me this morning, he said. I was walking the dog ...

But you don't have a dog.

OK, it's Mum's new dog. Anyway, I was walking the dog down this laneway and these people with a dog up ahead stopped and stepped aside onto the concrete apron of a carport. When I got close to them, they said, Sorry but this bulldog here can be aggressive. I must have looked concerned cos the woman said, It'll be fine, just walk through and I'll put my hands over his eyes. And she did and don't you think it's bizarre to obscure a minor sensory faculty when dogs have got a million times better sense of smell than humans and, anyway, the bulldog had already seen my dog and so what was he going to do when she had her hands over his eyes, pretend to be stupid and forgetful?

Don't you think that's amazing? he urged in an explosion of emotion for Mark.

It is, I said.

But I was thinking that his story, while undoubtedly bizarre, was nowhere near as amazing as someone who responds to an inquiry about his health with the story of the allegedly belligerent bulldog.

I eventually managed to piece together some snippets of Mark's recent life. It transpired that the stockmarket downturn, followed by the next upturn followed by the next downturn, had been so dramatic and unsettling that he'd been trying to control his confusion by playing Grand Theft Auto night and day. I should have guessed.

I waited in vain for the great conversationalist to ask me how I was, but I knew that was never going to happen. I started to feel impatient about the time I was wasting and resentful that what was supposed to be a significant moment in my life had been reduced to something about as special as watching a postman's pyjamas go round in the tumble dryer.

It was now or never. I decided to launch the unfolding of the end of my Master Plan in a suitably discordant manner. I raised my glass and made a toast.

To the beginning of the end of my Master Plan!

Mark took it in his stride. To the beginning of the end of your Master Plan, he repeated in a monotone.

I waited for the inevitable question. However, with Mark, such a question was highly evitable. So unlikely was he to ask me what I meant, that I paused for a few seconds only.

Then I scooped up my half-drunk bottle, saluted formally to Mark and split.

I began to feel a bit put out, I have to say. I could relate to how parents feel when the kids have moved out. After all you've done for them, you could be struck down by bubonic plague and they still wouldn't visit you. They're too busy. Making a career. Making a home. Making love. Fucking before family, that's their motto.

I felt a bit that way. My housemates were all too busy to bother with me. Sure, I'd made them busy and that was gratifying. But they were lost in their own mean, little worlds and I had things to do that required their attention now and again.

I was biding my time for the big bang, which in this case, was a monumental event that would finish rather than start things. But it was ridiculous. There was I trying to wave at these people, trying to flag them down, trying to warn them. The brakes on your bus have been tampered with and I'm the only one who knows. For God's sake, take some notice of me. I'm not some druggie on ice or some mental case without the medication, for Christ's sake, take some notice of me before it's too late.

But no, all the passengers on the bus had their heads down, had their eyes closed listening to their ipods or were just plain asleep. Basically they were asleep at the wheel. Or, to put it another way, they were in the toilet piddling while Rome burned.

Robert was moving out of home after all those years. Marjorie was being totally absurd. Frankly, she was cutting a ridiculous figure. What was the big deal? She'd known about his carryings-on over all these years and was choosing now to jack up about it. And why? Because the whole thing was out in the open? Stupid cow. Did she think she was the only one who knew about his philandering? It was so ridiculous. So bloody ridiculous.

I'm not moving *all* my bloody stuff out. It's still my bloody house. Who does she think paid for it? She hasn't done a day's work over the last twenty-five years. She conveniently forgets about that. And I'll still be bloody paying for it when I'm not there. Not likely. Anyway, I can see the boys rolling their eyes at her. They know it's all a bloody tantrum with a use by date that's long expired. Whatever I can carry in the car, that's as far as I'm prepared to go. And it's a bloody small car, anyway. She can have her way for a while, if that's what it takes.

I'll need a few more creature comforts in the flat at the RB, that's for sure. What's the name of that guy who furnishes apartments when they're up for sale? Henry? William? Some king's name? Maybe it was a pope's name, yes, that's it, Greg. I've got his number in the mobile, I'm pretty sure, so I'll get him onto it. He'll probably just go round and size it up and bring stuff round without me having to be there. He'll know what a guy needs in a pad like that. That'd be the go and then I won't have to worry about it given that I've got back-to-back appointments and procedures just about from here to eternity.

While Robert was sussing things out, Garry just couldn't think. Not with all that deafening background noise with the Kirsty situation. That lawyer woman sure was good, better than good actually, but so many bloody options to think through – and all of them bad. He spent a lot of time gazing into space. Furrowing his brow. Trying to work it out. All the guys down the station knew something was wrong, being men and sensitive as you'd expect them to be(!) But they all had the wrong end of the stick. They had his problems down as a simple boy meets girl, boy bonks girl, boy gets kicked out of home scenario or some such thing. Well, how could they think anything else? They couldn't imagine him being suspected of theft.

In the end, he had to defy Kirsty and do what was required. Why couldn't she understand that he was facing a jail term if the money wasn't returned? Why wasn't that obvious? But, for some reason, she didn't see it that way. Did she secretly want him to be banged up? For crimes against her? What crimes could they possibly be?

In the end he acted. He ransacked the house one morning when she was out with the kids to track down the money. It wasn't all there, by the way. Then he'd packed some things, just the bare essentials, and gave himself up at the police station. They made him wait for hours for his ritual humiliation, which culminated in him returning the money and receiving an official WA Police Service receipt for the proceeds of crime.

He'd hoped that finally acting out of integrity would improve things. It didn't. It just made his situation less bad than it would otherwise have been. He was still in the mire with the law and was given bail to appear for a further round of humiliation at the Fremantle Magistrates Court. He faced the prospect of suspension from duties at work until the case was heard. And he would have to exercise an option, as his female lawyer put it, about how he was going to plead. This was a fucked-up choice in itself. He could choose between owning up to something he didn't really do and getting a criminal record, or defending himself on the basis of a series of misunderstandings. His lawyer advised him on the range of likely outcomes from pleading not guilty. At best, he might get away with a fine and a spent conviction, but at worst, he might face a jail term and a lifetime of notoriety as the bastard who ripped off the elderly holocaust victim who'd devoted her life to saving lost souls. How fucking great was that, on top of losing his wife and probably access to his beautiful children?

I'm looking for my mojo, mate.

That was the only way he could think of explaining his sombre mood to the others in the pub, who couldn't reconcile the new Mario with his legendary status as life and soul of the party. For them to really understand, he'd have to explain the weird things that had happened to him recently, things weird even by his own exalted standards. He was so not up to that. His mates were suckers for the smart one-liner or the short anecdote. They were not the sort of people to pay attention to the physical and emotional saga that had been Mario's last hundred days.

It was a fact that he preferred his own company of late and that was really unusual. He didn't prefer it because it was better, but rather because he was the only person he didn't have to explain things to. And what exactly was there to explain? He'd got himself way out of his depth and he'd had to own up to not being the tough, cool hombre he thought he was. He'd been assaulted and hurt and terrified. Ditto repeato – so he wasn't the tough, cool hombre he thought he was. He'd crossed a poofter lawyer, who possibly was the tough, cool hombre Mario had once thought himself to be, or who, at the very least, had a very good mate who was a sadistic bastard rather than a tough, cool hombre. So the truth was he didn't know for sure any more whether there'd be another set of guys in black waiting for him in the liftwell to his apartment or whether anyone had believed his pathetic attempt to persuade them that his dirt file on the poofter lawyer was in safekeeping for transmission to the police and the Law Society in the event of something happening to him.

And, on top of all that, there was the bird. Yes, the bird. The smartest, tastiest, sexiest piece of arse he'd ever had. Within his grasp, so to speak. Maybe. He couldn't be sure. He'd been sure she was falling for his rough and ready charms at one time. But now? Who knows? That little poofter would have his claws right into her, for sure. And he was the managing partner, which is basically the boss, isn't it? So, loyalty would be the price of her job.

But, wasn't she too much of a free spirit to be tied to the company kitchen sink like that? Didn't she have that wild, Irish streak in her that ran a mile from someone trying to control her, especially a man? And wouldn't she do anything for a bit of excitement in her life? Maybe she would. Maybe she would break free. But, even if she did, what would she want of him? What would she expect of him? Would she even care about him at all? She may refuse to bow down and worship the male god of seniority, but that didn't mean she'd defy the partners and instead decide to run to him.

No wonder, he couldn't share all this crap with anyone else. He sucked on another fag and slugged down his latest beer. It's all bullshit anyway, that's what it is. Who gives a fuck anyway?

The dependency was really getting to Hannah. In truth, it was the *sense* of dependency, since there was no one for her to be dependent on. But there was no escaping the inescapable. All this nastiness and upset was taking its toll on her. She was tired and lethargic most of the time and, in layman's rather clinical terms, she felt depressed.

She lay there in bed, as the rising sun broke through her thin curtains. Today she had committed to dragging herself out of bed first thing, regardless of how tired she felt. But now, the moment had come and it was a battle of will between her intellect and her body. This situation was bread and butter, meat and drink for a spiritual guru. She had never in her life allowed herself to take the easy way out, to fool herself that the line of least resistance was the best course to take. So, having made the firm commitment today, there had been no doubt that, when the sun came up, she would get out of bed.

Hannah began to sweat. She felt quite faint. She was willing herself to move her legs, move the covers back, slide her bottom to the side of the bed and stand up. But nothing was happening. Her body felt weightless like an astronaut's. There was some sort of blockage between the impulses from her brain and the receptors in her limbs. Hannah was scared and the feelings of terror from childhood came flooding back. This time, there were no marauding, leather-coated purveyors of hate and revulsion. There was nobody there at all. It was just her – mind, body and soul – all three in turmoil.

By a tremendous effort of will, she forced herself to relax. She was relieved that she could at least achieve that. She breathed slowly and deeply with her mouth closed. She closed her eyes and transported her stilling mind to her favourite waterfall in the snow-capped mountains. She worked through the classic relaxation techniques she had used on her clients and patients a thousand times before. Eventually, her breathing came back under control and her heart rate slowed. She patted the sweat from her body with her top sheet.

She needed now more than ever for her body to obey instructions. Thank God, it did. She hauled herself from the bed as if dragging a heavy weight and shuffled her way along the corridor to the kitchen. Fortunately, the kettle was already full so it required no more of her than to light the gas. She finally lowered herself into the haven of her kitchen chair. She rolled her eyes and shook her head as if to some malicious deity. This is bad. All of this business is really bad. I am a foolish, foolish, stupid old woman to indulge in such nonsense. Such childish, ridiculous nonsense has laid me low. All this excitement has made me ill and old and weak. And all for nothing. Nothing at all. Foolishness and vanity, like a young girl. Can I get up to make the tea? Hannah raised herself and acknowledged the pathetic flush of success that accompanied the straightening of her stiff joints. How are the mighty fallen, she muttered as she headed to silence the whistling kettle.

Lost, Julia said to Lisa. That pretty much sums it up. I'm not happy. I'm not unhappy. I'm lost. I don't have a home. I don't really have a family. I don't have a husband. I don't really have a lover. I don't know how much money I've got. I haven't got a job. I'm not sure if I have a car. Actually, all I've got is you!

Lisa smiled sympathetically at her friend.

It's awful, but I hate going home at the moment. Stephen has been working his devious magic on the girls. It's so upsetting to watch them eating out of his hand, but I know there's nothing I can do.

Julia reached for her friend's hand. You're such a treasure, Lisa. I don't know what I'd do if I couldn't crash at your place when I'm not staying at Robert's apartment. Stephen is poisonous these days. He almost oozes hatred for me. That's why I like to meet the girls out somewhere. At the beach, at a café, at the movies or whatever. It's really sad how wary they are of me and it hurts like fire. But, slowly, slowly if we're out together for long enough, they thaw like snow on a sunny day when you're skiing and eventually they come back to me, just like they used to. But it doesn't last – that's the shame of it. He gradually gets to them again and brainwashes them so that when I see them they are distant strangers, again.

Lisa squeezed Julia's hand supportively.

And it's amazing, Julia continued, I don't feel like I own anything any more. Me! When they invented shopping, it had my name on it. But this new world is good for me, I think. I only have a few things with me, as you know. It's true I have some more gear at Robert's. But, compared to walk-in wardrobes full of haute couture, my dear, I am positively naked. And, as for jewellery, I just have these rings and these bangles with me and that's it. I noticed the other day when I was home that I didn't want to take any more of my jewellery with me. It was really interesting. I consciously thought of my jewellery box, but when I got to the ensuite and looked through those piles of beautiful things, I didn't actually want to take any of them with me. I've been thinking about it and I can explain it, I think. I fooled myself for a while that all this turmoil in my life had made me a new person. A new, less materialistic one. But, that's not it all, I came to realise. The bloody stuff has this powerful association with Stephen, that's the problem. Sure, he bought me some of it, but I acquired the trinkets mostly without anybody else's help. But, that doesn't seem to matter. It has been sitting for years in that bedroom and that bathroom. The one I have shared so long with that man. That man I truly despise.

Lisa kept playing her part. Nodding and smiling, not talking.

It's such a relief to be honest to use such a vile and hateful word as *despise*. It means that I've come to terms with something equally hateful and vile. Something that makes me uncontrollably sad, quite frankly, to admit. The sorry fact is that I've despised him for years. Maybe even ten years. So that means I've wasted ten years of my life – some might say my best! – spending every day, every hour, every dreary bloody second, connected to this excuse for a man. And that's all because I lacked the courage to admit the truth to myself and to summon up the guts to do something about my barren existence with this nothingness.

Tears welled up in Julia's eyes and Lisa knew just what to do. The tissues were readily at hand.

Kathleen was out on the town. She thought about that, dragging on a cigarette out the back of a club. What's happening to me? Housewives go out on the town. It's what you say to yourself when the bulk of your life is as boring as fuck and you've got a leave pass from mashing bananas and cleaning up vomit.

All work and no play *was* making Kathy a dull girl. Even the endless work part had changed. Not the work itself, but being at work. The atmosphere at work was unbearable. Max had changed and that was the problem. He was the one who'd always made the office fun. The old Max was exciting. Sure he could be serious, professional, meticulous – all of those things. But the Max of old was still always pushing the boundaries. Living in the fast lane. Taking a risk. Valuing the thrill.

Kathy sent her latest uber-Bruted suitor on his way. She was going to get laid tonight. It was the least she could do for herself. But, not with him, not with just anyone. Definitely with someone who is someone.

Max wasn't Max any more. Min perhaps, but not Max. He was a brooding, menacing, unforgiving mass of misery. Morose Max. His perfunctory dealings with Kathy were as minimalist as modern architecture. Giving instructions. Discussing briefs. Demanding answers as to why her billings were so low. She'd tried to get to the bottom of things with him, but to no avail. She'd tried to get some drinks into him to loosen his tongue, but that didn't work. She'd even plucked up the ultimate courage.

Max, we need to talk, she said.

No, we don't, he snapped back.

Of course, she knew what it was all about. Roughly anyway. It was true he was being the village arsehole with everyone, but he was reserving his best mooning moves for her. For her, substitute Mario. Kathy – friend of Mario; Kathy – fuck buddy of Mario; Kathy – everything of Mario; Kathy = Mario. Max = Arsehole. Kathy v Arsehole.

The problem defied solution. She couldn't work on Max to fix things up because he wouldn't let her near him. She hoped the other associates would help, but they were useless. She knew they were secretly pleased she was now public enemy number one. They were hoping she'd keep poking the bear with a stick. As a last resort, she contacted Sebastian.

She lured him to a bar on some pretext. She grabbed her opportunity.

Sebastian, can you help me with Max?

What can *I* do about him?

You've got to help me put this Mario business behind us. Mario's obviously bluffing, you know that. And, even if he isn't, he's not stupid – well, not *that* stupid that he's going to risk crossing Max when you're lurking in the background. Surely, Sebastian, you can talk some sense into Maxie?

Sebastian smiled back at her. He shot Kathleen that condescending, non-comprehending smile he reserved for his victims when they were begging for mercy.

No can do. It's your problem, sweetheart, Sebastian said, looking straight back at her with a smile on his face this time that said you don't know the half of it.

Kathleen shrugged off a passable suit. Not ready yet. Sebastian had frightened her. Surely Max wasn't going to be stupid enough to sic Sebastian onto Mario? Mario couldn't be worth all that, could he? It just didn't make sense. If *she* thought Mario had to be bluffing, why the fuck wouldn't the arsehole from hell think exactly the same thing?

And where was she with Mario anyway? Did she care? Yes, she knew she did care, but that didn't exactly help her answer the question. Basically, Mario deep down was the nicest guy she'd ever met, but unequivocally he was also the biggest schmuck. He was wonderfully uncomplicated, but pathetically shallow. He was incredibly sharp, but stupendously dumb. He was fabulously funny, yet embarrassingly crass. He was disarmingly honest, yet enormously untrustworthy. Innocently charming yet horrendously rude.

In any event, she knew tallying his ledger like this had no real bearing on the matter. Deep down, she wanted him around. She wanted to see him now and again, she wanted to have a laugh with him, she didn't mind fucking him on that basis. The thing was – she wanted him around, within limits. He was too much like a puppy dog to be safe. When she pushed him away, he would scamper off with his tail between his legs. But, if she encouraged him at all, he would be all over her again, tail wagging, tongue licking, eyes wide open. That was the problem. He didn't seem to do halfway. He was either not on or full on. He either wanted it all or would settle for nothing.

He was never going to get it all. She felt ashamed about the reason. He wasn't in her class. He lacked her style. He would never cut it with her friends and could never help her with her career. Particularly now that he'd caused such a rift for her with Max. So, if he couldn't have it all and couldn't deal with halfway, why couldn't she do the right thing and make him settle for nothing?

She'd found no resolution, but it was time to go back inside the club to drown her sorrows. Her two female lawyer mates disappeared onto the dance floor. She sipped at the dregs of her drink.

Can I buy you a drink?

If you must, she said, a Bolly if you're up for it.

Don't let him be another puppy dog, she prayed to any deity who would listen. Please give him the good grace to fuck and go.

I thought it through, without Mark's non-help this time. All roads led to Hannah's.

Her slow progress down the corridor to answer the door seemed more laboured and certainly slower than usual. When she eventually made it, she opened the door with the chain, which I'd never known her do before. I beamed at her from the doorway, but my superficial smile buried my inner thoughts. God, she looks awful. Not like her at all.

It's you. I wasn't expecting you. Just wait a minute. I'll get this infernal contraption off the door and open up for you.

After a lot of scratching and scraping, the door was free and ajar and Hannah was already scuttling her way back towards the kitchen.

She dumped herself into a chair as quickly as possible.

You can make the tea, she said.

This was amazing. It was appalling and magnificent. I filled the kettle as I'd seen her do a dozen times and fiddled around trying to get a match lit under it. She directed me to the real tea as I opened and closed doors looking for it.

I've got a surprise for you, I said.

Oh *Gott*, that's just what I don't need! I don't need any more surprises, any more excitement, any more comings and goings for a little while now.

I turned around and gave her my best, highly puzzled, deeply quizzical expression.

She clearly felt an obligation to elaborate. It's fine, you don't have to concern yourself with it, she said splaying her hands. It's just some things that have been happening recently. Don't worry about it. Put your concentration, for goodness sake, into making a decent cup of tea, which I seriously doubt any young person from the tea-in-bags generation can do, but try hard anyway, will you?

I poured the boiling water over the leaves, having warmed the pot. At least that was something she didn't have to coach me on. I rattled the cups and saucers, tracked down the sugar bowl and found the spoons. It wasn't that hard – the most logical drawer was the right one.

Shall I be mother?

She wasn't in the mood for humour. To be honest, her dark mood was making me nervous. I was wondering if I should abandon the play for the moment and retreat to live another day. I decided not to go for it straightaway and see if one of our usual 'intellectual' chats would brighten her mood and her likely receptiveness.

As everyone was talking about it everywhere, at work, at home, in the bank, at the café, everywhere, I asked her how long she thought the worldwide economic volatility would play out. This sort of question normally elicited some interesting historical perspectives. I don't want you to think me soft, but her monologues about yesteryear were really kind of fascinating.

Who knows? Who cares anyway? The only people who care are the excessively greedy who gamble with other people's livelihoods and the excessively foolish who trust charlatans and robbers with their cash.

This sort of reply was not her. It was dismissive and non-expansive. I had to get her going.

What about the super funds who invest for all those innocent mums and dads?

The government forces those hard-working mums and dads to put large amounts of money into super and that money inevitably goes into the hands of all these fraudsters I was talking about before. So, society compels people to entrust their life-savings to the fraudulent and the greedy.

This was better. I could tell she was warming to the task. I sat back and absorbed pre-war and post-war European policy-making aimed at making people do what's good for them. She was a passionate and convincing libertarian even at her age, and, if I'd been in the least interested in what she was saying, I'd have been persuaded that governments seemingly acting in the interests of the people are always covertly just working in the interests of themselves.

Her eyes were livelier and a healthy colour was returning to her cheeks. I judged it was now or never. I'd never seen her like this before and so I had no idea whether she was back to her normal self for good or whether she might shrivel up again like the broken old lady who'd opened the door to me. I went for it.

As I said, I've got a surprise for you.

I'd hoped you'd forgotten about that.

That response sounds bad, I know. But it was said with a playful smile on her face. I took that as a cue to flirt with her in return.

It's a good one. It's a really good surprise.

Oh, go on with you, enough of the big mystery. Spit it out and let me be the judge of how good it is.

Normally, I'd milk the moment, but I was resolved to head straight there while the going was good.

I haven't been quite straight with you, I'm afraid.

She laughed out loud. By the way, I hope that isn't the surprise!

No, that's not it. It's a bit better than that. Anyway, I haven't been quite straight with you, as I say, but only in a good way.

In a good way, of course. She was mocking me.

You see, I haven't really been writing this article about you. Well, I have actually, but that wasn't really my main purpose.

Oh re-ally?

No, you see, I had a tiny ulterior motive. I thought a book would be better.

Could you be overlooking the fact that there have been about ten books already?

There, she was sucked in by the master! She was knocked out, hog-tied and with a fucking big lemon in her mouth.

Right, I can see you're not impressed with my surprise about a book. Well, how about this, then? If you're not otherwise engaged at seven p.m. on the twenty-seventh, how would you care to attend an announcement?

I waved away her attempt at a response. How would you care to attend a media launch of the making of a film of the story of your life?

Wow, really, you're such a dark horse! How come you're keeping secrets from me and Lisa too? Well, yes, of course, I'll come. I think it's fantastic – she's such an incredible woman. I went to see her a couple of times and she was incredible – so calm, so serene I guess, so sharp for someone of her age. Anyway, let me just check my diary. Yes, it's terribly old-fashioned. The girls are always mocking me for not using the schedule on my phone. Anyway, I can never find anything in my handbag these days. It's terrible; this bag is more of a mess than it used to be. It sounds impossible, I know, but I'm a bit of a refugee these days so I have to take so much more stuff around with me all the time. Anyway, let's have a look – oh, I've got my hairdresser. But never mind, I'll change it.

By the way, Julia asked, can I bring someone?

It's a peculiar measure of success, I know, but I couldn't find anybody in person to invite. I'd just got Julia on her mobile, but I wanted the justifiable satisfaction of issuing my invitations to my housemates face to face. But, do you think I could find anybody? I'll give you a clue. No.

I decided to rest and have a coffee after I'd failed to find Mario at any of his usual haunts – yet again. It was soothing, I'll admit, to take the weight off the feet. I retreated to a mock French chain store café, where the leather was as fake as the croissants were faux, to contemplate my new frontier in management theory. For the very first time, I announced to myself, the key performance indicator of success is – absence.

Yep, thanks to me, no one seemed to live at home any more. OK, Hannah did, but if she'd been ten years younger, I reckon she'd have been a nomad as well. Julia was zigzagging between Lisa and Robert's apartment; Robert had been kicked out of his house; Garry had gone AWOL; Mario hadn't changed his address but was ducking and diving and changing his normal patterns like a Western diplomat in the Middle East; and Kathy was officially on leave for a few days and I couldn't track her down anywhere.

I savoured the winds of change that were blowing my waifs and strays hither and thither. At the same time, I was hoping for a modest breakthrough with someone so I could get the little rendezvous up and running in a personally rewarding fashion. And then my mobile rang. Yes, indeed, Mario's name flashed up. The very man I was looking for. I'd found someone at last. I'd have to settle for technology once again.

Sorry, matey, I'm not avoiding you on purpose or nothing. I've just got a few issues going on and I'm trying to lie low, if you know what I mean. No, mate, I wouldn't bore you with the details, but it relates back to the same issue I had. Yeah, it's over, but it's not over, if you get my drift. Let's just say that the solution brought its own problems with it, as these things tend to sometimes. Well, you being sorry won't help much. Nah, just kidding mate, forget about it, it's all good.

Say that again. Why would you want me at something like that? No, I'm not sure it's my style, to tell you the truth. Film stars, booze and tarts, you say. Funny man! OK, free booze and free tarts then. I still don't think it's my scene. I've never heard of her – you know that, don't you? Well, sure, if it's that important to you to get a good roll up, I'll do you the honour of gracing you with my presence. But, not my presents, naturally. You should be giving me presents for indulging you like this. No, I won't let you down. On my word of honour, I am putting the date into my scheduler as we speak. As we speak, my friend, it is going in. Wait a minute, yes, it is done. Don't worry, my word is my bond.

While I'm on the subject of critical success factors, I was exceeding performance targets in more ways than one. Not only were they all wandering like the ten lost tribes of Israel, but it was also hard to get a sensible conversation out of any of them when I did make contact. For some reason, and what a coincidence that the same affliction should have beset them all, they all seemed rather distracted. You'd have their undivided attention for a little while and something resembling a chat would ensue. It would have a coherent theme, a bit of interactional give and take. There would be something of the old I-speak-then-you-speak rigmarole and you'd think this is a bit better and then, suddenly, they've forgotten their lines on you and just when it's the next you-speak part, you see that their eyes have glazed over and they are miles away and basically pretty vacant, as the song goes.

Yes, it was a triumphant but troublesome time. I had the devil of a job trying to find any of my friends and, when I did, I inevitably found myself hanging on the telephone, as the other song goes.

A film launch *you're* connected to? Kathleen responded cautiously. I thought you were just into real estate. Frankly, it sounds pretty suss if you won't reveal the name of the film. You're not trying to ask me out, are you? No, I do appreciate that. Honestly, I do understand you're not coming on to me. All right, yes, I do see your point about the Chief Justice and the Attorney-General being there and, yes, I *am* grateful for the invitation. Yes, it does sound intriguing, so, yes, that's right, it's a yes. Yes, it sounds great. I'll be there, don't worry, I'll definitely make it.

Garry was undoubtedly the most itinerant and vacant of them all, yet I had no trouble finding him. Well, I did at first, when he didn't turn up to work on my house, wasn't answering his mobile and seemed to be on indefinite leave. Then he reappeared out of the blue, much as he had done before.

He looked like shit. So terrible in fact that he looked like a bad case of diarrhoea. Then once he'd returned, he took to working all the hours God's given us. I was happy at first to have someone dependably where I could find him, but then I started to smell a rat. He was very sullen and unforthcoming of course, but I eventually got an explanation. Kirsty had kicked him out of the house. Well, at least that's what he said.

Around that time I made it my habit to drive past the house on the way home from work because there had been a spate of thefts from building sites in the neighbourhood. On this particular night, I did my security check a little later on account of an evening meeting. My heart pounded at first when I saw from a distance that there were lights on at that time of night. But, when I got closer, I saw Garry's car pull out of the tilt-up garage. I pulled over so he wouldn't see me and waited until he was gone. I didn't know how long he was going to be, so I raced quickly and quietly into the house. It was ridiculous really to do this cloak and dagger stuff when it was actually my own house, but I needed to test my theory and I didn't want Garry to know I knew.

There were no outward signs to corroborate what I was thinking. For all I could see, he might just have been working late. Maybe just to make the most of the time he had off from work. But my theory was so watertight that I sensed it had to be true. He'd been kicked out of home or had left of his own accord, so why wouldn't he sleep at my house? It explained perfectly why he seemed to be there all the time. I systematically opened all the cupboards, but found nothing. I worked my way methodically from room to room trying to find some proof. Feeling totally frustrated, I decided as a final point of search to check the garage and, bingo! right on the top shelf, behind the paint-smeared cans, there was a backpack, sleeping bag and pillow.

I knew it. I felt vindicated, but at the same time betrayed. People are deceitful, aren't they? Why can't people be more straightforward these days? Why do they have to lie and cheat? What's so hard about asking if he could stay? Was I going to say no? Am I such an unreasonable person? Would I have bitten his head off?

Would I not offer the hand of friendship to someone in his hour of need?

Of course, I wouldn't. But he didn't know that. Garry was just being deceitful.

A house-sitting opportunity? Garry responded enthusiastically. For three months – that sounds great! Let me just make a note of the time and place. I'll be there for sure, it's the only piece of luck I've had in I don't know how long.

Hey, I'm really sorry about squatting in your place like that. I didn't know what else to do and I couldn't think of anywhere else to go that wouldn't lead to endless questions from my friends or workmates that I didn't want to answer. Obviously, that's no excuse and I feel really bad for not asking you.

I think my mind's gone to jelly, to tell you the truth. I seem to make nothing but bad decisions right now, such as camping there without asking you. If I'm honest, I suppose, I didn't want to ask you because I didn't want to get into the whole business with you either. But, let's face it, none of any of this adds up to an excuse. So, I'm really apologetic, you know that.

Anyway, I'm also incredibly grateful to you for letting me stay. Particularly after breaching your trust the way I did. And then, on top of that, you really didn't need to follow up on that housesit for me. Mind you, I don't blame you for a minute as it's the perfect way to get rid of me! I can't believe it, a three-bedroom house in Mosman Park for three months. That would be paradise, better than paradise, if there could be such a thing. Anyway, listen to me, getting my hopes up. You'd think I'd know better by now after everything that's happened to me. I suppose I just need something hopeful to cling to rather than mooch about the place thinking about what life used to be like with Kirsty and the kids and the good steady job and the moonlighting opportunities and the ordinary boring suburban life that I led what seems like a million years ago.

Do you realise that I could go to prison? She says it's a remote possibility, but I might actually be sent to jail. I might go directly to jail without passing go and without collecting two hundred dollars. That's ironic isn't it when collecting twenty thousand dollars was the root of the problem. How can the class goody goody, the only guy in the schoolwho never stole lollies from the corner shop, be the same guy who might be going to prison? Can that guy really be me?

Anyway, thanks for everything, mate, really thanks for everything. I'll be there to meet your friends and I will be on my best behaviour. No criminal acts, I swear!

At this point, I was exhausted and excited. I'd eventually tracked all my guests down except for Robert. It was obviously a fair assumption that Julia would be bringing Robert along. Put it this way, I didn't think she'd be asking Stephen. Still, I had a frisson of doubt that Julia might have had one of her girls in mind.

You probably feel a bit superior right now. I'm sure you do. You're probably thinking I bet it's Lisa, I bet it's Lisa, I know where this is heading, I'm so smart.

Well, I'm sorry to disappoint you, but deep down I'm sure you would've realised that I'd be one step ahead of you. Of course, Lisa was a monster risk. A risk that had to be neutralised.

As luck would have it, Lisa had announced some time ago that she'd arranged to visit her sister in Christchurch. What a pain life can be! What an absolute bummer that the film launch happened to fall on that very same weekend!

I'm as devastated as you are, darling, I said so sincerely, but the timing is determined by the studio and it's something way out of my control.

Beyond the Lisa prospect, I couldn't risk Julia bringing one of her girls. Potentially, she could've thought the opportunity to be educational and inspiring for one of her maidens of tender years. It wasn't a huge risk, as a radical feminist Julia is not. But, for a man who has come so far, any level of risk is just one scintilla of uncontrolled chance too far.

I thought carefully about which mitigation strategy could be deployed and then my PA provided what I needed.

You need to confirm really soon whether you're going to the Minister's cocktail party, she admonished me for the third time, as security needs a list of people to be allowed in.

It was *so* obvious.

Julia, sorry to be a pain about the film launch, but for security reasons the studio insists that guests will only be let in whose names have been left at the door.

Simple, but perfect.

I'm bringing Robert, if that's OK.

Absolutely, I just didn't want to make any assumptions.

No worries at all. I think Robert will find it interesting, she added.

I said nothing, but I could've confirmed without fear of contradiction that Robert *would* find the event interesting. Extremely interesting, as will you, Julia.

Oh, by the way, what's his surname again?

After all, how would I know that or, if I'd been told, why would I remember an irrelevant detail like that?

Hetherington.

Great, Robert Hetherington's name will be there at the door.

REALITY SPURNED

Where oh where to host the extravaganza? Should I hire a studio so the address would be authentic? Maybe a TV station would suit? Or should I just hire a function hall?

I pondered for a while some venue that would speak volumes about Hannah's life. A feminist centre – I couldn't bear the thought of that. A Jewish cemetery – appealing at one level, but very hard to arrange. Something at a publishing house – definitely plausible, but fraught with too many dangers that something might go wrong.

Those ideas were creative but mostly impractical or far too risky. I would have to settle on a safe and standard function room. I cast my mind back over all the parties and events I'd been to since arriving in Perth. Most of the venues were daggy, suitable only for a reunion of 1970s architects. I thought about the nightclubs – it would be a laugh, but Hannah might refuse to attend.

What about cultural centres? I wondered. There's the Museum, the Art Gallery, the Mint, but wait ... wait a little minute. What about the amazing Maritime Museum at the Fremantle port? What about it indeed?

I had a hunch and I went to the Museum's website. I clicked on the Welcome Walls register that lists all the migrants who entered Australia by ship through Fremantle port. It was a long list with tens of thousands of names. I didn't have far to scroll as I was only going to the Bs. There was a handful of Jewish sounding names starting with *Baum*, sandwiched between their more numerous Italian counterparts. I figuratively ran my finger down the page, moving the cursor down the screen until I was very, very close. Baum, Baume, Baumen, Baumgarten. And there was the name – Else Baumgarten.

I checked and re-checked the entries. An Else, but no Hannah. Maybe Hannah's real name was Else? If that was so, how come I hadn't picked up on that from my research and my meetings with Hannah?

I was puzzled and frustrated, but had to leave the problem at that point because something banal and irrelevant was required of me at work. As soon as I got home, I poured myself a glass of Brown Hill Estate shiraz and started filing through my paperwork on Hannah. I confirmed she did arrive through Fremantle as her cousin was living in Perth at the time. I knew she hadn't stayed very long, preferring to seek her fame and fortune in a real city rather than in a boring and ugly, racist country town. But, she had definitely migrated via Freo. There was definitely no record of an Else or of her calling herself Else. I spent several hours going through the paperwork, but to no avail.

I left my home office to make myself something to eat and, no sooner had I done so, than the answer came to me. Just like the final clue of a crossword that you have pored over and thought through for hours. Inevitably, when you stop thinking about it, the answer comes to you.

I checked back over my notes. I could pretty much remember the conversation we'd had. I found the relevant notes fairly quickly and there, scribbled in my appalling hieroglyphics, was a name I'd not associated with this issue just an hour before. I went to the website. It seemed to take an eternity to load. Once it opened up, I scrolled excitedly through the names. Soon I was at the Gs, and then the GOs, and then I was there. Hannah Goldstein, with name of the ship and the year.

Hannah had indeed told me that she'd married Jacob Goldstein, but the issue of her surname hadn't registered with me. She married the young Jacob out of loneliness and pity a year before she left, but it barely lasted six months. I reflected that Jacob was probably a mere mortal. Just a man of his time. An uncomprehending, innocent victim to be chewed up and spat out of the mincing machine that was the pre-feminist ball-bursting woman.

I was shown round the function room at the Maritime Museum with enthusiasm by a slim, young woman called Vanessa who no doubt would soon tire of the thankless task of running a commercial venture from a government instrumentality. I felt like warning her to get the hell out of there while her sanity was still intact. But, then again, I wondered why she shouldn't suffer like the rest of us.

Anyway, I was keeping my mind on the job. I was casing the joint for my grand finale. I was like a terrorist planning his attack with intricate precision. It seemed perfect. It was filled with light in the daytime, but was equally magnificent at night, according to Vanessa. I loved the way massive container ships seemingly made a beeline for the function room itself. Then, at the last minute, they would veer away and obey the little pilot boats that looked like plankton harassing a whale.

I made Vanessa's day. Yes, this will be perfect, I said.

Great. May I ask what kind of function it is, as weddings ...

It's for a film launch actually.

How exciting! Anything I would have heard of?

I rather doubt it. It's a film about a woman who migrated through Freo port, as it happens.

Fabulous.

Enthusiasm can be really annoying sometimes. I found myself wishing the dead hand of bureaucracy would strike her down any second.

Let me cut to the chase, I said firmly but with charm. There will be one hundred guests and I'd like the canapés and finger food you mentioned with the West Australian wines package.

Staff? Vanessa asked now in a more businesslike fashion.

Yes, plenty of waiting staff – we can't have the VIPs, WAGs and movie types going hungry and thirsty, can we?

Wonderful, she said backsliding again.

And I'll be needing a PA system. And ... a light show.

Not a problem, Vanessa said. So lovely to meet you, she added, spoiling everything.

I determined to spend a fortune as a fitting tribute to my guests at this gala event. Anything else would have been disrespectful. First impressions would be critical. When the guests arrived, I wanted them to check their watches in case they'd arrived early. Soon their questions and observations would start: Where is everybody else? Look at all those waiters buzzing around us like flies. I hope the media aren't going to miss the whole thing. What could've happened to the others? Maybe there's some mix-up with the date or the venue.

This gala event would be worthy of its name. No corners

would be cut. I was spending the best part of ten thousand dollars, and all for a handful of people. That's a small fortune each. But there would be no expense spared. They would understand that. They would see this unmistakable commitment to respect. This crowning glory of my enterprise would be done properly and, in being done so, my guests would understand that I was prepared to make sacrifices, too. Ten thousand dollars laid out for a function for a hundred, but with only six special guests invited. That is grand scale. That is deep respect. The waste would be spectacular. The waste was for a good cause.

My mood was upbeat. All the ducks had been lined up and my hunting gear was in perfect order, all ready for the shoot.

I allowed myself the little luxury of a teasing session with Hannah. I knocked on her door with a jaunty rat-a-tat-tat, poised to have some fun. I waited expectantly for the familiar creaking and scraping sounds of Hannah approaching.

I was in such a good mood. I felt in no hurry, enjoying the penetrating warmth of the mid-morning sunshine on my be-suited back.

I waited and waited. I knocked and knocked. Nobody came. No one at all. No one to even apologise for keeping me waiting.

Then I returned another day and then another. Not only no reply: no sign of life.

I imagine a lesser person would've crumpled under the weight of disappointment on finding their heroine had gone AWOL. It's not that I didn't experience moments of blackness and despair when I contemplated how cruel life could be. But I picked myself up and consoled myself that all historic achievements over time had encountered setbacks. Setbacks that seemed insurmountable at the time. Those were the occasions when heroes came into their own.

Hannah obviously wasn't at home. I racked my brains to work out where she could be. I drew upon my management background and experience. Rational process combined with creative problem-solving would get me through. As she'd never mentioned family or friends being in her life of recent times, I thought travel was unlikely. If she hadn't gone on a trip, which I felt sure she would've mentioned anyway, where would an old lady go without warning? There was an idea in my brain with its hand up trying to attract my attention. Please sir, I think she's gone to hospital.

The unthinkable crossed my mind. She might be dead. I tried to stay in rational mode. Let's try to exhaust more likely scenarios first. Let's check the hospitals. There could only be half a dozen of these at most where she could have been taken.

I phoned in sick. Me! The leader! It shows how serious things had got. I mapped out the various medical institutions and set off to pose as Hannah's concerned nephew trying to trace his favourite aunt. At the first location, Sir Charles Gairdner Hospital, I used my charm and good looks on the receptionist, whose beauty was fading in keeping with the government-issue flowers designed to reassure the unwell. No one could have been more helpful. If she could've produced Hannah by some magic, I'm sure she would have. But she couldn't.

No, I'm sorry, your aunt is definitely not here.

My second choice was Fremantle Hospital. To picture this place, you have to think of the building you hate most, and double it. It is a 1960s eyesore, built without windows during the oil crisis to save fuel. It stands there poking its tongue out at the heritage landscape of Freo. I hunted around for reception, which I should have known a State hospital planner had put round the back.

Once again, I posed as a concerned nephew.

Yes, your aunt is on the fifth floor, the lady with orange hair said peering over her half-moon glasses.

Fantastic! I was worried for a moment that I'd brought Vanessa's gushing disease into the hospital. Is it possible to see her?

Yes, you can go up. Follow the corridor round to the left, then you'll find the lifts on your right to take you to the fifth floor.

I emerged from the lift, blinking like a badger emerging from its burrow. I felt confused and disorientated, blasted by the smells, sights and sounds of a bustling medical ward. A young Asian nurse took pity on me.

Your aunt is in the shared room three doors down on the left.

I strode purposefully towards my goal, bursting with hope and expectation. I poked my head round the door. There she was, my beautiful, wonderful aunt. Her head was slumped to one side, her mouth was open and her eyes were closed.

My heart was pounding, full of dread. I dropped into the chair by the bed. I dared to look up. And there was a marvellous sight. Her chest was rising, and it was falling. Rising and falling. Rising and falling. There was Hannah. *My* Hannah.

So thoughtful of her to be asleep and not dead.

You've got to be joking. You must be fucking joking.

Suddenly I was doing a great impression of John McEnroe abusing a linesman as I listened to the ward sister tell me that there was no way Miss Baumgarten would be home by the twenty-seventh, let alone fit enough to attend a function.

The deflation of my elation with this distressing information pricked me to this outburst of indignation.

I couldn't believe it. My mood soon turned to frustration and I took it out on my PA in no uncertain terms. She flounced out in a theatrical huff.

I picked up my phone and walked out of the office and down the bustling city street to get some space. Some opportunity to think. How could the ungrateful old bag get sick on me? Now? Just when I need her most. Within metres of the finish line.

Jesus, what a mess. I kicked an unsuspecting stone that had innocently strayed from the roadworks into my path. I've been betrayed. When is the venue going to be free again? How am I going to get a time when they can all front up again? And what about Garry? Fucking hell, where is he going to stay? He'll have to stick around at the house, I suppose. And, what about Lisa? Oh my God, I hadn't even thought about her. Fucking Lisa will be back from NZ and how am I going to get rid of her another time?

I'd been fucking betrayed. After all this effort and genius and creativity. After everything I'd done to make this happen for them. What the fuck was I going to do?

There was nothing else for it. I had to sit by the bedside every inch the dutiful nephew.

Her room-mates left something to be desired. A woman grunted and snored from behind curtains that were never drawn back. It could've been a grunting and snoring machine for all I knew.

Another lady, who looked like death itself, smiled vacantly into the distance. To pass the time, I tried to work out what she was staring at. What was it about the empty bed opposite her with the hospital paraphernalia attached to the wall that she found so riveting? I guessed she was staring through some rip in the space–time continuum to contemplate some memorable times in her life. Whatever it was, it kept her attention forever.

And there was the obese, middle-aged talkative one, Molly. She told me her name after only thirty seconds. I will spare you the details, but suffice to say that she had women's troubles. She was forever complaining about the food. It was on the tip of my tongue to suggest that she could miss a meal or two without serious risk of malnutrition. I thought better of it.

Instead, I put my head down into my newspaper to avoid the third degree. It was as protective as paper armour from the verbal assault and battery from marauding Molly. Never have I been so pleased in my life to see someone wake up.

Wasser bitte – ich bin durstig, Hannah said to me behind uncomprehending eyes. I placed the drinking beaker to her lips and lifted her head from the pillow as any doting nephew would.

Hannah's brain snapped back into gear as if someone had flicked a switch.

What in heaven's name are you doing here? she said.

What are *you* doing here? I replied. That's more to the point.

The answer was that she'd seen her cardiologist for a six monthly check-up and he'd found some abnormal rhythm in her heart.

You know what they're like, they're panic merchants, she said. It's all driven by the fear of medical malpractice suits, of course, but anyway, I was admitted immediately and a social worker was sent to my house to get some things, lock up properly and so forth.

I looked concerned. Believe me, I *was* concerned. I was lost for words, to tell you the truth.

Well ... is it ... are you ... is there? I stammered.

Hannah waited for me to spit something out, clearly enjoying my loss of composure. As nothing sensible was forthcoming, she intervened.

You know, sometimes, you even have *me* fooled that you care about me. Maybe at some level you really do. I'm not sure, I'm really not sure, but no matter anyway. Well, young man, it won't surprise you to know that the boy has cried wolf once again. The esteemed doctor, or mister as he's called in this silly British system that pervades in the colonies, is now convinced it was just an infection. An infection for goodness sake that necessitated them locking me up here without going home.

Are you going to be OK then? I asked solicitously and even articulately this time.

She sighed and shrugged her shoulders. Well, who can say at my age?

Her eyes seemed fairly bright. She was fine, at least for now, I reassured myself, punching the air without moving a muscle.

I smiled at her. She smiled at me. It was game on once again.

Don't worry, I said, I'll rearrange the launch.

No, don't *you* worry, Hannah insisted, be a good boy and go ahead without me.

It was now a battle of wills. And not the battle of wills Hannah had dreamed up for Garry. I was determined she would attend the rescheduled launch. She was equally resolved that she would not.

I visited her every day in hospital. I went round to her house and left lights on, collected the mail and made sure everything was safe. She had nobody else to look after these things and she was in no position to prevent me from getting the moral upper hand.

I went out of my way to Kakulas Sisters and Kakulas Brothers (by the way, don't they talk?) to find European delicacies Hannah would like and I unveiled a new culinary delight to her every evening when I visited after work. Did someone say that if you wear clothes long enough they start to fit you? I might have made that up, but it actually might be true. In the course of playing the role of attentive relative, I found myself becoming that person in reality. I was quite enjoying it and Hannah clearly felt the same.

Through my diligent attention I was establishing a bond and, as a consequence, I felt I was gaining the ascendancy. She sensed that, but there was little she could do. Those cards of fate that keep recurring in this story were dealt in my favour and I was fated to win.

One Friday lunchtime, she was discharged with negligible warning, as is the practice of institutions governed by perverse KPIs. Once they got their tick for keeping her alive in hospital, she could die on her front doorstep for all they cared. Hannah needed some urgent assistance. I was no ghostbuster, but who was she gonna call?

I picked her up and drove her home. I made her comfortable and I presented her with her first ever mobile phone so she could ring me if she needed anything.

Make sure this contraption doesn't flash and beep at me all the time, she admonished me.

I kissed her on the cheek as I said goodbye. It was a declaration of victory on my part. Hannah got that, turning her cheek away just enough to show defiance but not rejection. Just as I got to the door of her bedroom, I cleared my throat and swivelled around just like they do in the movies.

Oh, I almost forgot to give you this, I said.

As my R. M. Williams boots clattered along the corridor, I heard her opening the envelope that contained her treaty of surrender.

It was the time and place for the launch that she knew she had no choice but to attend.

It was tedious and expensive to reorganise the launch. It involved a fair bit of toing and froing to get things organised, but eventually I managed to find a date and time the guests could come. I squared things away with the venue by graciously forfeiting a not inconsiderable deposit.

The situation with Garry was tricky. I explained that the event my friends were coming back to town for had been postponed, but that he could continue to doss at the renovation house for the time being. He was disappointed at the delay in his promised housesit, but was overjoyed when I was able to tell him told him that the event and the meeting with my friends had been rearranged.

Regrettably, the Lisa problem could not be dealt with by patience, money or offers of accommodation. There was only one way to resolve this problem and it had to come from her and not me. She had to refuse to come. It was as simple as that. She had to want to punish me. By not coming.

From months of painful experience, I had discovered that Lisa was ridiculously easy to offend, but also absurdly predisposed to forgive. So I had to repeatedly flip an *offend–forgive* coin making sure it came down decisively on *offend* at exactly the right time.

At first, I omitted to invite her. Julia spilled the beans. She was offended. Shortly afterwards, I was forgiven. The invitation that I'd promised wasn't forthcoming. She was offended. I re-promised it. I was forgiven. I refused to tell her any details about it. Offended. Time passed. Forgiven. I refused to go with her to shop for a dress. Offended. She bought one anyway. Forgiven.

Things went on like this for a while. You get the picture. Then, when the time was right, I prepared myself for the ultimate *offend-sive*. I can't invite you into the VIP section. Offended. Maybe could forgive. Finds out Julia and Robert are included. Can't forgive now. Why are Julia and Robert included? Robert's well connected. I see. Maybe I can forgive. But, I've been thinking about it. How come you can't add one more person, your girlfriend at that? You want the truth? Yes, of course. I'm sorry, but I think I'd be embarrassed if you were there.

You're a total bastard, she bawled, more in sorrow than anger.

Please come, I do want you at the launch.

No way, not now. If I'm not good enough in your eyes to mix with the rich and famous, I'm not bloody coming to your pathetic function at all, no way, forget it.

I was unforgiven but it was not forgotten.

REALITY REVEALED

CHAPTER WHO GIVES A FUCK ANY MORE?

I don't know what metaphor to use to describe the feeling. The feeling as I stood there, bright and early, surveying my field of Mars. A warlike one such as that? No, I don't think so. It was Venus rather than Mars. I could swear I was falling in love! Or as Dr Seuss once put it, 'You know you're in love ... because reality is finally better than your dreams.'

There was a tinge of sadness, too. I admit it. It would happen. It would be joyous. But, it would then be over. The *petite mort* again. What would I do then? How could anything later in life compare with a rush like this?

I did a final inspection to make sure everything was perfect. It had to be just so. My little lovers at least deserved that. After all, one way or another, they had all co-operated. They had all played their part in making this the happiest day of my life. That's it. Of course, I should make a speech to them. Dearly beloved – and you are – this is the happiest day of my life. Tears of joy – sincere and genuine tears – would roll down my cheeks and fall on the pages, smudging the little speech I'd prepared for tonight. But, never mind. It is better anyway to speak from the heart. The words will flow from an underground stream of emotion. They will well up, overflow and drown us all in a whirlpool of wellbeing.

Like any exciting event you've longed for, I kept running these little scenarios through my head. Who would arrive first and who would roll up next? How would they get on? The thought of innocent small talk between strangers was delicious. Or would the first arrivals be those I'd flirted with and allowed to meet? Julia with Hannah or Robert with Mario?

I'd obviously considered manipulating their arrival times. Hannah was a given, in that she wasn't likely to get there on her own. So, I went the whole hog instead. I organised a limo with a chauffeur. Well, how could I resist? Obviously, the bigger the build-up to the great event, the greater would be the let-down. As for the others, there would be no more manipulation. They had been thrown together by fate, so fate would determine the order of their arrivals and exactly how the great finale would ultimately unfold.

The preparations came and went and the clock marched on. The day arrived and then the afternoon and then the early evening and then the time itself.

I had dressed in a dinner suit, hired from the formal wear shop in Freo that seemed to cater for the totally *unsuit-able*. I preened for a while in front of the full-length mirror. I looked the part.

The drinks were laid out in serried ranks on the white linen covered tables. The waiters were poised outside the kitchen to start handing the food around. The decorations and lights were fabulous. The PA system had been tested with the usual *1-2, 1-2* and all was in order.

I gathered my thoughts. I adjusted the shirtsleeves within my jacket and made sure my hired cuff links were peeking from the hem of my sleeve. I straightened my bow tie. I took a deep breath. I set off. It's so true that a long march starts with a single step. I could feel each footfall on the stone floor and then the stairs. I could experience my weight shifting through the muscles of each leg as they supported me, down, down, step by step, ever closer, closer still, that much closer to the beginning of the end.

I allowed myself to be silently twirled through 180 degrees by the revolving door to find myself in the pleasantly warm evening air. So often it blows a gale down there by the port, but that night it was a rippling breeze. So perfect for such a perfect night.

Who would be first? Who might roll up just that fraction early, out of habit or thanks to the light traffic? I had calculated who would be first. I knew it wouldn't be Hannah as I had timed her limo journey so she would be fashionably late. I'd worked out who it would be from the meticulous psychological profiling I'd done of my wonderful housemates. And there was my first guest at last. And it was not she.

Mario defied the odds and was the first. I was so confident in my arrival projection that I didn't even see him approach. He shook my hand. I reciprocated warmly, using both hands over his one. I touched him with a warmth that, at that moment, I truly felt.

He had scrubbed up for the occasion. He was clean-shaven. His hair was freshly washed and not hanging limp and greasy as it often did. He was wearing a suit that looked out of place, if not embarrassed to be on him. His loud, purple tie was tightly knotted and languishing some centimetres from the shirt collar. He had set the suit off with outrageously pointy, patent leather shoes that allowed him to retain his preferred persona as a spiv despite the relatively conservative nature of the rest of his attire. And, of course, he was aftershaved and hair-gelled to such an extent that his natural body odour might never recover.

I led the way briskly towards the function room. I galloped up the stairs in the expected manner of a host with many things to do.

Come this way, I said in a businesslike, friendly tone.

I ushered him into the perfectly laid-out hall, which was exquisite and immaculate, but as empty as your average parish church. I didn't fail to notice his double-take. I let it register, but I didn't tarry. I resumed the air of a frantically busy host.

Excuse me, Mario, won't you?

I dashed back down the stairs. For the money I was paying, I expected the limo company to follow my instructions to the letter. I knew an old lady could put the whole thing out of kilter, so I sent them to her house at a ridiculously early hour. I told them to drive her around the streets if they had to, but on no account were they to drop her ahead of time. I checked my watch and confirmed that the appointed hour had come. As I walked through the air lock of the revolving doors again, I was gratified to see the black Mercedes pulling up at the ramp.

An immaculately dressed chauffeur opened the rear car door. A vision of mature loveliness struggled from the depths of the plush leather seats to gain an upright position. Hannah did look fabulous. She was an absolute picture of elegance. She had the air of a dowager heiress from a costume drama. I caught a distinct whiff of mothballs as Hannah took my arm to be escorted in the classic manner. She turned her nose up at the ramp and so I helped her slowly up the three stairs that led to the revolving doors.

I didn't doubt that her radar had detected the eery silence that prevailed where a hubbub would be expected for a film launch.

But the thing was – she approved.

You've excelled yourself, she said.

I have?

Of course. And there was I thinking you didn't have it in you.

What exactly?

Restraint, of course! A young man with such a quality is hard to find. I was dreading something commercial and gross, to tell you the truth.

Are you sure you're not disappointed?

Well maybe just a fraction. A little razzle-dazzle would be acceptable.

We arrived at the lift and it ascended the one floor unbelievably slowly for a modern glass and stainless steel box. I motioned to a waitress, who was standing just outside the function room, to take the old lady's arm and show her into the hall.

Watch out for the paparazzi inside, I called back to her.

I made my way back downstairs and then the rest of the meet and greet went by with a rush. At the bottom of the stairs, I bumped into Julia hand-in-hand with Robert. They were both looking chic. I showed them the way to go and then made my way back out through the revolving doors again. No sooner had I emerged into the night air than a taxi drew up and the sleek and sexy Kathleen stepped out. Her shimmering, metallic dress was so short that I didn't need to guess the colour as she climbed from the car.

I knew her reaction to the lack of vibe would be the opposite of Hannah's so I had set myself to greet her so I could deal with it.

She didn't disappoint. What's this, Deadsville? she asked.

Very funny, I replied, but this is how the star wants it.

I continued my explanation, shepherding her towards the entrance so she couldn't cut and run. Stars shine bright on a moonless night, I said.

Spare me the poetry, buddy, just point out the way to the champers.

This way, madam, I said bowing like a lackey. What the lady wants the lady gets.

By some miracle, but probably out of sheer boredom, a gaggle of underemployed waitresses had gathered outside the function room. Fortunately, they descended on Kathy and she moved on happily with a Pol Roger in each hand. A lecherous waiter rushed to open the door for her and I made myself scarce for the final introductory play of the night.

As you can imagine, I was looking forward to Garry's arrival with great anticipation. Not only was he the lucky last, but he was to be doubly duped. I'd given him an arrival time safely later than Hannah's grand entry. I expected him to arrive on foot as I felt sure he'd stop for a couple of beers with his firefighter mates at the pub down the road.

He was a bit late and I was starting to worry a little. I hoped his unreliability wouldn't bring me undone. It occurred to me to text him but then I saw a figure, casually dressed in check shirt and jeans, emerge from the darkness of the wharf sheds into the Maritime Museum lights. He looked anxious as he got closer and then he apologised, having clocked the resplendent gear I was wearing.

Shit, I'm sorry mate – you didn't tell me to tart myself up.

No worries, I reassured him. Just hang around inside the entrance to the function room and I'll get Tony to come over and chat to you.

We walked towards the building. Garry was nervously garrulous.

I've been worrying all week that something would go wrong with this again at the last minute. I guess that's how you feel when you're hoping against hope that your luck might have turned.

I gave him an avuncular pat on the back.

I reckon you deserve a little bit of luck, I said.

What is this do, anyway? It must be something pretty special by the look of you.

We trotted quickly up the steps. I was setting the pace as the excitement of my impending triumph was getting the better of me.

Have a drink. I handed Garry a white wine from a laden tray. Actually, it's a kind of surprise party.

For anyone I know?

Could be, I said, could be.

CHAPTER CROWNING GLORY

As Garry walked slightly ahead of me through the function room door, I had the sensation of a simmering pot finally coming to the boil. I caught a passing glimpse of my gaggle of guests huddling by the doors, severely outnumbered by the relentless forces of hospitality. The slight incline of my head was the limit of the acknowledgment I afforded them.

I soaked up the incongruity of the scene. An impressively spacious hall, resplendently lit, presiding over the fascinating landscape of the port, decked out with elaborate decorations fit for a queen, with a hunched and bedraggled group of guests hunkered in a corner surrounded by service staff and drinks, food and trays and starched tablecloths galore. The scene was one of beauty. The contrasts were something to behold.

I strode forward, proud and erect so to speak, looking neither left nor right. My eye was fixed on the microphone, so thoroughly tested just minutes before. I walked as slowly as a pallbearer and with requisite dignity up the black-carpeted stairs. Once on the stage, I allowed my footsteps to echo round the near-empty hall as I approached the lectern.

I produced my notes from the inner pocket of my dress suit coat. I laid them carefully out in front of me, smoothing the creases as I went. I cleared my throat – a fruitless but satisfying gesture as there was only silence.

Good evening, ladies and gentlemen.

I stand before you a happy man. When I set out on this grand enterprise, this Master Plan, I dreamed, but didn't dare even to hope, that I could pull off such a glittering triumph. But thanks to you all, thanks to your participation, as unwitting as it may have been, people everywhere will marvel at what has been accomplished.

When you exercise your freedom and embark on an epic journey like this, you are inspired by your vision of what it might be like to reach your destination. Yet life is beset by twists and turns. However carefully you plan – and I'm sure by now you appreciate that I left nothing to chance – unanticipated events conspire to trip you up. But life wasn't meant to be easy. When we overcome the pitfalls and challenges, the joy of achievement is magnified, as it is for me today.

As I gaze down upon you now, I recognise you all as family. It is hard to believe that such a short time ago, I was a stranger to you all and you were all strangers to each other.

I once was lost, but now I'm found. But not you, not now. Take a moment to look inside yourselves and tell me honestly whether twelve months ago you could possibly have imagined where your lives would be today. It's unimaginable, isn't it, how far we've come? We have been involved in something magnificent and as a result have transformed ourselves from the ordinary to the extraordinary. We have evolved from the bland to the passionate. We have dared to live life to the full. To fully experience life with all its violent pendulum swings of emotion. We have finally stepped to the abyss and dared to look over. And, what we have seen has scared us, but not cowed us. That which hasn't killed us, has made us stronger.

So we are family and we are one. And yet I beg to separate myself from you. The fact is that what you have all resigned yourselves to call fate, I have reason to call reality.

This, my friends, is a critical point. Fate is the hand that gets dealt to you. By contrast, reality is the hand I create. I have changed your lives. I have brought you together and changed you from complete strangers to lovers and into enemies, clients and admirers. For each other, you have experienced the full gamut of human relationships. Your lives have been enriched. Not by fate. But by me. I have created your reality and you have me to thank for the fact that, at last, you are living life.

But, listen to me, waxing lyrical. This is a party and you are here to celebrate. So, my friends, all good things must come to an end. There is nothing left but to thank you all for playing such an important part in my life. All of you familiar people, who were once nothing more than a list of names. Not people to me then. Imagine the joy it was for me, having selected you all at random, to find you, get to know you, open doors for you, develop you and finally honour you at a gala function such as this.

My dearest friends, this party is all for you. I am deeply appreciative of your participation in my Master Plan. So please enjoy. Make yourselves at home. Savour the impressive wines and the sumptuous food. You are special people now, who deserve all this. You are my people. You are my chosen ones.

EPILOGUE

As you can imagine, it was a wonderful experience to step down from the stage and mix and mingle with my guests. While I'd hoped for their adulation, I didn't get it. Instead, once they'd overcome their shock and denial, I was on the receiving end of their anger and insults. But I remained calm and did not rush to judgment. I was confident they'd come to appreciate my achievement in time.

Despite the overly aggressive tone some of them adopted when I joined them, I patiently answered their questions. That's right, I selected you all at random. From the Perth telephone directory. Yes, I found ways of entering your lives. It wasn't always easy, but I kept at it. Yes, I manipulated you, but it's not a word I particularly care for.

And then there were their particular questions:

How did you get Hannah to engage me to do her work?

How did you get Mario to use me as his lawyer?

And the one Julia obviously thought I was dreading. So, where does this leave Lisa?

Pretty much where she was before, I suppose.

You bastard, she said in a very unladylike way.

I explained with exaggerated tolerance. You must understand that Lisa isn't one of you. Her name didn't come from the book.

So you have no feelings for her, Julia concluded, walking away.

Once the penny dropped and they were able to piece together how I'd been pulling their strings, they refused to believe it. They were shaking their heads muttering that this was some kind of sick joke or maybe a set-up to test people's reactions under stress. However, as all of you students of Kübler-Ross would now be predicting, their denial phase was soon to be replaced by anger.

I thought several of them might spit on me or even hit me. There was one exception. While the others carried on like pork chops, Hannah sat on a chair thoughtfully provided by an underemployed waiter and observed proceedings with a wry smile on her face. As a mature woman in every sense, she seemed content to be part of history in the making.

The collective angst was clearly directed at me. Yet I was loath to claim all the credit. How could I, in all conscience, accept the credit for the decisions they'd made of their own accord? Garry, what kudos attaches to me for Hannah testing you like that? Can *I* reasonably boast about how you and Kirsty kept the money? Did I advise Mario on the strategy for his case? Similarly, did I decide to take Julia to Bali when my son's engagement party was on?

Over time they drifted away. Some of them left together, others stayed miles apart. I did my best, but I couldn't drink the booze for a hundred people. I snacked on the canapés for a while, but hardly made a dent in the mountain of food. The function manager came up to me very concerned.

What happened, did something go wrong with the invitations?

Quite the reverse, I reassured her. Everyone turned up and, let me assure you, this event has been the night of nights.

Fortunately, I had a couple of days to savour my success before the circus started. On the Monday, I tendered my resignation. I gave the honest reason that I'd achieved everything I'd set out to do. Although my western quest was accomplished, I stuck around in my adopted State of Wondrous Achievement.

At first, I was subjected to recriminations and backbiting from the housemates. It was the tall poppy syndrome I'd prepared for.

How could you do this to me? How could you deceive me like this? What have I ever done to you?

The answers were simple and straightforward. I was creating reality, which part of that don't you get?

After the backbiting, came the confrontations. I was bailed up outside my apartment and even downtown in Freo. They shouted at me and somehow expected me to make amends. But I couldn't take them seriously.

How can I compensate you for something you did yourself? I asked.

My factual response made them angrier still.

Then came the threats. To this day, I can still only guess where they came from. You would probably have your own ideas, just as I have mine. But, they just didn't get it. I didn't care what they did to me because I had created reality. Why was that so hard to understand?

Then, it was the turn of the police. They questioned me in relation to conspiracy to commit an impressive array of crimes.

Since when is it a crime to select people out of the telephone book and put them in touch with each other? I asked. Did I force anyone to do anything against their will?

Don't let me give you the impression that the aftermath of the night of nights was all negative. Far from it. With it, came fame and notoriety. I became a media darling.

This was only right and proper given that a callow youth with supersized yellow sunglasses had only recently become an overnight celebrity for holding a party that trashed his parents' house. I'd resented that until my own moment in the limelight came around. After all, mindless vandalism should not be condoned in any civilised society. Even by the media. And how could that stupidity be compared with the guile and genius of my undertaking?

Appropriately, I was an overnight sensation on social media. On Facebook, I out-friended cult-leaders and I trended worldwide on Twitter, garnering more followers than a miniskirted supermodel on a steep staircase.

My Master Plan fitted the double standards of the mainstream media to a tee. While *The West Australian* railed at this depraved act of deception and despaired at the alarming decline in community standards, its co-owned shock-horror current affairs program celebrated my 'coup' with a heavily cross-promoted 7.30 Sunday night special.

That program, where you probably first came across me, blitzed the ratings for the whole quarter. I hope you won't think me immodest if I reproduce the transcript of the interview here.

I sat in the green room watching the show live on the monitor. From memory, I think an intrepid journalist with a camera crew in tow was chasing a Middle-Eastern landlord down his home driveway asking why he hadn't returned the bond to a homeless family just because they'd used his rental house as a meth lab. Anyway, an ad break came around and then a kid dressed entirely in black with earphones on his head and a clipboard in his hand came to get me. I was escorted into the studio and sat patiently through my introduction, which was part nasty and part laudatory. The camera panned out and then the glitzy host got our interview underway.

Well, you're an overnight celebrity. How does it feel?
Pretty good actually, I'm enjoying it.

Did you expect the story to get so much coverage?
I certainly hoped it would.

Let's be honest, though, a lot of what's been written and said has been critical, if not totally scathing. How do you react to that?
It really doesn't worry me. There are always people who are jealous of your achievements. They always want to pull you down.

But, in this case, don't they have good reason to? I mean, how would you have felt if the boot had been on the other foot?
That's not the point. I achieved an incredible feat, that's what's important.

So, do you dismiss the moral angle completely?
No, not at all. Everyone is responsible for their own morality. Let those who are without sin, as the saying goes. All I did was exercise my freedom. In this case, to create a new reality for people. What they chose to do within it was their own affair.

OK, let's take another tack in relation to the morality of your behaviour and ask you about what the Premier of WA had to say in Parliament the other day. I won't read it all, but I just want to select one quote. The Premier said, This despicable act of manipulation is one of the saddest things I have come across in a long time. For someone to use human lives as his playthings turns my stomach, quite frankly, and I despair yet again at the decline in moral values in our society. *Turning the Premier's stomach is pretty bad, don't you think?*
No, I don't. To me, it means nothing at all. I think politicians are consistently rated by the public as the group with the lowest moral values in society, about on a par with journalists, from

memory. So the Premier is not in a position to talk down to anyone. Again, he is someone who clearly doesn't understand. This is about greatness. This is about achievement. This is about seeing a goal out there that looks impossible to achieve and going for it and making it happen. That's what I did and I'm proud of it.

OK, let's leave the moral angle for now. After all, while your actions have been roundly condemned by many in the community, it would seem that your exploits have caught the imagination of many others and that, in some quarters, you're being elevated to something of a cult hero. How do you react to that?
How do I react to it? I thinks it's due recognition for a great achievement.

There have been a lot of rumours and stories about exactly how you planned this and carried it off so I'd like to separate fact from fiction, if I may. Would it be all right to ask you about your modus operandi?
Sure, go ahead.

You're not worried about people stealing your trade secrets?
Not at all, plagiarism is the sincerest form of flattery.

Right, then, is it true they were all selected at random from the Perth phone book?
Absolutely true.

You didn't throw any back cos they were too hard and stick your pin in again?
Not at all. That would be cheating and I have a strict moral code on these things.

Is it true you came over from Melbourne to run this scam?
You'll offend me if you call it a scam. I didn't come over to enact this particular Master Plan, but I did leave Melbourne to separate myself from the familiarity of my surroundings. I moved so I could be free to achieve my potential.

And I read that you were inspired to do this by watching Big Brother? That can't be true, surely.
Well, it's basically true.

How did that come about?
I was casting around for some great enterprise that might be worthy of my talents and then I happened upon Big Brother, which I'd never seen before. It struck a chord with me immediately. At first, it appalled me because people were living such pathetic lives that they were prepared to move out of home and go and live in an aquarium for people to gawp at on national TV. And then it fascinated me because these individuals would respond like rats in a laboratory to every introduced stimulus in their environment and, just like laboratory rats, they would do whatever it took to get the pellet of food and win the prize.

It's a bit like an experiment, I can see that.
And, after all that, I was inspired by the rat cunning of the housemates and the way these fairly unsophisticated people would develop complex behavioural strategies to get themselves closer to winning and their opponents further away, while maintaining every outward appearance of being best friends with them.

So, you were inspired to conduct some sort of social experiment?
Yes, in a way, but I was taken specifically by the way these programs create reality and by how people are prepared to go along with it.

OK, so creating a new reality was the thing that turned you on. I can follow and I guess understand that. But, the bit I don't understand is this. You said yourself just now that Big Brother creates a new reality and you were struck by how people will willingly go along with it. But surely the scenario you created was entirely different. After all, your participants weren't willing players and they were effectively duped by you into falling into the web you were creating?
I seriously think you're missing the point. You see, programs like Big Brother, and actually the name clearly implies this,

allow us to see society as it really is. Not some version created for television as some would have us believe, but a picture of how it is and what people are like. I learned from Big Brother that people are up for having a reality created for them and they will go along with it. So, once I realised that, I wanted to create a reality for people, but I had no obligation to spoil things like the programs do and let them in on the secret. Society these days gives permission for realities to be created for people and the people have given their permission that they will go along with it.

You have no qualms about intruding in people's lives like you did?
None at all.

What about the poor woman you conned into becoming your girlfriend? Do you not feel anything about how much you would've hurt her?
I reject completely the idea that I conned her into becoming my girlfriend. She voluntarily became my girlfriend. She was totally free to be my girlfriend or not. She chose that status for herself.

But you must accept that you befriended her and got close to her to get to one of the people you'd selected to be part of your experiment?
Absolutely, but what's your point?

The point is surely obvious: you deceived her.
Look, I think most people realise that relationships are a complex, subconscious tangle of needs and wants. Many of our purposes and desires are made plain to the people we relate to and many, many are not. So, I don't see this as so different to most other relationships.

Surely, you can see why people see you as immoral or at least amoral?
No, I can't. My morals are completely irrelevant. Truly, they are. Why is this so hard to understand? I say again, I merely exercised my freedom. It was an incredible achievement to create a new reality within which people could continue to act as they pleased, to exercise their own freedoms as they wished.

This is fascinating, but we're running out of time. So what's next for you after this? Is it true you've been approached about the rights to a book?
Yes it is.

What about a film?
A film would be the natural thing to do. After all, the best films are about greatness, one way or another. They are about people doing extraordinary things and usually triumphing against great odds. This is what I did. I pulled off a great coup and created my own reality for some lucky people.

And after that? Any more ... I won't call them scams ... any more experiments?
Why not? I'm convinced that people want more of what I do. They dread a dull, predictable, entrenched life. People don't stick around in a job for twenty years these days. They have trouble staying married for more than two. That tells you they want discontinuity, not continuity. But they want to be led. Led towards the new. Not only have they lost the acceptance and patience of their forebears, but they have also lost their courage. So they lack the guts to achieve what they need. They crave but they're craven. That's where I come in. I lead them to the life they covet. And the beauty is I seek so little in return. All I charge is admiration. Where else can you get such value?

Where indeed? Well, we really do have to wrap it up. But I have to ask you one last thing: Do you have a message for any of the people involved?
All I can say to them is this. Don't be ungrateful. People always talk about looking for a life-changing experience. They didn't have to go searching for one. I brought it to them. Most people resist change. Even the change they desperately need. This way, they had nothing holding them back from a new direction. I gave them that. At random. They should thank their lucky stars they were chosen.

As you probably would recall, that interview was great for me. Millions of viewers got to hear me put things in my own words to provide some sense of balance about the whole affair.

Thanks to that outing on TV, I attained celebrity status. I became a hero for the generations at the bottom of the alphabet. The Xs, Ys and Zs identified with me. They saw my striving for greatness and my flouting of convention as akin to their own forms of self-expression, such as head-to-toe tattooing and train surfing.

When it came to the book rights, I couldn't believe the goings on. All the major publishing houses were vying for me. After everything I'd achieved, can you believe that some publishers wanted to use my story but have it written by somebody else? A ghost-writer was something I would never accept. So I stuck to my guns and held the nerdy publisher types and their corporate lawyers at bay until I could secure the deal I wanted – to write this great book myself.

This book has been a labour of love. I have toiled long and hard over it, searching for exactly the right word. I wanted to create a work of art that would both educate and entertain. A book about great deeds is not an easy thing to write for the masses. The most difficult part for me was laid out at the very beginning. I knew every reader would want to judge me. Not only that, but they'd find themselves rushing to judgment before the full facts had been laid out before them. They would want to adopt some moral superiority before they fully understood the reasons I did what I did. Now, at last, you are in a position to see the full picture and to understand from the horse's mouth things you only thought you knew from reading the papers and watching TV.

The purpose of this book is to have you marvel. I took the trouble to explain everything to you because understanding normally breeds greater appreciation. But, at the end of the day, I actually don't care what you think. This book has made me famous and it will make me rich with a film of the book in the wings.

Alas, I can't be everywhere for everyone. I was able to create reality for these few lucky people and I've been able to show the rest of you how it's done. Basically, what it comes down to is that there are those who make things happen and those who don't. I don't want to moralise to you because it's not my style. But, if you don't make it your business to do things to other people, they sure as hell are going to do it to you.

POSTSCRIPT FOR THOSE WHO HAVE TO HAVE ONE

I don't really want to write this bit. I can't see why you should care what happened to my housemates. But I know there are people out there so lacking in imagination that they have to know the ending of a book or a movie before they can feel satisfied. So, I'm doing this for them. That might be you. I am all heart.

It would be nice to invent some *happy* endings for you, but this story has had too much publicity for me to be able to lie to you like that.

I'll start with the good news first. It will come as no surprise that Hannah has gone from strength to strength. By confronting the real motivation behind her inappropriate behaviour in relation to the money and the ring, she has become an even more enlightened person at her advanced age. As you saw before, she was full of admiration for what I did. And thanks to the stimulation my intervention provided, Hannah remains as active and engaged as she's ever been.

I can't say what's happened to Garry recently. He seemed to blame me for how things turned out and yet I had nothing to do with any of the decisions he made. I'm pretty sure he was allowed back in the family home for a short while, but the bond of marital trust was well and truly broken. Garry avoided prison by the skin of his teeth, but the conviction put paid to his chosen career. The best thing to come of all this was that he finished the work on my house. He did it under considerable sufferance, I might add. Then again, he had nowhere else to go.

The lovely Julia has recently returned to the loathsome Stephen. Far too predictable, I know, but that's how boring life can be. In the end, it seems that the public limelight on my story proved too much for her to bear. She rationalised things to herself, saying she couldn't put the girls through it any more. So she returned to her Cottesloe life with her Cottesloe husband. A cott-case, I guess you could call it. Around the same time, the impacts of the end of the resources boom tore through the leafy western suburbs like a plague. The Lees lost a fortune on their shares and had to sell their winery. These are the harsh sacrifices that some people have to make.

For Robert life goes on as it always has. The gynaecology game is recession-proof so his income remains impressively high. On top of that, the RB is going gangbusters after the bar extensions. Naturally, his apartment above the bar gets plenty of use. Can you guess who still visits him there from time to time? Come to think of it, there has been one significant change to his lifelong routine. Marjorie kicked him out for good. It was a shock to the system no doubt, but Marjorie and Robert will get by – their kind always do.

I have left the most salacious part to last. I know some of you are dying to find out what happened between Mario and Kathy. I guess you're hoping that the nice guy got the girl.

As it happens, I bumped into Kathy about a month ago. She was at the opening of yet another trendy bar. She noticed me from a distance and sought me out to buy me a drink. I wasn't sure if it was me she was after, or the notoriety that now surrounds me. I didn't care terribly much either way.

Oh, I almost forgot to tell you. Kathy dumped Mario long ago and has now taken up with a famous dreadlocked DJ from Jamaica. I met the guy later at the bar. He's a fan of mine, what more can I say?

I see Mario now and again in the corner of his Fremantle pub, where I know he can be found. He looks older these days after his ordeal and his smile and his cheery disposition seem that much harder to maintain. He tells me he hates me every time I see him, but he tolerates me because he would never have met Kathy but for me. Even with her gone, there must be happy memories, right?

Mario remonstrates with me at every opportunity. When I tell him I merely exercised my freedom as we all do, he has one thing to say.

Do that to me again and I'll break your fucking neck.

ACKNOWLEDGMENTS

I'm very grateful to those who suffered for my *Reality*. Warm thanks to Greg Caswell who first loved the book, and to Jane Nolin for her generous professional critique. I greatly appreciate the faith that Fremantle Press placed in me and the amazing guidance and support afforded by my editor, Georgia Richter. Thanks also to our boys – Jack, Jack, Tom & Rohan – for indulging me in my fantasy that I could write a novel. Above all, what can I say about my beautiful Carol? Without her love, encouragement, endurance and belief, this crazy notion of mine could never have become *Reality*.

First published 2014 by
FREMANTLE PRESS

Fremantle Press Inc. trading as Fremantle Press
PO Box 158, North Fremantle, Western Australia, 6159
fremantlepress.com.au

Cover design Ally Crimp
Cover photograph Daniel Craig, Matsu Photography

 A catalogue record for this
book is available from the
NATIONAL
LIBRARY National Library of Australia
OF AUSTRALIA

ISBN 9781922089373 (paperback)

 |

GOVERNMENT OF
WESTERN AUSTRALIA

Fremantle Press is supported by the Western Australian State
Government through the Department of Cultural Industries,
Tourism and Sport.

Australian Government

Publication of this title was assisted by the Commonwealth
Government through Creative Australia, its arts funding and
advisory body.

Fremantle Press respectfully acknowledges the Whadjuk people of
the Noongar nation as the Traditional Owners and Custodians of the
land where we work in Walyalup.